Paint Her Dead

By

Wanda Shelton

Chapter One

Leah headed back through the woods, over the footbridge and down the hill toward the inn. As she drew near the cove, she noticed the tide had gone out leaving some brightly rags behind. But, a closer look caused her heart to pound and her knees to grow weak, it wasn't rags, it was a body.

A familiar face gazed up at her. One blue eye held an expression of horrified surprise. Red-gold strands of hair streamed across the once attractive face.

The rain had stopped and the sun was shining. Butterflies fluttered around nearby wild flowers. Bird songs filled the air. So much beauty and normality.

If I look back, she'll be gone. It can't be real. Things like that don't happen at places like this. Leah glanced up the hill and saw the tall man coming down the path. He stopped and looked in the direction of the cove. She watched his expression change. She knew then, it was no dream. The body was real, and the woman's death was no accident.

Three Days Earlier

Leah rolled over and hit the snooze alarm. The loud buzzing stopped, but she was wide awake now. No more sleep for her. She slid out of bed and headed to the kitchen. While the coffee brewed, she checked each item on her to-do list. She'd packed everything except her toiletries, and those would go in her carry-on bag. She shipped her painting materials last week. They should already be at the Inn.

Leah tingled with excitement, anticipating the coming week.

I can't believe I'll actually be studying under Andrew Barzetti, she thought as she poured a cup of coffee. And, I'll get to visit with Sandy, my best friend ever. Thank goodness, I'll get away from that creepy John Phelps. Hopefully, he'll find someone else to stalk while I'm away.

Leah took a taxi to the airport and directed the driver to America Airline's curb side check in. She handed the skycap her ID; he glanced at her picture, then at her, then pecked several keys on his computer. "Looks like you're going to Portland, Maine with a connecting flight in Detroit."

"That's right," she said.

"How many bags are you checking today, young lady?"

"Just the one," Leah said.

"You'll be departing from gate B27," he said, handing back her driver's license, along with a boarding pass and baggage receipt. "Have a good flight," he said

As she hurried through the terminal, she noticed a man seated in a row of chairs lined along one of the walls. The m appeared to be about the same size as John Phelps, but he held a newspaper in front of his face. Leah was sure his suit was a Hermes, John's favorite brand. She stared at the seated man asmemories flooded her mind.

She thought of the first time she met John Phelps. It was only three months ago at a friend's tenth wedding anniversary celebration. She was talking to several friends when a man joined them, and spoke to several in the group. They appeared glad to see him, and one of the ladies asked where he'd been fso long.

"Oh, just doing some wheeling and dealing in foreign lands. You know I have to keep beating the bushes to keep the wolf away," the man had answered with a grin.

"Yeah, right," the woman had said with a laugh. "If the wolf ever came to your door, it would be to a masquerade party."

Leah stood there watching the comradery between the unknown man and the woman she knew as Barb. They seemed to share a rapport, giving Leah the impression they were romantically involved. But suddenly, the man made excuses to Barb,and walked over to where Leah was standing.

"I don't think we've met. I know I'd never forget such a lovely face. My name is John Phelps."

He was a little over six feet tall and immaculately dressed. Leah was sure his blond hair had been professionally styled. His smile revealed perfect white teeth, and charm oozed from him like syrup from a bottle.

Leah felt uncomfortable, thinking maybe he was involved with Barb. But, when she glanced in her direction, Barb was laughing and talking with another man. They seemed to share the same comradery she had with John.

So, Leah looked at him and said, "Hi, nice to meet you. I'm Leah Dawson."

He took her hand and raised it to his lips. "You know, you're the most beautiful woman in this room," he said, while looking at her as if she was the *Venus de Milo* and he was a collector of fine art

His smile was warm, but his eyes were cold as the Arctic Ocean. They were almost colorless, like ice with a touch of blue. When Leah looked into those colorless depths, she felt a chill run up her spine and prickle her neck. She should have followed her instincts and avoided John Phelps like the plague. But, he'd been so attentive and charming. He had a knack few people possess. He had an incredible ability to make you feel both beautiful and brilliant. She'd ignored her gut feelings and began seeing him. She wondered how many times she'd done the proverbial, "hind sight is perfect, kick in the rear-end. He'd been the escort of every woman's dreams, until his true colors were exposed.

The day they had lunch at the Brushmark restaurant in the Brooks Museum of Art had been the coup de grâce. They were discussing George Rodrigue's "Blue Dog" exhibit currently on display when a man sitting at the next table spoke to Leah. He recognized her from an article in the *Architectural Digest* magazine. She had won an award for the design of her current home, and the magazine had done a great write-up with pictures of her and her house. The man said he was considering a renovation project and asked for one of her cards. Leah reached into her purse, pulled out a card, and thanked him for his glowing remarks. Meanwhile, John had become very quiet. He said something had come up, and they must leave right away. Leah was puzzled by his actions. *What had come up, and how did he know? He hadn't received a phone call or any other communication that she was aware of.* Nonetheless, she had dutifully left her half-eaten lunch and gone with him.

When they reached his car, he got in the driver's seat and waited for her to seat herself. *Very unlike Mr. Perfect Manners,* Leah thought, as she got into the passenger seat. Before starting the engine, he turned to her and between gritted teeth said, "Don't ever do that again."

"What are you talking about? Never do what again?"

"Talk to another man when you're with me." His pale blue eyes were filled with rage and seemed to shoot icy darts at her.

"You're out of line. Your actions are totally unacceptable. Please take me home," Leah said in a cold voice.

"The man was obviously flirting with you; he used his renovation project as a ruse to get your phone number."

"I won't dignify that comment with an answer. Take me home, NOW." Leah could feel anger growing in her chest and knew her face was turning red. She looked at John's handsome profile and wondered, *What has happened to the charming, thoughtful man I've been dating?* There'd been a few subtle hints lately, but she'd ignored them. Why? Was it because she didn't want to admit she'd been taken in by his smooth-talking, charming manners? *No,* she decided, *I truly enjoyed his company.* Under the anger, she felt disappointment and a sense of loss.

When they arrived at her home, she opened the car door, got out, and turned to the man behind the wheel.

"Goodbye, John. Today's been a real eye-opener. Don't bother calling me again."

He looked at her with an icy glare and drove away without saying a word.

The next morning, she received a bouquet of two dozen daisies. John knew they were her favorite flower. He had chosen well; they were a beautiful mixture of yellow and white. A handwritten card read, *these lovely flowers dim next to your beauty. Please forgive me. I acted a fool, and I promise it will never happen again.* The card was signed, John.

Her phone began ringing as she started out the door. She was on the way to work and was running late, so she let it ring. When she arrived at her office, her assistant was on the phone and indicated the call was for her.

She took the receiver. It was John, and he was asking her forgiveness.

"You have my forgiveness, and I want to thank you for the beautiful flowers. You shouldn't have bothered, though."

"It was no bother. I want you to know how sorry I am for my behavior yesterday. I hope you'll forgive and forget. I promise it will never happen again."

"I forgive you, John, but I think it will be better if we don't see each other anymore."

He didn't say anything for such a long time, Leah had begun to feel uncomfortable and started to babble.

"I wish you well and hope you'll be happy."

"Oh, I'll be happy," he'd interrupted, "I'll call back in a few days after you've had time to cool off."

"Don't call me again. Goodbye, John." She'd hung up, her hands trembling as she replaced the receiver.

****

Leah looked again at the man who reminded her of John. He put the paper down, stood and walked away. He had dark hair, dark eyes, and was at least ten years older than John.

Leah shook her head, her thoughts returning to the present, and hurried down the concourse to her departure gate. After a short wait, the passengers began boarding, and she was soon buckled in her seat. When they were airborne, she leaned her head back and closed her eyes. She let her mind wander back to memories of the last few days.

John seemed to have an uncanny ability to appear at every function she attended. He would smile and greet her as if they were long lost friends, sometimes kissing her on the cheek or her hand. But, when she looked into his eyes, the cold, ice-blue depths were filled with a challenge and an unspoken message, "You'll come around; it's just a matter of time."

She had dinner with an old friend earlier that week, and when he arrived home, he was mugged and beaten. The thugs were hidden in the shadows and attacked him when he got out of his car. He was now in the hospital with two broken ribs, a concussion, and multiple bruises. Leah had gone to visit him, and he assured her he would be alright. When she suggested John may have been responsible for what happened, he'd looked at her with a guarded expression.

He already suspects that. For crying out loud, he could have been killed because of me. She started apologizing, but he'd stopped her.

"Leah, it's not your fault. You can't help what that crazy psycho does. Besides, it may just be a coincidence. We have no way of knowing if John was responsible for what happened."

Was it a coincidence? Maybe, she thought, *But, last night was real.* Last night had made her blood run cold. When she got into bed and opened the nightstand drawer, a daisy was lying on top of her book. *My God, he's been in my house. He could still be here.* She immediately called 911, and the operator stayed on the line until the police arrived. While waiting for the police, she went to the window and peeked through the blinds. John's Jag was parked across the street in front of her house. He waved and drove off. When she told the officers about seeing him, they sent a squad car to his place. He had come to the door in a robe, looking disheveled, like he'd just crawled out of bed. The police had been very condescending to her, suggesting perhaps she put the flower in her nightstand and forgotten about doing it. She didn't know how John did it, but she knew he was in her home sometime that day or night.

Leah shoved the thoughts of John out of her mind and tried to relax. She could feel the tension flow from her body as they drew closer to Portland. She would be safe when she got to the inn. Sandy and the other guests would be there. Sandy always made her feel better. Regardless the circumstances, she felt more optimistic when she was with Sandy.

****

They landed with a bump, and Leah watched as markers on the tarmac whizzed by. Soon they were at the arrival gate, and passengers began spilling into the aisle, pulling luggage from overhead compartments. As soon as people started moving, Leah hurried from the plane and up the jet walk, following the signs to the baggage area.

Riding down the escalator, Leah spotted Sandy standing at the foot of the stairs. Her red hair and pixie face with a sprinkling of freckles across her nose stood out from the crowd. She was wearing a casual black pants suit and a sea foam green blouse that matched her eyes. She loved Sandy like the sister she'd never had, and her heart swelled with warmth at the sight of her.

Leah and Sandy had been friends since first grade. Leah could never understand how their friendship had come to be; they were different as night and day. Sandy was so outgoing and full of confidence, while Leah was shy, self-conscious and unsure of herself. But, they seemed to be drawn to each other, and they became closer than most sisters. Sandy would take up for her when the other kids made fun of the way she dressed or the way her hair was fixed. Leah's grandmother had raised her, and she made most of Leah's clothes. They were usually too long and old-fashioned. One time, she and Sandy cut about four inches from the bottom of Leah's dress. Her grandmother had scolded her severely, but she got the message. She started making Leah's dresses shorter and more stylish.

Sandy caught sight of Leah on the escalator, and a huge smile spread across her face. She began waving and almost bouncing with eagerness. As soon as Leah stepped from the stairs, the two friends grabbed each other in a bear hug, laughing and crying, both talking at once.

"You are a sight for sore eyes, girlfriend. It's been too long! Just look at you," Sandy said, while turning Leah around in circles. "You never change. Still slim as ever and even more beautiful!"

"Look who's talking! You still look like the prom queen who broke all the boys' hearts back in high school. "You're just as petite and pretty as ever."

"Yeah, but I have to work at it, while you could eat everything in sight and still stay slim and trim."

"So how are Al and the boys managing without you for a whole week?

"They're probably glad to be rid of me for a while. They'll eat junk food and watch nonstop football. It'll probably take me a month to get things back in order, but it'll be worth it. How's your business doing? How'd you manage to get away this long?"

"Whoa, slow down! My business is doing great. Charlie's taking care of everything. We're kind of between jobs right now, and he can handle anything that might pop up. We just finished a project for someone I bet you've heard of," Leah said with a grin.

"Hmm, someone I've heard of…give me a clue," Sandy said.

"Well, he used to be a big-time rock and roll star, and there was a Broadway hit play about him and three other stars who got together at a famous recording studio in Memphis and…"

"Wait, don't tell me. Was it 'The Killer,' Jerry Lee Lewis?!" Sandy asked with disbelief. "I saw that play, *The Million Dollar Quartet*, and I know he's the only one of the four who's still living."

"The one and only," Leah said. "We built a sunroom and salon bath off the master bedroom in his home in north Mississippi. I'll have to say, it was one of the most interesting jobs I've ever done. Mr. Lewis is a very entertaining person, even off stage. But, bottom line, he was pleased as punch with the results."

"I want all the juicy details, from start to finish," Sandy said.

"We've got all week to catch up on everything," Leah said as a loud buzzer sounded and bags began spewing from an opening in the wall. Leah's was the fourth to hit the moving belt, and she grabbed it as it went by. Sandy had already retrieved her bag, so they headed out the door into the bright September sunshine. The earlier clouds had dissipated, leaving a clear, brilliant, blue sky.

Standing at the curb in front of a taxi was a man holding a sign that read Rocky Ledge Inn.

"That's got to be our man," Leah said, as they started walking in his direction. At the same time, a man rolling a large bag approached the taxi driver, said a few words, and started to get into the back seat. He appeared to be about forty with dark, shoulder-length hair tied back into a ponytail. He was wearing designer black jeans, a black turtle neck sweater, a pair of Adidas Yeezys, and no socks. He had dark, brooding eyes, prominent cheekbones, and a full, sensuous mouth.

About that time, the taxi driver saw Leah and Sandy walking toward them.

"Are you Leah Dawson and Sandy Carlton?" he asked.

"Yes," Leah replied. "We reserved a taxi from the Ocean View Cab Company."

"These are the two ladies I'm taking to Rocky Ledge Inn. Apparently, there's been some mix up about your transportation," the driver said.

"I'm terribly sorry," the man said, backing away from the cab. "I was also expecting transportation from Rocky Ledge Inn, so I just assumed you were it."

"Well, there's enough room for you to join us. My name is Leah Dawson, and this is Sandy Carlton. We're attending a workshop at the inn this week. Are you attending the workshop also?"

"I guess you could say I am. I'm the instructor, Andy Barzetti. It's very nice of you to offer to let me join you. I would be honored to ride with two such lovely ladies."

He had just gotten the words out of his mouth when a limousine pulled into the parking lot. A man wearing a chauffeur's cap got out of the car and looked around. He spotted the people by the taxi and approached them.

"Any of you go by the name Andrew Barzetti?"

"That would be me, but I'm not expecting a limo. What's going on?"

"Your friend Calvin Ross hired me to pick you up. Apparently, he's under the impression you're spending the night with him in Portland. He has retained me to take you to the inn tomorrow."

"That sounds like Cal. Seems he failed to inform me of the invitation," Andy said with a laugh. "I greatly regret that I won't have the privilege of riding with two such charming ladies. But, I look forward to meeting you again tomorrow and having a wonderful week of painting instruction at the beautiful Rocky Ledge Inn."

He bowed with a flourish and, taking their hands in his, kissed each one. "Ci rivediamo," he said and got into the limousine.

Leah and Sandy stood with wide eyes and open mouths as they watched the long car drive away.

"What a charmer—it should be an interesting week," Leah said.

"Yeah, I think I'm in love," Sandy said with an impish grin.

They crawled into the backseat and the driver started the motor and pulled away from the parking area. Following the signs to exit the airport, they were soon on the road, leaving Portland behind. They passed through several small villages and towns. By now, the sun had set, and a full moon was rising in the east. "You ladies ever been to Rocky Ledge before?"

"I was here two years ago," Leah said. "I thought it was great and talked Sandy into coming this year."

"Yeah, it's a pretty popular place. I haul people up here several times each year."

About forty minutes later, the driver turned off the highway onto a secondary road. Soon, they turned onto what appeared to be a private drive with a sign saying Eagle Nest Estates.

"Is this the place?" Sandy asked.

"No, this is a resort we drive through to get to the inn property," Leah replied.

They went by a club house, some shops, a restaurant, and some condos, then turned onto a drive with a sign saying Rocky Ledge Inn. The road curved and wound its way through an open gate and up a slight incline. They could now see the main house where a weak light illuminated a small front porch. Everything had a silvery tinge in the moonlight.

"Quaint and homey, and they left the light on for us," Sandy said.

The cab driver pulled up to the front steps, got out of the car, and opened the rear doors for the ladies. He then fetched their bags and carried them up the steps, setting them by the front door. They paid him, giving him a generous tip, and thanked him for a safe and enjoyable trip. Once inside, they were greeted by a lady standing behind a counter at the opposite end of the cozy room. There was a fireplace, comfortable chairs, and side tables with lamps that cast a soft glow and seemed to beckon for you to come sit, relax, and enjoy.

"Hi, you must be Leah Dawson and Sandy Carlton. We've been expecting you. I'm Joan Hataway. I can get you checked in and show you to your cottage," said the lady behind the counter. When the paperwork was completed, Joan led them out the back door and around to their accommodations. She said they would be staying in Gray Dove that night but would move to Broadview Cottage the next day. "Broadview is larger, and each room has its own bath. You'll be much more comfortable there. Sorry it's not ready yet, but we had guests who just checked out this afternoon. I know you must be starved. The dining room is closed, so I'll have George bring dinner to your room."

She continued her monologue, telling them breakfast would be served from 7:30 until 9:30 the next morning. The inn wouldn't be serving lunch, but there was a nice restaurant in the resort where they could eat. The workshop did not officially start until the next afternoon, when it would kick off with a wine and cheese reception to get acquainted with the other participants.

At Gray Dove cottage, Joan opened the door and helped them in with their bags. "Your painting supplies arrived yesterday; they're in the office. We'll move them to your rooms at Broadview tomorrow. Just let me know if you need anything."

"What about the key?" Sandy asked.

"Oh, we don't have any keys; the doors are never locked here. You can bolt your door from the inside if you want to lock it," Joan replied as she turned to leave.

"But," stammered Sandy, "anyone could go into the rooms when we're not in them."

"Don't worry, my dear. We've had workshops here at the inn for 22 years, and there's never been any problem with thefts or break-ins. This is a laid-back country inn. Unlike cities, where crime is rampant, it's practically non-existent here. But, we want you to be comfortable and at ease here, so if you have any valuables, we'll be happy to put them in the safe in the office."

Joan smiled and patted Sandy on the shoulder. "Just let me know if you have any more concerns, and I'll see that they're resolved." She bid them a good night and went out the door.

The cottage consisted of a large main room with a sofa and several comfortable-looking chairs, two bedrooms and one bath. Leah kicked off her shoes, "I don't know about you, but I'm getting into something more comfortable." She rolled her bag into one of the bedrooms, opened it, and dug out a pair of jogging pants and a sweat shirt. Sandy appeared in the doorway, looking at Leah with a concerned expression.

"Okay, my friend, tell me what's going on with John Phelps. I know he's been driving you crazy, but you've got that deer-in-the-headlights look, so what's he done now?"

"You always could tell when something was bothering me. The fact that I've been complaining about him every time we talk on the phone *is* a pretty good clue that things are no better. I'm so afraid John will follow me up here. He was in my house yesterday. I don't know how he got in, but I know he did. He left a daisy in my nightstand."

"Did you call the police?"

"Of course—a lot of good it did. They chalked me up as a hysterical woman, imagining things. I looked out the window while I was on the line with 911, and John was parked in front of my house. He just waved and drove away. When I told the police about that, they sent an officer to his house and…"

"Wait, let me guess. He was at home in bed."

"Right, and that was the icing on the cake. I've never been so patronized in my life. I expected them to pat me on the head and tell me to be a good little girl and quit making up stories."

"John sounds like a slick character, but we'll figure out a way to get rid of him," Sandy said.

"I feel better already. And…" Leah started saying, but was interrupted by a loud knocking. She walked over and opened the door. A man about fifty, with graying hair, wearing a pair of overalls and a plaid shirt, was standing there holding a cloth-covered tray.

"Hi, my name's George. I'm the handy man here at the inn. I've brought your dinner. Where would you like me to put it?"

Leah moved some books from the coffee table and told him to set the food there.

"Well, I've got to run, but you'll probably see me puttering around this week. I fix things—guess that's why they call me the handy man. If you need anything, just holler," George said, opening the door to leave.

"Thank you so much. We really appreciate it," Leah said, as she closed the door and bolted it. "What do we have?" she asked, going over to join Sandy on the sofa. "I'm so hungry I could eat a horse."

"It looks like a chicken casserole," Sandy said, removing the coverings from the food. There were two salads and two small casserole dishes containing something that smelled heavenly. Also included were napkins, silverware, two bottles of water, a basket of homemade rolls and salad dressing. "Yum, this is delicious," Sandy said as she dug into the food. "I feel like I've died and gone to gourmet heaven; I better plan on starting a diet when I get home. I'm going to enjoy every meal, and I'll probably gain ten pounds."

They finished eating and put the empty containers and utensils back on the tray.

"It's been a long day," Leah said. "How about us calling it a night and finish our talk tomorrow?"

"Sounds good to me," Sandy said, giving Leah a hug. "And don't worry about John, we'll figure out something."

Leah opened the windows before she crawled into bed. There was a cool breeze with a promise of rain in the air. She could smell the crisp, algae scent of the ocean and hear the steady rhythm of waves breaking against the rocky shore. She snuggled under the covers and, for the first time in days, felt safe and secure as she drifted off to sleep.

****

Leah awoke to the steady sound of rain falling on the roof of the cottage. She lay there stretching and enjoying the fresh, clean smell of rain-drenched foliage and the distant sounds of squawking gulls. She looked at the clock on her bedside table—7:35 was glowing in large, red numbers. She could hear Sandy moving about in the next room and then the sound of the shower. *Guess I better get up too*, she thought as she crawled out from under the warm covers, shivered, and closed the windows.

Sandy came out of the bathroom, followed by a cloud of steam. "Good morning, sleepy head. Did I wake you?"

"No, I was awake, just didn't want to get out of the warm bed. Are you through in the bathroom?"

"I've got to dry my hair, but I'll do it in my bedroom," Sandy said as she grabbed the hair dryer.

Leah took a quick shower and got dressed in a pair of jeans and a long sleeve, red top. She ran a brush through her hair and looked at her reflection in the mirror. "Oh, great day, now I've got bags under my eyes," she said to herself. Sandy came out of her room wearing jeans and a bright yellow sweater.

"I heard that! You don't have bags, just a little puffiness that'll go away after you've been up awhile. You know, you have beautiful eyes. I've never seen anyone with that shade of turquoise blue."

Leah smiled, "You always could make me feel good about myself, even when I was young and so insecure."

"I just pointed out the facts. You're smart, beautiful, kind, and compassionate—that's what you were then, and it's what you are now."

"You just described yourself," Leah said, giving Sandy a hug. "So, let's take this mutual admiration society down to the dining room and feed our beautiful faces."

The rain had stopped, but the air was still heavy with moisture. When they arrived the night before, the tide had been out, leaving only rocks and mud visible in the moonlight. The tide was in now, and they stopped to admire the view. Fog hovered over the bay, and boats appeared as ghostly apparitions emerging from the water. Gulls seeking food swooped and dived, their squawks muffled by the fog.

Rocky Ledge Inn was located on a peninsula, surrounded on two sides by Eagle Nest Bay and a cove on the third side. Large boulder-sized rocks covered the steep incline from the ledges above to the water below, hence the name Rocky Ledge Inn. Impatiens, Petunias, Periwinkles, and other perennials grew in beds interspersed along the lane that led to the main house. Flower boxes added bright splashes of color to the cottages located around the outer edges of the peninsula. "What a beautiful and charming place," Sandy said in an appreciative tone of voice.

As Leah and Sandy drew near the house, they could see a man standing on the small patio just outside the back door. He was feeding a large white dog tied on a leash.

"What a beautiful dog," Leah said, as she approached the man.

"This is Sasha, a Siberian husky," the man informed her.

"She has such beautiful, blue eyes. Is she friendly?" Leah asked.

"Yes, she's very friendly unless she senses hostility or evil in a person."

"My name's Leah Dawson, and this is my friend Sandy Carlton. We're here for the workshop," Leah said, extending her hand.

"My name's Jason Atwell. I'm the breakfast chef," he said, shaking hands with Leah and Sandy. "Sasha and I do sled dog racing in Alaska sometimes. We've won a few races, but we mainly do it for fun. She's very smart and loyal. She likes both of you. She knows good people when she meets them."

As he leaned forward to untangle Sasha's leash, his lightweight jacket slid up. Leah caught a glimpse of a pistol in the back of his pants. The sight of the gun made Leah a little nervous, and she wondered why he was carrying it. But, she instinctively trusted and liked this man. She thanked him for allowing them to pet Sasha.

"Something sure smells good. Are you ready for coffee and food?" she asked, looking at Sandy.

"You know I'm always ready for food," Sandy replied as they headed toward the back door. They entered a sunporch, which led into a large sitting room containing a television, sofa, chairs, and side tables. The room had a comfortable, welcoming ambience. Leah and Sandy passed through it and down a short hall to the dining room. As they passed the open door to the office, they could see Joan Hataway sitting behind a desk. Another woman was leaning over her shoulder, looking at some papers. Joan looked up as Leah and Sandy walked by, "Good morning ladies! Did you have a good night?" They both assured her everything was very comfortable and the dinner had been delicious. "This is Liz Walker, the owner of Rocky Ledge Inn," Joan said, introducing the other lady.

"It's so nice to meet you," said Sandy, extending her hand. Leah said hello and reminded Liz they'd met two years ago when she'd attended a workshop here. "I'm so sorry to hear about your father passing away last year."

"Yes, I do remember you, and it was a shock. Who would have ever thought by the time I saw you again my father would be gone. I guess you're never ready to lose a parent, but when it's so sudden and unexpected, it really hurts," Liz said, with a sad introspective look.

"Did you have a nice flight in yesterday?" she asked, suddenly changing the subject.

"Very uneventful," Leah replied. "Oh, I forgot, we did see Andrew Barzetti, our instructor in the airport parking lot. He was picked up by a limo sent by his friend in Portland."

"Yes, I understand he has a friend who has a home in Portland as well as an art gallery and apartment in New York."

Leah was a little puzzled by Liz's tone of voice. She didn't seem to approve of Andy's friend.

"Enjoy your breakfast and have a wonderful day. Don't forget the wine and cheese reception at five this afternoon," Liz said, turning back to her work.

Chapter 2

Nathan Parker pushed his car seat back and stretched out his long legs. He'd been driving since he and his sister Becky left her home in North Conway, New Hampshire that morning, about the same time Leah and Sandy were having breakfast. When they stopped for lunch, Becky offered to relieve him for the remainder of the trip. "We shouldn't be more than an hour away from the inn," she said, while adjusting her seat.

"Alright," Nate said, "let's go over our story again. I don't want any slip-ups this week."

"I won't have any trouble remembering my part since we're using my real name and background. I've just got to remember to call you Hal, or honey, the way I do my husband. I don't want to slip and call you Nate."

"Yep," replied Nate, with a concerned expression, "It's important I maintain my cover. I don't know what to expect, could be a precarious situation."

Becky would be attending the acrylic painting workshop at Rocky Ledge Inn and was due to check in no later than 2:00 PM that afternoon. Her brother was going under the guise of her husband in order to keep a low profile and track down art thieves. He was one of sixteen special agents with the FBI making up a team of dedicated art crime investigators.

Based on reliable sources, the person or persons responsible for several recent art thefts were expected to be at Rocky Ledge Inn the coming week. Nate's job was to find evidence that would expose and convict that person or persons. He or she was like a chameleon, changing their appearance the way some people change clothes. This last heist had been one of their biggest. The thief had walked away with a Jan Van Eyck painting worth somewhere in the neighborhood of $2.5 million, leaving an empty frame hanging on the museum wall. The theft took place at the Uffizi Gallery in Florence, Italy, one of the oldest galleries in the world but with updated, high-tech security.

There was one commonality in all the thefts: the criminal always bought a print in the gift shop, using the tube the print came in to conceal the stolen painting. The gift shops equipped with surveillance cameras had videos of all the purchases made the days the crimes took place. The images were grainy and, even though experts had enhanced them, it was impossible to get a good description. Only by the movements and mannerisms could they tell if it was the same person. Sometimes it appeared to be a man and other times a woman. They sometimes wore pants and a loose-fitting jacket and sometimes a dress. At times they wore a hat. Other times, the person appeared to be an older, plump woman with gray hair or a younger, slim blond or redhead. However, one thing never changed: the person who bought the print was always left-handed. Nate was inclined to believe the videos were of one person. And that person probably had an accomplice who managed a distraction while the painting was quickly sliced from the frame. Nate's gut feeling told him he was looking for two people. It could be two men, two women, or a man and woman, but Nate felt sure they would be closely connected somehow.

"I know you're investigating an art heist, but just what do you expect to find at Rocky Ledge Inn?" Becky asked.

"I'm not sure yet. All I know is the person or persons behind this latest art crime is supposed to be at the inn or somewhere in the immediate vicinity. The Bureau sent three other agents to assist me. They should already be there."

"Are they attending the workshop?"

"No. One of them is working as a chef at the inn. The other two are a married couple, supposedly on vacation, relaxing and soaking up the local color."

"Becky, never, under any circumstances, show or say anything that will portray us as anything other than an average couple on vacation, you painting and me photographing. I know enough about photography and birds to pose as an enthusiastic ornithologist. That'll give me an opportunity to be out nosing around and poking into places without causing suspicion."

"Bird watchers don't poke around just anywhere," countered Becky.

"I can always come up with a logical excuse for whatever I'm doing."

"Yeah, you always came up with a good story when we were kids and got into trouble. And, don't worry about me; I'm good at improvising and I'm a pretty good actor, too. Remember what a good job I did as the lead in our high school senior play?"

"Yeah, the way I remember it, you forgot your lines in the third act, and Paul Holcombe had to whisper them to you."

"Well, I *was* only seventeen, and I still did an excellent acting job. Besides, you'll be nearby and can send me signals if I mess up," Becky said with a grin

Nate and Becky were fraternal twins but looked nothing alike. Nate had dark hair and hazel eyes, about 6'4" and a solid 220. Becky was tall and slim with sun-streaked, light brown hair and smoky gray eyes. Like most siblings, they'd fought like cats and dogs growing up. But if anyone else did something to hurt one of them, they'd fight like a tiger to defend or protect each other. They seemed to know what the other was thinking without saying a word.

Nate laughed, but then his face grew somber. "We don't really know what to expect, but the people we're looking for could be very dangerous. Anyone who would pull off the daring robberies they did will probably do anything to avoid being exposed. Bottom line, Becky, watch what you say and do at all times."

****

The dining room was empty when Leah and Sandy entered for breakfast and sat down by a window. They had just placed their order when a couple appearing to be in their mid-fifties came in and sat at the table next to them. The woman was around 5'3" and looked physically fit, like someone who worked out regularly. She had red-blond hair, cut in a flattering style. The man also looked physically fit. He was around 5'10", medium build with salt and pepper hair that was beginning to recede. They were dressed casually, both wearing hiking boots, cargo pants, tee shirts and hooded jackets.

"Good morning," the woman said with a warm smile. "Are you two here for the workshop?"

Leah and Sandy said yes, they were, and soon the four of them were chattering away like old friends. The couple introduced themselves as Ron and Sheila Rhodes from Houston, Texas. They were there just to relax and do some sightseeing. Their food had just been brought out when another couple entered the dining room. They also looked to be mid fiftyish. The woman was around 5'5" and very slim. She had medium-length brown hair and was dressed in tight, designer jeans, a white silk blouse, and a denim jacket. She had diamond studs in her ears that were at least a carat each. The man was around six feet, medium build with white hair and a moustache. He looked debonair in khaki pants, a Ralph Lauren polo shirt, and a Rolex watch.

"Good morning, everyone," the woman said as they sat down at the table next to the Rhodes. "Isn't this the most divine place? So quaint. It reminds me of a place in France where we stayed once.

"My name is Susan Porter, and this is my husband Wayne. We're spending the week at the inn and attending a wedding being held here on the grounds next Saturday. What about all of you? Are you here for the workshop?"

Sandy, Leah, and the Rhodes introduced themselves, and the group continued to chat until Leah and Sandy excused themselves.

"Well, that was an interesting breakfast," Sandy said as they headed back up the lane to Gray Dove to get their things and move to Broadview, their location for the rest of the week.

"Yeah, the Porters are obviously very wealthy, and Susan seems to like to flaunt it," Leah said.

"Oh yes, my dear, wasn't that 500-year-old castle we stayed in while in Italy just too magnificent for words," Sandy said, trying to mimic Susan's voice.

Leah laughed. "Well, the Rhodes are probably as wealthy as the Porters, but you'd never guess from their down to earth attitude. They seem like a very nice couple."

At Gray Dove, they packed their belongings and rolled their bags up a slight incline to Broadview, which was located on the point of the peninsula. Eagle Nest Bay spread out as far as the eye could see with sail boats and colorful buoys moored just off shore. Most of the clouds had dissipated with only a few cotton puffs remaining. The rain had cleared the air, leaving the sky a brilliant cobalt blue. Several Adirondack chairs scattered about the lawn seemed to beckon to come sit and enjoy the view.

"What a beautiful sight. I can see why it's called Broadview cottage," Leah said, turning and looking out over the bay.

They entered the building that would be their home for the next week. A sunporch with a sink, refrigerator, microwave, and several chairs led into a comfortable sitting room. A split hallway led to their respective rooms. Rooms one and two were on the right, while three and four were on the left. Leah was in number four, Sandy in number three. Each room had a private bath and a radio, but that was the extent of the amenities. There were no phones, televisions, or air conditioners.

"I think I'll get unpacked and settled in," Leah said, standing in her doorway.

"Good idea, think I'll do the same," Sandy said, entering her room.

Leah closed the door and looked around. There was a twin-size bed, nightstand, dresser, and chest of drawers—her home away from home for the coming week. Several watercolors hung on the walls. Leah knew without checking the signature they were painted by Liz's father, Charles Walker. He had been a well-known watercolorist and was often featured in *American Artist* magazine and *American Art Review*.

"It must have been devastating for Liz when he died here at Rocky Ledge Inn after slipping and falling in the bathroom," Leah thought as she unpacked her bags.

Leah finished unpacking and stowed her empty bag under the bed. The box of painting materials she'd shipped in advance sat in the corner of the room. Leah opened it to make sure nothing had broken in transit. She'd packed a heavy jogging jacket in with the supplies to allow more room in her luggage and provide padding for the painting materials. Everything seemed to be intact; nothing had opened and spilled.

She went into the bathroom and brushed her teeth, then went next door and knocked. Sandy opened her door almost immediately.

"Would you like to take a walk and do a little exploring?"

"I'd love to," Sandy said, "just let me get my Nikes and I'll be ready to go."

As Sandy got her shoes, Leah looked around. "This is the room I had two years ago. It's almost identical to the one I'm in now except the paintings are different. But, they're also by Liz's father."

"They've got to be prints. His originals must be worth a mint now that he's deceased. They already cost an arm and a leg when he was still living," Sandy said.

"I think Liz is an only child, so it must have left her pretty well off. But, I'm sure that doesn't compensate for the loss of her father," Leah said.

"How do you feel about not having a door key and leaving your room unlocked when you're not in?" Sandy asked.

"I think this is a safe place and I don't have anything of real value, so it doesn't bother me. Unless, on second thought, if John Phelps was hiding inside when I returned from an outing."

As they left their cottage, they noticed Ron and Sheila Rhodes, their breakfast companions, standing outside of the cottage next door to theirs. They were involved in a discussion with Jason Atwell, the breakfast chef. Leah noticed that Sheila seemed to be upset and distraught about something. Ron cleared his throat and Sheila looked up and saw Leah and Sandy coming down the lane towards them. A smile spread across her face as she waved a greeting. "We meet again. Looks like we may be neighbors. Are you in Broadview cottage?"

"Yes," Sandy said, "We just got settled in and thought we'd do a little exploring."

"Are we interrupting anything?" Leah asked.

"Oh, no. Jason was just telling us about his mushing days," Sheila said.

"Would you like to join us for a walk?" Leah asked.

"We'd really love to, but we've already made plans to run over to the village."

"Well, guess we'll see you at the reception this afternoon," Leah said as they walked away.

They walked past the main house and down the road that led to Eagle Nest Estates. A path veered off to the right and curved around the north end of the cove, and they turned and headed in that direction. The path led up an incline and into some woods. It wound around through the trees and over a footbridge that spanned a narrow bubbling creek. A little ways past the bridge was a gazebo. They stopped and sat down there to rest,

"Wonder how far we've walked? Seems like miles. You know I'm not used to all this activity. You may have to send a rescue squad to carry me back," Sandy said.

"It hasn't been that far, probably no more than a mile," Leah said with a laugh. "We'll rest awhile and head back. It'll be time to go over to the estate and have some lunch by then."

"Guess I really needed the walk." Sandy said with a moan. "Seems all we do is eat, but I am getting hungry. All this activity has given me an appetite."

They walked back to the inn, made a pit stop, and then headed to the Ledges restaurant in Eagle Nest Estates. The restaurant was built beside a lake with part of the building extending out over the water. The hostess seated them beside a window with a spectacular view. They both ordered a salad and the soup of the day, which was organic carrot and ginger. Sandy was a little skeptical about the soup, but when it arrived, she found it to be delicious. Leah had been looking out the window watching a cripple gull limping around searching for food when she caught sight of a familiar-looking person. He was standing by a light pole talking to another man. She turned pale as the blood drained from her face and she dropped her spoon back into the soup. She rose from her seat and headed to the door.

"What is it? What is wrong?" Sandy asked in a startled voice as she jumped up to follow Leah.

Leah rushed out the door, looking to the right where she'd seen the two men. She scanned all the people as far as she could see, but the man she'd seen was not among them.

"What is it? My God, you're pale as a sheet! What is wrong? What did you see?" Sandy asked as she grabbed Leah by the arm, "Please tell me what is going on!"

"It's John Phelps. I saw him standing out here talking to a man. He's followed me here! How does that slime-ball manage to follow me everywhere I go?!"

"Leah, calm down. Do you see him anywhere now? If he has followed you, we'll go to the authorities and charge him with stalking or get a restraining order or something. Where is he?" Sandy said, scanning the people in the area.

"He's gone. I don't see him anywhere now. But, I know I saw him! He was standing right over there," Leah said, pointing in the direction of the light pole by the dock.

"It was probably just someone who favored him, and you've been so upset your imagination overreacted. Come on; let's go finish our lunch. They'll think we're trying to skip out without paying."

After they were back in their seats and Leah had calmed down somewhat, she started trying to rationalize the situation. "I think you're right; it was someone who looked like John and I overreacted. He can't have just disappeared."

"What does he do for a living?" Sandy asked.

"He has an import business. He travels extensively, going abroad very often. He imports the 'finest olive oil from Italy, the best quality Oriental rugs from Persia and India, among other things,' to quote John. I'd say he's fairly successful, based on his lifestyle.

"Sandy, I'm not totally convinced that wasn't John. When we were still seeing each other, I mentioned that you and I had enrolled in Andrew Barzetti's workshop in Maine. John is very tech savvy, so it would be incredibly easy for him to find out when and where the workshop was being held. He's a very clever man."

"We'll keep our eyes open. If he's here and causes you any problems, we'll do something. Surely, he wouldn't try to hurt you physically; it sounds like he is trying to intimidate you into a relationship, regardless of what you may want."

"I don't know *what* he's capable of doing. I just know he scares the hell out of me."

Leah and Sandy finished their lunch and walked back to the inn without seeing anyone resembling John. They were both tired and decided to go back to their rooms to rest until time for the reception later that afternoon.

Once in her room, Leah turned the hot water faucet on and poured bubble bath into the tub, adjusting the temperature as the foamy bubbles rose and a pleasant fragrance filled the air. She shed her clothes and, with a sigh, slid into the water. She didn't realize how tired she was until she leaned her head back and began dozing as she relaxed in the hot water. When the water began to cool, she climbed out of the tub, dried off, and wrapped a towel around herself. She pulled the covers back on the bed, let the towel fall to the floor, and slid in between the sheets. She was asleep by the time her head hit the pillow.

****

John stepped out of the boat house that was down the incline from the light pole where he'd been standing when Leah spotted him. He had been talking to a man about renting a boat when he saw Leah through the restaurant window. He saw her when she'd looked in his direction and jumped up from her seat. He'd told the man he needed to look at his equipment again and quickly headed down the incline, into the boathouse. He was completely hidden by the time Leah exited the restaurant. *The stupid bitch never saw me*, he thought, *but she'll see me when I'm ready for her to see me. No one dumps John Phelps. I'll have her or I'll see to it that no one else does.*

Chapter 3

The fog had moved back in, and Leah could barely make out the trees as she ran through the woods, a wet limb occasionally slapping her in the face. She could hear the sounds of footsteps behind her, but no matter how fast she ran, the sound of the steps grew closer and louder. She kept looking back to see who was pursuing her, but she could only see a dark outline in the heavy mist. The footsteps grew louder until they became a pounding in her ears, and, over the pounding, someone was calling her name.

Leah's eyes flew open as she became fully awake and realized someone was knocking on her door. Her heart was still pounding as she got her bearings. *What a dream—more like a nightmare!*

"Are you alright," Sandy asked from the other side of the door.

"I'm fine, you just woke me from a bad dream. Hold on while I grab my robe."

"That's ok. It's ten minutes until five, and I thought I would walk on down to the reception, but I'll wait for you if you like."

"No, go on, I'll get dressed and be down in about fifteen minutes."

Leah crawled out of bed as the sound of Sandy's footsteps receded down the hall. She slipped into a pair of black silk pants and a cream-colored silk blouse, added a little blush and lipstick and ran a brush through her dark brown, shoulder-length hair. She grabbed a black beaded jacket and headed down the hill to the main house.

Leah entered the large room she and Sandy had passed through that morning on the way to breakfast. The room was now filled with people. She scanned the faces of those milling around but saw no one she recognized. Then, she caught sight of a long, dark ponytail. The ponytail turned, and there was Andrew Barzetti. His eyes lit on her, and a smile spread across his face as he headed in her direction. He had a glass of wine in his left hand, which he set on a nearby table. Spreading his arms, Leah thought he was going to hug her. Instead, he grabbed her hand in both of his and raised it to his lips.

"I must apologize for the confusion I caused yesterday. I was suffering jet lag and wasn't my usual astute self. It was so very sweet of you to offer to share your taxi, and it would have been a pleasure and honor to ride with two such lovely ladies. I'm looking forward to the coming week—I love teaching and observing the growth of budding artists."

"Thank you, Mr. Barzetti. I'm excited and very much looking forward to the workshop also," Leah said with a smile.

"Please call me Andy, and yes, I will teach with patience and forbearance all week. Eager students shall garner my most secret techniques, and I will impart my painting knowledge to all who will listen and learn."

Leah, thinking perhaps he had imbibed one glass of wine too many, said, "That's wonderful, Andy. I hope to learn a lot from you this week." Spotting Sandy coming into the room, she excused herself and went over to her friend.

"Have you talked to our *patient* and *forbearing* instructor yet," she asked Sandy with a smile.

"Oh yes, I have been most graciously begged forgiveness and informed of his eagerness to impart knowledge to those willing to learn. Did he tell you why he was not his usual astute self at the airport?"

"Only that he was suffering jet lag."

"Well, he told me all about being abroad the last two weeks. He taught a workshop in France for a week, and then visited relatives in Sicily. He assumed the inn would send transportation. His friend in Portland had failed to inform him of his invitation, but everything was 'in bocca al lupo,' whatever that means," Sandy said.

There was a makeshift bar set up in the front room and a table containing several delectable looking hors d'oeuvres. Leah headed in that direction and ordered a glass of white wine. She retrieved a small plate and napkin and helped herself to some olives, stuffed celery, and a few nuts and grapes, trying to ignore the rich looking dips and pastries.

"Don't you know that stuff will make you fat?" A tall man said, pointing at Leah's plate.

"Excuse me?" Leah said, turning and looking at the man who'd just spoken to her. He had thick, dark, unruly hair and hazel eyes with flecks of green. Those eyes were now locked on hers with an intensity that sent shivers down her spine. She tore her gaze away from his, feeling her knees grow weak.

"I'm sorry," the man said with a grin. "My name is Hal Lawson. Are you here for the workshop?"

"Yes, I am. My name is Leah Dawson. What about you? Are you attending the workshop?" Leah said, trying to regain her composure.

He laughed, "How about that. We rhyme. Our last names, that is. No, I'll be on my own photographing and enjoying the scenery."

An attractive woman walked over, stood beside him, and said, "He's just along for the ride. I'm Becky Lawson. I'll be attending the workshop."

"Becky, this is Leah Dawson—we were just talking about the fact that our names rhyme."

"Only one letter makes the difference," Becky said with a laugh.

"Have you been painting very long, Leah?"

"Most of my life, but I just started painting with acrylic about two years ago. How about you?"

"Same here. I started painting in junior high with watercolor, switched to oils later, and just started with acrylic about a year ago. I'm really looking forward to the workshop."

Sandy walked up about that time with a man and woman who looked vaguely familiar to Leah.

"Do you remember Louise and Joe Williams? Louise was at a workshop with us in Greenville, New York three or four years ago," Sandy said to Leah.

"I knew you looked familiar. I remember now. That was a great workshop," Leah said and then introduced Becky and Hal to the group.

They all acknowledged each other and chatted for a while about the workshop, the inn, and various other topics. Another couple came over and joined the group and introductions were made again. The entire time the group was conversing, Leah was aware of Hal Lawson's intense gaze. When she glanced his way, she'd catch him staring, but then his eyes would slide to a point somewhere beyond her. She could feel his presence as strongly as if there were an electrical current running between them. It seemed everyone in the room should be receiving shock waves from those currents. She excused herself and went into the next room. She had to get away from the tall man with the hazel-green eyes and unruly hair.

Damn, what is wrong *with me? The wine must have gone straight to my head.* But she knew it wasn't the wine. She couldn't remember when she'd experienced such excitement when she looked at a person of the opposite sex. *Well, I'll just have to avoid Mr. Lawson this week because there's a Mrs. Lawson, and she seems like a very nice person.*

Leah saw Ron and Sheila Rhodes across the room. They were talking with two women, who both appeared to be in their early thirties. She drifted in their direction, speaking to several people along the way.

When she reached the group, Sheila introduced her to the pair.

"This is Mary Jane," she said, "a pathologist from Boston, and this is Linda, an attorney from New York. I think they are your cottage mates."

"Yes," Mary Jane said, "we have rooms one and two in Broadview Cottage."

"You must be in the ones with a private deck. I'm so jealous. Would you like to swap rooms?" Leah asked with a grin.

"No, but you're welcome to join us anytime. I'm sure it'll be nice to sit out there, relax, maybe have a glass of wine and enjoy the scenery after a hard day of painting."

"Thanks, I may take you up on that; it's very nice of you to offer to share."

"You must be from the South," Linda, the lawyer, said with a slightly patronizing smile.

"Why, yes, I live in Germantown, Tennessee, a suburb of Memphis, but I grew up in Kentucky. Have you always lived in New York?" Leah asked, sensing a hostility emanating from the woman.

"No, actually I grew up in Georgia, but I moved from there as soon as possible," Linda said, as if "Georgia" was a dirty word she spat from her mouth.

"What area of law do you practice?"

"I'm in civil litigation with the firm Jamison, Jamison, and Mason. You've probably never heard of them, but they're very well known in the Northeast."

"No, afraid not," replied Leah, "but then again, I don't keep up with what's going on in the world of litigations. I stay pretty busy with my interior design business."

"Oh, I'm surprised there's much demand for that type of service in Tennessee," Linda said with a disdainful expression.

"I manage to keep myself occupied," Leah said, trying to maintain her composure and wondering what was eating at this woman.

****

Nate Parker, masquerading as Hal Lawson, had just entered the room and, noticing Leah talking to the four people, turned and left. He wanted very much to get lost in the depths of those tantalizing blue eyes. *It's like looking into the waters of a Caribbean Sea.* He shook his head to rid himself of the vision filling his mind and the warmth spreading over his body. He couldn't afford to get involved with a woman. He had a job to do and she was much too distracting. He could hardly tear his eyes away every time he got near her. It made him angry. Angry at himself, and angry at her. *Why the hell did she have to be here? For all he knew, she could be the art thief. Yeah, right, and bears don't crap in the woods.*

Nate helped himself to a glass of wine and started back to where Becky was still chatting with the Porters. They all seemed very amused by the story Susan Porter was telling.

"Sounds like I've missed something very amusing," he said, rejoining the group.

"Wayne and Susan were just telling me about getting lost while in southern France," Becky said.

"Yes, absolutely no one spoke English and our French leaves much to be desired, but Wayne managed to communicate with pantomime, gestures, and a few words of French. I was telling Becky, I would love to have had a picture of him trying to get the locals to understand that we were lost."

"Well, at least I managed to get us back on the right track," Wayne said.

"Do you travel often?" Nate asked

"Yes, we've covered most of Europe several times and have taken one trip to Africa."

"What kind of work do you do that gives you the freedom to travel so much?"

"I dabble in a number of things but mostly real estate development. What line of work are you in?" Wayne asked.

"I own the local NBC affiliate TV station in Conway, New Hampshire," Nate said.

"Are either one of you attending the workshop?" asked Becky, interrupting the conversation, afraid Nate was getting in over his head.

"No, we're going to the wedding being held here next Saturday. We decided to come early and make it a vacation," Susan said.

"There's that darling man who's teaching the workshop. He has family in Italy, and I've got to ask him about something he was telling us earlier this afternoon. Please excuse us," Susan said, grabbing Wayne's arm and propelling him in the direction of Andy, who was standing at the bar getting his wine glass refilled.

****

The dining room was full when everyone gathered for dinner that night. Leah sat at the table with Sandy, the Williamses, and Andrew

Barzetti. She was very much aware of the Lawson's sitting at the second table over from theirs. Fortunately, Andy turned out to be very entertaining. He was telling them all the different things he'd done to scrape by until his art was recognized. He'd actually had one painting sell for almost $45,000 and, according to him, a gazillion prints of the same painting and still counting. *He certainly is not modest*, thought Leah as he told them he only did workshops for the enjoyment of teaching others, not because he needed to.

"Yes," he said with a laugh, "I've waited tables, sold children's books, and worked as a short order cook. While I was doing those odd jobs, I cleaned and restored rare paintings. I even worked as a magician, entertaining at children's parties and carnivals," he said, reaching behind Sandy's ear and pulling out a coin. Everyone laughed and applauded softly.

When Leah looked in the direction of the second table, her eyes locked with Nate Parker's. He had been watching the instructor's performance, but when his gaze swept over Leah, it stopped as if pulled there by a giant magnet. She turned her face away, but not before she noticed a look of determined resolve replace the expression of desire burning in his eyes. She felt a flush creeping up her cheeks as she looked across the table and saw Sandy watching her with a concerned expression.

"Okay everyone, listen up," Andy said, while clicking a spoon against a glass. "There is rain in the forecast for tomorrow morning, so we will meet in the studio at 9 AM. I'll do a demo painting, and— if the weather permits—we'll go out on location and paint; if not, we'll paint in the studio. I'm looking forward to working with all of you. We're going to have a fun and instructive week."

"Hear, hear," said several of the people, lifting their wine glasses and drinking a toast to the instructor. There was a light sprinkling of applause from the group, and a few people came over, apparently to ask more questions about the workshop.

Leah eased out of her seat and headed toward the door. She felt a need to get away from the crowd, breathe some fresh air, and clear her head. Sandy was talking to the Williamses, so Leah didn't wait for her. She stepped outside and took a deep breath. Most of the people were still inside; only a few had left early. Leah started up the lane to Broadview. There was a full moon, and lights twinkled from the windows of several cottages. The air was cool and crisp, and she could hear the distant sound of the surf. *The tide must be coming in or going out,* Leah though as she approached Broadview. She sat down in one of the Adirondack chairs and pulled her jacket closer. She was beginning to feel the bite of the cool air, but she hated the thought of going inside right now. It looked as though the moon had cast down golden jewels, spreading them across the dark water of the bay. She could see a few boats moored out from the shore, bobbing in the water, their masts pointing towards the moon like fingers from a giant hand. She could hear the eerie sounds of the buoys as they rose and fell with the waves, and she thought of the person she had seen at lunch. *Could it have been John Phelps? Surely and hopefully I'd been mistaken.*

She thought of Hal Lawson and the way his piercing gaze had made her feel. He made her heart beat faster and her body tingle with warmth. She felt an excitement and desire she'd not felt with any man in her adult life. He looked at her as though he could see her thoughts so clearly, as if they were printed on her forehead. She felt a warm glow, but then anger took its place. Anger at herself and anger at him. How could she have these feelings, knowing he was a married man? She remembered the way his expression had suddenly closed and a hard, determined look had spread over his face. *Well, maybe he does have a conscience, but I will not think about him*, she told herself as she started to rise from the chair and go inside.

She heard the cottage door open and the sound of footsteps. Thinking it was one of the other occupants, she turned to say hello when the word froze on her lips. A man was coming out the door and heading down the lane. He had not seen Leah. She hunkered down lower in her chair. She didn't think he was anyone she knew; he was too thin to be George the handy man. He had on a cap and a jacket pulled up around his ears. It could have been someone she'd met, but she couldn't see well enough in the moonlight to know for sure. She couldn't think of any reason why a lone man would have been in Broadview cottage when none of the occupants were home. Thank God she'd sat down outside for a few minutes, or else she would have walked in while he was still there. And, she reminded herself, none of the doors were ever locked, which made it easy for anyone to enter the rooms. She shivered, and not from the cold. She felt apprehensive about going into the cottage alone. *The intruder is gone and I can go in my room and lock the door. I need to try to determine if anything is missing.* She eased out of the chair and headed to the door.

****

Nate and Becky had left the dining room shortly after Leah's exit. They were staying in Rosewood cottage, located near the front of the inn property and on the bay side of the peninsula. It consisted of a sitting room and two bedrooms, each with its own bath. There was a screened-in porch at one end of the sitting room. Becky and Nate were sitting on the porch rehashing the events of the day. The air was cool and crisp, but Nate didn't seem to notice. Becky was wrapped in a furry throw from the foot of one of the beds. The full moon was sparkling across the bay, and they could hear the waves pounding the rocky shore. Rosewood cottage was about two hundred feet from the ledge that dropped down to the bay, with rocks and boulders all the way to the water.

The Porters had been Becky and Nate's dinner companions, and, as they later discovered, were also occupants of Rosewood cottage. When Nate left the reception, he'd researched Wayne and discovered he was a very wealthy man—the owner of some prime real estate in Manhattan, and an investor in numerous other businesses. Nate had tried to learn more about Porter's business concerns while conversing with him at dinner, but Susan Porter was constantly interrupting with some anecdote about their travels.

"What do you think about the Porters?" Becky asked, while adjusting the throw around her feet.

"They give the impression of a bored, wealthy couple. Susan an airhead and Wayne a preoccupied, tolerant husband going along with whatever Susan wants. I think we need to keep an eye on them. Appearances can be deceiving."

"I met the couple who is here to assist me," Nate said

"When and how did you meet? You've been with me most of the night. Do I know them?"

"You met them at the reception, same time I did."

"Well, you were slick. I had no idea you'd made contact with any of the other agents."

"Yeah, that's part of our training. We learn to be sneaky and sly."

"Seriously, now. How did you connect?'

"Mostly eye contact and speaking in unknown tongues known as FBI language."

"You're hopeless. Did you find out if they've made any progress on the case while speaking this mysterious language?"

"They just arrived yesterday and met the other agent this morning. I'll meet with the three of them tomorrow morning and set up an agenda."

"I have no doubts you'll have this case wrapped up in a matter of days. You were always so determined and hard-headed. You never gave up on anything you started."

"Thanks, I hope you're right. I have enhanced photos from the surveillance videos, and I've studied the videos themselves. The problem is, it could be most anyone we've met. The thief has a different appearance on each one. Hopefully, I'll pick up on his or her mannerisms and movements. This is such a rural area. I can't imagine why they'd choose this place."

The sound of someone approaching the cottage interrupted their conversation. They heard the front door open, and a woman's laughter filled the air. Wayne Porter's muffled words were indiscernible. Then, Susan's loud, high-pitched voice answered, "Don't worry, honey. He's nobody's fool." Wayne's muffled reply was lost as their footsteps faded down the hall.

Chapter 4

Leah heard the welcome sound of voices and saw Sandy and Mary Jane coming up the hill. She could have hugged them when they reached Broadview.

"I sure am glad to see you two," she said, opening the door to the sunporch.

"It hasn't been long since you've seen us. What's up? Has something happened? You're pale as a sheet," Sandy said, with a concerned expression.

"I've been sitting out here enjoying the moonlight and the sounds of the bay. Guess I got a little chilled," Leah said, as they all entered the sunporch and went on into the sitting room.

"Would you like for me to build a fire? Looks like they have everything we need," Mary Jane said, indicating the stack of wood in the alcove beside the fireplace.

"No, I'm kind of tired, and we have an early day tomorrow. Think I'll call it a night, but y'all go ahead; I'll see you in the morning."

Leah went down the hall and entered her room. She switched the light on and looked around. Nothing seemed to be disturbed. She started to close the door, but Sandy was standing there.

"Okay, what's going on? You weren't just chilled; you were frightened. Tell me what happened. Surely you haven't seen John again."

"I saw a man come out of the cottage while I was sitting outside. I have no idea who it was."

"Could it have been George, the maintenance man? Why didn't you mention it to Mary Jane? Maybe she or Linda has a friend who was looking for one of them or bringing them something or who knows what. I really think you should tell Mary Jane and Linda just to be sure it wasn't a friend of theirs."

"You may be right; perhaps I should tell them. I didn't want to get anyone involved in case it was John."

"Okay, let's go talk to her now," Sandy said, leading the way back to the sitting room.

Mary Jane was sitting in one of the chairs looking through an art book. She looked up as the two came back into the room. "Oh, did you change your mind about retiring now?" she asked with a warm smile. Leah couldn't help but think of the difference between Mary

Jane and Linda. Mary Jane was so friendly and thoughtful, while Linda seemed like a real bitch with a big chip on her shoulder.

"Well, I guess I should have told you when you first got back, but I didn't want to upset you. Sandy thinks I should tell you now. You may have some ideas about it."

"About what? What should you have told me?" Mary Jane asked with a confused expression.

"When I left the dining room, I came straight up here and sat outside. I just wanted to sit and relax, unwind. But, when I started to go into the cottage a man came out the door. I couldn't see well enough to tell who it was. He was too slim to be George the handy man. Sandy thought maybe there was a possibility he could be a friend of yours or Linda's."

"I don't know about Linda, but he certainly wasn't a friend of mine. I'm not expecting anyone. I came up here to get away from everything. Maybe we should go back to the house and report it to the owner."

Just then, the sunporch door opened, and Linda walked into the room. "Am I crashing a party? I thought everyone would be in bed by now. Mary Jane explained about Leah coming back early, sitting out front for a while, and seeing a man coming out of their cottage.

"Well, is anything missing or disturbed, any signs of an intruder?" Linda asked in a miffed voice.

"We haven't checked everything, but on the surface, nothing seems to be out of place. Were you expecting anyone?" Mary Jane asked, looking at Linda.

"Why would I be expecting anyone? I'm here to paint, not rendezvous with some man. Maybe some of us are here for other reasons—maybe some of us have an over-active imagination."

Leah couldn't understand Linda's hostility. It was beginning to get under her skin, but she maintained her composure and responded in a soft voice, "I saw a man I didn't recognize leaving this cottage, and I think we should report it."

"Well, you won't be reporting anything tonight. The main house is closed; there's no one there. Unless you want to call 911 and bring out the local troops."

"No, I'll mention it to Liz tomorrow; meanwhile, I think we should lock the sunporch door, and we can each lock our bedroom doors. It's probably just someone helping George with some kind of maintenance."

"Mary Jane and I both checked our rooms and nothing's missing—everything seems to be in order," Sandy said, coming back into the sitting room.

Leah locked the door to the sunporch and the door to the sitting room.

"This is supposed to be a safe place. Don't you think you're being a little paranoid?" Linda asked, looking more puzzled than hostile now.

Leah ignored her comment, bid them all goodnight, and went to her room.

"What is it with the legal beagle?" Sandy said, following Leah into her room. "She seems to have a vendetta against you."

"I have no idea what her problem could be; she doesn't know me from Adam's house cat, but she never misses an opportunity to throw digs at me."

"By the way, what is it with the goo-goo eyes with Mister Tall, Dark and Handsome?"

"Nothing! He's a married man, and I plan on steering clear of him. I like his wife, and they seem to have a good relationship."

"Maybe, but sparks were flying between you two all night."

"I'm sure Becky had to have noticed the way he looked at me and the tension between us. I don't understand her indifferent attitude," Leah said with a puzzled frown.

"Just be careful, Leah. I don't want to see you get hurt again."

"I do seem to have bad luck when it comes to men. Sandy, do you have any idea how fortunate you are? You and Al have such a good marriage with two good looking, well-behaved sons."

"Yeah, no telling what direction my life would have taken if I hadn't met Al. He's a wonderful, loving husband and my best friend. I'd be lost without him."

Leah gave Sandy a hug, and they bid each other good night. After Sandy had gone to her room, Leah lay in bed trying to sleep, but thoughts of the man she had seen leaving the cottage kept running through her head. Could it have been John? What would she do if it was?

****

Linda went down the hall to her room, opened the door, and switched on the light. She looked around, but when she saw the piece of paper on her bed, she knew the intruder had been looking for her. Maybe Leah wasn't the type of person she'd thought she was. She'd handled herself with dignity and class, and she'd obviously been very frightened the way she locked all the doors. The man wasn't looking for Leah, he'd come to the cottage looking for her. God, she felt like she had an albatross around her neck.

****

After tossing and turning for what seemed like hours, Leah fell into an exhausted, restless, dream-filled sleep. When her alarm clock went off at 7 AM, she hit the snooze button, rolled over, and dozed again, wishing she could sleep all day. The alarm sounded again—she groaned and crawled out of the warm bed and got into the shower, letting the water run hot and then cold until the fuzziness cleared from her mind. She put on a pair of comfortable jeans, a sweatshirt, and athletic shoes, tied her hair back into a pony tail, and grabbed her jacket. She knocked on Sandy's door but got no answer. Sandy had probably gone for coffee already.

There was a heavy drizzle, and the sky was laden with dark clouds promising more rain to come. Leah raised the hood of her jacket. She could see Jason Atwell and Hal Lawson standing on the back patio; they seemed to be engrossed in a serious conversation. Hal was bending over petting Sasha. Neither man seemed to be aware of the rain. When she drew near, they both wished her a good morning. Hal Lawson addressed her as Ms. Dawson—she nodded her head curtly and bade them a good morning. She felt a flush creeping up her neck into her cheeks. She quickly looked away, though not before catching the flicker of an expression in Hal Lawson's eyes, an expression she couldn't define. But, if she had to describe it, she would probably call it desire.

Stopping by the office, she found Liz Walker seated behind her desk. Leah said good morning and told her about the man she'd seen the night before. Liz apologized for any upset it may have caused and promised to check with George to find out if he had someone helping him. She also assured her it could have been one of the other guests who had inadvertently gone into the wrong cottage. Liz asked if anything was missing or out of place. Leah said that nothing appeared to be amiss, thanked her, and headed for the dining room.

The room was already filled with people. Leah spotted Sandy sitting at the table with Louise and Joe Williams and Becky Lawson. Sandy waved and beckoned for Leah to join them.

They were talking about the workshop, and everyone seemed to be excited about the prospect of getting to paint for a week with no other obligations. Joe said something about exploring the surrounding area, but he wasn't sure what he would do now that it looked like such a crummy day. He turned to Becky Lawson and asked if her husband would be out photographing in the rain. She replied that Hal loved rainy days, and it would take a monsoon to keep him inside. There was obvious affection in her voice when she spoke of him. Sandy looked at her and asked, "How long have you two been married?"

Leah was surprised that Sandy asked such a direct question, but she waited eagerly for Becky's reply. "Seems like all my life, but actually only six years. Hal owns the local NBC affiliate television station, and I started working in the advertising department the summer after graduating college. That's when we met. He was my boss, but we got married and I became the boss," Becky said with a laugh.

Becky was telling the truth about what her real husband did and how they had met, but was having trouble separating facts from the fiction that she and Nate had created. To get the topic of conversation away from herself, she asked, "How about you, Sandy?

How long have you been married, and how did you and your husband meet?"

"Al and I met in college. We were both attending the University of Kentucky. I was a freshman, and he was a junior. He was the best quarterback UK had seen in a long time, such a hunk. But he was a goner once he met me. We dated for three years and have been married ten."

"What about you, Leah? Are you married or have a significant other? Becky asked, turning to Leah.

"No, there's no one in my life at the moment. Seems like I'm married to my business. I work six or seven days a week," Leah said

"What kind of business do you have?" Becky asked.

"I'm an interior designer. I also own an upholstery business."

"That does sound like a full plate. Do you own your interior design business also or work for someone else?"

"I used to work for a firm of architects, but I branched out on my own about five years ago."

"Sounds like you are one busy lady. You must have some good help to be able to leave for a week."

"Yeah, I have an assistant, Charlie. He's a jewel. I don't know what I'd do without him. But, we're between projects right now, and I've got some really good employees working in the upholstery shop."

Breakfast was served about that time, and everyone began eating. Some disappointment was expressed about the rain and not being able to go out on location. But, the thought of painting was exciting, inside or out.

Andy Barzetti reminded everyone to meet in the studio at 9:00 sharp. Leah and Sandy went back to their rooms to get their supplies, use the bathroom, and brush their teeth. Leah noticed that Hal Lawson was gone when she passed the patio where he and Jason Atwell had been standing. He was still nowhere in sight when she came down the hill on the way to the studio, which was located in a large building a short distance from the main house. Andy was already looking through a selection of photographs that were spread out on a table. He chose one and clipped it to the top of his easel.

"Okay, everyone. I'm going to paint a seascape with rocks as the focal point." He placed a large canvas on the easel and began putting out his paints. "As you all know, acrylic paints dry rapidly, but I'm going to show you a trick to keep them wet much longer." He placed a disposable paper pallet in a plastic box, folded several paper towels, and placed them on one end. He poured some water on the towels wetting them thoroughly, then squeezed his paints out in large dollops on the wet towels. He then took a spray bottle filled with water and lightly misted the glops of paint.

"Misting your paints every so often will keep them from drying out. When you're finished painting for the day, mist the paint and put the lid on the pallet box. They should remain moist for several days. You'll notice I've arranged my paints from left to right, starting with warm colors on the left and going to cool on the right. I always put out a lot of white on one side and black on the other. Don't be stingy; there's nothing more frustrating than to have to stop in the middle of painting to put out more paints." He took a large brush, dipped it in water, then in black paint. Then, he plopped the brush on the disposal paper pallet, mixed in a small amount of burnt sienna, and began sketching. With quick, bold strokes, he soon had a rough drawing. He then began painting in the dark areas of the picture.

Leah watched in fascination as the painting took shape. She was amazed at the clean, bright colors and light effects he achieved with minimal brush strokes. Andy was about halfway finished with the demo painting when the studio door opened, and an older woman walked in.

"I'm so terribly sorry to interrupt, but my daughter had an emergency and couldn't bring me to the inn yesterday. My name is

Mattie Wainscot. I'm enrolled in this class. I've checked in at the office, and Liz said for me to come on to the studio and that George would bring my supplies later. I shipped them last week, and they have them in the office."

"Well, come on in Ms. Mattie," Andy said, getting a chair and placing it in an open space near Leah and Sandy.

"Please, call me Mattie. I may be ninety-nine, but you make me feel one hundred and ninety-nine by calling me Ms. Mattie. When I was growing up, we always had to call our elders Ms. or Mr. or aunt or uncle, but I don't feel like an elder yet."

"Okay, Mattie it is. How long have you been painting?" Andy asked with a broad smile.

"Well, I had to quit playing tennis when I was ninety-three, so I decided to take up painting. My college art teacher told me I'd never be any good as an artist, so I just decided I'd prove him wrong."

"You seem like a lady with a lot of determination, so I wouldn't be surprised if you do just that," Andy said. He went on to explain what he'd done so far and then continued with the demo.

Andy finished the painting around 11:30 and told the group he would sell it for $200. He explained he sold all his demos at bargain prices. Mattie raised her hand, indicating she'd like to purchase the painting. Andy said he'd sign it, and she could collect it when it was dry. Everyone began looking through the pile of photos, trying to select one to paint. Andy had said he'd like for everyone to paint something with rocks, so Leah found an ocean scene with waves and large rocks in the foreground.

George came through the door about that time, pushing a cart loaded with their lunches and Mattie's painting supplies. Everyone had received a card at breakfast with a selection of lunch items. Leah had chosen turkey on wheat with provolone cheese, lettuce, tomato and mayo, chips and sweet tea to drink. There was also an assortment of homemade cookies for dessert. Andy told everyone they would start painting at 1 PM promptly. Leah noticed that Linda Baker and the two local commuters were the only ones leaving to have lunch elsewhere.

Leah caught George before he left and asked him if he had sent someone to their cottage the previous evening. He told her that Liz had already asked him about that, and no, he hadn't sent anyone. He said someone had more than likely gone into the cottage by mistake.

By one o'clock, everyone had finished eating, cleaned up their mess, and set up their easels. Leah followed Andy's instructions and put her paints out on folded paper towels saturated with water. She did a rough sketch and started blocking in the large dark areas. She was so engrossed in her painting, she couldn't believe it was already after two o'clock when Sandy walked over and looked at what she'd done so far.

"Wow, that looks great! Good job, girlfriend. How about taking a little break to stretch your legs?"

Leah cleaned her brush, arched her back, stretched, and looked around. "I think I do need to get away from this for a few minutes. What did you choose to paint?" Sandy had chosen a lighthouse located on a rocky island.

"Hey, that's looking good—you've got a great start."

They stopped at Mattie's easel and were amazed at what she'd done. She'd captured the feeling of storm-tossed waves crashing against foreground rocks.

"Your painting is very good! I've never seen a seascape that looked more wet and stormy," Leah said.

"Thank you, young lady. What is your name—how long have you been painting?" Mattie asked.

"Leah Dawson, and I've been painting most of my life. I just started working with acrylics about two years ago, though. Your college professor must have been blind, by the way. You're an excellent artist."

"Ah, I'll have to give the devil his due. I wasn't really interested in painting back then. My passion was tennis. I did play professionally for a number of years and then just for fun, until a bum knee made me give it up. I had to have something to keep me busy and out of trouble, so I took up painting. I thought I'd just show that arrogant art teacher I could paint if I chose to."

"You're an interesting person, Mattie. I'd like to hear more about your life sometime when we're not involved with painting," Leah said, as she and Sandy moved away. They went around the room, looking at everyone's work.

When they stopped at Becky Lawson's easel to admire her sunset seascape, Becky laughed and said, "You know, I'd really get pissed if I was forced to work this hard, but, I truly love to paint. I get so absorbed that time stands still."

"I know what you mean," Leah replied. "It seems as though we've only been painting a few minutes, and it's been over an hour."

"Have you noticed that Linda never came back after lunch?" Becky asked.

"I hope nothing's happened. Maybe she had a previous appointment or some business to take care of. She *is* an attorney; maybe something came up," Sandy said.

Leah and Sandy returned to their paintings, and by 3:30, they had finished. Some of the other students completed their work earlier and placed them against a wall where Andy had instructed everyone to leave their finished work. He said he would critique them that night after dinner and show slides of the work of some of the earlier New England painters.

Sandy and Leah left the studio and headed back up the lane toward their cottage. The rain had stopped, but the air felt heavy, and clouds were hanging low in the sky.

"I think they're having happy hour at the main house around four. You want to go mingle and see what everyone has to say about their first day of painting?" Sandy asked

"I need to get some fresh air and exercise. I'm going to my room for a pit stop and then go for a walk. I may stop by when I get back."

"Okay, I'll fill you in if there's anything worth repeating. Maybe I'll find out what happened to Linda. You be very careful, and watch your back at all times," Sandy said as they went into the cottage.

Leah put on her rain slicker and borrowed an umbrella from a stand in the sitting room. She went down the lane and headed in the direction of the path that led to the woods. As she turned towards the cove, she saw Hal Lawson and Ron Rhodes standing by a tree near the entrance to the inn property. Neither one of them looked in her direction. Leah continued on the path through the woods, crossed the little footbridge, and walked past the gazebo. The path wound around, and she could now catch a glimpse of the bay through openings in the trees. Large rain drops began plopping on the ground in random patterns as though a giant hand were squeezing the clouds, indiscriminately directing the drops. Suddenly, the clouds burst open, and the bottom fell out in an almost solid sheet of water.

Leah had opened the umbrella she'd grabbed as she was leaving the cottage. It was almost useless in the downpour, though. She starting running back to the gazebo and almost collided with the man she knew as Hal Lawson. He caught her as she slid through a mud puddle, preventing her from falling. He pulled her up onto the platform of the gazebo. Her umbrella had fallen to the wooden floor, and she realized he was still holding her. He had drawn her so close she could feel his heart beating against her chest. A tingling warmth engulfed her body, and she had to struggle with herself to keep from wrapping her arms around his neck. She raised her arms to push him away. But, when she looked into his eyes, her heart seemed to momentarily stop beating. He was staring at her with such intensity she felt a shiver of fear, but then his eyes dropped from hers and a deep sadness seemed to engulf his large frame. He stepped back, putting distance between them, and led her to the bench seat.

"I'm sorry, I didn't mean to alarm you. That shouldn't have happened. Please forgive me, you look so much like Jackie; it just happened before I realized what I was doing."

"Who is Jackie?" Leah asked in a puzzled voice.

"She was my wife. She died six years ago."

"But, Becky said you'd been married six years. You must have …"

"Leah, when you look at me with those blue eyes that I could drown in, I can't think straight. By the way, you do look so much like Jackie you could be her twin, but her eyes were brown. I apologize again for upsetting you, but I'm not exactly sorry it happened. You just looked so damn fetching in that slicker with rain dripping off your face."

"How can you say that? You're a married man, and Becky is such a nice person."

"You're right, Becky is about the nicest person I know and I love her dearly, but there are things you don't know that I can't explain right now. I wish I could tell you everything. I know I'm asking a lot, but try not to hate me. I promise I'll explain everything as soon as possible."

Leah looked at him with confusion, not understanding what he meant. *What could possibly excuse the fact that he's a married man?* She thought, as she grabbed her umbrella and ran down the path towards the main house. When she got closer to the cove, she noticed the tide had gone out, and there was clothing caught in the rocks not far from the shore. As she drew nearer, she came to a sudden stop. A blur of horror—sight and smell joined together—caused her heart to leap and begin pounding in her chest as if it would burst apart. The clothes took shape, and she could see an arm extending out, as if reaching for help. Help she was powerless to give. Like tendrils of seaweed, red-gold hair streamed across a familiar, bloated face. One blue eye was fixed in a sightless, accusatory stare, an empty socket where the other eye had been. Leah cried aloud, "Oh, my God, no!" but her tormented cry was lost in the wind. The smell of the mud filled her nostrils until she could barely breathe. She must be caught in a nightmare, a terrible dream. She'd awaken and everything would be normal, no grotesque body caught in the rocks.

She saw the tall man coming down the path toward her. She knew by his expression when he looked in the direction of the cove that it was no dream. And, she knew the woman's death was no accident.

Chapter 5

Leah squared her shoulders and stiffened her spine. *I've got to be strong. I can't let him see me like this*, she thought, turning her face away as Hal drew near and slid his arm around her waist. He held her close and stroked her hair, murmuring soft words of comfort. Despite her resolve, a shudder ran through her body, and she clung to him. He was stability and sanity in an irrational, nightmare world. She needed his strength right now. She'd worry about her other needs later.

*****

Although the day had ended on such a horrifying note, it had started with promise. Nate awoke early, eager to get the ball rolling with his investigation. He'd called Ron and Sheila Rhodes and Jason Atwell the night before and arranged to meet with them at 6:30 that morning. Since Jason didn't begin his breakfast duties until 7:30, this allowed enough time for the group to get acquainted and set up an agenda. Nate slipped quietly into the bathroom, showered and shaved, dressed quickly, and eased out the door into the hall. The cottage was quiet as a tomb—hopefully the Porters, who occupied the other apartment in Rosewood, were sleeping soundly. Nate stepped out the front door and started up the path to the Rhodes' cottage, their designated meeting place.

The sun was just breaking over the horizon, turning the eastern sky a vivid red, shot with streaks of gold. *What was that old expression?* Nate thought. *Red skies at night, sailors' delight; red skies in the morning, sailor take warning.* Nate shivered as a chill ran up his spine, and the hairs on his neck prickled with a sense of foreboding. The air was still and heavy with the promise of rain. Nate could smell the ozone as lightning flashed across the dark waters of the bay, followed a few seconds later by the distant rumble of thunder. He didn't see anyone as he hurried past the main house and up the incline to Fernwood cottage. As he drew near, a man stepped from the shadows, a white dog by his side.

"You must be Jason Atwell," Nate said, as the man approached.

"Yes, and this is Sasha," he said extending his hand. Nate studied him as they shook hands. He looked to be about six foot two with broad shoulders and a slim athletic build. His hair was light brown, and his eyes appeared almost black in the early morning shadows. He returned Nate's look, as though he was sizing him up, too. He had a firm handshake and an openness that appealed to Nate.

"It's good to meet you, Jason, and you too, Sasha," Nate said, bending forward to pet the dog and scratch behind her ears.

"She likes you," Jason said.

"She seems like a good dog," Nate replied.

"She is a good dog. She's smart and loyal as the day is long. She'll be a real asset to us. She has another talent you probably won't believe, but I swear it's the truth."

"What in the world can she do? She's not a talking dog, is she?" Nate asked with a grin.

"Nope, she hasn't started talking yet, but I wouldn't be surprised if she started any day now," Jason said laughing. Then, turning serious said, "You've heard of dogs that can detect cancer in a person or warn an epileptic if they're about to have a seizure. Well, she senses when someone is about to do something bad. For example, we were in a convenience store one time when two men came in. She immediately started growling, and her hackles came up. She started toward the men, and one pulled a gun. She was so fast, she lunged and had his gun hand in her mouth before he knew what was happening. The clerk had a weapon under the counter. He held it on the men and called the police. Turned out they were behind a string of recent robberies. She also can detect a good person. She took right up with you. I figure you've got to be an okay guy. She's never wrong about a person's character."

"That's good to know," Nate replied. "Maybe she can find the thief for us."

"I wish that was true, but she senses their evil intentions before the act, not after," Jason said, as he tied Sasha's leash to a small tree before entering the cottage.

They found Ron and Sheila drinking coffee at a table in the small dining area.

"Would you guys like a cup?" Sheila asked, as Nate and Jason pulled out chairs and sat down.

"I'd love some; smells delicious," Nate said.

"Same here," Jason replied.

Sheila got two cups, filled them with the steaming liquid, and slid a tray containing cream and sugar in front of them. "Would you like something to eat? I've got some fresh doughnuts."

"Thanks," Nate said, "but, I thought I'd let Jason cook me some real food."

"You're in for a treat," Sheila said. "We ate breakfast at the inn yesterday, and it was one of the best I've eaten. That includes our European travels when we've eaten at places that boast they have the world's finest food."

Jason grinned, his cheeks turning pink, and mumbled a modest, "Thanks."

"I think we need to get a little better acquainted before we proceed," Nate said, taking a sip of coffee. "Could you two tell me a little more about yourselves?" he said, looking at Ron and Sheila.

"There's not a lot to tell," Ron answered. "We both grew up in Houston, Texas, attended the same school, and started dating in high school. We attended different colleges and both dated other people. But we'd see each other on holidays and summers. We finally figured out we were in love and wanted to spend the rest of our lives together. We married the summer we finished college. I have a master's degree in business, and Sheila has a BA in fine arts. We've been married thirty-two years; I'm 56, and Sheila's 55. We have a very successful real estate & development business, which our son now runs. We spend most of our time traveling—we both love art and have been to most of the well-known museums in the world."

"Thanks for the info. You sound like two lucky people to have found each other. Not everyone's that fortunate," Nate said. "I think you all know my background, so for now let's get down to business."

"I'd like to get everyone going on this investigation today," he continued. "Ron, I understand you've done surveillance work in the past, so I'd like for you to keep an eye on the Porters. If they leave the premises, follow them and see where they go, what they do, and whom they talk to. Sheila, I understand you're a real tech wiz, so you can do some background checking. Find out where the Porters were when each of the robberies occurred. The same for Andrew Barzetti."

"Okay," Sheila replied, "but I'll need to go over to the resort to the Ledges; they have free Wi-Fi and it's much faster and more reliable than what I can get here."

"Do whatever you have to, just be sure you cover your tracks." Nate turned to Jason and asked what time he'd be finished with his breakfast duties.

"I'll be free for the day by 9 am," Jason replied.

"Good, I want you to go into Portland and find out everything you can about Andrew Barzettis' friend or friends who sent a limo to the airport to pick him up Saturday. He spent the night with them and was delivered here yesterday via said limo."

"I'm impressed," Jason said. "You've already accumulated a lot of information. Apparently, you're good at what you do."

"Elementary. I learned everything yesterday afternoon at the reception by keeping my eyes and ears open and making a few subtle inquiries. Okay, that's it for now. Any questions?" asked Nate.

"Only one," said Ron. "What are *you* going to be doing?"

"Right now, I'm going down to the main house and let Jason cook me an early breakfast, and then I'm going to do some checking on the other workshop students," Nate said, getting to his feet and heading for the door. "I'd like to get an update from everyone tonight—hopefully we'll get this case wrapped up by the end of the week."

Nate and Jason walked down the hill to the main house, and Jason got busy in the kitchen. He brought two mushroom, bacon, tomato, and cheese omelets, wheat toast, juice, and more coffee into the dining room, which was empty except for the two of them.

"That is undoubtedly the best omelet I've eaten in my entire life," Nate said pushing his chair back and rubbing his stomach. "If you're half as good an investigator as you are a cook, we'll have this case wrapped up by tomorrow. Where did you learn to cook like that? Do you have any family? Where do you call home when you're not on a job?"

"Whoa, one question at a time. I grew up on a ranch in North Dakota. It was a rough life; guess it contributed to my survival abilities. My parents still live there, and my dad is tough as rawhide. I got a football scholarship but injured my knee my senior year of high school, so I never got to use it. I was in R.O.T.C and studied electrical engineering for three years at a local college. I joined the Army and, thanks to R.O.T.C, made Second Lieutenant. I was assigned to a criminal investigation unit, but military life wasn't for me. So, I got out after two years on an early-out program. It seems the Army had overloaded themselves with officers. I attended a culinary school in New York. My military stint as a criminal investigator led to my work with the FBI, and my cooking abilities provide a good alias. How about you? How'd you wind up with the Bureau?"

"Kind of like you, I grew up on a farm in Pennsylvania and got a football scholarship to Penn State, but only played one year. I got a BA in—believe it or not—art history. However, I went on to attend law school and became a licensed criminal attorney, as well as an FBI agent.

"The art degree is surprising; it sure doesn't fit with your persona," Jason observed. "Guess I better feed Sasha and get busy in the kitchen. The workshop group will be coming for breakfast soon. I sure would like to hear the rest of your story and how you wound up with this international art crimes unit. I guess your knowledge of art had a lot to do with it."

"Yeah, it helped," Nate agreed, as they headed outside.

Two helpers were already making preparations for the upcoming breakfast as the two men passed through the kitchen to the back patio. The skies had darkened, and it was drizzling rain when Nate and Jason went out the back door. Jason put a bowl of food in front of Sasha, and she eagerly began chowing down the kibbles. Nate looked up the lane and saw Leah hurrying in their direction. She had on jeans and a slicker with a hood pulled over her head. Nate's heart did flip flops—she looked so much like Jackie it took his breath away. He squatted down and began petting Sasha to distract himself. Jason said good morning to her and Nate managed a, "Good morning, Ms. Dawson." She smiled at Jason and returned his greeting, gave Nate a curt nod and said, "Good morning, Mr. Lawson."

After she disappeared inside, Nate could still see her face in his mind's eye. She looked enough like Jackie to be her twin, and yet she was so different. The way she walked and talked, the way she held her head. And her eyes…they simply blew him away. He'd never seen that shade of blue before. He'd gotten married shortly after graduating from law school. He and Jackie had been so much in love, and when they found they were going to have a baby, they'd been ecstatic. When Jackie developed diabetes, she just had to be more careful. But he came home that day and found her unconscious, and by the time he rushed her to the ER, it had been too late. She never came out of the coma. She was three months pregnant and 25 years old. He blamed himself for a long time. If he'd just checked on her more often or gone home earlier that day. He didn't want to get involved with another woman. He was too guilt-ridden, and deep inside he was afraid of falling in love, afraid he would jinx the relationship. He felt responsible for Jackie becoming diabetic, no matter how many times he told himself that couldn't be. But when he'd met Leah Dawson, he was drawn to her like a magnet. Perhaps it was her resemblance to Jackie, but he felt it went deeper than that. He felt a connection to her, as if he'd known her most of his life. When he'd first seen her at the reception and made a joke, he just wanted to see her smile. Then, God help him, when she turned and looked at him, he wanted to take her in his arms so badly it was like a physical pain. He felt as if he could drown in the depths of those intriguing eyes.

Damn it, Nate thought as he headed back to his cottage. He didn't want or need this distraction. Becky was gone to breakfast—*good,* he thought. The cottage was empty, and he could work with no distractions. He went into the sitting room and booted up his computer.

When Becky checked in yesterday, she'd received a list of the people attending the workshop. The list consisted of the names, addresses, and phone numbers of all the students. Nate called Harry, his contact with the agency, and gave him the list of names, asking him to check them out. He then began a methodical search; the names were in alphabetical order. The first on the list was Jeanette Ames. She lived in Bath, Maine, and drove back and forth each day. She had meals and attended any functions at the inn, but she wasn't an overnight guest. Nate drew a line through her name. Her life was pretty much an open book. Next on the list was Linda Baker, in her thirties, an attorney from Manhattan, New York. She'd grown up very poor in a small town in Georgia, attended the University of Georgia on an academic scholarship, and graduated from the school of law with honors. She then moved to New York, passed the bar, and was now with a prestigious law firm. He put a question mark by her name. This lady was going to require some in-depth research— maybe Harry would come up with more information on her background. Sandy Carlton and Leah Dawson were next on the list. Nate discovered they had both grown up in a small town in Kentucky and had been close friends since first grade. Leah's mother had died when she was less than a year old, and she had been raised by her paternal grandparents. Leah's grandparents both died when she was in her teens, leaving only her and her father in the household. He never held a job for any length of time, so it was a struggle to make ends meet during Leah's high school years. Her father never remarried, lived in his parents' home, and drank himself to death when he was in his early 50's. Sandy, on the other hand, had come from a fairly affluent family. *Well*, thought Nate, *Leah certainly didn't grow up in a privileged household. Seems she's had a lot of obstacles to overcome.*

Both attended the University of Kentucky. Leah, with the help of an academic scholarship and a part-time job, had graduated with a BS degree in interior design. Sandy finished with a BS in business, met her future husband, Al Carlton, and married him the year she graduated. Carlton was from upstate New York and had attended UK on a football scholarship. After marrying, they moved back to his hometown. He now owned a successful accounting firm.

A year after graduating, Leah married Richard Samuels, a wealthy, spoiled playboy. They separated a year later, and Leah filed for divorce, but he was killed in a car accident before the divorce became final. She had her name legally changed back to Dawson and now owned an interior design and upholstery business in Germantown, Tennessee.

Nate began to have guilt feelings. He felt as though he was intruding into Leah's personal life, but also felt he was getting to know what made her tick. He reminded himself he was investigating everyone at the inn and moved to the next name on the list. Lucile Friedman, also a day student, had always lived near Portland and led an exemplary life. He drew a line through her name. He also marked through the next name, Sally Hines from St. Louis, a retired school teacher. No red flags there. Following Sally was Judy Mansfield, age 42. She was also a local who commuted to and from the inn. She had been married four times, divorced once, widowed twice. Her current husband, who happened to be very wealthy, was suffering from some mysterious aliment doctors had been unable to identify. He put a question mark by her name. He continued down the list of names, checking each one. *Well, here's a really interesting character,* Nate thought, as he read about Mattie Wainscot. She was 99 years old and had taken up painting when she was 93 because she had to give up playing tennis. She said her art teacher told her she'd never make an artist and she wanted to prove him wrong. *I'm looking forward to meeting her*, Nate thought

There were ten people enrolled in the workshop, and Nate had gone through the entire list by noon. He put a question mark by three of the names for further research. He would also pass their names on to Harry and have him use all his resources to find out everything he could. He also gave Wayne and Susan Porter's name to Harry and, as an afterthought, told him to get all the information on Ron and Sheila Rhodes. When and how they came to be working with the FBI and how many projects they had helped on.

He stood up and stretched and thought about his options for lunch. He could drive over to the next village and see if there was anything there, but decided instead to walk over to the resort and have lunch at the Ledges. Maybe he would see Sheila and find out if she had made any progress.

It was still drizzling rain as he walked over to the resort, but the clouds had thinned and a weak, watery sun was struggling to break through the mist. When he entered the restaurant, the hostess greeted him with a smile and asked if he would prefer a booth or table. He indicated a booth by a window. She led him to the designated seat, handed him a menu, and said his server would be right with him. A girl with curly blond hair and a cute perky face bounced over to his booth. She walked as if she had springs on the bottom of her shoes. "Hi, my name is Melanie, and I'll be your server. Could I get you something to drink?" she inquired in an equally perky-bouncy voice. Nate asked for a glass of tea. He studied the menu and, when Miss Bouncy returned, he ordered a Ruben sandwich with a side of potato salad.

He let his eyes travel around the room, searching for Sheila, but she was nowhere to be seen. To his surprise, he did see someone he recognized. In the back of the room was Linda Baker. She was sitting at a table with a well-dressed man. His blond hair was combed to perfection. *Probably has a hair dresser and uses hair spray*, thought Nate. He estimated the man's age to be somewhere in the early 30's. But, he could be older or younger; it was hard to tell. He appeared to be in very good physical shape. Nate took out his cell phone and furtively held it down close to the table to snap two or three pictures of the couple. He then texted the photos to Harry with a note asking him if he could identify the man and to send him any info he could dig up.

When the waitress returned, Nate asked if there was another area in the restaurant for Wi-Fi users. She said there was a small room in the back where most people sat when accessing the internet. He described Sheila and asked if she'd seen her or if she knew if she was back there now. The waitress said, no, she didn't remember seeing her, and she wasn't back there now because no one was back there.

That's strange, thought Nate, *but then maybe she had decided to work from home.* His sandwich came and, as he ate, he kept his eyes on the couple. The waitress had left their check and the man placed a credit card on the table while he and Linda Baker continued an animated conversation. The waitress took the credit card and bill, returned shortly, and laid them on the table. The man signed the receipt, put the card back in his wallet and, getting up, gallantly pulled Linda's chair back as she rose to her feet. Nate turned his head as though looking out the window and put his hand beside his face. He could see their reflection as they walked past on the other side of the room and left the restaurant. Nate went to the door and watched as Linda headed down the street in the direction of the inn. The man stood watching for a few moments and then followed after her.

About that time, Nate's phone beeped an incoming text. He pulled it out of his pocket and read Harry's reply. "The man's name is John Phelps. I found him through the lady he's with, Linda Baker. Her law firm defended him in a lawsuit two years ago. An upscale shop in Manhattan that specializes in oriental rugs claimed he sold them about 100 inferior, fake rugs. They sued him for $250,000. That included the cost of the rugs, damage to their reputation, etc. The firm Jamison, Jamison and Mason handled the case and your

Ms. Baker was the attorney in charge. Seems they reached a settlement out of court. Mr. Phelps claims he was also deceived, but he took back the rugs and reimbursed the company the amount they paid him, plus $25,000 to soothe their ruffled feathers, for a total of $125,000. I don't have any further information on John Phelps. It could be an alias, so I'll keep digging."

Nate went back into the restaurant and finished his lunch. After paying his bill, he walked outside and glanced at his watch. He was surprised to see it was almost two. He decided to walk around and check out the resort. He walked up the street, passing a gift shop, an ice cream stand, another restaurant, several condos, and a golf pro shop. When he turned around to head back, he noticed John Phelps going into the Ledges. It was almost three now, and there was still no sign of Sheila Rhodes. He decided to go back into the restaurant and see what Mr. Phelps was up to. About that time, a black Hummer passed him, driving about 5 or 10 miles per hour. Nate could see two men in the front seat—both appeared to be looking for something, scanning the passersby with intense stares. Their eyes slid over Nate as if he wasn't there, so obviously they weren't looking for a tall man. They looked like thugs straight out of a 1940's gangster movie with overblown steroid muscles. Nate wondered if they could be connected with the art heist but then discounted that idea. They didn't really fit the profile of an art thief. He went into the Ledges and took a seat up front where he had a good view of the street and could also see Phelps sitting in one of the booths by the windows. Nate ordered coffee and sipped it slowly. John was on his cell phone having a very animated conversation with someone. He was also drinking what appeared to be coffee and eating some kind of dessert. Nate had been sitting there about ten minutes when the Hummer came back by, driving much faster now, and heading toward the highway. *Wonder if they found what they were looking for*, Nate thought. Something wasn't right. Those guys just didn't fit in a place like this.

Nate decided he was wasting time sitting there watching Phelps, paid for his coffee, and headed back to the inn. As he approached the entrance to the inn property, he saw Ron Rhodes coming down the lane. They met at the light pole, just past the Rocky Ledge sign. Ron had a worried expression on his face as he greeted Nate. "I was just headed over to the Ledges to see if I could find Sheila. I'm really worried about her. She sent me a text about 11:30 this morning, asking how the surveillance was going. She said she thought she was on to something and would tell me more when she saw me.

"Sheila's not at the Ledges. I just left there," Nate said. "Did you learn anything from your surveillance of the Porters?"

"They never left the premises except to run over to the fishing village. They spent about an hour there, browsing in an antique shop and having some coffee in a grocery store. It was around 1:45 when they left, and they've been back in their cottage since they returned around 2:45. No one else entered or left the building except the cleaning lady. She came out around one and went back in with some towels about thirty minutes later. The Porters left shortly after that."

"I'm going to walk over to the resort and browse around, see if I can find out what's happened to Sheila," Ron said

"Okay, let me know what you learn," Nate said, walking towards the lane. He wasn't ready to go in yet, so he veered to the left to the path that led to the woods. He had not seen Leah pass by while he was talking to Ron, and he took the same route she'd taken. He walked through the woods, crossed the little footbridge, and continued to the gazebo.

He stepped up onto the wooden floor and took a seat, stretched his long legs out, and leaned his head against the post as he thought about the past events of the day. The rain had stopped, but the sky had darkened again. Storm clouds where hanging low, racing across the bay, swirling like his thoughts. Where could Sheila Rhodes be? Why did Leah Dawson make his heart beat like an

Indian tom-tom war dance? Why did things have to be so complicated? He came here to do a simple investigation and the very first day, there she was, beguiling him with those bewitching eyes. Why couldn't she have gone to a different workshop? Then he'd never have met her, never seen her smile, never heard her laugh. His life would still be on an even keel, safe, no unwanted disruptions. But, despite all his objections, he wanted her. Wanted her arms around him, looking at him with the same need in her eyes that he felt in his heart, mind, and body.

The wind picked up. Suddenly, the clouds burst open and rain came down in a solid sheet of water. He couldn't believe his eyes; his imagination must have run away with him. There was Leah, and she was headed in his direction. He must be dreaming. But no, she was real, and she was sliding through a mud puddle, about to fall. He caught her just in time and lifted her into the protective covering of the gazebo. When she looked up and their eyes met, he saw fear mixed with desire. The drumming of the rain on the gazebo roof seemed to be in rhythm with the pounding of his heart, and he realized he was still holding her. He stepped back and apologized. He told her about her resemblance to Jackie, trying to explain his actions, but it had only confused her more. He wanted so badly to tell her the truth, that he wasn't married, that Hal Lawson was actually his brother-in-law. But he couldn't do that, at least not now.

She grabbed her umbrella from the floor and ran down the path leading back to the inn. The rain that had come so suddenly stopped just as quickly, leaving the tree branches drooping almost to the ground. Nate followed Leah down the lane and watched as she stopped abruptly, staring at something in the cove. As he drew closer, he understood why she looked so terrified. The sad, desolate body of Sheila Rhodes lay in the mud. One arm extended, one blue eye staring in disbelief, one side of her head bashed in. He hurried to Leah's side and slid his arms around her waist, pulling her close, wishing he could obliterate the horror and soothe away her fears.

Chapter 6

"Leah, do you want me to call Becky to come and walk you up to the house? You need a stiff drink, maybe a hot toddy and a warm fire," Nate said, removing his coat and placing it around Leah's shoulders.

"I'll be okay, I just need to get my bearings. Too many shocks in one afternoon," Leah said, pulling his jacket up around her neck.

Nate took out his cell phone and punched in a number. "Becky, are you in our cottage?" Nate asked and waited a moment for a reply. "Good, something terrible has happened. I need you to bring a thermos of hot coffee and an afghan down to the bench by the cove. Leah and I just found Sheila Rhodes' body, and we need to stay here until the authorities arrive."

"Oh, my God, Nate, what are you saying? Was it an accident?" Becky asked.

"No, I don't think it's an accident. Becky, don't say anything to anyone, and try to get down here without being seen. Hurry!"

Nate hung up and dialed 911.

"They're sending the county sheriff," Nate said, looking at Leah. She was still pale, but her eyes were more focused.

Nate saw Ron Rhodes about that time. He was on his way back to the inn when he spotted them sitting on the bench and headed in their direction. "I couldn't find any trace of Sheila, and no one I talked to remembered seeing her," Ron said as he approached them.

"Ron, you need to come and sit down," Nate started saying, but Ron had already spotted Sheila's body. "What the hell, what's going on?! Oh no, God no, that can't be Sheila. She can't swim," he said, as though he thought she was just going out for a casual swim and had an accident. He started to go out into the cove where she was lying.

"Wait, we can't move her. The sheriff and the coroner are coming," Nate said, grabbing Ron's arm and pulling him back. "Becky's on her way down here with some coffee; maybe you should walk back to the house with her."

"I'm not leaving Sheila! Let me get her out of that mud," Ron said, starting in her direction again, tears streaming down his face.

Nate took his arm and led him back to the bench. Ron was dazed and disoriented, and Leah took his hand and pulled him down beside her. Putting her arms around him, she made soothing sounds, patting him on the back as if calming an upset child. It seemed his grief and suffering had given her strength. Her concern for Ron had temporarily assuaged her own distress. He laid his head on her chest and sobbed, his tears soaking the jacket Nate had placed around her shoulders.

They heard the sound of approaching footsteps, and Becky came around the path carrying a thermos and a large afghan. She took in the scene before her but quickly averted her eyes from the muddy cove. If she let herself acknowledge the reality of the situation, *she* would need the coffee and afghan as badly as Leah. She sat down beside Leah and poured some of the coffee into the lid and handed it to her. "Drink this. It'll warm your insides and help you feel better," she said, as she wrapped the furry throw around Leah's shoulders.

Leah took the coffee and took several sips, then handed it to Ron. "I think you need this more than I do," she said, wrapping her arm around Ron's shoulders and hugging him. "I'm so terribly, terribly sorry. I wish there was something I could do."

About that time, they heard the sound of a siren and saw the flashing blue lights as a patrol car came around the bend and up the lane. The car came to a stop about 50 feet from where they were sitting. The sheriff got out on the driver's side of the car and hitched up his pants. He appeared to be about 50, almost bald, with broken capillaries on his nose and cheeks. He was around 5 foot 8 with a belly that looked as though he'd consumed too much beer and rich food over his lifetime. He was winded by the time he reached the group sitting on the bench. A deputy got out of the passenger side and followed the sheriff. He looked to be about 30, around six feet tall, with an athletic build, dark hair and dark eyes.

"I'm Sheriff Jack McMullen and this is my deputy, Earl Watson. What happened here? Was there an accident? Dispatch said a body had been found. Who found the body, and do you know who it is?"

"We found her," Nate said, indicating himself and Leah. The body is Sheila Rhodes, and this is her husband Ron Rhodes."

"Who is this other lady?" the sheriff asked, looking at Becky.

"This is Becky Lawson. She just came down with some coffee; she doesn't know anything and probably needs to get back to the house," Nate said.

"I'll let you know when anyone can leave—everyone just stay put for the time being," the sheriff said with an arrogant attitude.

Jack McMullen took a closer look at the body, then snapped, "Watson, call the police! Tell them we've got what appears to be a homicide." Then, as if adding more authority to his command, he spit a disgusting wad of tobacco juice at the deputy's feet.

"I'm sorry folks but looks like there may have been foul play here, which means it's a case for the Maine State Police investigative unit."

"What do you mean, foul play?" asked Ron

"Well, I'm real sorry about your wife, Mr. Rhodes, but the police will get to the bottom of what happened. In the meantime, no one is to go near the scene. We don't want to contaminate the area. I don't know, what with all the rain, there may not be much to find. But, those guys with the state are pretty good at what they do. They can find evidence in places you'd never dream possible. Like the old saying, 'they can find a needle in a haystack,'" Sheriff McMullen said with a chuckle. His humor was lost on the despondent group, sitting with silent, glum faces.

Apparently, some of the people at the main house heard the siren, and several were walking down the lane heading in their direction.

"Go tell those nosy busybodies to get their asses back to the house," the sheriff said to Deputy Watson, as he wiped tobacco juice from the corner of his mouth. "We don't need them snooping around here. Tell them to sit tight. The police will probably want to question everyone," he said, hitching his pants up again.

Leah watched the deputy as he jogged toward the group of people. She could feel Ron moving as if he were going to get up. She put her arm back around him and tried to think of something soothing to say that would ease his pain. She couldn't think of anything that seemed appropriate, so she just hugged him. He sat back and shuddered, and Leah took the afghan Becky had wrapped around her shoulders and placed it around Ron's.

It had been almost an hour since the deputy called the police. The clouds had thinned and the rain had moved out, but the air was still heavy with moisture. A rainbow appeared in the sky, only to disappear when the sun slipped below the rim of the earth, casting an ethereal rosy glow over everything. *How ironic*, thought Leah, *so much beauty in such a macabre situation. Perhaps nature is paying a final tribute to Sheila.*

Just then, two blue cruisers drove in and parked behind the sheriff's car. The doors opened, and a uniformed man emerged from each one. They approached the group, first stopping to speak with the sheriff and his deputy.

The light was fading fast and the temperature was falling, causing a misty fog to form in the low areas around the cove. The two policemen had powerful flashlights, which they switched on and swept over the group huddled on the bench. Leah put her hands over her eyes to shield them from the glare. Ron sat motionless, unaware of his surroundings. He had withdrawn into his own private hell. Nate stood and walked over to the men, spoke, and shook hands with them. Leah watched as he talked to the law officers. They were too far away and speaking too softly for her to understand what they were saying. Now and then, she would catch an occasional word. She heard her name and saw Nate gesturing in her direction; he mentioned Ron and Sheila, pointed to the cove and back toward the main house.

After a few minutes, the three men approached the group sitting on the bench. The officer who seemed to be in charge told them they could go up to the house now. He said the forensic unit was on the way from Augusta and should be there soon. In the meantime, they had some preliminary work to do. They'd come and take their statements after the unit arrived.

Nate helped Ron to his feet and started in the direction of the house. Ron hesitated and said he didn't want to leave Sheila there in the cold and dark all alone.

"There's nothing you can do now, Ron. The forensic unit will take her to the crime lab in Augusta. They'll get to the bottom of what has happened."

"Nate, that text I told you about. Do you suppose she found out something about someone? Something that may have put her life in danger?"

Leah looked at Ron, then Nate. "What's he talking about? Who is Nate?" she asked.

"He's confused and upset. After the shock he's had, I don't think he realizes what he's saying," Nate explained.

When they got to the main house, most of the occupants were gathered in the front room, full of questions and concerns. Sandy broke away from the group and came over to put her arms around Leah. "What has happened? You look like you've seen a ghost. And why are the police here?"

"Oh Sandy, it's Sheila Rhodes. She's dead. We saw her body caught in the rocks in the cove. Her head was all bashed in. The police think she was murdered. I can't believe she's dead. Just last night we were talking and laughing in this same room. I can't understand why anyone would want to harm her."

"I'm so sorry you had to witness that. I know it's been a terrible shock. Sit down here by the fire, and I'll get you a glass of wine." Sandy said, leading Leah to a chair by the fireplace where a welcoming fire was blazing. The logs were crackling and popping, filling the room with the autumn smell of burning wood.

Mattie Wainscot came over and took Leah's hand. "I didn't have the pleasure of meeting Sheila, but I've talked to her husband. He seems like such a nice person. The poor man is devastated. I'm so sorry you had to be the one to find her, I know it was a terrible shock." She put her arms around Leah and hugged her.

"Thank you, Mattie," Leah said.

"I know you don't want to think or talk about it right now, but when you feel like talking, I'm a very good listener. Sometimes talking helps to purge the mind and heart."

"Yes, I'll remember that. Thanks again, Mattie."

Leah leaned back against the chair and took a sip from the glass of wine. Her thoughts whirled as she tried to sort things out. She kept hearing Ron Rhodes questioning Hal Lawson, addressing him as Nate. What was he talking about when he mentioned the text from Sheila, possibly putting her life in danger? *What is going on here*, she wondered.

About that time, Nate made an announcement to the group. He told them about Sheila and said the police were doing some preliminary work while they waited for the forensic unit to arrive. He also said they would want to take statements from everyone. He also let them know that he'd been instructed to ask them not to leave the premises until they'd been questioned.

Someone had given Ron a glass of Jack Daniels, neat. He gulped it down in almost one swallow and was well into a second one. Dinner was announced and they all shuffled into the dining room. Leah and Sandy had the same table companions as that morning, Louise and Joe Williams and Becky Lawson. So much had happened since then.

To Leah, it seemed like it had been a month instead of a day. Leah looked at Becky and felt a flush of guilt, but Becky smiled at her and took her hand and squeezed it. "I'm so sorry you had to witness such a tragic scene," she said with a concerned expression.

"Thank you," Leah mumbled.

"You know, Na—Hal really admires you," Becky said, with an expression Leah couldn't interpret. "He told me how brave you were. So many women would have had hysterics under the same circumstances."

Leah didn't know what to say, so she remained silent. They had just finished dinner when one of the police officers came to the house to begin the questioning. He indicated he would like to speak first with the ones who found the body.

He started with Leah. He led her to the back sitting room and told her to have a seat. He pulled one of the chairs around and sat down facing her. He asked her what time she had first seen the body and what she was doing in that area. Leah told him about going for a walk after the workshop, going by the cove and up through the woods. She told them how a downpour had come and she had run into Hal Lawson at the gazebo and, when it stopped raining, they'd headed back to the house. When they came to the cove, the tide had gone out, and that was when she first saw the body. He asked if she knew the victim prior to seeing her in the cove. Leah explained that she met her for the first time the day before at breakfast and again at the get-acquainted art reception that afternoon. He took her name, address, and phone number and told her they would probably have more questions, not to leave the area.

Leah left afterwards and went to her room. She just wanted a hot bath and a warm bed. Sandy walked up with her to make sure she was ok.

"I know you've been through hell today, sweetie, so I'm not going to hammer you with questions, but I think there's more bothering you than finding a dead body. When you get ready to talk, you know where I am."

"Thanks, Sandy. I really appreciate that. We'll talk tomorrow. I'm so tired and confused right now, I probably couldn't speak coherently."

****

The policeman questioned Nate next. "Your name is Hal Lawson?" he asked Nate.

"Yes, that is the name I'm going by while I'm here," Nate replied.

"What do you mean, 'going by?' Is it your name or not?" the officer asked in a disgruntled tone.

Nate explained that he was an undercover agent with the FBI, working on an art heist and gave him his real name. "I would appreciate you keeping that fact under wraps. It's very important that I remain incognito." He also told him Ron and Sheila Rhodes were working with him.

"Are they FBI agents also?" asked the officer.

"No, they're part of a special unit that assists the Bureau with certain cases."

The officer said he had no reason to inform the other guests of Nate's true identity. "I will need to use your real name in my official report," he said, looking over the paperwork. He asked Nate about his actions prior to finding the body. After a few more routine questions, he told Nate he would be back in touch once they had the results from the lab. Nate gave him his cell phone number and said he would be glad to assist in any way possible. The police officer asked Nate to keep him informed about anything he discovered concerning the art heist. "It might help lead to the identity of the killer," he said, handing Nate his card.

The officer talked to Ron Rhodes next. He asked him what time he had last seen Sheila alive.

"When I left the apartment around 8:30, she was doing some research on her laptop, but she was planning to go to the Ledges where she could get better service. She probably left around 9:30. She sent me a text around 11:30 saying she may have found something important and would tell me about it when she saw me. That was the last I heard from her."

The officer asked if he knew if she took her purse with her when she went to the Ledges. Ron said he didn't know for sure since he had already left. "She probably put some money in her pocket and only took her laptop. That would have been more typical of the way she did things."

"We would like your permission for the forensic unit to search your cottage before you return to it," the officer said.

"Sure. If it will help you find the person who killed my wife, do whatever you need to do."

"Thank you, Mr. Rhodes. This is just standard procedure. I'll have a couple of the guys from the forensic unit take care of it. You can make yourself comfortable here, and I'll let you know when they're finished. I would also like to look at your cell phone. You said you received a text from your wife around 11:30. Was that the only time you heard from her after you saw her last?"

"Yes, that was the only time I heard from her after I left the cottage this morning. I think the battery is about to die and the charger is in my bedroom."

"Don't worry, we'll take care of it and get it back to you, probably by the time the guys are through going over your cottage. Thank you, Mr. Rhodes. That's all for now," the trooper said, dismissing Ron.

Nate had overheard most of the inquisition and felt a pang of sympathy for Ron, but knew the officer was only doing his job.

After questioning Leah, Nate, and Ron, the officer requested the names of the guests staying at the inn. Joan Hataway prepared the list and gave it to him. He did a roll call, placing faces with names. Everyone was present or accounted for except Linda Baker and Wayne and Susan Porter. Joan explained that the Porters were there earlier and said something about going to the Ledges for dinner. It seemed no one had seen Linda since she left the workshop at noon. Nate told the officer about seeing her at the Ledges having lunch with a man and the two leaving together.

"Did you recognize the man she was with?" the officer asked Nate.

"No, but I did some checking; his name is John Phelps. He has an import business based in Memphis, Tennessee."

"What was your take on their relationship? Did they appear to be romantically involved? Maybe she took off somewhere with him."

"No, definitely not romantic. They were having a very animated discussion, and she seemed to be upset about something. When they left the restaurant, she headed toward the inn. The man started in the opposite direction but changed his mind and followed her."

"I'll stop by the Ledges when we leave here. I need to talk to this John Phelps." He began gathering up his paperwork and handed something to his partner. It was a plastic bag containing something Nate couldn't identify. "Okay, we'll be back tomorrow. No one is to leave the premises until they've been questioned and received clearance," he said before leaving.

Nate and Becky left the house and went to their cottage. There were no lights on in the building, and none of the occupants appeared to be at home. The temperature had dropped, and it was much too cool to sit out on the porch. There was a chill in the air inside the cottage, so Nate built a fire in the sitting room fireplace using the wood and kindling already stacked in the grate. The kindling caught quickly, and flames licked around the logs until they were ablaze, filling the room with warmth and the pleasant aroma of burning wood.

"I don't remember seeing the Porters tonight. Did you notice if they were at dinner? Becky asked.

"No, they weren't in the dining room. I overheard the police asking about them. According to Joan Hataway, they went to the Ledges for dinner," Nate said.

"According to Ron, they were at home all day except for their brief trip to the fishing village. Of course, they could've left any time after Ron went looking for Sheila. I'm going down to the parking area and see if their car is there," Nate said, putting on a jacket and heading for the door.

He returned after about five minutes and told Becky their car was not in the parking lot. "I'd think they would walk over to the Ledges. Seems kind of strange. According to Joan, they must have left shortly after the police arrived."

"Wonder what could be so important they would leave. Surely they would know the police would want to question them," Becky said.

"I'd like to see what they have to say, if they return before we go to bed," Nate said.

"Nate, are you going to tell Leah who you are and what you're doing here?" Becky asked, changing the subject and surprising Nate with her question.

"Why do you ask that?"

"Because it's obvious as the nose on your face that you are more than just attracted to her, and she seems to feel the same way about you. I like her. She seems to be a genuinely nice person."

"I've thought about it. I would like to tell her, but I don't think the time is right yet. I'm sure she suspects something though. Ron called me Nate on the way back to the house tonight. I tried to make excuses for him, but it sounded pretty flimsy even to me. I know she's wondering what's going on. But, she could be the art thief for all I know."

"You don't believe that for a second. I think you should tell her."

They heard voices about that time and the front door opening. Nate went out into the hall and caught the Porters as they were entering the building. "Hi, do you mind joining Becky and me for a few minutes? I'd like to talk to you."

"Sure, we'd be glad to," Wayne Porter said.

Becky offered them something to drink when they entered the apartment. They both declined, saying they had just finished eating and having some wine at the Ledges. They took a seat on the sofa in front of the fireplace.

"That fire feels good tonight," Susan Porter said with a smile

Nate got right to the point, "Did you know about Sheila Rhodes?"

"Yeah, we heard the sirens and saw all the police cars. We talked to the owner, Liz Walker, and she told us what happened. We decided to go to the Ledges and have dinner to stay out of all the confusion. We told Joan we were going to the Ledges," Wayne explained.

"Did the police come in while you were still there?"

"Uh, no." Susan said. "We left about thirty or forty minutes ago. We rode over to the village to pick up a few things from the grocery store, but it was already closed."

"You know the police will want to get a statement from you. They're talking to everyone staying at Rocky Ledge Inn, and I'm sure they'll question people at the resort, probably the surrounding area also," Nate said.

"Well, we'll be glad to help any way we can," Wayne said, and Susan nodded agreement.

"Were you here all day? Did you leave the premises at any time?"

"We were here most of the day. We drove over to the fishing village, browsed around, and had some coffee in the grocery store, but we were only gone about an hour, maybe an hour and 15 or 20 minutes," replied Wayne.

"Did you see anyone or anything that looked suspicious or out of the ordinary?" Nate asked.

"No, nothing unusual. We did see Ron Rhodes going into the post office, but we didn't think anything about that."

They stayed another ten minutes or so and then bid Nate and Becky good night, saying it had been a long day and they were headed for bed.

"I wonder why the Porters would need to go back to the village tonight when they were there this afternoon?" Nate asked.

"They could have forgotten something, or maybe they just wanted to get away," Becky suggested.

"Maybe," Nate said with a thoughtful frown. "Ron didn't say anything about the Porters spotting him. I guess that's why he went into the post office—so they wouldn't suspect he was tailing them."

"Well, it has been a long and very stressful day. You can sit here all night and ponder over everything, but I'm off to bed," Becky said, getting up and heading to her bedroom.

"I'll keep an eye on the fire. As soon as it dies, I'll call it a night." He sat by the fire another thirty minutes, watching the logs as they collapsed and sparks flew out against the fire screen. Soon there were only glowing embers that quickly turned to gray ash. Nate thought about the events of the day, trying to make sense of

124

everything. Did Sheila discover something about the art crimes that put her life in danger, or was it something else that had nothing to do with the art thefts? Maybe someone from Sheila's past. Someone with a vendetta, who followed her here and took revenge. And what about the cleaning lady Ron saw leaving the building? She didn't sound like anyone Nate had seen around the place, and when did she go inside, Ron only mentioned seeing her come out. He would have to question Ron more about her.

Nate's thoughts whirled, but regardless of what direction they took, there was always a picture in his head of Leah's eyes staring at him with questions and accusation

Chapter 7

A subdued group gathered for breakfast the next morning. Everyone seemed to be in a state of suspended shock and confusion. After all, what did they really know about each other? Most of them had only met for the first time Sunday afternoon at the reception.

Leah noticed that Linda Baker was not amongst the crowd in the dining room and wondered if she had returned and just didn't come to eat, or if she was still missing. One or two of the more bold and nosy guests attempted to ask Leah questions about discovering Sheila's body. She shrugged them off, saying she didn't know anything and preferred not to talk about it. *They're probably the kind that stop and stare at a gristly car accident*, she thought.

Andy Barzetti came into the dining room and joined the group. He seemed to be in an upbeat mood, considering the situation. "All right everyone, let's lighten up. There's been a tragic event, and my sympathies go out to Mr. Rhodes, but we can't just sit around with our chins hanging to our knees. I think we should go on with the workshop. When the police come for questioning, we will cooperate and help them in every way possible." There were a few murmurs and objections among the crowd. Some of them approved the idea, while others thought it was showing disrespect.

"Look, there's nothing we can do to change the situation. I wish there was, but unfortunately, there's not. I think it will be better for us to keep busy and focus on our painting. It could provide a temporary distraction from the shock and sadness. I do hope all of you will join me in the studio at the usual time."

"I think he's right. What else are we going to do? Sit here and stare at one another?" Becky Lawson piped in. Several others agreed, and soon the group was making plans to meet in the studio at 9 AM.

Leah and Sandy walked back to their rooms before heading to the workshop. Leah told Sandy about her encounter with Hal Lawson at the gazebo. She also told Sandy about the slip Ron Rhodes made calling Hal, Nate and the strange way Becky acted, telling her how much Hal admired her.

"That is a strange thing for a wife to tell another woman," Sandy said. "There's something going on here besides a workshop, and I'm not sure I want to know what it is," Leah said with a shudder.

As soon as Jason Atwell completed his breakfast duties, he and Nate met to rehash the previous day's activities. "I sure am sorry about Sheila and sorry you had to be the one to find her."

"Better me than some of the others. No telling what might have happened. I'm really thankful Ron didn't find her. I can only imagine how he would've reacted. I feel sure her murder is tied in with the art heist, and I'm going to do my damnedest to find out who did it and why."

Jason finished feeding Sasha and attached her long leash. "She needs some exercise. Could we walk and talk? I've got a lot to tell you about yesterday."

"Sure, I'm eager to hear what you discovered, and we won't have to worry about being overheard."

The rain had moved out, washing the air clean and leaving the sky a clear, brilliant blue. There was a light breeze blowing inland, making for a cool, crisp day. Nate pulled the collar of his jacket up and shoved his hands in his pockets. They headed down the lane, turned and walked up the path leading towards the woods. Yellow tape stretched along the bay side of the path at the spot where Sheila's body had been found. The tide was almost in with sun sparkles across the water. A sailboat was gliding out to the bay. *Such an idyllic setting*, thought Nate, *Hard to believe it's the same site where Sheila's body was found caught in the rocks and mud.*

Jason pulled Sasha back as she started in the direction of the tape. They hurried past the spot and on through the woods, pausing by a tree as Sasha squatted to do her business.

"What time did you leave for Portland, and what time did you return?" Nate asked.

"I left around 10:00 and didn't get back until after the police arrived last night."

"Can you prove you were in Portland all day if you're asked to? The police are going to check everyone's movements. After they establish the time of death, they'll zero in on that particular time frame. Ron received a text from Sheila around 11:30. The murder could have occurred any time after that up until around three. Ron and I were talking at the entrance to the inn about 3:30 yesterday, and then I went for a walk through these woods afterwards. The rain began to pour while I was at the gazebo, and that's when I ran into Leah Dawson. We found the body on the way back to the inn."

A songbird trilled a happy sound from the tree overhead, and the leaves rustled as a breeze stirred the air. Jason looked down at the sun-dappled shadows on the ground. He then looked up into Nate's eyes and said, "Yes, I can prove I was there. I talked to several people. I started with the limo companies. There are three in Portland, and I hit pay dirt at the second one. It was the company hired to pick up Andrew Barzetti at the airport. I had to show my creds, but I got the name and address of Barzetti's friend. I went to his house, if you can call it that; mansion would be more appropriate. Mr. and Mrs. Baskins, a married couple, live there year-round and serve as housekeeper and maintenance man. I spent some time talking with them, pretending to be a reporter doing a story on Barzetti. They were very accommodating. The friend's name is Calvin Ross. He owns an art gallery in New York, and Barzetti's paintings are the main attraction. There are also several other very well known artists represented in his gallery. Here's the strange part though—Ross seems to have a knack for discovering old paintings, most of them painted by fairly well known artists. Barzetti restores and cleans the ones that are not in prime condition. They're usually auctioned at Christie's or Sotheby's for a 'big chunk,' according to Mrs. Baskins."

"Good job, Jason," Nate said. "I think we need to dig a little deeper into this Ross and his connection with Barzetti. I'll have Harry run a background check on them."

Nate's phone buzzed about that time. He pulled it out of his pocket, and looked at the caller ID. "Speaking of the devil," he said, hitting the answer button. "Hey, Harry. What's up? Tickle my ears with some good news."

"I don't know how helpful it is, but Ron and Sheila Rhodes have only worked on one other project prior to this one. They were instrumental in helping one of our agents retrieve a stolen painting. They happened to be in the museum when the heist occurred and came forth with information that led to the identity of the thief. They offered their services for any future projects. That's how they came to be at Rocky Ledge Inn assisting you."

"Did the Bureau do a complete background check on them?"

"Does a squirrel eat nuts? You know the Bureau. They check everyone with a fine-tooth comb and then put them under a magnifying glass to check some more. They both checked out squeaky clean. I also have more information on John Phelps."

"Well, don't keep me in suspense. Tell me what you've found."

"He owns a business named JAP Imports based out of Memphis, Tennessee. It's an import business that deals with high-end specialty items. You already know about the lawsuit over the oriental rugs and the outcome."

"Yeah, and the attorney he was having lunch with yesterday, Linda Baker, did a disappearing act. As far as I know, she's never returned," Nate said.

"Seems John Phelps is quite the man about town. He has been dating another one of the ladies attending the workshop," continued Harry.

"Who is the lucky, or perhaps I should say, unlucky lady?"

"Her name is Leah Dawson, and she lives in Germantown, Tennessee, a suburb of Memphis."

"I know where Germantown is. Remember, *I* sent you the list of those attending the workshop," Nate said in an irritated voice.

"Hey, I'm just giving you the facts. What did I say that lit your fuse? Something to do with Leah Dawson? Do I detect an interest in the lady that goes beyond a general investigation?"

"Never mind, I'm sorry, just a little on edge. I came here to find an art thief, and now I've got a murder to deal with. Keep digging, Harry, and let me know what you find." Nate hit the off button on his phone and slipped it back into his pocket. Nate asked himself why the hell he got so damned upset. Leah Dawson had been or probably was still dating John Phelps, so what! It was none of his business what she did. He had no claims on her. But who was he fooling? He wanted her; he wanted to have claims on her. *I've got to get her out of my head. She clouds my mind. I can't think straight where she's concerned.*

Back at the workshop, Andy was almost finished with the demo painting. He was doing a portrait of Liz Walker. He called it a portrait sketch. He explained that it was rougher, not as detailed and finished as a formal portrait.

Leah was amazed as the painting took shape. He not only captured Liz's likeness, he had painted her attractive face with an expression of inner contemplation. Almost as if she were guarding a secret behind those dark, brooding eyes. They held a mysterious depth that made you want to know what made her tick. He had placed her in front of a window using the natural light, casting one side of her face in shadow. The light effect was perfect, adding to the mysterious effect.

"Finito!" shouted Andy, turning the canvas to allow Liz to view the finished portrait.

"Oh, my! Just look at what you've done. You're a genius!" Liz exclaimed, giving Andy a big hug. "I don't know how you managed to do such a fabulous painting in only two hours."

The rest of the students were also in awe. "I feel like I should throw my paints away and start knitting or something. I'll never be able to paint that well," Becky said.

"Don't fret, my sweet lady. No one can paint the way I do. I am gifted, and I work very hard to learn and improve. You may never paint like me, but you can paint your way and you can learn and improve and do beautiful work. But, you must work and practice and never stop learning and working to paint better and better," advised Andy, looking at Becky, then scanning his eyes over the entire group.

"Young man, you are a wonderful, gifted artist and I am honored to be in your class," Mattie said, walking up to the portrait for a closer look. "You not only capture a likeness. You capture the soul—something a photograph, and most artists, can never do."

There was a knock at the door; it opened and two men entered the room. The one in front was tall and thin. His hair was almost completely gray, although he appeared to be no older than 35. He introduced himself as Detective Powell with the police. He apologized for intruding but said they needed to ask some questions and would like to speak with each of them. He introduced the other man as Detective Mayo, who appeared to be in his late 20's, medium height, and looked as though he spent a lot of time at the gym. They were dressed casually in khaki pants and sports jackets, no ties, their shirts open at the throat.

"I want you all to go to the main house," Detective Powell said. "I need to get a statement from each of you. It shouldn't take long, and your help will be very much appreciated."

Nate and Jason were on the path back to the house when the unmarked car pulled into the drive and the two men got out and went into the main house. "Those guys are detectives with the police," Nate said. "I'm going to have a word with them, and then I'm going over to the Ledges to see what I can find out about Linda Baker and John Phelps. I also want to search the Porter's apartment, and I'll need your help when I do that."

"Don't you need a warrant?" Jason asked.

"This will be an unofficial search. If I should find something that could be used as evidence, I'll worry about getting a warrant later," replied Nate. "You'll have to hang around here for a while until they question you. In the meantime, I'm going to see if I can find out what the police have come up with so far. They don't particularly like working with the FBI, guess they feel it's their case and we're interfering. I'll try and stress the fact I'm trying to find an art thief, and the murder is probably connected in some way."

Just as Nate and Jason reached the end of the lane and started up the road toward the main house, the two detectives came out and entered the studio. Nate and Jason hurried to the back patio, and Jason tied Sasha and gave her some water. Lunch was already being prepared when they entered the kitchen. Jason got two cups and filled them with coffee, handing one to Nate. They heard the group from the workshop entering the backdoor and being ushered into the front room. Detective Powell informed everyone that he and Detective Mayo would question them in the back-sitting room. He had the list of the ten people attending the workshop and said he would start with the first one on the list. He called Jeanette Ames, and she got up and followed him to the back. She was gone about five minutes, and when she came out, Sandy was called. After another five or six minutes, Sandy came out, and Leah's name was called. She followed the detective to the back room. She noticed that the younger man was not in the room, and they had skipped Linda Baker's name. *She must still be missing,* thought Leah.

"Have a seat, Ms. Dawson," Detective Powell said, indicating a chair opposite him. "I appreciate all of you taking time to talk to us. We'll try not to inconvenience you too long," he said with a friendly and open look. He had intelligent, soft brown eyes that didn't seem to miss anything. "I understand you were in the workshop class all day yesterday. Could you tell me what time you arrived and what time you left?" Powell asked in a routine manner.

"I got there a few minutes before 9 yesterday morning and left around 3:30."

"Did all the students remain in the workshop all day?"

"No, the two ladies who live nearby went home for lunch. They were gone about thirty minutes, and Linda Baker left at lunch time and never returned," Leah explained.

"Where did you go when you left the workshop and what did you do up until the time you found Sheila Rhodes' body?"

Leah told him about going back to her room, getting her rain slicker and the umbrella, and then going for a walk. She told him about walking up through the woods and the cloud burst and running into Hal Lawson at the gazebo. She said they left the gazebo when the rain slacked, and when they got back to the cove, the tide had gone out. That was when she saw the body. He asked if she remembered seeing anything unusual or out of the ordinary prior to that. Leah thought back over the preceding day and couldn't think of anything unusual other than Linda Baker leaving the workshop when lunch was delivered and not returning.

"Can you tell me what time Sheila was murdered?" Leah asked.

"I'm sorry, Ms. Dawson, we're not allowed to discuss the case."

"Well, can you tell me if you've found Linda Baker? You know it doesn't make a person feel very comfortable having a murder on the premises and one of the guests disappear," Leah said in an exasperated tone.

"We don't have any information yet, but we're checking every possibility. I'm sure we'll come up with something soon. Thank you, Ms. Dawson. You're free to go. If you think of anything that may be helpful, please call me," he said, handing her his card.

Leah returned to the front room and found Sandy waiting there. They were told they could hang around and have lunch at the inn once the questioning was completed, or they were free to leave if they wanted to eat elsewhere.

Detective Mayo had gone to the kitchen for coffee prior to Leah being questioned, and Nate had intercepted him, showing him his credentials and telling him about the art heist. He said he was sure the murder of Sheila Rhodes was connected in some way, and that she had been assisting him with his investigation. "I will be glad to help you and share any pertinent information I come up with," said Nate. "In return, I would appreciate it if you would keep me in the loop on your investigation."

Mayo said he had no problem with that, and Nate asked him if they had determined the approximate time the murder had taken place. Mayo informed him it had happened sometime between 11:30 and 2:30 yesterday.

Leah and Sandy decided to go to the Ledges for lunch. After returning to their room to freshen up, they walked over to the restaurant. The hostess greeted them and led them to a table by the window and handed them menus. A perky waitress bounced over and took their drink order. Leah was reading the lunch specials trying to decide what to order when she had an overwhelming, uncomfortable feeling of being watched. She lowered the menu, looked across the room, and saw John Phelps sitting at a table in the back of the restaurant. He was looking directly at her with a sardonic smile on his face. He lifted his hand in a mock salute.

Chapter 8

Leah stared as John Phelps lowered his hand and picked up his drink, his ice blue eyes glued to hers. He raised his glass as if drinking a toast to her. Her heart seemed to sink to the pit of her stomach as a claustrophobic feeling engulfed her.

"Sandy, don't look now, but John Phelps is sitting in the back of the restaurant. He's staring directly at us! God, will I never be rid of him?"

"Maybe we should go to the police, charge him with stalking," Sandy said.

"I don't think it would do any good. He hasn't done anything yet. It's a free country, and he has as much right to be here as I."

"Maybe you could get a restraining order."

"It'd probably be a waste of time. Police seldom take things like that seriously. I'll just have to handle this myself. I've got to figure out some way to get him out of my life."

"What will you do?" Sandy asked in a concerned voice.

"I don't know, but he's headed in this direction."

John Phelps sauntered up to their table. "Well, well, what a pleasant surprise. Imagine seeing you here. How are you doing, Leah? Who is your lovely friend?"

"That's really none of your business, John. Now if you'll excuse us, we're having lunch."

He pulled out one of the chairs and, uninvited, seated himself. "You've got to be Sandy. I've heard so much about you. I know you and Leah have been friends most of your lives," John said with a charming smile.

"Okay, John. Enough of the BS. What the hell are you doing here? Did you follow me?" Leah hissed. She was so angry and frustrated she wanted to reach across the table and slap his smirking face.

"My, my, I do believe the lady is riled. But don't flatter yourself, my sweet. I have business in the area, but I can always find time for you. How about having dinner with me tonight?"

"Drop dead, you arrogant, demented, delusional…" Leah spluttered, seeking more adjectives to throw at John when she saw Hal Lawson enter the restaurant and look in their direction. She stopped in the middle of her tirade and stared. He had on jeans and a cotton shirt that emphasized his broad shoulders, flat belly, and narrow hips. Her cheeks, already flushed with anger, grew warmer at the sight of him. She forgot about John Phelps as a memory filled her mind. The memory of rain pelting her as strong arms lifted her into the gazebo. She remembered how good it felt being in those arms, and then she remembered the shame and anger she'd later felt. *Damnation, why did he have to be here this week?* Why couldn't she just ignore those flashing hazel-green eyes and the hair that fell across his forehead, making her want to brush it back from his face?

Leah took several deep breaths, ridding her mind of unwanted thoughts. She made the muscles in her face relax into a nonchalant expression as Nate approached their table.

"Good afternoon, ladies. May I join you?" He asked, pulling out the empty chair and sitting down without waiting for a response. He looked across the table at John Phelps. "My name is Hal Lawson. Are you a guest here at the resort?"

John was fully aware of Leah's flustered state as she'd stopped mid-sentence and stared at the tall man as he approached their table and sat down.

"As a matter of fact, I am. My name is John Phelps, and Leah and I are old friends, both from Tennessee. Imagine my surprise when I ran into her. It is truly a small world," he said looking at Leah with feigned adoration in his eyes.

Leah tried to maintain her calm facade and ignore John's innuendo, but Hal was obviously holding back pent up anger. *Against who, why is he so angry?* she wondered.

Nate's amber eyes flashed green sparks. "So, what brings you to this part of the world?" he asked, looking at John.

"Combination of business and pleasure," John said in a cold voice.

"What kind of business are you in?"

"I have an import business, specializing in unique and high-end merchandise."

"I'm surprised there'd be anything in rural Maine interesting or valuable enough to be of benefit to your import business," Nate said, cutting his eyes in Leah's direction.

Leah did not miss the barb, and neither did John. A devilish glitter filled John's eyes, and he opened his mouth to make a snide remark. But, before he could speak, Leah pushed her chair back, dropped her napkin on the table, and stood up. "If you'll all please excuse me, seems I've lost my appetite and don't feel like eating." She then turned and walked out of the restaurant, her back ram-rod straight and her head held high.

"I've got food coming, so I'll bid you both a good day. It was a pleasure meeting you, Sandy." John ignored Nate as he left them and sauntered back to his own table.

Sandy looked at Nate, "What was that all about? Did I detect a note of jealousy? By the way, have you forgotten you're a married man?"

"I just made a damn fool of myself," muttered Nate. "That's why it's no good to let yourself get emotionally involved."

"Wait a minute…you are emotionally involved? You have a wife, a very nice wife," Sandy said with an emphatic tone of voice.

"Becky's my twin sister. I don't have a wife. It's just a cover so I can be here at the inn to investigate an art heist," Nate said, looking into Sandy's startled eyes.

"Who are you?" asked Sandy.

"My name is Nate Parker. I'm an FBI agent with a special unit that investigates international art crimes."

"Why are you telling me this now?" asked Sandy.

"I think Sheila Rhodes' murder is connected to the art heist. I've talked with my superiors, and we agree it may be necessary for me to reveal my true identity. Sheila was a special FBI agent assisting me with the art crime. The Bureau will be involved in the investigation of her murder, making it necessary for me to come out of cover. I would prefer that you keep it under your hat for the time being, though."

"Don't worry, mum's the word. My lips are sealed, but what about Leah? Don't you think she should know the truth?"

"I'd appreciate it if you didn't say anything yet. I know you two are close friends, but I'd like to tell her myself. She's got a low opinion of me, and I don't blame her. I'm sure it's plummeted even lower after the way I acted just now."

"She was kind of upset," Sandy said.

"I know. I came over here specifically to talk to John Phelps and then got side tracked when I saw him sitting there with Leah. I don't know what it is, but I'm sure he's knee deep in some kind of illegal activity. I'll have to do some back-pedaling with him now to have any kind of credibility in his eyes."

"Be careful. He's shrewd and cunning and probably a very dangerous man," Sandy warned.

"I'm not worried about John Phelps. I can handle him, but I thought he and Leah were an item," Nate said.

"Only for a very short time, until Leah saw through his guise. He's been stalking her and making her life a living hell. She was afraid he may have followed her to Maine and thought she saw him Sunday when we were eating lunch. She'd about convinced herself it was a mistake, and then she saw him here today. When he came over to our table acting so cavalier, she was angry and upset, and then you walked in with a big old chip on your shoulder."

"Man, I really screwed up. I could kick my ass from here to the middle of next week. Guess that's what I get for jumping to conclusions before I have all the facts."

"Yeah," Sandy said, "you're supposed to be a professional."

"Even professionals screw up when they let their emotions get involved."

"Nate, it's obvious you and Leah have a strong attraction for one another. I was really concerned about that when I thought you were married. Now that I know that's not the case, I just want to say one thing. Well, maybe two things."

"And what might that be?"

"First of all, I think you and Leah are great for each other. Second, John Phelps is a thorn in Leah's side. She's sure he followed her here with no good intentions. I am worried about what he might do, and I'm hoping you'll keep an eye on Leah. You know, kind of watch out for her."

"I'd love to keep an eye on Leah; she's great to look at. But she's also very stubborn and hard headed, and right now, can't stand the sight of me."

The perky waitress who'd taken their order earlier returned with the food and put it on the table. They'd each ordered the lunch special, haddock chowder and a side salad.

"Yum, this food is delicious. Would it embarrass you if I licked the bowl?" Sandy asked taking the last bite of her food.

"Be my guest. That chowder *was* delicious. It almost made me forget my worries," Nate said with a grin. He pulled out some money and put it on the table. "This should cover the tab. I'm going to talk to Mr. Phelps before he gets away. I'll see what I can do about Leah's problem with him."

Nate approached the table where John Phelps sat nursing a cup of coffee. "Well, well, Mr. Lawson. I thought you might be wanting to continue our conversation," John said in a sarcastic tone.

"And what makes you think we had a conversation to continue?"

"I think you have a thing for the lovely Leah and you want to pull the macho man stuff and tell me hands off."

"I intended to talk to you before I knew you were upsetting Leah, but since you brought it up, if you do anything to harm her, I will do more than pull 'the macho man stuff.' I will make you wish you'd never been born."

"That sounds like a threat to me, and I don't like threats," John said, his icy eyes locked on Nate's. "So, what else did you have on your mind?"

"Linda Baker," Nate said, watching the other man's expression closely.

There was a flicker of surprise in John's eyes, but just as quickly as it came, it vanished, replaced with a nonchalant smirk.

"If you're wanting her telephone number, you'll have to get that from her yourself," John said in a taunting voice.

"Look, Phelps, cut the crap. Linda Baker is missing, and the last time she was seen was yesterday having lunch with you."

"I don't know anything about where she is or what's she's doing. She handled a lawsuit for me a couple of years ago, and her law firm does some legal work for me occasionally. We ran into each other and had lunch, period, end of story."

"Not quite," Nate continued. "The two of you left the restaurant together. She hasn't been seen or heard from since."

"Look, I don't owe you any explanation. I don't even have to talk to you. Matter of fact, it's none of your damn business."

"I suppose you know there was a woman murdered at the inn yesterday."

"Yeah, I heard about that. Too bad, but I sure as hell don't know anything about it, and I'm through talking to you. So, you have a nice day, Mr. Lawson.

"I was in the restaurant yesterday and saw you and Linda in a very animated conversation. I also watched you when you left and saw the two of you walking towards the inn. But, she never made it back to the inn," Nate said.

"Who the hell do you think you are? I told you, I'm through talking to you; so, once again, good day, Mr. Lawson."

Nate sat and looked at John Phelps, studying his face. A face most would consider handsome. Blond hair, combed and styled to perfection, his features almost patrician. *Almost too pretty*, thought Nate. He pondered whether he should reveal his identity and push the issue but decided it would be better to wait.

Nate rose from his chair and turned to leave, "You have a good day, Mr. Phelps. Sorry if I've inconvenienced you, but remember, Big Brother is watching."

John sat and watched Nate as he walked out of the restaurant. *Who the hell is he and just how much does he know?* he thought, as he reached for his phone and punched in a number

****

Linda Baker didn't know what time of day it was or how long she'd been in this dark place. It must be sound proof or so far from everything no one could hear because she'd screamed until her throat was raw. There was a bed with a lumpy mattress, and she was lying on it with her wrists and ankles bound with duct tape. Every so often, someone came to bring food and water. They would release her hands and allow her to eat and use the bathroom which consisted of a tiny closet with a toilet and sink. She couldn't tell if the person was a man or woman. They had a hood over their head, and the only light was a flashlight they carried which turned on only long enough for her to see the food. The room she was in must be in a house or building because there was nothing visible except another dark wall when the door opened to allow her visitor to enter. She had begged and pleaded with them to tell her who they were, what they wanted, and why was she being held prisoner, but there was never a response. Linda racked her brain trying to remember what happened, how she came to be in this dark room. She remembered having lunch with John Phelps, they were discussing something, but she couldn't remember what it was. Everything was still so fuzzy. She wondered if they were putting something in her food, keeping her drugged. She remembered leaving the restaurant—she was going back to the studio, and John followed her. They stood at the edge of the inn property and argued about something. John was trying to talk her into doing something. She couldn't remember what it was, but she knew it was something she was opposed to.

Her head seemed to clear a little, and she could now remember John telling her they would talk about it more later on. He walked back toward the resort, and she started in the direction of the inn. A black Hummer came along about that time and stopped beside her. A big, tough-looking man got out of the car and said something to her. The next thing she knew, she was in this dark room, lying on this bed, taped up like a mummy. There was something very important, if she could only remember. If there was some way she could avoid eating the food, maybe her mind would clear and she could remember. If she could just get her hands loose…but she felt so weak, it was almost impossible to walk. She had to crawl when she tried to explore the room.

She heard a sound, and the door opened. She was expecting a flashlight to be turned on and shined into her eyes. Instead, there was a click, and an overhead light came on. She blinked her eyes several times trying to adjust to the bright light. When they finally focused, she could see a person standing in front of her. The person was not wearing a hood this time, and she knew who it was.

****

Leah went back to the main house in a huff. *I wish I had never laid eyes on John Phelps! He is the devil incarnate, a truly evil man,* she thought. *As for Hal Lawson or whoever he is, I wish I knew what kind of game he's playing. Then again, maybe I don't. He's a married man who acts less like a married man than anyone I've ever known, and yet he seems to have high principles in other ways. I wish I could just put it all out of my mind.*

When she entered the house, she found that the detectives had completed their questioning for the time being and lunch was being served in the dining room. She realized she had not eaten and was hungry. *I need food to calm myself,* she thought. She spotted Louise and Joe Williams and Mattie Wainscot at one of the tables and asked if she could join them. They were all having turkey and avocado sandwiches with tomato basil soup.

"Yum, that looks and smells delicious," Leah said as she sat down next to Mattie.

"There's nothing like good food to comfort the heart and warm the soul," Mattie said, squeezing Leah's hand. "You look like you could use some comfort right now," she continued, taking in Leah's pale face and worried expression. "I know you've experienced a terrible shock, but I detect something else is troubling you. Is there anything you would care to talk about?"

"Trouble seems to follow me wherever I go," Leah said, looking into Mattie's kind and concerned face. She felt so drawn to the older woman's sympathy and kind words that, before she realized what she was doing, she told her all about John Phelps.

"My dear child, I know exactly how you feel. Frustration and helplessness doesn't come close to describing what you're going through."

"You sound like someone speaking from personal experience," Leah said.

"There was a young man I dated a few times while attending Simmons College in Worcester, Massachusetts. He lived in the area, and he decided he was going to have me or no one would. He made my life a miserable fiasco. I became so paranoid I was afraid to go outside. He would be lurking around every corner."

"What happened? Did he finally give up, or did you have him arrested, or what?" Leah asked.

"No, I knew it would be useless to go to the police, especially back then. They would have just thought me a hysterical woman, and that would've been the end of it. I decided to take matters into my own hands, and I had that young man wishing he'd never laid eyes on me before it was all over."

"What in the world did you do?"

"I'll tell you all about it, but right now you need to eat. Rest assured though, my dear, you can have that overzealous suitor high-tailing it right back to Tennessee."

About that time, Mary Jane walked into the dining room and asked if the people there were interested in continuing with the workshop.

"Well, I'm all for continuing, and I know Andy wants to keep teaching. In fact, he said he would be in the studio this afternoon if anyone wants to paint. I'm going as soon as I finish eating, and I know Mattie is planning to go to the studio. I was hoping Leah and Sandy would be there also," Louise said with a hopeful smile.

"You can count me in, and I know Sandy will be all for it," Leah said.

****

When Nate left the Ledges, he went in search of Jason. Nate knew he was renting a small house located just past the inn property. It had a small, fenced-in back yard, and Nate could see him and Sasha there playing catch.

"How did the questioning go?" Nate asked, walking up to the fence. Sasha ran over to where he was standing, and he reached over and scratched behind her ears. "How you doing girl, you taking care of this big guy?"

Jason walked over to where Nate was standing. "The questioning went fine. I've been eliminated as a suspect."

"That's good to know. I'd like to search the Porters' apartment now if they're not there. Have you noticed if they're at home or not?

"No, I had some lunch and walked back here to check on Sasha. I figured you'd be by when you finished. Did you find out anything from John Phelps?"

"Afraid not. The only thing I found out about John Phelps is he's a sneaky bastard with something to hide," Nate said as they started walking up the path that skirted the inn property and led around to Rosewood cottage.

The bay was a brilliant sapphire blue, and the sky was a few shades lighter with a few wispy clouds streaking across it, like vapor trails of forgotten jets. The surf was up, and the sail boats moored off shore were rising and falling with each wave that washed ashore.

When Nate and Jason reached the parking area for Rosewood, the only vehicle parked there was the Jeep Cherokee SUV he and Becky had arrived in.

"Well, doesn't look like anyone's home," said Jason.

"Yeah, we'll go into my apartment. Since it's on the front of the building, you'll have a vantage spot to keep a lookout while I search the Porters' apartment."

They'd brought Sasha with them, and Jason asked if it would beokayto take her inside. Nate said it would be fine. It was always good to have an extra set of eyes and ears.

They entered the apartment Nate and Becky were occupying, and Jason made himself comfortable in a chair by a window that overlooked the area in front of the building. Nate went down the hall and knocked on the Porters' door. He waited a few seconds and knocked again. He put his ear to the door and listened. There was no sound from within. Nate eased the door open and called out a hello. There was only silence in return. He scanned the front room, which was a duplicate of the one where he was staying. He saw nothing of interest there and went on into the first bedroom. There was nothing of interest there, either. It had an unoccupied air. The closet was bare, and the dresser was empty. He went to the second bedroom. Clothes were scattered across the bed and on the floor. *Messy*, he thought, as he carefully stepped over them and went to the nightstand, where a Harlan Coben mystery was lying. A slip of paper was stuck in between the pages, probably marking the reader's place. He removed a pen from his shirt pocket and flipped the book open. He removed the paper, careful not to leave any prints. Numbers that appeared to be a phone number were written in black ink. He added the number to his contact list in his cell phone and put the slip of paper back into the book. He opened the drawer on the nightstand and found allergy medicines, a sleep aid, what appeared to be some receipts, and, nestled amongst them, a 9 mm Sig Sauer. Nate didn't touch it and tried to leave everything as it was. He wondered if they had a permit for the gun and why they would find it necessary to have one at a laid back, rural, New England painting workshop inn.

He went to the closet and opened the door. His heart skipped a beat, and his eyes did a double take. Someone appeared to be standing in the shadows of the closet, but he quickly realized he was looking at a wig head sitting on the shelf above the bar with clothes hanging from it. Upon closer inspection, he found three wigs, each a different color. *Susan Porter is a brunette, if she's not currently wearing a wig,* thought Nate. There was a blond, red, and gray wig in various lengths and styles. Why in the world she would want all those different colors and styles, Nate couldn't understand, unless maybe she was trying to disguise herself.

Suddenly, Nate's phone vibrated with a text from Jason: *The Porters are back!*

Chapter 9

Nate closed the closet door and hurried across the bedroom, through the sitting room, and out the door. He had just made it down the hall to his apartment when the Porters entered the building. Sasha started barking. Wayne and Susan both looked surprised and said they didn't realize he had a dog. Nate told them Jason and Sasha were visiting with him.

"Oh yes, I remember seeing them around. He's the breakfast chef, isn't he?" Susan asked with a disdainful expression on her heavily made-up face.

"That's right, and you can consider yourself lucky that he enjoys this place enough to agree to come here for a week. He's a fine chef. He studied at the Miette Culinary School in New York and worked with some world-renowned cooks. He's also published a book on early American recipes with lots of interesting anecdotes and illustrations." Nate felt like kicking himself after he finished talking. It sounded like he was trying to make Jason look good in Susan Porter's eyes, when he didn't really give a rat's ass what she thought about anything.

"I never learned to cook. My mother wouldn't allow me in the kitchen; she thought cooking was for the working class and, anyway, we had a great chef," Susan said with a bored expression.

Nate looked at Susan's smooth, pampered face with its vapid countenance, and thought, *What a waste of humanity. I wonder if she ever thinks of anything beyond herself and material possessions.* "Are you two staying the rest of the week, now that everything is so chaotic?" Nate asked, changing the subject.

"I'm afraid we have no choice. Seems everyone without an iron clad alibi has been asked not to leave the area," Wayne replied.

"We still have a wedding to attend this weekend, so I guess it's just as well," chimed in Susan.

"Well, try to enjoy yourselves and take care," Nate said, opening the door to his apartment and going inside. When Nate entered the apartment, Sasha was standing by the door, her hair bristling and a low growl coming from her throat. "What's wrong girl? Did you smell something that got your dander up?" Nate asked, rubbing Sasha's head.

"She started growling as soon as she saw the Porters. I'm pretty sure this is the first time she's been around them, but she sure didn't like their looks. Did you find anything interesting in their apartment?"

"Yeah, a couple of things. There's a 9mm Sig Sauer in their nightstand, and I found a slip of paper with what looks like a phone number. I'm going to have Harry run it through his database, see if he can find who it belongs to," Nate said, as he pulled his phone from his pocket and punched in Harry's number.

Harry answered on the third ring, "What can I do for you G Man?"

"What makes you think I want something, big guy? Maybe I just want to shoot the breeze."

"You always want something, so what's up? Tell Uncle Harry what's on your mind."

"I've got a phone number for you. Hope you can find who it belongs to. I know if anyone can do it, you're the man. Also, while you're checking, see if Wayne or Susan Porter have a permit to carry a weapon." Nate gave Harry the number and disconnected the call.

"Think I'll try calling the number, just for the hell of it. Who knows, I might get lucky and get an answer." Nate punched *67 to prevent his number from showing on the caller ID. He then entered the phone number. It started ringing on the other end. "That's strange," Nate said, pushing the off button.

"What happened?" asked Jason.

"Someone answered but they didn't say anything, just an open line, and then they hung up. There was a sound in the background. I've heard it before, but I couldn't identify it. I doubt they'll answer again, but it's worth a try. I'd like to listen to that background sound again," Nate said, while punching in the numbers. Much to his surprise, the phone was answered on the second ring, but it was as if they were waiting for him to speak first. Nate listened to the background noise the few seconds the line was open but still couldn't recognize the sound. "Well, hopefully Harry will come up with something. It's probably a burner, but Harry has a way of finding out things," Nate said, while putting his phone back into his pocket. "I did find something else in the Porters' apartment that was interesting or at least puzzling."

"What did you find?"

"Susan Porter has three wigs in her closet—a red one, a blond, and a gray, all different styles and lengths."

"That is kind of strange. I could understand having some the same color as your hair. Maybe she and Wayne like to play games. You know, pretend they're with a stranger. Who knows what goes on behind closed doors?" Jason said.

"Changing the subject back to John Phelps, if you're not busy this afternoon, how about hanging around over at the resort, see if you spot him and keep an eye on his movements?" Nate pulled up the pictures he had taken of John and Linda the day before at the Ledges and showed them to Jason.

"You got it, chief. I don't think I'll have any trouble recognizing him, but you better text me the picture, just to be sure."

Nate's phone buzzed about that time. "Must be Harry," he said, pulling it from his pocket.

"Hey, what you got for me, Answer Man," Nate said.

"Well, not many answers. I'm afraid the number you gave me belongs to a throw-away phone, no way to trace who it belongs to. But, I did find out where it was bought."

"Where was it bought?" Nate asked in an impatient voice.

"It was purchased at a Walmart in Portland," Harry replied, "and there's no record of a permit to carry for either of the Porters. I'm checking with Walmart about getting a copy of their surveillance video the day the phone was bought."

****

After finishing lunch, Leah went to her cottage for a pit stop before going to the studio. Sandy had just returned from the Ledges and was already in her room. Leah told her about Andy being at the studio and asked if she would like to go and paint. She agreed it would be a pleasant diversion. While walking to the studio, Leah asked Sandy if she had a nice lunch with John and Hal. It was all Sandy could do to keep from telling Leah Hal's true identity. "John left right after you did and went back to his table in the back of the restaurant. Hal and I had a very tasty and interesting lunch," Sandy said.

"What do you mean, interesting?" asked Leah.

"Just that he's an interesting person, and that's all I'm saying right now. Let's talk about what we're going to paint this afternoon. I think maybe I'll set up a still-life arrangement. There's all kinds of vases, fruit, and flowers in the studio."

"Sounds like a good idea," Leah said with a distracted look. She was finding it difficult to concentrate on painting or anything for that matter other than the murder and the enigmatic Hal Lawson.

When they entered the studio, Mattie, Becky, Mary Jane, Louise, and two other ladies Leah couldn't remember were already set up and painting. Sandy started arranging some fruit and an interesting vase on a checkered cloth. Leah started looking through the photographs and picked out a landscape with a rustic barn reflected in a lake with mountains in the distance. She and Sandy got their painting materials ready and began working. Leah did a rough sketch and started blocking in the large, dark areas. Andy went around the room making constructive comments and suggestions to each of the painters. He stopped beside Leah and studied her work. "That's coming along great! You're starting with the large shapes— keep up the good work and save the details for last, kind of like putting the icing on the cake. Remember, the first thing the viewer sees is the last thing the artist paints," he said with a grin.

Leah was trying to get the reflections in her painting perfected when someone asked if Linda Baker had been found.

"Her car was found at the airport in Portland, and they have an APB out for her. I think the police have talked to some people at her law firm and a neighbor where she lives. Apparently, no one has seen or heard from her," Andy informed the group.

"How did you find out so much?" Becky Lawson asked. "Well, the police were questioning me, asking what I knew about her, which is zilch, and I just asked. They were very informative and asked me to let them know if I heard anything from her. She is supposed to be taking a workshop with me after all," Andy said in an indignant tone.

Leah finished laying in the dark shapes in her picture and then began working in lighter tone values and adding more detail. She was about two-thirds finished with the painting when everyone started putting their materials away and cleaning their brushes.

"You ready to call it a day, or would you like to keep painting awhile?" Sandy asked, walking over to where Leah was staring at her painting with a brush poised in mid-air.

"Seems I've reached a snag, or I'm so keyed up and restless I can't concentrate on painting another brush stroke."

"It's almost happy hour. Maybe a glass of wine would help you unwind," Sandy suggested.

"I don't want to sit inside. I'm going to change my shoes and go for a walk. Maybe I'll join you when I get back."

They packed away their painting materials and went to the sink to clean their brushes to be ready to use the next day. Mattie was just finishing cleaning hers and she smiled when she saw Leah.

"How are you feeling? Are you still fretting about your tormentor, that John person?"

"Yes, and you're supposed to tell me how you solved your problem when it happened to you," Leah said.

"It's really very simple, my dear. You just have to change the direction of his object of affection," Mattie said with a grin and a wink.

"You make it sound simple, but I'm afraid it's not that easy when it comes to John Phelps.

"Sweetie, you know, women are naturally smarter than most men. Or perhaps I should say, men are less complicated than women. You just have to outsmart him."

"But, I've tried everything. I've blocked his calls; I've told him repeatedly, I no longer want to see him. It seems the more I try to be rid of him, the more determined he is to keep seeing me."

"Did you ever think of trying reverse psychology?" Mattie asked, her eyes filled with the wisdom of age.

"Reverse psychology, in what way?"

"You have to make him think you want him more than anyone or anything else in the whole, wide world. Tell him you want to get married right away. You want to have ten children and that now you can go to court and fight to get your illegitimate child back. You'll quit your job and help him with his business because you want to be together twenty-four, seven. This worked great for me. My stalker took to the hills so fast. It was really funny; all of a sudden, he was sick, his mother was sick, and he had to spend all his spare time doctoring himself and looking after his ailing mother."

Leah laughed and felt some of the burden lift from her shoulders. "Mattie, you are a jewel. But, that would never work with John.

Maybe if I'd tried it at the beginning, it may have sent him running. I'm afraid it's too late to use that strategy on him now. You sure know how to make a girl feel better. Thank you for telling me your story."

"Honey, worry never did anything but make you grow old faster. It won't solve your problems. My mother was a very wise woman and she always told me: Worry is the interest you pay on trouble before it's due."

"I'll remember that," Leah said, giving Mattie a big hug.

Sandy had cleaned her brushes, put everything away, and left while Leah and Mattie were talking.

Leah hurried up the lane to Broadview, changed into sweatpants, a t-shirt, and a pair of reeboks. She grabbed her jogging jacket as she went out the door and headed back down the hill.

Nate was sitting in one of the Adirondack chairs in front of Broadview, waiting for Leah to return from the studio. He'd been sitting there about ten minutes when he realized he was hearing the same sound he'd heard in the background of the phone call he'd made earlier. He listened carefully; it was something like a whistle and a sigh, and then he realized it was coming from the buoys out in the bay. The person who answered the call without saying anything had been near the bay or some body of water with buoys the same as the ones he was hearing.

Leah did not see Nate when she came up the path and entered the cottage, so when she came back out the door, he called to her.

She turned and looked at him and started to walk away.

"Leah, please, I need to talk to you," Nate said.

"I really don't have anything to say to you," Leah said, as she started walking down the path.

Nate caught up with her and grabbed her arm, "Leah, I'm sorry for anything I may have said or done to upset you. I owe you an explanation."

"You don't owe me anything," Leah said, jerking her arm free from his grasp.

She continued down the lane, past the main house, and followed the path around the cove and up into the woods. The yellow tape was still stretched along the edge of the cove where Sheila's body had been found. Leah shuddered as she passed the spot. Nate was walking alongside her, even though she acted as if he wasn't there.

"Please go away and quit following me," she said, giving Nate a scornful look.

"It's a free country, I can walk anywhere I choose," he replied with a mischievous smile. The golden afternoon sunlight turned his eyes to amber with sparks of green, causing Leah's heart to skip a beat.

"Well, I'll just go back to my room and--," Nate took her arm and spun her around, pulling her close until her body was pressed against his. He slid his hand up her spine and tilted her head back until she was looking directly into his eyes.

"You're not going anywhere until I've had my say, and then you can do as you please," he said in a husky voice. Leah's blue-green eyes were shooting daggers, but he could feel her heart racing against his chest. Before he realized what he was doing, his lips closed over hers. She struggled for a moment, but then her lips softened and she returned his kiss, her body melting into his.

"Leah, you drive me crazy. I can't think straight when I'm near you, and I can't get you out of my head when I'm away from you."

Leah tried to regain control of her emotions as anger and passion battled within her confused brain. "I wish I had never laid eyes on you," she said, enunciating each word slowly.

"I don't believe you mean that, but before you say anymore, let me explain. I'm not married; Becky is my twin sister, and Hal Lawson is her *real* husband. My name is Nate Parker, and I'm an FBI agent with a special unit that investigates international art thefts. We've got information that leads us to believe the person or persons responsible for a recent art heist is here at the inn or somewhere in the immediate vicinity. Sheila and Ron Rhodes were here in a special capacity to help with the investigation. I feel sure her murder is somehow connected to the art crime."

"Why didn't you tell me this sooner?" Leah asked.

"I wanted to, believe me. I wanted to so badly. I was supposed to remain undercover, but Sheila's murder changed all that. I'm going to have to reveal my true identity now. I told Sandy at lunch today, and I would have told you sooner if you hadn't run off in a huff."

Leah opened her mouth to object, but Nate interrupted her, holding his hand up as if he were surrendering. "Now, I know, I acted like a fool. But I thought you and John Phelps had something going, and I was bitten by the green-eyed monster. I know it's no excuse for my actions, but it could have been a lot worse. I didn't really say anything, just made those nasty looks," Nate said, doing a Groucho Marx eyebrow imitation. "I'll get down on my knees and apologize if it will help."

"This is too much for me to absorb all at once. Give me time to think about it," Leah said, but the corner of her mouth twitched in a little smile.

"I understand. Take your time, but be careful; John Phelps is a sly character. I wouldn't put anything past him. And, we've got a murderer running around with no idea who it is. At least, not yet."

****

Back at the inn, the two policemen had returned and were questioning Ron Rhodes again.

"What time did you say your wife left the apartment?" Detective Powell asked.

"I told you, I don't know for sure. She was still there when I left, but she was planning to go to the Ledges to do some research," Ron replied with an exasperated tone.

"Where did you go when you left, and what time did you leave?" Ron went on to explain about doing surveillance, watching the building where the Porters' apartment was located.

"Did anyone see you while you were watching the Porters' building?"

"I don't know; I doubt it. I was trying real hard not to be seen. Why are you asking me all these questions? Am I a suspect? If so,

I'm not answering anymore of your questions. Either charge me, or quit badgering me," Ron said.

"We'd like for you to go to headquarters with us and clear up a few things," Powell said.

"You can go voluntarily, or we'll charge you with suspicion of the murder of your wife and take you in for questioning."

"Okay, I'll go, but I have the right to an attorney. I want to call Nate Parker to meet me there and act as my lawyer," Ron said, as he took out his phone and punched in Nate's number.

Nate had barely uttered his last words to Leah when his phone vibrated. Pulling it out of his pocket, he saw Ron's name on the caller ID. "What's up Ron?" he asked. He listened for a few minutes then said, "I'll be right there."

He turned to Leah and said, "The police are taking Ron in for questioning about the death of his wife, and he's asked me to meet him at headquarters to act as his attorney."

****

Linda looked at the person standing in the doorway of what she had come to think of as her cell. She couldn't believe her eyes.

"John, what are you doing here? What am *I* doing here? For God's sake get these bonds off me."

"I'm afraid I can't do that Linda. Someone thinks you know too much about things you shouldn't know."

Chapter 10

Jason put Sasha in the back of his Ford Explorer and drove the short distance to the resort. He parked in the guest parking area and opened the back windows about half way, got out of the SUV, and filled Sasha's water bowl. He placed the bowl on the back floorboard and told her to be a good dog. She cocked her head to one side and looked at him with her intelligent blue eyes. Her expression seemed to say, "You know I'm always good, but please hurry back."

Jason stepped inside the door at the Ledges and looked around. He knew it was too late for lunch and too early for dinner, but he wanted to cover all bases. When the hostess approached, he told her he was meeting someone and described Phelps. She said he'd been there for lunch earlier but left about two hours ago. Jason thanked her and said he'd return later. He then headed for the clubhouse.

Jason entered the clubhouse and walked to the bar, noticing that Phelps was not among the few people scattered about the room. When the bartender brought his beer, he took it to a table by a window overlooking the golf course. He watched two men tee off and then climb into a golf cart to ride to the next hole. Another cart was coming in from the links carrying a man and woman. They both looked tired and frustrated as they clambered from the cart and came into the clubhouse. They looked familiar to him, but he couldn't place them. The man went to the bar and ordered two beers. The woman sat down at the next table and smiled. When spoke to him, he realized it was the Porters from the inn. Jason thought, *Hell and damnation! The last thing I need is to run into someone from the inn, especially the Porters.*

"Are you a golfer?" Wayne Porter asked, as he sat their drinks on the table and took a seat.

"Now and then. I'm just enjoying the beautiful weather and relaxing this afternoon. You two have a good game?" he asked, trying to appear relaxed and casual.

"If every day was like today, we'd probably give up golfing," Porter replied.

Jason had almost finished his beer and was trying to decide what to do next when he spotted Phelps. He was walking down the sidewalk that led to the condos. Jason wished the Porters a good day and better luck next time and hurried from the clubhouse. Phelps had disappeared from sight, so Jason walked in the direction he'd seen him going. As he rounded the corner, he saw Phelps getting into a black BMW parked in front of a condo about half way down Green Tee Drive. Jason made a mental note of the street's name and hurried back to his Explorer. Sasha was lying in the back seat. She sat up and made happy noises as Jason climbed behind the wheel. He saw the BMW pull out of the side street and head toward the highway. Jason backed the Ford out of the parking space and turned in the same direction, allowing Phelps enough time to get to the exit before pulling out and following him. The BMW turned right on the highway, and Jason followed a short distance behind. Phelps went about a half mile and turned onto a small lane on the right side of the road. Jason drove on by and turned into a small park just past the street where Phelps had turned. *Where the hell is he going?* He was familiar with that lane; you could reach it by walking through the woods on the north side of the Rocky Ledge Inn property. He had discovered it by accident one day while taking Sasha for a walk. He had continued walking in the direction away from the inn and had stumbled upon the lane and found there were four or five houses there. The bay was behind the houses, allowing the owners a spectacular view.

Jason had to know which one of those houses Phelps was headed to and why. He got out of his vehicle, grabbed Sasha's leash, and opened the back door. Sasha jumped out, eager for a walk. He attached her leash, and they started walking back towards the lane. A big black Hummer seemed to come out of nowhere, going fast and driving close to the edge of the road. He and Sasha had to jump into the ditch to avoid being run down. Jason turned and watched as it went around the corner and disappeared from view. He tried to get the license number but could only make out the first two letters, RA, on a vanity plate. He and Sasha jogged to the entrance of the lane and walked about 300 yards before coming to the first house. The BMW was nowhere in sight. Jason walked to the end of the lane, where it narrowed down to a path that meandered through the woods located on the north side of the inn property. He could see the bay through the trees and a sailboat gliding across the choppy waters. It had a bright orange and blue insignia on its sails which were bellowing to full capacity. He could hear the surf and the sound of the buoys sighing in the wind. He felt the chill in the air as the breeze stirred the tree branches overhead. He had on boots and jeans, a lightweight cotton shirt, and a windbreaker jacket, which he zipped and pulled the collar up around his neck. He walked farther into the woods trying to find a vantage point where he could watch the houses.

He knew Phelps had to be in one of them with his car either in a garage or hidden in the back. There was no way he could see all the houses, so he walked back up the lane towards the highway, studying each house as he went. The first house had no garage, only a carport with a white Volkswagen parked in it. The second house had a garage with the entrance on the side. There were no signs of life, and it had an unoccupied appearance. The third had a pickup truck and a Toyota in the drive. There was a garage on the front, but Jason didn't think the BMW would be there. The fourth house also had a garage, and it also had a deserted look. The fifth and last house had a station wagon in the drive, a basketball hoop on the front of the garage, and several toys lying around the yard.

Jason was betting Phelps was in either the second or fourth house, but he was going back to the inn to leave Sasha. He would walk back over through the woods and check out numbers two and four.

The name of the street was Bay View Lane. The first house from the highway was number 30 and the numbers increased in increments of six. That made the second house number 36 and the fourth 48. Jason sent Nate a text asking him to have Harry check the ownership of those two addresses. He also told Nate about following Phelps and was sure he was inside one of the houses. He said he was taking Sasha back to the inn and would walk back over to see what he could find.

Nate was on the way to Portland to meet Ron at police headquarters when he received the text. He found a place where he could pull over and send Harry the request. He also asked him if he had come up with any more info on Linda Baker and John Phelps. Nate had just pulled into the parking lot at police headquarters when his phone beeped. He pulled it out of his pocket and looked at the long text from Harry.

I was waiting on one more piece of information before texting you. I've found a whole shit load of stuff on Linda. It's too long for a text. I'll email it as an attachment. As for the property on Bay View Lane, number 36 belongs to Horace and Carol Campbell. They live in South Carolina and pretty much use the house as a vacation and summer getaway retreat. Number 48 is a little more complicated. A corporation owns it. When I checked out the corporation, it turns out to be a dummy front for another corporation. I'll keep digging.

Nate sent Harry a thanks and then texted Jason to concentrate on number 48 and be very careful.

Jason went back to his house, fed Sasha, and changed into jogging shoes. He checked his Colt 38, snapped on a shoulder holster, and slid the gun under his arm. He put on a heavier jacket, clipped a flashlight to his belt, and headed towards the woods. By the time he reached the gazebo, the sun was setting, casting a golden glow through the trees. An owl hooted its eerie sound from a nearby branch and was answered somewhere deep in the woods. A chill of apprehension prickled his skin. By the time Jason reached the edge of the woods, the sun had slipped below the horizon, leaving the sky a deep navy blue, filled with twinkling stars. It reminded Jason of a velvet blanket sprinkled with diamonds. He could see the ocean through the trees and a gibbous moon appeared to rise out of the dark water, casting a silvery path across the bay.

The first house at the end of the lane was shrouded in darkness, as was the next one, number 48. Jason eased from tree to tree, working his way to the back of the second house. As he approached, he could see a large object in the back yard. When he drew nearer, the object took shape, and he could see it was the BMW. There was a large deck across the back of the house with French doors leading inside. Jason stepped upon the deck and, staying close to the wall, moved silently to the doors and reached for the knob on the first set. It was locked. He tried the knob on the second set, and it turned. Jason gave a gentle push, and the door opened soundlessly. He released his pent-up breath, stepped inside, and closed the door. He stood perfectly still and listened. He could hear the murmur of voices, but they were so far away he couldn't tell if they were coming from inside or outside. He eased away from the door until his back was against solid wall. As his eyes adjusted to the darkness, he could tell he was in some kind of sitting room with large pieces of furniture draped with sheets or dust covers. They looked like pale monsters hovering, waiting to pounce. He stepped carefully around them and silently drifted into the next room. As his eyes became more accustomed to the darkness, he could see a large kitchen off the sitting room. He saw a door in the far wall that more than likely went into the garage. He was standing in a hallway, and the voices were much louder now, though still muffled. There were several doors leading off the hall, but what caught his attention was the one at the end. The door was slightly ajar, and a pale light was glowing around the opening. Jason moved in that direction, stepping slow and easy to avoid squeaks. He reached under his arm and patted the Colt 38, hoping he wouldn't need it, but glad it was there.

Looking through the partially open door, Jason could see a flight of stairs going down into a basement. He slid the door open an inch and held his breath—no sound, another inch, still no sound. He stepped through the door and stood at the top of the stairs. The light was coming from a room at the opposite end of the basement. The door to that room was half open, and the voices were coming from inside. Jason slowly descended the stairs, careful to step on the outside of the tread, hoping to prevent any squeaking. He stood at the bottom of the steps and considered his options. He wanted to hear the conversation coming from the room at the end of the basement but did not want to be discovered. There was a large object on the left wall, and he carefully picked his way in that direction. Upon closer inspection, he found it to be a furnace with enough space between it and the wall for him to squeeze behind it. He could hear the conversation clearly now. A man he assumed to be John Phelps was speaking. Jason couldn't make sense of what he was saying until a woman's voice said, "When you called me a few months ago, you said you were involved with Leah Dawson and were considering marriage. Now, you show up here and she doesn't even seem to know you're around. I can't believe that John Phelps the Romeo got dumped."

"No woman ends a relationship unless I choose to do so. Leah Dawson just *thinks* she's through seeing me. She just doesn't know her own mind. She needs a little attitude adjustment. She seems to have moon eyes for that big nosey hick staying at the inn, but that will change once she sees the light."

"That big nosy hick has a wife," the woman said, interrupting him.

Just as Jason stepped behind the furnace, his foot stepped on a small object and sent it skittering across the floor. The conversation coming from the room came to an abrupt halt, and Jason held his breath.

"Did you hear a noise?" Phelps asked.

"I always hear noises—this place must be infested with mice...probably even rats. How can you leave me here in this dark room, tied up and helpless? If your friends are going to kill me, tell them to do it! I'd rather be dead than go mad in this hell-hole, wherever or whatever it is."

"Get a grip, Linda. I've told you, I'm working on it. Seems you've been running your mouth too much," the man replied.

"I don't even know who your friends are, and I don't really know what I've done. Please, John, at least take the tape off my feet so I can walk to the bathroom."

"I can't do that, Linda. I would be in trouble if I did."

"John, please for old times' sake, help me."

"We have no 'old times' sake.' Where were you when I needed you?"

"I did what I had to do," she replied in a dejected tone.

"Are you through eating? I've got to get out of here. I have things to do," Phelps said in an impatient voice.

Jason hunkered down behind the furnace and listened with amazement. So, this must be the missing Linda Baker and that is John Phelps. What were they talking about? He was hoping they would continue their conversation; instead, he heard the clatter of dishes and the light was extinguished. Phelps walked out carrying a flashlight. He locked the door to the room and walked across the basement to the stairway. Linda was screaming his name, but he might as well be deaf based on his actions. He went up the stairs and closed the door. Jason heard the lock turn.

Great, he thought, *Now I'm locked in the basement with a screaming woman.* He wasn't worried about getting out. He was pretty good at picking locks, and he had his handy set of lock picks. What he was concerned about was what he was going to do about Linda Baker. Should he release her, call 911, or do nothing? He sent Nate a text and told him about finding John Phelps talking to Linda Baker who was being held captive in the basement of the house at 48 Bayview Lane. Did he have any suggestions as to what he should do?

****

Nate and Ron were shown into an interrogation room. A long metal table was bolted to the floor with three metal chairs on each side and a large mirror on one wall. Nate walked over to the mirror, put his face close to the glass, pulled out his comb, and ran it through his unruly hair, wet his fingertips and ran them over his eye brows, then winked and smiled.

"What the hell are you doing?" asked Ron

"I want to be sure I look pretty for our audience on the other side of the mirror," Nate replied with a grin.

"You think we're being watched?"

"Sure, we are, and if someone doesn't come in here and do their interrogating within five minutes, we're out of here," Nate said, looking at the mirror.

The door opened about one minute after Nate made the threating statement, and two men walked into the room. The first to enter was a big, burly, red-faced man about 45. His pants were stretched tight across his stomach, and his shirt buttons looked as though they were barely hanging on to the fabric. He introduced himself as Detective Sam Spencer. It was hard to judge the age of the second man. He had a Dick Clark, perpetually young-looking face. He was dressed in khakis and a Ralph Lauren button-down shirt. He had a friendly smile and compassionate eyes. He introduced himself as Detective Ray Thompson and asked if they would like something to drink. *Good cop, bad cop,* thought Nate.

Detective Spencer glowered at Ron, "Why did you kill your wife, Mr. Rhodes? Is there another woman, or did your wife have a boyfriend? Did she say something that set you off and you bashed her head in?"

"Why, you scum bag. How dare you accuse me of killing my wife? I wouldn't harm a hair on her head!" Ron shouted, jumping to his feet.

Nate grabbed his arm and told him to sit down and keep quiet. "Detective Spencer, do you have evidence to support such a claim? If so, please make your charges; otherwise, we're gone."

"I'm sure Detective Spencer didn't mean what he said. He gets a little premature with his thoughts and accusations," Detective Thompson said. "I don't believe you would deliberately hurt your wife. Maybe in the heat of the moment, without realizing what you were doing, you struck her," he said in a soothing voice.

Nate looked at Ron, "Don't say anything."

"It'sokayNate. I've nothing to hide." He then turned to Thompson, "Speak for yourself, Detective. I've never struck my wife in my entire life, and I would never do anything to harm her. I loved her dearly; she was my best friend. My life will be an empty void without her," Ron said, as his shoulders slumped and a dejected expression spread across his face.

"Now, tell me again. Please retrace your movements between the hours of 11:30 AM and 2:00 PM yesterday," Sam Spencer said in an accusatory tone.

"I've told you, I was watching the building where the Porters are staying."

"Did anyone go in or come out of the building while you were watching?"

"The cleaning lady came out of the cottage around noon, then came back about thirty minutes later with clean linens and went back into the building."

"Did anyone see you during those hours?"

"I was trying real hard not to be seen. I had backed my car into the parking lot in front of the building and scrunched down in the seat. I adjusted my mirrors so I could see anyone leaving or entering the building. The Porters left about fifteen minutes after the maid returned, and I followed them to the fishing village. We were over there a little over an hour. I was afraid the Porters had spotted me, so I went into the post office, but I think it was 2 PM or later by then. I waited a few minutes after the Porters left, then followed them back to their apartment. I continued my surveillance until 3:30 or 4:00. I was worried about Sheila; she'd told me she'd get back in touch with me and let me know what she'd found. I walked over to the Ledges looking for her," Ron explained.

"What did you do with her phone and laptop?" Spencer demanded.

"She had them with her. I don't know what happened to them. Maybe you should try looking for the real killer, and you might find them."

Detective Spencer brought a plastic bag over to the table and set it down. The bag contained a black granite paperweight slightly smaller than a football. "Ever seen this before?" asked Spencer.

"It looks like the paper weight in my apartment."

"I guess you *have* seen it before, since that's what you used to bash your wife's head in. Your fingerprints are on it, along with hair and blood belonging to your wife, Sheila," the detective said, glaring at Ron.

"Why you--," Nate grabbed Ron as he jumped from his chair. "Sit down, Ron, and don't say another word."

"Mister Rhodes, I'm sure it would go easier on you if you confess and tell us what happened," Thompson said in a conciliatory tone.

"My client has nothing to say. Either charge him or let him go," Nate told the detective.

"Mister Rhodes, you are being charged with the murder of your wife, Sheila. You have the right to remain silent. Anything you say can be held against you . . ." Sam Spencer continued reading Ron his Miranda rights.

Nate looked at Ron and said, "Don't say anything. Let me work on this and get back to you tomorrow."

"Do whatever you have to, but get me out of here as soon as possible," Ron said, as he was handcuffed and led away.

****

Jason climbed out from behind the furnace and went to the door of the room where Linda was being held prisoner. He took out his lock picks and went to work. It was a simple lock, and he had the door opened in about thirty seconds. He flipped on the light, and Linda stared at him from the bed where she was lying.

"Who are you? Are you here to kill me? Oh, I know you! You work at the inn!" Jason pulled his knife out of his pocket and started toward Linda. She drew up in a knot and cringed. "Please don't!" she screamed.

"Hush. I'm not going to hurt you. I'm going to cut that tape off of you. We've got to hurry. Someone else may return anytime."

"They usually only come twice a day, and someone was here this morning."

"Who was it and who did this to you?" Jason asked.

"I don't know. They must have drugged me. I can't remember what happened. I just woke up and I was lying here on this bed, trussed up like a Thanksgiving turkey."

Jason cut the duct tape away from her ankles and started on her bound wrists. "Are you going to be quiet and not make a run for it when I release you?"

"I don't know where I would run, and there's someone out there who seems to want me dead. Where do you plan to take me when we leave here?"

"I'll take you to my house until I can figure out a safe place for you."

"How did you find me and why are you doing this?" Linda asked with a puzzled expression.

"We'll talk when we get to my place. Right now, let's just concentrate on getting out of here."

Jason removed the tape from Linda's wrists and helped her stand. She was a little shaky at first, and Jason held her arm as they left the room. Something told him to relock the door before they climbed the stairs. He used his picks on the door at the top of the steps, and within a few seconds they were in the hallway. He relocked the door, and they headed toward the sitting room. Just as they rounded the corner and started to the French doors, car lights swept across the back yard, and Jason recognized the black Hummer that had almost run him down on the highway earlier. Both front doors of the Hummer flew open, and two muscle-bound thugs climbed out. Jason grabbed Linda's arm. "Wait, let's try the front door."

They retraced their steps to the hall and found the front door, but it had a dead bolt lock and no key in sight. Jason knew he wouldn't have time to pick the lock before the goons got into the house. There was a table to the right of the door and Jason started feeling around, hoping to find a key. Linda was searching in the kitchen and found a set of keys in a small bowl on the counter top.

"See if any of these fit," she said, handing Jason the keys.

They heard the men walking across the deck, and Jason grabbed Linda's arm and whispered, "We don't have time to get out the front door. Let's duck into one of the bedrooms." They ran back down the hall and opened the first door on the left, stepped in, and closed the door. The men were in the house now, and their footsteps were loud as they went down the hall to the door leading to the basement. They heard the rattle of keys as the men unlocked the door and then a loud clattering sound as the men lumbered down the steps. Jason went to the bedroom window and opened it. He stepped out onto the front porch and helped Linda through before closing it.

They ran across the road and into the woods. After they got farther away, they turned and looked back at the house. Lights were on in every room. "They must be searching for you. They'll probably talk to John and find out when he was here, and they'll know you haven't had time to get very far. We've got to hurry and get to my place. I don't think there's any way they can connect you to me, but we cannot trust anyone except Nate. You've got a lot of explaining to do, but first we've got to get you hidden."

"Who is Nate?"

"You met him Sunday. He's an FBI agent and was posing as his sister's husband, Hal Lawson."

"But why was he doing that? Why is he here?"

"I'll fill you in on everything when you answer my questions," he said, taking her arm and telling her to hurry.

Jason was afraid to use his flashlight, but the moon was bright enough for them to see the path and make their way through the thicket. The owl hooted its creepy call from a nearby tree and, like an echo, an answer came from deep within the woods. Linda grabbed Jason's arm and shuddered. "It's just an owl," Jason said in a reassuring voice.

They hurried past the gazebo and across the wooden footbridge down out of the trees to the path that circled around the cove. When they came to the spot with the yellow tape stretched along the bay side of the path, Linda stopped and gasped. "What happened here?"

"This is where Sheila Rhodes' body was found."

"What do you mean, her body?"

"Oh, I forgot. You disappeared before she was found. Someone bashed her head in and apparently threw her body in the bay. It was caught in the rocks close to the shore here. Leah and Nate found her yesterday," Jason informed her.

Linda looked pale as a ghost in the moonlight. She put her hand to her mouth to keep from screaming. "Oh my God, what is going on here?" she said, almost in a whisper.

Chapter 11

Nate watched as the detective led Ron away. *I'll push for a hearing tomorrow and hopefully post bond and get him released,* Nate thought as he went to the parking lot and got into his car. He took out his phone and pulled up his emails. He found the one from Harry and opened the attachment. Harry had done his homework—the attachment was two pages long. Nate scanned it, reading the highlights. Linda came from a very dysfunctional family. She had an abusive father, James Pruitt, who was mean and ornery and even meaner when drunk. The mother, Irene, was browbeaten and scared to open her mouth. There were two girls and one boy. The oldest girl, Peggy, was 14 when Linda was put into a foster home at age 12. A few months later, at age 11, the boy, James, Jr. was also put into a foster home. Peggy married at age 15 to escape her environment and still lives in Georgia. James, Jr. joined the military when he turned 18. He stayed in the army four years, received medals for marksmanship and was honorably discharged ten years ago. He then disappeared from the face of the earth. Linda received an academic scholarship to University of Georgia and went on to law school. She was married to a man named Robert Baker, the marriage lasting a little over a year. She kept his name when they divorced.

As Nate perused the document, his phone beeped a notice of an incoming text. It was from Jason. Nate closed the email, careful to save the document, and opened the text.

It was short and to the point. *Please stop by my house when you return from police headquarters.*

What's up? Nate texted back.

I'll explain when you get here. Park in your regular place and walk over. Avoid being seen, was the reply.

It took Nate almost an hour to get back to the inn. He parked the Cherokee in his usual parking spot in front of Rosewood cottage. He walked down the lane toward the main entrance to the inn. The resort was to the right, but he turned left and walked down the road to Jason's rented house. He saw no one along the way. When the house came into view, it appeared to be in total darkness. As he drew near, though, he could see a faint light in the back. *Probably the kitchen,* he thought, as he stepped up onto the small porch and knocked on the front door. Sasha barked once, and then he heard footsteps. The door had a glass pane on the top half with a closed blind. Nate saw the blind move as someone peeked out, and then the door opened. Jason stepped aside and beckoned for him to enter.

"What's with all the cloak and dagger?" asked Nate

"Come on back to the kitchen and we'll talk," Jason said. "Would you like some coffee?"

"That sounds good. I could use something to eat too, if you have anything," Nate said, petting Sasha and scratching behind her ears as she nuzzled up to him wagging her tail.

"I'm making an omelet, French toast, and a salad," Jason said, leading the way back to the kitchen.

"My mouth's watering already," Nate said as he followed Jason to the back of the house.

Linda Baker was sitting at the table with a cup of coffee between her hands, rubbing the cup as if she could absorb the warmth of its contents.

"You remember Linda," Jason said. "She's had a rather harrowing experience. Matter of fact, I think we're both still in a state of shock."

"I can understand that. You've both been though a lot today." He turned to Linda and said, "The police have an APB out for you. They found your car at the Portland airport. Do you feel like talking about it now?" he asked.

"Give her a little time," Jason said, breaking eggs into a bowl and adding a pinch of salt and pepper and a dash of cream. He whisked them until they were light and frothy and then dumped the mixture into an omelet pan sizzling with butter. A tray containing crumbled bacon and various vegetables and cheeses was on the counter beside the stove. Jason added them to the eggs at just the right moment. Nate watched in amazement as Jason juggled the French toast and omelet and soon had it all assembled on the table. He put out plates, napkins, and silverware and retrieved a Caesar salad from the fridge.

"I hope this will help Linda feel stronger and more like talking. She's only had cold canned food since she was kidnapped," Jason explained. He went on to tell Nate about following Phelps to the house on Bay View Lane, the conversation he overheard, and his and Linda's narrow escape when the two thugs showed up. "I'm afraid John Phelps is a dangerous man, and he's also a man with a vendetta," Jason said.

"Vendetta? Against whom?"

"Leah Dawson because she dumped him, and now you because he thinks she's interested in you. He has no conscience, and I truly believe he derives pleasure from hurting people," Linda said, speaking for the first time.

"What's your connection to him? How long have you known him?" Nate asked.

"I've known him all my life. He's my brother," Linda said in a flat monotone.

"I don't understand. You don't act or look like brother and sister," Jason said in a voice filled with surprise.

"We were put in foster homes when I was 12 and he was 11. I never knew what happened to him until about five years ago when he showed up at my office one day. He had somehow managed to find me, and he told me about being in the army. He said he learned a lot during that time, including how to make money, big money. He had changed his name and had some plastic surgery done. He looked completely different from the way I remembered him, even considering the fact he was only 11 the last time I saw him. He just looked different. His nose was broken when he was eight, and it had a bump and was crooked. Now he has a perfect nose. He needed legal help and seemed to think I owed him."

"Why would he think that?" asked Jason.

"I was put into a foster home first, and he thought I had abandoned him. I used to try to divert our father when he was on a rampage. He especially liked to pick on John. I think that and the military contributed to John's lack of conscience and cold bloodedness."

"Do you think he killed Sheila Rhodes?" Nate asked.

"No, I don't really think John is capable of murder. He's the type to hire someone else to do his dirty work, and I don't know what the motive could possibly be. I don't think he even knew Sheila Rhodes."

"Did he kidnap you? If so, what was his motive?" Nate asked.

"My head is clearing now, and I can remember pretty much everything that happened prior to waking up in that horrid room. John had left a note in my room Sunday night asking me to meet him at the Ledges for lunch. I thought I would meet him and tell him I was through helping him with any kind of legal problems concerning his shady activities. He can be very persuasive, and he was making a very good case for me to help him. I finally told him I would think about it and headed back towards the inn. He followed me, and we stopped at the edge of the inn property while he continued to try and convince me to help him. He started talking about our youth and how I used to intervene between him and our father. I noticed him looking towards the inn with an interested expression, and I turned and looked in the same direction but didn't see anything. John always had extremely good vision, so I just chalked it up to him seeing some interesting or unusual occurrence that would be of no interest to me. Then he told me he'd be back in a few minutes, and he went up the lane to the second cottage. I watched him open the door on the screened-in porch. It looked like he knocked on the door, then poked his head inside. He came back down the hill and told me he thought he'd seen someone he knew. It was between 1:30 and 2:00 by then, and I stood there debating whether to go back to the studio or not. I didn't want to go back to my room, but I felt it was too late to start a painting. I'd probably been standing there about ten minutes when a black Hummer drove up and stopped, and a big, rough-looking man got out and came toward me. That was the last thing I remembered until I woke up in that dark room, my feet and hands bound with duct tape."

"Hold on, back up," Nate interrupted, "you said John went up to the second cottage and went in?"

"Well, he went into the screened-in porch, and it looked like he knocked and then opened the door. He may have called out something, but he closed the door and came right back."

"Hmm, the second cottage is Fernwood, the cottage the Rhodes are staying in. I wonder what he saw that caused him to go up there. You're sure he didn't go inside?"

"Yes, it was kind of hard to see what he was doing through the screen. But, I'm sure he just opened the door and, if he did go in, he came right back out because he was only gone a few minutes.

"I think maybe Mr. Phelps has a lot of explaining to do."

"Had John been to the house where you were being held before tonight?" Jason asked.

"No, tonight was the first time I'd seen him since I was abducted. I don't know who the other person was—they never said anything and it was so dark. I couldn't see. They never turned the light on, just used a flashlight."

"Why did he come tonight? He'd been there at least thirty minutes by the time I found you," Jason said.

"I got the impression someone had sent him. He'd been questioning me a lot about what I knew of the stories I was talking about at the reception. Someone seems to think I know something, but I have no idea what they think I know."

"Did he mention what stories you'd discussed at the reception that had someone upset?"

"He said I talked about a movie I'd seen about an art forger and about a murder that was made to look like an accident."

"Can you remember who was around when you were talking about those things?" Nate asked.

"No, I know Sheila and Ron Rhodes were there and the Porters at least part of the time, and there were others coming and going. It could have been most anyone. I don't even remember what all I said that would cause someone to think I know something important."

"Whoever it was must have sent those goons," Jason said.

"I think they were probably going to torture me until I told them what they wanted to hear and then probably kill me. Thank God you came when you did," Linda said, looking at Jason.

"By the way, I saw Sheila yesterday when I first went to the restaurant to meet John. She came out of the gift shop and headed toward the inn; there was a woman with her," Linda said as if in an afterthought.

"A woman—did you recognize her?" Nate asked with suppressed excitement.

"No, I've never seen her before," Linda replied.

"What did she look like? Can you describe her?" asked Nate.

"She was an older woman, in her early to mid-sixties, gray hair, and heavy set. She and Sheila seemed to be having a disagreement of some kind."

"It doesn't sound like anyone from the inn. We should canvas the area tomorrow and see if anyone remembers seeing her. We need a composite drawing. Think you could do that?" Nate asked.

"Yeah, I think I can do that."

"Okay Jason, that's a job for you tomorrow. I've got to work on getting bond posted to get Ron out of jail. Be very careful; watch who you talk to. We don't really know who the bad guys are in this case, and Linda, you better stay put. Don't even stick your head out the door or get too close to a window. I have a feeling John will be looking for you at the inn. I'm also worried about Leah, after what Jason told me of John's vendetta. I'll kill that S.O.B. if he lays a hand on her."

"Nate, I'm so sorry I acted like such a bitch towards Leah. I thought she was involved with John, and I just naturally thought anyone who would get involved with him would be a no good person," Linda said with a shamefaced look.

"That's water under the bridge. The main thing now is to keep you hidden and hope you remember something that will help us find whoever is behind all of this."

They finished the meal and Nate complimented Jason, telling him again what a fabulous cook he was. Linda agreed that the food was spectacular and if she could just have a nice long, hot bath, she would feel like a human again. Jason showed her where the bathroom and clean linens were located and told her he would put clean sheets on the bed in the extra bedroom. "I know you're exhausted. We can talk tomorrow after you've had a good night's sleep."

Jason came back into the kitchen after making up the bed in the guest room. He sat down across the table from Nate, who was just finishing his coffee. "Well, we have a lot more information but still don't know much."

"Actually, we know a lot more. I think we need to make a list of everything and see if anything jumps out at us."

Jason got up and rummaged around in a desk drawer. He pulled out a composition notebook and a pen. "Okay, start talking, and I'll take notes," he said, opening the notebook and writing, "What We Know" across the top of the page.

"Number one," said Nate, "Sheila Rhodes was murdered by someone because she had found some important information about that person or persons. She sent Ron a text telling him she was on to something and would get back in touch. Did she confront the person or persons? If not, how did they know she was on to them?"

"What if Ron really *did* murder his wife?" asked Jason. "He may be involved in the theft for all we know, or maybe he got angry and hit her. Harder than he really meant to."

"My gut tells me he's innocent," Nate said. "At any rate, let's go on the assumption that he's innocent."

"Number two, Sheila's phone and laptop are missing. Did the killer destroy them or hide them someplace? Number three, John Phelps is somehow involved with the person or persons responsible for kidnapping Linda. Number four, Linda knows something.

Something she remembers and is lying about or something she thought was so trivial at the time that she's not associating it with the murder or theft. Number five, Sheila was with an unknown woman just prior to being murdered. Number six, Sheila was murdered in her apartment with a granite paperweight. It has Ron's fingerprints on it, so the killer was wearing gloves. Otherwise, their prints would be on it or it would have been wiped clean."

"Do you have anything to add to our list?" Nate asked.

"I have a question," Jason said.

"What is it?" Nate asked.

"How did Sheila's body get all the way to the end of the cove if she was murdered in her apartment?"

"Something to do with the tides. If the body was thrown in the bay while the tide was coming in, it could have washed up into the cove. Apparently, the body got caught in the rocks, so when the tide went out, it was left exposed."

"Another piece of information we have: the phone number I found in the Porters' apartment who someone answers but doesn't say anything. I believe whoever answered was somewhere close by in this area. We need to check with Linda and find out what her number is. The phone could belong to her. Phelps or whoever kidnapped her may have taken it," Nate said. "It's been a long day with many emotional upheavals. I'm going to call it a night and let you get some rest. Hopefully tomorrow will bring more answers," Nate said, grabbing his jacket and heading for the door.

Nate took the path along the side of the bay back to the inn. The moon was high overhead now, surrounded by a circle of mist. Nate counted three stars within the circle. *What was that old saying?* he wondered. *It would rain that many days or it would be that long before it rained.* He didn't remember, but the sound of the buoys sighing and moaning out in the bay reminded him of the phone number. As he approached Rosewood cottage, a woman came out the front door.

"Oh, hello, Mr. Lawson. You startled me. I wasn't expecting to see anyone," said Liz Walker, the owner of Rocky Ledge Inn.

"I'm sorry if I startled you. I was just stretching my legs before I call it a night," Nate said.

"No problem. Is everything okay? I'm so sorry about everything that's happened—the murder and then the kidnapping. I do hope everything will soon be resolved. I understand the police arrested Mr. Rhodes today."

"Yes, I'm acting as his attorney and just returned from Portland a short while ago."

"Well, as they say in show biz, 'The show must go on,' so hopefully the workshop will continue without further incidents," Liz said with a smile.

"Hopefully. Have a good night, Ms. Walker," Nate said, entering the building.

Nate found Becky in the living room sitting in front of a crackling fire looking through an art book. He removed his jacket and boots and sat down in the chair opposite her. He stretched out his long legs and propped them on a foot stool, enjoying the warmth and comfort of the fire.

"Well, hello stranger. This is the first time I've seen you all day," Becky said with a smile.

"Yes, it's been a long day. I guess you know the police arrested Ron and charged him with the murder of his wife. He asked me to act as his attorney."

"Do you believe he's innocent?" Becky asked.

"If he's not innocent, he's the best actor I've ever seen. I believe he's totally devastated over the loss of his wife, and I'm a pretty good judge of character."

"They did seem to be very close," Becky said.

Nate debated telling Becky about Jason following John Phelps and rescuing Linda Baker. He'd think about it, maybe tell her tomorrow. "Was Liz Walker here just before I came in?" he asked.

"No, I haven't seen her. I did hear someone in the hall and the front door opening just before you arrived."

"She must have been to the Porters' apartment."

"I couldn't really tell. I just heard the footsteps and then the front door opening," Becky said.

Nate told Becky about talking to Leah and telling her his true identity, as well as the conversation he'd had with John Phelps at the Ledges restaurant.

"John is a deceitful, cunning man, and he's angry and seeking revenge. He followed Leah here to do God only knows what. He now has it in for me because he has it in his head that Leah wants me. I don't trust him as far as I can throw him, so be very careful. He may decide to try to hurt me by hurting anyone close to me. But, he doesn't know that you're my sister. So, with his warped way of thinking, he'd probably think he was doing me a favor if he harmed you."

"I think you need to concentrate on covering your own butt and watching out for Leah. I'm glad you told her who you are and why you're here. She's a very nice person, and she's also very attracted to you," Becky said.

"I don't know about that. She didn't exactly do flips when I told her I wasn't married."

"She just needs a little time to adjust and let everything sink in. She's had a lot of emotional upsets in the last two days," Becky reminded him.

Nate told her about searching the apartment earlier that day and what he'd found.

"I think I'll try that number again," he said, pulling his phone out of his pocket and dialing *67 and the number. It rang four times. Nate was about to hang up when it clicked and the line opened. He thought there would be only silence on the other end as before, but to his astonishment, a voice said, "Speak." Nate couldn't identify the voice. It was low and raspy. It could belong to a man or woman. He lowered his voice to a whisper and said, "Where shall we meet?" There was a pause. Nate could hear low music in the background and then a click when the phone was disconnected.

Chapter 12

Leah went straight to her room after her encounter with Nate Parker. She needed to think and sort things out, but her thoughts were swirling. Too much was happening too fast. She opened the door to her room and went inside, now wishing she could lock it when she was away. She'd been right—John Phelps was in the area. She didn't know if he followed her or if it was a coincidence. Whatever the reason, it didn't bode well.

She changed from the sweatpants and shirt into jeans, boots, and a blue turtleneck sweater. As she brushed her hair, she could almost see Nate Parker standing behind her, reflected in the mirror. His eyes filled with questions as they stared back at her. A flush spread across her cheeks as she remembered how good it felt in his arms, his hard body pressed against hers. A warm glow spread over her, and she caught herself smiling at the shadowy reflection in the mirror. Then, an uninvited voice whispered in her mind, *What if it's his dead wife he's attracted to and not the real you. I can't think clearly now. I need to get him out of my mind, concentrate on something else.* Her thoughts swirled as she watched the amorphous shape vanish, leaving only the room behind her reflected in the mirror.

When she arrived at the main house, she found Sandy sitting in the front room by the fireplace. The fire had burned down, leaving only glowing embers in the grate, but warmth still emanated from the cinders. The Porters were sitting on the loveseat, and Liz Walker was standing by the mantle. "Hi Leah, how are you doing? Would you care for a glass of wine?" she asked as Leah entered the room.

"I'm doing fine, thanks for asking. I'd love a glass of white wine."

"Make that two, or you can let me pretend I'm a gentleman and I'll get one for you, Leah, and myself," Andy Barzetti said, entering the room.

"No, no, you're a guest. Make yourself comfortable, and I'll be right back with the wine," Liz said.

Andy walked over to the fireplace where Leah was standing looking at a painting hanging over the mantle. "That's a beautiful painting, but it pales in comparison to you. I'd love to paint you in that blue sweater," he said, studying her face. "It would be quite a challenge to capture the color of your eyes. They're almost the same shade of blue as the water on a Caribbean beach."

"Thank you. I would be flattered to have you paint me, but I'm sure you could find a much better subject. Besides, if you were painting me, how could I watch and observe your marvelous talent?"

"You would have the end result to study and admire," Andy said.

"Touché," Leah replied.

"Did you know the police took Ron Rhodes in for questioning?" Sandy asked, interrupting the exchange between Leah and Andy.

"Yes, I feel so sorry for him. I don't believe for a minute he murdered his wife. They seemed like such a devoted couple."

"You can't always go by appearances," Andy said with a mischievous grin. "I'll bet none of you would ever guess that I was once a male stripper. I'd strip down to my G-string. Boy, you should have seen some of those sedate, conservative women screaming, 'Take it off! Take it *all* off!' and putting five, ten, and twenty-dollar bills in my jock strap." Everyone laughed, not knowing if he was really serious or making a joke. It did lighten the mood, though. Dinner was announced about that time, and they all trouped into the dining room.

Liz wished everyone a good evening and hoped they enjoyed the meal. As she started to leave the room, Sandy stopped her at the door and asked if she had heard any more about Linda Baker.

"No, only that the police found her car at the Portland airport. Seems she's disappeared without a trace," she said with a concerned expression. "I hope this doesn't create fear and anxiety among the group. I feel sure it must have been something in her personal life that brought this on and has nothing to do with the workshop or anyone here."

"I'm wondering if her disappearance is connected to Sheila Rhodes' murder somehow," Leah suggested.

"Oh, I don't see how it could be. They didn't know each other and had no connection other than both staying here at the inn. Maybe Linda had a misunderstanding with someone and just decided it would be better to leave. After all, the police seem to think Ron Rhodes murdered his wife, and he *does* seem to be the most likely suspect. Who knows what went on behind their closed doors…" Liz said in a cool voice, but her eyes held a concerned expression.

Leah looked at Liz and wondered what she was really concerned about. It didn't seem to be about Linda's disappearance and safety. Maybe it was about the effect it may have on future workshops at the inn. She was definitely very concerned about something and seemed overly eager to let the matter of the murder be closed and wrapped up with the arrest of Ron.

Leah and Sandy went into the dining room as Liz headed to her private quarters upstairs.

****

John Phelps was sitting at a table in the Ledges having his dinner when his phone vibrated. Taking it from his pocket, he looked at the caller ID and felt a spark of apprehension and irritation.

He hit the on button and asked, "What's up, why are you calling me instead of your boss?"

"I don't have a boss. I'm a self-employed facilitator."

"Okay, Jagger, whatever you want to call it. Why didn't you call the person who hired you?"

"Your little chickadee has fled the coop," said a gravelly voice on the other end of the line.

"What the hell do you mean, fled the coop?" John asked, trying to keep his voice in a normal tone.

"Just what I said. Knox and I just come from 'the place' and there's no one there. The doors were all locked and nothing disturbed, just a pile of duct tape where the chick should be."

"Did you search the house and area?"

"Well now, you think you're dealing with a couple of shitheads? She's nowhere to be found, Einstein. Maybe you know where she is; you were the last one there and the doors were all locked. Maybe you felt sorry for her and let her go," Jagger said in a sarcastic tone of voice.

"I don't feel pity. There's no room for it in my character and you'll do well to remember that. If you bumbling idiots have let her escape, you'll regret the day your mama and daddy got together and conceived your worthless ass. I've got to give this some thought. In the meantime, see if you can get your little gray cells working and try to remember anything that will explain how she got away," Phelps hissed into the phone.

"You better watch your mouth, pretty boy. We didn't just ride in on a load of pumpkins, and we don't take no shit off pricks like you."

"Okay, stay cool. I'll talk to the one who hired you and let you know if you're needed," Phelps said in a conciliatory tone. He disconnected the phone and took several deep breaths trying to calm his jangling nerves. After his heart rate slowed down and his anger settled to a quiet simmer, he thought about the situation. Where could she be? She had to have had help. One name kept popping up in his mind. *Nate Parker.* He would bet his condo Nate Parker was behind Linda's disappearance. *I think I know how to make Mr. Parker return her—I think I can make him want to return her real bad. I think he would be more than happy to exchange her for the lovely Leah Dawson.*

He picked up his phone and punched in a number he had committed to memory. It was answered on the second ring.

"Why are you calling? Don't tell me you didn't get the information I sent you to get."

"No, I didn't get any information. I think you're over reacting; I don't think she knows anything, whatever it is you're so worried about. The reason I'm calling is because those bumbling idiots you hired just reported to me that she's fled the coop."

"So, did you let her go?" asked the voice on the other end of the phone.

"Don't be ridiculous. Why would I do that?"

"She's your sister. I've always heard blood is thicker than water."

"There's no family ties here. As far as I'm concerned, I have no family, and compassion is not part of my make-up. You'll do well to remember that."

"*You* will do well to remember that blackmailers don't usually get what they want, but they often get what they deserve."

"If that's a threat, you better remember that if anything happens to me, even if it appears to be natural causes, the police will be receiving some very incriminating information about you."

Phelps heard a click and the line went dead on the other end of his phone.

****

Leah and Sandy walked back to their rooms after dinner. Leah had told Sandy about Nate revealing his true identity to her that afternoon.

"How do you feel about him now?" Sandy asked.

"I can't deny, he curls my toenails every time we get near each other, but I'm afraid of him. I should say afraid of getting hurt. I've always had bad luck with men, and he looks like trouble with a capital T."

"How do you figure that?" asked Sandy

"He's an FBI agent. He travels constantly, and has probably been involved with countless women."

"So, he investigates art crimes, and he's also an attorney. He's not on the road all the time, only when there's a need for his special services. He has a law office in Williamsburg, Virginia with a couple of associates who handle things when he's away. He loves kids and dogs."

"Well, anyone who loves kids and dogs can't be all bad," Leah said with a laugh.

"How did you learn so much about Mr. Parker?" she asked.

"I've talked to Becky a lot. She's a really nice person, and she and Nate are very close. She thinks he's crazy about you. She says that since his wife died, he's never looked at another woman the way he looks at you."

"That's another one of my fears. He says I look like his deceased wife. I'm afraid he sees her in me, and that's why he's attracted to me."

Her phone beeped an incoming text. Leah looked at the screen and saw an unfamiliar number. She opened the message and read, "Leah, I need to talk to you. Will you meet me tomorrow morning around seven in front of your cottage?" It was signed Nate.

"What is it? Is there something wrong?" asked Sandy.

"It's from Nate. He wants me to meet him tomorrow morning. He says he needs to talk to me…that it's very important."

Leah woke up around six the next morning. She lay there thinking about what Nate had on his mind. Why did he want to talk to her? She would have liked to sleep another hour, but her mind was too active to allow her to even doze, so she crawled out of the warm bed. She filled the bathtub with hot water and added some concoctions while the water was running. Bubbles and steam rose from the tub as she slid into the water. She leaned her head back and closed her eyes. As her body relaxed in the soothing water, her mind drifted. She began to doze and dream. She and Nate were in the woods, and he was walking in front of her. He stopped and turned his head, and the face looking at her belonged to John Phelps. His eyes were blazing, and his mouth was twisted in a cruel smirk. She jerked awake, her heart pounding as she opened her eyes and took in her serene surroundings. She climbed out of the tub, dried off, and slipped into a soft terry robe. *What in the world could that crazy dream mean? What in my subconscious mind would make me correlate those two men? They are as different as night and day.*

Leah slipped into a pair of jeans, boots, and a bright red sweater. It was almost seven when she opened the door and stepped outside. The air was cool and crisp and Leah took a deep breath, thinking how clean it felt going into her lungs. The sun was sending sparkles across the bay. Boats moored offshore were bright splashes of color reflected in the calm water where seagulls swooped and dipped, searching for food. Their loud "haw-haw" reminded Leah of the sound crows made back home in Tennessee.

"It's a beautiful sight, isn't it?" Nate said as he walked up to Leah.

"I wonder if I would ever get tired of looking at all the beautiful views. Regardless of the weather or time of day or night, there is a special, unique beauty in this place," Leah said.

"Kind of like you, Leah. I know I would never get tired of looking at you. You have a special, unique beauty, and not only the outer package. You have an inner beauty that touches my heart," Nate said, reaching for Leah's hand.

Leah was speechless—she stared at Nate, looking into his eyes, which were more green than usual. He smiled, and Leah noticed for the first time that he had a dimple in his right cheek, but it did nothing to take away from his rugged good looks. Just the reverse; it added to them. His dark brown hair was unruly as usual and still damp from a recent shower. He kept it cut short enough to keep the wayward strands out of his eyes. Leah felt her insides melt as her stomach did flip flops; she caught her breath and tried to assume a cavalier attitude.

"You've never seen me first thing in the morning," she said with a laugh.

"I sure would like to," Nate responded.

Leah felt heat rising from her middle, and her lips parted as her tongue licked them. Her eyes grew moist with desire, but she stiffened her spine and, ignoring his statement, asked, "You wanted to talk to me about something?"

"Yes. I've got something really important to ask you, but, you look so amazing in that red sweater, I just completely forgot my reason for coming here."

"What is it you wanted to ask me?"

"I had to think about this a long time before deciding to get you involved. I would never forgive myself if I put you in danger and something happened to you. There's no one else at this inn that I would trust, with the exception of Becky and Sandy."

"What in the world are you talking about?" asked Leah.

"Linda Baker," Nate replied

Leah gasped, "Did you find her? Is she all right?"

"Jason found her yesterday. She was being held like a prisoner in a house on the other side of the woods. Jason took her to his house until we can decide what to do."

"Don't you think you should tell the police?" Leah suggested.

"Even if the police caught the kidnappers, the person who hired them would probably just send someone else. She was drugged and apprehended by two thugs driving a black Hummer. John Phelps is involved somehow, but he's not the one who hired those goons to grab her and take her to that house. And we have no idea who that person is. We figure the best thing to do to keep her safe is to keep her hidden."

"Why are you telling me this? What do you want me to do?"

"Since you're in the same cottage where Linda's room is, I was hoping you could get her some clothes and toiletries. You walk a lot anyway, so no one would suspect anything if they see you out walking."

"Where does Jason live? Is he in one of the cottages here at the inn?"

"No, he lives in a rental house down the road to the left of the entrance to the inn. You can reach it by taking the path that goes from the cottage where I'm staying along the cliff above the bay. I can show you the way, if you'd like. I've got to leave pretty soon for Portland. I'd like to be there by 9 AM to try and get bail posted for Ron."

"Okay, do you want to come in and help me pick out some clothes and toiletries for Linda?"

"I've still got things to do before I can leave for Portland. I'm going back to my cottage, but I'll be watching for you and join you when you come by. I'll take you the rest of the way to Jason's. It would be good if Sandy could go with you."

"I'll get some stuff together and talk to Sandy. Shouldn't take more than fifteen minutes."

"Leah, be very careful and be aware that John Phelps is a very dangerous man. Linda can tell you more about him. Have her tell you her story—you're in for a surprise."

He took her hand and squeezed it gently, flashing his killer smile that turned Leah's insides to mush.

She jerked her hand away and headed back inside the cottage. With a carefree attitude that she didn't really feel, she said, "Don't worry. I'm a big girl. I can take care of myself."

Leah stopped by Sandy's room and told her everything Nate had said and asked if she could go with her to Jason's house. Sandy said she'd be glad to—she'd love to hear Linda's story. The two of them went around to Linda's room and eased the door open. They didn't know if Mary Jane was in her room next door or not, but they didn't want to take a chance on being overheard.

They quickly collected some underwear, jeans, sweaters and warm-up pants and tops. They gathered some toiletries and put everything into their painting supply bags. "If anyone sees us, they shouldn't suspect anything unusual with us carrying these bags,"

Leah said, as they left the cottage and headed down the lane. They passed the main house without seeing anyone and went past the studio, on around to Rosewood cottage, where Nate and Becky were staying. As they neared the cottage, Nate stepped out the front door and greeted them.

"Good morning, ladies. Mind if I join you?" he asked.

"We're always happy to have the company of a good-looking man," Sandy teased.

"Just in case the Porters or any of the other tenants are watching: I don't want to arouse suspicion with the wrong person, especially since we don't know who the 'wrong' person is," Nate said with a smile, as though they were out for a casual walk.

Unknown to them, someone *had* seen Leah and Sandy walking down the lane with their painting bags. The person first thought they were taking supplies to the studio, but when they went on past the studio and around toward Rosewood cottage, they began to wonder what they were up to. They watched as Nate Parker came out, greeted the ladies, and the trio continued on to the path that ran along the edge of the inn property, parallel with the bay. The person watched until the three disappeared from sight. It could be an innocent morning walk. *Then again, it could be something else,* thought the onlooker.

Nate continued walking with Leah and Sandy until they were past the inn property and the road leading to Jason's house was in sight. He pointed to the house and cautioned them again to be extremely careful. He had to leave for Portland and do all he could to get Ron released, or else he would go with them. He sent a text to Linda telling her that Leah and Sandy were on the way, then headed back to his cottage.

Leah and Sandy approached the house located at the end of the road. The blinds were closed, giving the appearance that no one was home. They stepped onto the small front porch and knocked. Sasha began barking from within, and the blind on the front door moved as someone peeked out. The door opened, and Linda beckoned for them to hurry and come inside. She quickly closed the door and told them to come on back to the kitchen.

"Would you like some coffee?" she asked over her shoulder while walking to the back of the house.

"I'd love some, but we don't have much time," Leah said.

"Yeah," Sandy said, "We need to get back to the inn for breakfast. We don't want to cause anyone to get suspicious."

"Jason is already over there doing his breakfast duties," Linda said while getting two cups and filling them with coffee. She placed a tray with cream and sugar in front of them. Sasha was prancing around, wagging her tail, and making happy noises. Leah and Sandy petted her and told her what a good girl she was and how pretty she looked. She wiggled and pranced, the expression on her face almost like a smile of appreciation.

Linda turned and looked at Leah, "I want to apologize for being so bitchy to you. It was all uncalled for. I didn't really know anything about you, and I assumed you were in a relationship with John and that made you a bad person."

"Don't worry about it," Leah replied. "Can you tell us what happened? How were you kidnapped? Who did it, and why?"

Linda explained all she could remember about being abducted. "As far as the reason it happened, I don't know. Apparently, I've said something to someone that led them to believe I have information that could be a threat to them."

"Think back over all the conversations you've had since you've been here. Maybe something will ring a bell," Leah suggested.

"I've racked my brain, but I'll keep trying," Linda said.

"We need to get back to the inn for breakfast and the workshop—we'll keep our eyes and ears open," Leah said.

Linda quickly told them about John being her brother and how dangerous he was. "He's going to be furious when he realizes I've escaped. He will retaliate and do everything in his power to find me.

The two muscle-bound men who arrived about the time Jason and I were about to leave the house were driving a black Hummer. Whoever hired them, be it John or someone else, will probably have them searching the area." As they got up to leave, Linda gave Leah and Sandy a hug and thanked them for bringing the care package.

"You be very careful! Do you have a weapon or any kind of protection if someone should show up?" asked Sandy.

"Jason left a gun with me, but I don't really know how to use it. He also showed me a secret hiding place. This is a very old house, and there is a hidden door with a small space behind it. If someone should come, I would get in there."

Leah and Sandy hurried back to the inn the same way they had come. They stopped by the studio and dropped off their painting supply bags, then went on to Broadview before going down for breakfast.

The person who had observed them leaving watched as they went into the studio and came out without the bags they had been carrying. *Well, perhaps they were just taking some painting materials to the studio and took a roundabout walk to get there. You'd think they would've dropped the materials off before going for a walk, though. What could those two be up to?* the silent observer wondered.

Chapter 13

Everyone was already gathered in the dining room by the time Leah and Sandy arrived for breakfast. They sat down at the table with Mattie, Becky, Mary Jane, and the Porters. The conversation soon drifted around to Linda's disappearance. Several among the group were speculating as to what could be the reason for her vanishing so suddenly.

"Have you heard anything from Linda since she left?" Susan Porter asked, looking at Mary Jane.

"No, but she probably wouldn't contact me anyway. We met for the first time Sunday at the reception. However, I did think I heard her phone ringing last night, but it must have been coming from somewhere else. I'm thinking she would have taken her phone with her."

"Oh, what do you think it was? Could you have dozed off and been dreaming?" Susan asked.

"No, actually, it was only a little after nine, and I was reading. I figured maybe the sound was coming from somewhere outside. I did have my window open and sound can play tricks on you."

"Yes, that's true, but did you check her room, just to make sure?" Susan asked.

"No, because I knew she wasn't in her room. I had knocked on her door earlier and peeked in to make sure she wasn't in there," Mary Jane replied.

Leah watched Susan as she questioned Mary Jane—she seemed to have an inordinate amount of interest in the ringing phone. Leah looked at Wayne and found him also staring at Mary Jane with an intensity that seemed a little strange. Why would he and Susan be so interested in whether Mary Jane had heard a phone ringing in Linda's room? After all, it wasn't like they knew her that well or were close to her.

Mattie was also watching the exchange between Susan and Mary Jane. She vaguely remembered Linda from the Monday morning painting class. She'd noticed that Linda had seemed a little preoccupied during the painting demonstration and then didn't return that afternoon. "Do you know if the police searched her room?" Mattie asked, directing her question to the table in general.

"Yes, I'm sure they did, and they talked to her friends and co-workers. She seems to have vanished into thin air. There is simply no trace of her anywhere. Her car was found at the Portland airport, but apparently she didn't take any flights from there," Mary Jane said.

"Well, obviously there are only two options for what happened to her," Mattie said in a no-nonsense voice, looking around the table as she spoke. She directed her gaze at the Porters and held it there as she continued. "Number one, Linda went somewhere on her own and didn't want anyone to know where she was going, so she left her car at the airport and took some other means of transportation to her destination. I hope the police checked with cab and limo services. Number two, someone took her against her will and left her car at the airport to divert suspicion, and she is either dead or being held captive."

"Oh my," Susan said, "what a gruesome thought."

"Young lady, I've been on this earth ninety-nine years, and I've learned a little about human nature in that time. Using common sense, those are the only two logical explanations for the poor girl's disappearance. I've also noticed that you and your husband have an unusual amount of interest in the girl's whereabouts. That tells me you either have a ghoulish curiosity or you're concerned that she knows something that you would prefer not to be known."

"How dare you insinuate such a horrid thing. We're only concerned about her safety," Susan said in a huffed, indignant voice.

"Ms. Wainscot, due to your advanced age, I will overlook the insults you've directed at me and my wife. But, you are totally out of line," Wayne Porter said in an equally indignant voice.

"Don't worry, young man. I'm not accusing you of anything," Mattie said, barely suppressing laughter. "But as Shakespeare so aptly said, *the lady doth protest too much, methinks.* However, I know that you have no knowledge of where Ms. Baker is, so let me soothe your ruffled feathers and apologize for my outspoken behavior. I sometimes forget myself—maybe I've read too much Agatha Christie and consider myself an amateur sleuth."

Susan and Wayne huffed a few times, mumbled a good day to everyone, and left to go back to their cottage.

After they'd gone, Leah leaned over to Mattie and squeezed her hand. "You're something else, Mattie. I hope I'll be half as wise as you someday."

"You will probably surpass me in intelligence by the time you reach my age. You're already well on your way. You are a very smart and talented young lady."

"Thank you, Mattie. I sure have my doubts at times." Leah paused and then continued. "I've just got to ask you, why did you tell the Porters you were sure they didn't know where Linda is?"

"They wouldn't be so curious about everything if they knew where she is. They would probably have played it cool and said very little," Mattie replied.

"You make everything sound so simple. And, by the way, I think you would make a great sleuth," Leah said.

About that time, Andy called for everyone's attention. He pronounced it to be a beautiful day and asked the group if they would like to go out on location and paint. The suggestion met with everyone's approval, so he said they would meet in the studio at 9:00 and decide where they would go.

Leah excused herself and went out the back door hoping to find Jason on the patio, but no one was there. She stuck her head in the kitchen door. Jason was talking to one of his assistants but excused himself when he saw Leah. He stepped outside and asked if anything was wrong. Leah told him no, there was nothing wrong, but she needed to talk to him. She just didn't feel comfortable talking out where everyone could see them.

"We're going out on location to paint and since we don't have a car, Sandy and I will need a ride. If you just happened to come along and offer us a lift that would give us an opportunity to talk."

"I'll be finished with breakfast by the time you leave, so I'll be glad to do that," Jason said.

"I would like to know if Linda has her phone with her. Nate sent her a text letting her know Sandy and I were on the way with her things." Leah said

"No, I left my phone with her in case she had an emergency, so she could call me here at the inn."

"At breakfast this morning, Mary Jane mentioned hearing a phone ringing in Linda's room last night. When the Porters questioned her, she passed it off as probably a phone ringing somewhere else. I have a feeling it was Linda's, though."

"You're right, Linda put her phone on the charger before she went to class the day she was kidnapped. She went directly from the studio to the Ledges to meet John. He had gone to her room the night before and left a note for her to meet him during her lunch break the next day."

"That explains who I saw coming out of our cottage Sunday night," Leah said, thinking back to how apprehensive she'd felt when she'd seen a man leaving Broadview cottage. Several of the students came out the back door about that time, and Leah wished Jason a good day and returned to join the group. She, Sandy, and Mary Jane walked together back to their cottage. Leah contemplated telling Mary Jane about Linda, but she discarded the thought as quickly as the thought entered her head. She remembered Nate's warning to not trust anyone other than Sandy and Becky. As soon as Mary Jane went into her room, Leah told Sandy about her conversation with Jason.

"I'm pretty sure Linda's phone is in her room, and I want to go back in there and look for it. I don't understand why we didn't see it when we were in there earlier."

"It might be on the floor by one of the electrical outlets. There's not many of them in our rooms," Sandy said.

"You're probably right. When Mary Jane comes out, why don't you walk down with her and make some excuse for me being late. That will give me time to go back into Linda's room and look for her phone."

Leah told Sandy about the plan to ride with Jason when they went out on location. "We've got to make it appear natural and unplanned even if we miss the opportunity. I don't want to arouse suspicion in any way or cause anyone to suspect Jason of any involvement." Leah went on to tell Sandy about an idea she had as to how Linda could change her appearance completely. "Jason will need to go to the nearest Walmart and buy several items, and Linda will have to be willing to cut and color her hair."

"Surely she'll be willing to do anything to avoid being seen and recognized," Sandy said.

After Sandy and Mary Jane left, Leah went around to Linda's room and knocked on the door. She stood there and listened for a moment, then opened the door and stepped inside, quickly shutting the door behind her. The blinds were closed and the drapes were pulled to on the sliding door that opened to the small deck shared by Mary Jane. Leah walked around the room. She didn't see anything in the bedroom or bathroom. *I'll bet whoever kidnapped her has already been here,* she thought. There was only one outlet by the dresser and one in the bathroom; both were empty. About six inches were between the bed and the wall. Leah didn't expect to find anything, but just to be sure, she slid the bed out a little farther. She looked in the open space and there, lying on the floor, plugged into an outlet, was a black phone. Leah pulled the plug out of the wall and shoved the phone and charger into her pocket, pushed the bed back to its original position, and opened the door. There was no one in sight. The cottage had a deserted feeling, and Leah hurried back to her room, where she grabbed her jacket and headed down the lane to the studio.

The group was standing outside in a circle around Andy, who was discussing different locations for their painting outing.

"There's a village about seven or eight miles from here with an old-fashioned grocery store. They have tons of lobster traps and a boat rental service. There's a small island there about a mile out in the bay. It's a painter's dream—you could do a still life of the lobster traps or the colorful floats. Then there's the village with picturesque streets and quaint houses. I'll do a demo painting first, and you can decide what you want to paint and be ready to start right after lunch," Andy explained

"Sounds great," said several of the people in the enthusiastic group. Leah noticed that Jason had walked down to the studio and was listening to Andy's speech. He caught her looking his way and nodded imperceptibly.

Everyone gathered their painting materials and started to their cars, which were already parked in the lot next to the studio. The local ladies all piled into the same car. Louise, Mattie, and another lady Leah couldn't remember got in the car with Mary Jane. They invited Andy to ride with them, and that was when Jason said he would be glad to take anyone who didn't have a ride. Becky, Leah, and Sandy got in Jason's Ford Explorer after putting their painting supplies in the back cargo area.

"Looks like everyone is situated, so we'll meet at the grocery store in North Pointe," Andy said, as he loaded his painting gear into the back of Mary Jane's Ford Edge.

Leah got out of the car and said she needed something else from the studio and went back inside. By the time she came out, all the other cars had left the inn property. She climbed into the front seat and pulled Linda's phone out of her pocket as told them where she'd found it. "We need to take this to Linda before we head for the village. I'm not very tech savvy, but I think it would be a good idea to keep it turned off. I'm pretty sure she could be tracked via her phone," Leah said, looking at the missed call that had come in at 9:08 the night before.

"I'm surprised someone hasn't already searched her room and found the phone," Jason said

"They probably have, but they would've been careful to go when everyone was away from Broadview. They probably had to do a quick search and overlooked it because it was behind the bed," Leah said.

"I don't know...it just doesn't seem right," Jason pondered. "They could have just called her number while in her room and found it that way."

"Maybe they don't have her number," Becky suggested.

"That could well be true. Apparently, John didn't have her mobile number. Otherwise, there would have been no need for him to slip into her room and leave a note," Leah said.

"Wonder how he knew which room was hers..." Sandy said.

"He probably just looked into each room until he found something he recognized as Linda's," Jason suggested.

They parked in front of Jason's house, and the trio all went inside. Linda met them in the front room with a relieved smile. "Thank God! I've been on pins and needles, jumping at every sound. I think it's rubbing off on Sasha. She's barking or growling every time we hear a noise."

"She's very protective, and she knows you're upset," Jason said with a reassuring smile.

Leah took Linda's phone out of her pocket and handed it to her. "I found this behind your bed right before we left. Mary Jane heard it ringing last night and was talking about it at breakfast. The Porters seemed to have an abnormal amount of interest in whether the ring was coming from your room or somewhere else."

"Can you tell who called you last night? Do you recognize the number?" asked Jason.

"It's probably John. I gave him my number when we had lunch, and he gave me his, but I didn't put it in my contact list," Linda said, looking at the display on her phone.

Jason jotted down the number and put it in his pocket. "I'll try calling it later, but you better turn your phone off now. I need to take my phone with me; I'll call and leave you a message if anything comes up that you need to know. Turn your phone on every thirty minutes, just long enough to check for calls. If you need me, turn it on just long enough to send me a text."

"Okay, but give me your number so I can add it to my contacts." Linda quickly programmed Jason's number and turned her phone off.

"Did you draw the profile picture of the person you saw with Sheila Rhodes the day she was murdered?" Jason asked, suddenly noticing a drawing on the table.

Linda went to the table and picked up the sheet of paper. "Yes, I drew a close-up of her face as well as I could remember, and also a full body sketch."

Jason took the drawing, "Wow! You're very talented. This is terrific." Leah looked over his shoulder.

"Her face looks so familiar. I'm sure I've seen that person before."

"I better get you gals to the painting site, or they'll start thinking I've kidnapped all of you," Jason said, heading toward the door.

"Before we leave, I wanted to ask Linda about changing her appearance. If you're willing to cut and color your hair, I think we can make you look completely different."

"I'll do anything to keep from being recognized," Linda said with a hopeful look.

"Okay, I'll have Jason or Nate pick up some stuff and get back to you later," Leah said.

By the time they arrived at North Pointe, the rest of the crew were already gathered on the dock at the grocery store. Leah wrote out a list of things needed to alter Linda's appearance and gave it to Jason. She, Sandy, and Becky retrieved their painting gear from the back of the SUV and joined the group on the dock.

Back at the inn, the person who had watched Leah as she went down the lane was now entering Broadview cottage. The intruder went through the sitting room and down the hall to Linda's room. Opening the door, stepping inside, and looking around, the inquisitive eyes of the curious onlooker could see nothing out of order or different from the day before. But, turning on the bathroom light, the trespasser noticed the absence of Linda's toiletries. *Not good*, thought the intruder. *Our Ms. Baker must be somewhere in the area. Someone here at the inn is helping her, and I've got a good idea just who that someone is.*

Nate had been very busy and lucky. The bail officer was at the police station, and Nate managed to get a hearing set for 10 o'clock that morning. Because Ron had no previous violations and was not a flight risk, bail was set at $10,000. Ron was able to post the $10,000 required. His personal belongings were returned to him, and he was free to go. He and Nate arrived back at Rocky Ledge Inn around 1:00 PM.

"I need a shower and change of clothes," Ron said, as they drove through the entrance to the property.

On the way back from Portland, Nate told Ron about Jason finding Linda and rescuing her. He told him about Linda seeing Sheila with a woman around 1:00 PM the day she was killed. The news upset Ron and made him more aware of the reality of the situation. "If I knew who killed Sheila, I believe I could strangle them with my bare hands," he said in a choked voice.

"I know how you feel, and we're going to find the person responsible. But, you can't be judge, jury, and executioner—it would land you right back in jail. I know you're hurting, Ron, but try to keep a cool head. If you need a shoulder to cry on, I'm here. And just remember, it's okay for men to cry. Keep your eyes and ears open, and watch your back. The killer may think you know more than you do."

Nate sent Jason a text asking where he was and, if possible, to meet him at the Ledges at 1:30. He dropped Ron off at his place and went around to Rosewood cottage, where he parked the Cherokee in his regular parking spot. Getting out of the vehicle, he noticed the Porters' car was not in its usual place. Once inside, he booted up the computer and sent Harry an update, telling him about getting Ron out on bail and asking if he'd come up with any more information on John Phelps.

Nate's phone buzzed with an incoming text from Jason saying he would meet him at the Ledges at 1:30.

Nate left his car in the parking lot and walked over to the restaurant. The sky was a robin's egg blue with a few puffy white clouds. The temperature was up from yesterday, and the sun felt warm on his skin. He thought about Leah and visualized her busy painting. She was so smart and talented. Just thinking about her brought a smile to his lips. His curiosity was insatiable. He wanted to know everything about her. What were her favorite foods; what did she love to do beside paint; what did she sleep in? Did she like to read? What her childhood was like? He grinned at the thought of Leah as a little girl.

As he approached the lane that led out of the property, he saw Ron coming down the path. He stopped and waited for him.

"I knew you were going to the Ledges and thought maybe I'd walk over with you and get a bite to eat. Maybe we'll see Phelps and have a talk with him," Ron said as he approached Nate.

Jason was waiting in front of the restaurant, and the three men went inside. The hostess seated them by a window, and the waitress took their drink order. Nate looked around the room but didn't see John Phelps or any other familiar face.

Jason reached in his pocket and pulled out the sheet of paper with the drawing Linda had done. He unfolded it and put it on the table.

Ron grabbed the paper and studied the picture. "Oh my God," he said, "that's the cleaning woman I saw coming out of Rosewood cottage the day I was watching the Porters...the day Sheila was killed."

Chapter 14

"Are you sure that's the same person?" Nate asked

"I'm positive! If this drawing is an accurate depiction of the person Linda saw, then she and the woman I saw are one and the same," Ron replied.

John Phelps entered the restaurant just as Nate looked up from the drawing. When the hostess approached, he pointed to the table where the three men were sitting and headed in their direction. Nate folded the paper with the drawing and put it in his pocket. "I need to borrow this for a while," he told Jason.

"Good afternoon gentlemen. Do you mind if I join you?" Phelps asked, pulling out a chair and sitting down without waiting for a reply.

"Please, be our guest," Nate said, eyeing the man closely and wondering what he was up to now. The waitress came back to their table and took the lunch order from the three men. John ordered a Guinness black lager.

"I thought you were behind bars for the murder of your wife," Phelps said, looking at Ron with a belligerent sneer.

Ron's face turned red, and his eyes snapped with anger. He opened his mouth to reply, but Nate interrupted him. "News sure travels fast. How did you know Ron had been arrested?"

"I heard it through the grapevine. How'd you manage to get out so fast? I thought Maine had tough laws when it concerns wife killers? Did your slick attorney pull some strings?" He seemed to be deliberately trying to provoke Nate with his derogatory remarks. He was looking directly at Nate, his eyes cold and piercing with a challenging expression, as if he wanted some kind of confrontation.

Nate studied the other man's patrician, pretty-boy good looks that contradicted his fiendish, ice blue eyes and the cruel twist of his mouth. *This is a dangerous man*, he thought, *I would never turn my back on him or underestimate his ability.* Phelps never looked away or dropped his gaze as Nate studied him.

"It's really none of your business," Nate finally said, watching the other man's cold, arctic eyes, which never changed or shifted. "By the way," Nate said, removing the drawing from his pocket. "Do you recognize this woman?" He spread the paper on the table keeping his hand on it, continuing to watch Phelps's eyes as he looked at the picture. A flicker of recognition passed over his face so quickly, Nate wasn't sure he had actually seen anything.

"No, I've never seen that woman before. Why do you ask? Is she another missing person?"

Nate ignored his question and asked, "Where were you this past Monday afternoon between 1:00 and 4:00 PM?"

"Like you told me, it's really none of your business," he said with a sardonic smile. "Well, I've got places to go and things to do. You guys have a wonderful afternoon and try to stay out of jail. By the way, tell your girlfriend I said hello, and I hope she's staying healthy and out of trouble," he said, looking at Nate with a veiled threat in his eyes and a malevolent grin. He drained the last of his Guinness, set the empty glass on the table along with a ten-dollar bill, and walked out of the restaurant.

It was all Nate could do to remain outwardly calm. He wanted to go after the arrogant bastard and rip his face off, but he knew that was just what Phelps was hoping he'd do, lose his temper and do something stupid.

"I wouldn't be surprised if Sheila had discovered something about him that put her life in danger. Wish I could find her computer. I'll bet it holds a lot of answers to our questions. I wonder if there's any possibility she could have hidden it somewhere before she was killed. The police searched the cottage thoroughly, but maybe Sheila found a place no one would think of looking." Ron said, as if thinking out loud.

"Good luck. I hope you find it. I'm sure it would answer a lot of our questions. What she may have discovered about someone that got her killed *could* well be on her computer. Finding it may be just what we need," Nate said. "I think Phelps recognized the woman in the drawing. I'm going up to the inn and talk to Liz Walker and Susan Porter. They may be able to identify this woman. Especially Liz. She should recognize anyone who works at the inn."

"I've got two sacks full of stuff for Linda. Leah gave me a list of things this morning that should change her appearance. Guess I need to take it to her and let her get started on the transformation. I think Leah is planning to cut her hair, and she said something about deciding if it would be better to make her look like a boy or a completely different type of woman," Jason laughed.

"That's a good idea. Maybe I'll come around tonight and see if I would recognize her," Nate said. Thinking about Leah cutting Linda's hair and helping her change her appearance relieved his tension and brought a grin to his face.

The three men paid their check and left the restaurant. Jason went to his house and Ron to his cottage. Nate went to the main house looking for Liz Walker. He found Joan Hataway in the office and asked if Liz was there.

"No, she had to go to Portland to take care of some business. She left around nine this morning," Joan said with a warm smile.

"Any idea when she'll be back?"

"No, but she often makes a day of it when she goes to the city. Is there anything I can help you with?"

Nate took out the drawing and showed it to her. "Do you recognize this woman? She was seen coming out of one of the cottages dressed like a maid."

Joan took the drawing and studied it. "She looks familiar, but I don't think she's anyone I've ever seen around here. Liz takes care of all the hired help, but I've never seen that woman. Do you think she had anything to do with the terrible thing that happened to Sheila Rhodes?"

"No, but she may have seen something that would be helpful. Right now, I'd just like to find out who she is and have a talk with her."

Nate walked around the path to Rosewood cottage and noticed the Porters' car was back in its regular parking space. He went into his room first and checked his emails. There was one from Harry with more information about Judy Mansfield, one of the locals that commuted back and forth to the workshop. She had attended at least one workshop at the inn every year for the past seven years. She had been involved with Calvin Ross, Barzetti's friend, before husband number four. Nate sent a reply to Harry to keep digging on all the people at the inn. He also told him to see what else he could find on Calvin Ross. He turned off the computer and went down the hall to the Porters' apartment and knocked. Susan opened the door, looking surprised to see him.

"Oh, hi Hal. I thought you would still be in Portland. Come on in. Would you like something to drink?" she asked as he entered the room.

"No, thank you. This isn't a social call. I wanted to ask you a few questions," Nate replied.

"What did you have on your mind?" Susan asked as Wayne came into the room and spoke to Nate. He also looked surprised to see him. They both appeared to be uncomfortable, and Nate wondered if they were expecting someone.

Nate took the drawing from his pocket and unfolded it. "Do you recognize this woman?" he asked.

Susan's face became pale as a ghost, and her hand trembled as she took the sheet of paper and studied the face.

"No, uh, no, I've never seen her before," she stammered.

"Are you sure? She was seen coming out of this building dressed like a cleaning lady."

"No, I don't pay much attention to the hired help around here." She handed the drawing to Wayne, "Do you recognize this person, honey?"

Wayne took the paper and studied it. He was obviously nervous—he kept avoiding eye contact with Nate. He looked at Susan and handed the drawing back to her. "No, I don't remember seeing anyone that looks like that."

"That's strange," Nate said, looking directly into Susan's eyes. I could have sworn this is a picture of you." He had just realized while looking at Susan and the picture together that it did look like her.

"That's ridiculous," Susan said with a nervous laugh. That woman is 30 pounds heavier than me and she has gray hair, nothing like mine."

"How do you know she has gray hair, this is a black and white drawing. Her hair could be any color," Nate said.

"Well, I just assumed it's gray; that's the way it looks in the picture." Susan was becoming even more agitated.

"Now look here, what do you mean coming in here and making these absurd accusations to my wife? Who the hell do you think you are anyway? I think you better leave, now!" Wayne said, his voice rising.

Nate took out his credentials and flipped it open. "My name is Nate Parker, and I'm an FBI agent with a special unit that investigates international art crimes. I understand you've just returned from a trip to Italy."

"That's right, and also France. What of it?" Wayne said in an indignant tone.

"Susan, did you kill Sheila Rhodes?" Nate asked unexpectedly.

"How dare you! Are you crazy? Why would she kill Sheila Rhodes?" Wayne's face was red, and his eyes bulged with anger. "I think you better leave now."

"Okay, you don't have to answer my questions now, but you better get an attorney. I could charge you with suspicion of the murder of Sheila Rhodes. I have a witness who saw you with her the afternoon she was killed. You had on a wig and some padding to make you appear heavier, but you'd be asked to wear a wig and let my witness look at you in a lineup."

"I didn't kill her; I just went to talk to her. I couldn't hurt anyone—she was fine when I left her in front of her cottage."

"Why did you wear that get-up as a cleaning lady, and what did you talk to her about?" Nate asked.

"Don't say anything else, Susan. I'll call our attorney." Wayne said, getting more disturbed.

Susan continued talking despite her husband's warning. "I wore the disguise because I knew her husband was in the parking lot watching the building, and I didn't want him to see me leave."

"That doesn't explain why you wanted to talk to her and why you didn't want anyone to know it was you talking to her."

"She called me and said she had something she wanted to discuss with me and could I met her at the Ledges. She had started back to her cottage when I met her, and she seemed in a hurry to get there. She said she would get back to me later."

"You were gone at least thirty minutes. It wouldn't take fifteen minutes to do what you just described. Are you sure that's all you did?"

"You've said enough, Susan. Don't say another word," Wayne warned her.

Nate looked at the couple standing in front of him, and suddenly he knew what Sheila Rhodes wanted to talk to Susan about. He remembered something and it all came together. But he didn't think Susan was the killer. She wasn't gone long enough, and she would have been more disheveled and probably would've had blood on her clothes. Wayne didn't have the opportunity because Ron was watching the building all day. If neither one of the Porters killed Sheila, then who did?

****

It had been a good day for Leah. Andy did a demo painting that morning of the dock with boats and some colorful floats. She was amazed at how quickly he could capture the mood and essence of a place or person. Lunch was delivered from the inn about the time he finished the demo. Leah, Sandy, Mattie, and Becky went across the street from the grocery store to a small park. There were a few picnic tables, several shade trees, and a spectacular view of the bay. They chose one of the tables, sat down and opened up their lunch boxes. "Yum, this smells delicious. All this fresh air and sunshine makes me ravenous," Sandy said as she pulled out a chicken salad sandwich and a bag of chips.

"You're always ravenous," Leah said with a laugh.

"Yeah, I'm afraid you're right. When I get back home, I'll be counting calories for two months to make up for this one week," Sandy said with a sigh.

"I know you gave Jason a list of stuff to buy today in order to change Linda's appearance. What do you have in mind to make this transformation?" Becky asked Leah.

"The first thing is to change her hair color and style. She has long blond hair, so if we dye it dark brown and cut it short that will make a big difference. She has a fair complexion and blue eyes. Wish she had some brown contact lenses. I thought if she tans her face with sunless tanning lotion, she'd look more like a natural brunette."

"That's very clever, and she could either tone down her bosom with loose fitting clothes, maybe wear glasses and look like a boy or wear a lot of padding and look like a buxom matron," Becky suggested.

"You two are full of ideas, and all of them sound great," Sandy said, finishing the last of her lunch. She put the paper wrappings and empty drink cup in the cardboard box her lunch came in. Leah, Mattie, and Becky did the same, and Sandy tossed them all in a nearby dumpster. Leah filled Mattie in on everything that was going on. She told Mattie about Jason finding Linda and how they narrowly escaped when the two thugs showed up. She also told her about Nate. Becky took up the narrative and told Mattie that Nate was her brother and his real reason for being there.

"Mattie, we don't want to put you in danger by telling you everything that's been going on. But, I've seen how observant and clever you are. I think you could be a real asset in helping to find out who killed Sheila Rhodes *and* who the art thief is. It could be the same person and it could be several different people," Becky said, taking Mattie's hand. "Be very careful. I would never forgive myself if something happened to you because of what we've told you."

"My dear, I am 99 years old. I've survived many dangers, heartaches, and catastrophes. I appreciate you trusting me with this knowledge. I assure you, I can keep my mouth shut and my eyes open. Just think of me as a modern-day Ms. Marple. She understood human nature and believe me, young lady, if anyone knows human nature better than I, you will have to look long and hard to find them. Now that we have that settled, I have only one more thing to say."

"What is it you want to say?" Leah, Becky, and Sandy asked almost in unison.

"Let's paint!" Mattie said with a grin.

They all laughed and started setting up their easels and putting out their painting materials.

Leah opened her French easel painting box and set it up close to one of the tables. She'd brought a gallon jug of water, which she used to wet her pallet and clean her brushes. She put a 16-by-20 canvas on the easel and began sketching the grocery store with the bay in the background. Several people were sitting on a bench in front of the store which she hoped to capture. If only she could work as fast and sure as Andy, it would be no problem. Soon, she was lost in her painting, and the afternoon sped quickly by.

The front of the store had been in the shade when Leah started painting, and it was now in full sun. *Oh well,* she thought, *I just need to make a few minor changes and it will be even better. I can show more detail on the front of the store and emphasize the people with cast shadows.* Her thoughts continued to wander as she considered that life was kind of like that. Sometimes you need to make adjustments in the direction you're headed in order to fit into the changing circumstances or maybe detour around them. And then what, you're right back in the shade again or the same old rut. *But, I like my rut. It's comfortable,* she told herself. Then, unbidden, Nate's face loomed before her. Smiling, his eyes twinkling with humor and mischief, he seemed to be chiding her for her fears and doubts. She could almost hear his voice—the way he said her name, a pleasant sensation spread over her entire being and the thought of seeing him again filled her with excitement.

I'm falling in love, I don't know how it happened. I've only known him a few days. But, I was lost the first time I laid eyes on him. She remembered how disappointed she'd been when she thought he was married and how she had fought her feelings. *If he's seeing his dead wife in me and he wakes up to that fact and moves on, I'll never let him know how deep my feelings go,* she told herself. She shook herself out of her reverie and concentrated on finishing her painting.

Andy came by and looked at what she'd done. "Very good! The light effect is excellent, really makes you focus on the store and the people. You didn't put too much detail in the people, adding interest but not distracting from the main subject. *Very* good. I think you've captured the mood and essence of the place very well. My only suggestion would be to put more color into the shadows."

Leah thanked him and started cleaning her brushes and putting her supplies into her paint box. She noticed Becky and Sandy also putting their materials away, and Mattie was adding the finishing touches to her painting. She walked over to where they had set up at nearby tables. Becky was moaning that she didn't capture the color she was striving for with the bay, and her sun sparkles didn't sparkle.

"You are your own worst critic," Leah told her. "Your painting is beautiful! You have actually captured the emotional essence of the area. I can almost smell the salt air when I look at it."

Sandy had painted a scene looking up the street with quaint houses on each side, trees with a hint of fall colors, and shadows from the trees falling across the street. Leah complemented her on what a good job she'd done.

Mattie had painted one of the other students standing in front of an easel, also painting a view of the bay. Mattie had captured the student with her back turned, facing her canvas, paintbrush in hand, the bay and the island in the distance. The colors were clean and bright, the shadows and lights drawing your eye into the painting.

"Mattie, that is amazing," Leah said, walking over to where Mattie was finishing up. "You've got a beautiful, loose style that sparkles with light and color. I think we've all had a very productive afternoon. I guess I'd better call Jason and see if he can come and get us," Leah said, pulling out her phone.

She sent Jason a text, and in less than a minute a reply came back saying he was on the way.

Leah asked Mattie if she'd like to ride back with them, but she said she still needed to clean up her materials and get everything packed away, so she'd ride back with Mary Jane. When they reached the inn, Jason stopped at the studio so the ladies could unload their painting gear. Leah and Sandy walked up the lane to Broadview, and Becky headed to Rosewood cottage. They told Jason they would see him around five, after they rested and freshened up.

****

Nate left the Porters' apartment. He didn't believe either of them guilty of murder. However, he was sure they were guilty of stealing the Jan Van Eyck painting from the Uffizi Gallery in Florence, Italy. He was going to watch the surveillance video again. He went down the hall to his and Becky's apartment and booted up the computer. He found the disk he needed and slid it into the slot. He watched as the images flashed across the monitor and then froze it at a certain point. There, the person in the gift shop buying a print had turned, and it was Susan Porter's profile. The same nose and chin, and she raised her hand exactly as Susan had just done and flicked her hair back. He didn't have enough evidence to charge them, but hopefully he had given them enough rope to hang themselves. They had no idea he was on to them for the art heist. They thought he suspected them of murder. He was sure they were here to make contact with someone, probably a buyer, and he needed to know who that person was. So many thoughts and possibilities ran through his mind, but it was all speculation. Who was behind Linda's kidnapping, and what did they think she knew? He needed to talk to her and see if she had remembered anything more about whom she had talked to at the reception and what they had talked about. He got a beer out of the small refrigerator and went out to the screened porch. He heard someone enter the building, and a minute later, the door to the apartment opened and Becky called, "Hello? Anyone here?"

"I'm on the porch. Come on out," Nate answered.

Becky stuck her head out the door and, seeing Nate's beer, poured herself a glass of wine. She stretched out on the chaise lounge and sighed. "This sure feels good—it's been a long day slaving over a hot canvas."

Nate laughed and then grew serious as he told her about his discovery. "The Porters are guilty as sin. They've probably been doing this for years. I want you to keep your eyes and ears open. I know how perceptive you are, and you may see or hear something that may seem trivial to most people but could be very important."

"That comes natural for me; I do it every day anyway. You learn a lot about people listening to the things they don't say." She went on to tell him about them bringing Mattie into the loop by giving her all the information about Linda and the art crime he came here to investigate.

"Sounds good to me. I think she's a wise old bird, and she might even be more perceptive than you."

"Gee, thanks. By the way, Leah's going to Jason's around five. That'll give her a couple of hours before dinner to work on Linda. What say we go and see how the makeover goes?" Becky asked.

"Sounds like a good idea. I'd like to take a quick shower first."

"Okay, save me some hot water. I need one too." Becky said as he got up and went inside.

Leah walked down the lane to Jason's house a little before five. Sandy stayed behind and went to happy hour at the main house. She could keep an eye on everyone and make excuses for Leah. When Leah arrived at Jason's, she found Linda had already dyed her hair and applied the sunless tanning lotion. Leah was amazed at the difference the changes had made.

"Wow," she said, "who are you and where is Linda?"

Linda laughed and handed Leah a pair of scissors. "Well, let's see if we can make even more changes."

"I wish you had some brown contact lenses," Leah said.

"Actually, I do wear contacts, and I have several different colors, just not with me. I thought I'd wear my glasses and no eye makeup; my eyes are totally unnoticeable then. They're almost the same color as John's, our only resemblance to each other."

"Except his are cold and inscrutable, while yours are warm and open. It's hard to believe he's your brother," Leah said in a baffled tone.

"He's our father made over. He was the devil incarnate, and John inherited all his bad traits, plus a few of his own."

"Have you thought any more about who you talked to at the reception and what you talked about?"

"Yes, I remember talking to the Porters about watching the movie, 'The Art of Forgery," a documentary about Wolfgang Beltracchi, the world's most famous art forger. They remembered the film, and I also said something about famous art heists. That led to a discussion about a few famous artist who had been murdered. Something was said about Liz Walker's dad being a very well-known artist, and we looked at some of his prints hanging on the walls. There were several other people in the group—I can't remember who right now, and someone said something about what a shame that Liz's dad had such a tragic accident two years ago. I think I made some off-the-wall comment about how easy it would be to make murder appear to be an accident."

"Can you think of anything else?" asked Leah.

"Oh, I remember someone in the group saying our instructor, Barzetti, was as good as Beltracchi. He could duplicate any of the old masters or impressionists, then they laughed and said he probably thought he was better than any of them and would think it beneath him to do forgeries."

Leah had been snipping away at Linda's hair the whole time they had been talking. Her long tresses were now lying on the floor. The person who was once a blond with long straight hair was now a brunette with very short curly hair.

"You've got naturally curly hair!"

"Yeah, I work real hard to straighten it every time I shampoo, and when it's long, the weight helps straighten it out."

Someone knocked on the front door. Jason went to see who was there—he came back to the kitchen with Nate and Becky.

"Oh my! You look like a completely different person," Becky said with an amazed expression.

"You've done a great job, Leah!" Nate said smiling, his eyes looking at her the way a starving man would view a banquet of delicious food.

"Thank you," Leah said, a flush spreading over her face. "Linda had already done a lot of the work, so she deserves most of the credit. By the way, she's been telling me about the conversations she had at the reception Sunday afternoon."

"I want to hear everything she can remember, but first I have a question for you," he said, taking Leah's hand in his.

"What is it?" she asked.

"May I walk you back to the main house and sit with you at dinner?"

Leah's heart did flip flops as she looked at the sincere expression on his face and the desire in his eyes. "I would like that very much," she replied with a smile.

"She's right," Leah said. "I can't believe the difference."

"Why don't we put it to the supreme test and take her to dinner at the inn," suggested Nate.

"Uh, I don't know," stammered Linda. I'm afraid I would give myself away."

Chapter 15

Jason had bought two pair of men's pants, a pair of jeans, and a pair of khakis. Linda was tall and slim, so he guessed at the size and bought 30 inch waist and 32 inch length. They were large in the waist, but wearing them low on her hips, which seemed to be the style now, the length was perfect. He'd also bought some shirts, a jacket, and a ball cap, plus a pair of western boots that had a heel almost two inches high making her appear even taller. He'd thrown in a package of tee shirts, size small. Linda had on one of the tee shirts, which fit very tight and, minus a bra, minimized her bosom. She'd chosen the jeans, a white cotton shirt, and a windbreaker jacket. When she walked out of the bedroom, everyone was aghast.

"I can't believe it," Becky said. "You look completely different. I would never recognize you."

"You grew up in the south. Can you revive your southern accent?" asked Jason.

"Well now, y'all jess give little ole me a few minutes, and I think maybe it might come back," Linda drawled.

"That's great! The only thing that worries me, you still have a feminine persona," Jason said.

"So, she'll just appear to be an effeminate man or a masculine woman," laughed Nate.

"I'll try walking different, more like a boy. I'm pretty sure I can do that," Linda said.

"Okay," Jason said. "I'll introduce you as my nephew, Billy Joe, from Alabama, who prefers to be called B.J. Is that okay with you, Linda?

"Why, yes, it is, Uncle Jay. I think B.J. fits my new look very well."

"It's almost 6:30. We probably need to get back to the main house and put B.J.'s name in the pot for dinner," Becky suggested.

"We'll come up with a good background story for you on the way up to the inn," Jason said. "Just keep a low profile until you have everything straight."

Everyone began making preparations to leave. Leah was cleaning up the hair from the floor and putting all the paraphernalia away. Nate pitched in and helped her quickly finish tidying up the kitchen. He took her hand and said, "Remember, you're walking with me. Let the others go ahead; we'll take the path that skirts the bay."

As Leah and Nate walked along the path that ran parallel with the shoreline, a three-quarters moon lit their way. The fragrance of a nearby summer sweet shrub, mingling with the briny smell of the ocean, was an ambrosia of sweet fragrances filling the air. The sound of the buoys sighing as each wave washed upon the rocky beach below gave Leah a surreal feeling. The night took on a magical fairytale appearance in the silvery glow of the moonlight.

"There's a falling star!" Nate said pointing to the sky. "Make a wish, and it'll come true."

"I wish I could catch it and put it in my pocket and never let it fade away," Leah said, quoting the line from an old Perry Como song.

"And save it for a rainy day," Nate said, finishing the lyric.

"Wouldn't it be great if we could do that? Always have a pocket full of star light that we could pull out on a rainy night."

"Do you remember the next line to that old song?" Nate asked.

"Let me think. No, that's all I can remember. What is the next line?"

"For love may come and tap you on the shoulder, some starless night, and just in case you feel you want to hold her…"

"You'll have a pocket full of starlight," Leah finished the lyric for him.

"Leah, I want to hold you; God, I want to hold you. I don't want to scare you away, but I think love has come and tapped me on the shoulder."

Leah was speechless. She didn't know what to say. She wanted to believe he was falling in love with her. She knew how she felt about him, and she wanted him to feel the same way more than anything else, but she was still so afraid he was transferring his feelings for his dead wife to her. Leah's heart was pounding so hard, she felt sure Nate could hear it. Never had she wanted so badly to be in someone's arms as she now did.

Nate bent his head and touched her lips softly with his and whispered in her ear, "I can't kiss you the way I want to; we'd never make it to the inn."

Leah's fears kept her from letting go and responding to Nate's words the way her heart longed to. Instead, she pushed him away and, trying to sound indifferent said, "We live in two different worlds—you're just caught up in the magic of the night and this beautiful place."

"No, I'm not caught up in some magical moment. I think about you day and night. I know how I feel, and I was hoping you felt the same. We don't have time to talk about it now, but I'm not letting you go out of my life."

When they arrived at the dining room, everyone was already there. Jason had told the dinner chef to make an extra plate for Linda and Becky. Sandy had introduced Linda as Jason's nephew,

B.J. No one seemed to notice anything unusual about her. Conversation continued pretty much as usual. Andy was in the middle of a story about some of his earlier exploits when two more people entered the room. Leah couldn't believe her eyes. Judy Mansfield and John Phelps were sitting down at the next table with the Porters and Mary Jane. Judy introduced John and spoke loudly enough for everyone to hear. She explained that she had spoken with Liz earlier that day and made arrangements to bring a guest. She went on talking about how she had known John since before she married her last husband. Seems John and Calvin Ross were friends, and she met him when she was dating Calvin. "I ran into John over at the resort as I was coming out of the gift shop this afternoon," she explained. "We got to talking about old times, and I suggested he join us tonight. I figure he gets lonely over there at the resort all by himself. Liz said it would be no problem and he would be welcome."

Leah stiffened, and a look of apprehension spread over her face. Linda kept her head down and moved nervously in her seat.

Nate looked at Linda with a broad smile on his face. "What do you think of Maine so far B.J.?" he asked, as if he were deliberately trying to call attention to her.

"Well, I haven't had a chance to see much of it yet," she drawled nervously, trying to lower her voice to a more masculine pitch. John looked at her, but only with an uninterested passing glance as Mary Jane explained to him and Judy that this was B.J., Jason's nephew from Alabama.

It was obvious to everyone at Linda's table that John Phelps didn't recognize her. Nate had intentionally called attention to her in order to find out if he would recognize her. He figured Phelps had a reason for coming to dinner at the inn other than to eat and socialize, and he wanted to know what it was. He had to get the fear of discovery for Linda out of the way. Nate knew he could read Phelps's expression well enough to know if he recognized her or not.

Nate was sitting between Leah and Becky, and apparently Phelps wasn't sure if he was with Leah or just happened to be sitting beside her.

Phelps looked directly at Leah and said, "Good evening, Ms. Dawson. How are you doing? Are you learning a lot from your revered instructor? Judy's been telling me what a wonderful artist Mr. Barzetti is. I would love to see some of your endeavors since you've been here. I'm a great critic. I could tell you if your work has improved over the work you showed me when we were in Tennessee."

Phelps's congenial tone of conversation belied the belligerent look in his eyes and the words which were meant to antagonize Leah and Nate. His malevolent glare moved from Leah to Nate. Moving his eyes from Nate to Leah, he said, "I would be honored to walk you to your cottage after dinner."

Leah was so angry she could hardly maintain her composure. She didn't want to call attention to their table, so she clenched her teeth and replied in a controlled, low voice, "Thank you very much for your kind offer to critique my work and walk me to my cottage, but I'm sorry I can't accept it. In fact, I will be unavailable for any future offers you may have."

"Are you *really* sorry?" Phelps asked, looking at Leah with an expression that caused a chill to run up her spine.

"You heard the lady, so buzz off. It would probably be a good idea for you to go back to Tennessee," Nate said in a quiet, measured tone.

"Are you threatening me?" Phelps asked with a sneer.

"No, just making an observation," Nate replied in a nonchalant tone of voice.

Nate and John continued to maintain hostile eye contact, and Judy looked from one to the other. She laughed, trying to break the tension and started talking about an encounter at Calvin's gallery back when they were an item. "You remember the time Calvin found what he believed to be a lost Correggio at an estate sale and it turned out to be a fake? Boy was he ever bent out of shape."

"Yeah, but he was very lucky at finding a lot of genuine missing master pieces," Phelps laughed, as if the previous conversation had never taken place.

Andy had overheard their discourse and joined in with some reminiscing of his own. "I remember him doing rather well finding the real thing a number of times." Everyone seemed to relax and enjoy the rest of the meal. During dessert, Andy rapped his spoon on a glass to get everyone's attention. "I'm sure you're all aware that tomorrow is the last full day of the workshop. Friday, I'll do a critique in the morning, and I think the inn is treating us to a lobster bake that afternoon. There's rain in the forecast for tomorrow, so we'll plan on meeting in the studio. If it clears up by the time I do my demo, anyone who wants to paint outside will find lots of subject matter right here on the grounds of the inn."

Judy left, saying she had to get home and see about her husband. John Phelps lingered, talking to Andy.

Sandy and Mary Jane walked back to Broadview together, and Mattie walked with them as far as Gray Dove, where she was staying. Jason came out of the kitchen where he had been assisting the dinner chef. He and Linda bid everyone good night and headed back to his house.

Nate's phone beeped an incoming message just as he, Leah, and Becky were leaving the main house. He took his phone out of his pocket and looked at the screen. The message was from Ron, asking Nate to come by his cottage.

"I'm not letting you out of my sight with that snake Phelps on the premises," he said, looking at Leah. "You and Becky come with me and let's find out what Ron has on his mind." Ron met them at the door of his cottage. He gave Leah and Becky a questioning look. "It's okay. You can talk freely in front of them," Nate assured him.

Ron looked up and down the lane, then urged them to come inside. "I have some good news and bad news," he said. "The good news is I found Sheila's laptop—the bad news is the data has all been removed."

"I'm sorry to hear that. How in the world did you find it, though?" asked Nate.

"Well, I looked everyplace I could think of where Sheila may have hidden it. Places the police wouldn't look. I looked for false bottoms in drawers and hidden spaces in the walls but found nothing. I sat down in the recliner where I usually sit and leaned back and closed my eyes and tried to think. When I opened my eyes,

I looked up at the ceiling and noticed a little heart drawn on one of the ceiling tiles. Sheila and I used to write notes to each other in school, and she would always draw a heart on her notes. I felt sure she had put it there as a message to me. I climbed up on the table and removed the tile, and there was the computer. I had to put it on a charger and wait for it to charge enough for me to turn it on. Unfortunately, as I told you, it had been wiped clean."

"We should be able to retrieve the data," Nate said. "I'm sure a real tech savvy person would have no problem doing that. I can send it to headquarters and…"

"Nate," interrupted Ron, "I'm sure Sheila cleared the data to prevent it falling into the wrong hands, but knowing her I know she would have backed it up. I'd bet my last penny there's a flash drive hidden somewhere in this cottage. She put that heart on the ceiling tile so I would find the computer, and she knew I would understand she had saved all the information and would continue looking. She probably left another clue somewhere, I just have to find it."

"You knew her better than anyone, so you could be right," Nate said.

"I'll find it if I have to turn this place upside down."

"I think she found something about the Porters that made her suspect them of being the art thieves," Nate said. "The cleaning lady you saw coming out of Rosewood cottage was Susan Porter. Susan told me Sheila called and asked her to meet her at the Ledges, but she said Sheila was on the way back to her cottage when she met up with her. I accused Susan of murdering Sheila, but I don't think she did. In fact, I would stake my career that she didn't do it, but she's lying about how long she talked to Sheila."

"I think when I find that flash drive, it'll tell us exactly what Sheila discovered that got her killed," Ron said with a determined expression.

Nate, Leah, and Becky bid Ron good night and good luck, and Nate asked Leah to come with him to walk Becky to Rosewood. He didn't want either one of them to be out alone. When they got to the cottage, he told Becky to lock the door and don't open it to anyone until he returned. He and Leah retraced their steps back to the lane leading to Broadview cottage. They didn't see anyone along the way. When they reached Leah's cottage, Nate took her hand and led her over to the Adirondack chairs facing the bay. He sat down in one and pulled her down onto his lap.

"You're a big guy, but I'm not exactly petite," laughed Leah. "I think we would be more comfortable inside, plus it's getting pretty chilly out here."

"I can keep you warm," Nate said, wrapping his arms around her and nuzzling her neck.

"No question about that. You could make me spontaneously combust," she said, feeling warmth and a tingling sensation emanating from the pit of her stomach. Leah stood up and, taking Nate's hand, tried to pull him to his feet. "Come on 'Double O Seven,' we need to call it a day. You've got bad guys to catch, and I've got a workshop to finish." He laughed at her efforts. She put her hands on her hips and, with a disgruntled sigh, said, "I might as well try to move that tree, so just sit there. I'm going inside and go to bed."

Nate rose to his feet and, taking her hand, pulled her into his arms. He bent his head and nibbled at her ear, "I want to go to bed with you." Leah leaned her head back until she was looking up into his eyes. She could see his face in the moonlight, but his eyes were in shadow. She knew their amber depths would be filled with green sparks of passion. If only she could be absolutely sure that passion was for her and not his dead wife. She put her hand on his cheek, tracing his face and outlining his lips. He took her hand in his and still holding it, slid his finger over her mouth. "I want you so badly. I want to melt into you and become one, but I don't want to just have sex with you; I want to make love with you. Leah, I think I'm falling in love with you. This is all new to me. I'm experiencing emotions I haven't felt in a very long time. I'm so comfortable with you. I feel I can talk about anything, and I trust you completely. And yet, you thrill and excite me to the point of distraction."

"Nate, I feel like I've known you all my life, and yet I'm also experiencing emotions that are new to me. I feel so safe and secure when I'm in your arms. When I see your face and your smile, my heart stands still and then pounds so hard, it seems it will explode. But, like I told you earlier, we live in two different worlds."

"I'm not going to let you get away; if I have to move to Tennessee, I can't see me without you ever again." He placed his hand under her chin, raised her face, and looked into her eyes. The moonlight lit her face. "You are so beautiful," he said in a husky voice as his mouth claimed hers.

Pulling away, he said, "This is going to be the hardest thing I've ever done, but I'm going to see you safely to your room, and then I'm going to my cottage. I want our first time together to be special and beautiful, not a stolen moment with people in the next rooms."

Nate walked Leah to the door of her room. After she turned the light on and he checked the bathroom to make sure no one was there, he told her to lock her door and keep her phone close. He was only a phone call away if she needed him.

Nate left Broadview cottage and walked down the lane that went by the main house and around to Rosewood. A few clouds were beginning to gather in the eastern sky, and Nate saw a flash of lightning out over the bay. A few moments later, he heard the low rumble of thunder. When he reached the place where the path turned in the direction of Rosewood, someone stepped from behind a tree growing beside the lane. A gusty wind blew in from the bay, and capricious clouds scuttled across the moon, casting shadows that raced along the path. When the moon peeked out again, Nate could see the man standing in front of him. John Phelps stepped in the middle of the path, blocking his way.

Nate reached under his arm and touched the Glock holstered there. "Get out of my way, Phelps," he hissed at the man standing in front of him.

Phelps swayed on his feet, and his voice was slurred when he spoke. "That's what I'm here to tell you. Get out of *my* way. You're stepping on my toes and becoming a pain in my ass."

"You're drunk. Go home and sleep it off," Nate said, trying to push by him.

John Phelps was a little over six feet tall, but Nate had almost four inches and twenty pounds on him. Nate was aware of Phelps's expertise in martial arts, but it didn't concern him. He knew he could take John Phelps down any time, even when he wasn't drunk.

Nate started around him when Phelps's right hand came up and Nate caught the glint of moonlight on metal. Instead of jumping back as Phelps expected him to do, Nate moved in closer, making it difficult for Phelps to strike at him. Nate grabbed Phelps's wrist and twisted it and kneed him in the groin at the same time. A switchblade knife fell from his hand as he doubled over and dropped to the ground. Nate picked up the knife and tossed it into the bushes on the far side of the lane. He went on to his apartment, leaving Phelps lying on the path in a fetal position.

Becky was up and waiting for him when he entered the sitting room. "I was getting worried about you! What took so long?"

"Leah and I talked awhile, and then I encountered John Phelps on the way back here."

"Are you okay? What did he want? What happened? You don't look so good."

"I look a lot better than Phelps. He pulled a knife on me, and I had to use a little force to relieve him of it. I wouldn't want him to accidently cut himself."

"Where's the knife? What did you do with it?"

"Threw it in the bushes where he'll have a hell of a time finding it again."

"Shouldn't you have kept it for evidence or something?"

"Evidence of what? He didn't get a chance to even scratch me. He was so drunk he may not even remember the encounter. I'm sure he's involved with someone who's involved in the art heist or maybe murder, and right now he's frustrated about Leah. I don't want to charge him with some petty crime. I want to give him enough rope to hang himself."

Nate lay awake a long time thinking about Leah and trying to make sense of everything that had happened.

He slept late the next morning and had to shower and shave quickly. Becky was ready and waiting for him when he came out of the bedroom. It was almost 8:15 by the time they left the cottage and headed to the main house for breakfast. Clouds were hanging heavy in the sky, but there'd been no rain so far. As they neared the bend where John had stepped from behind the tree and accosted Nate, they saw something on the path. Nate had a feeling of déjà vu, as he looked at what appeared to be a bundle of clothes. When they got closer, Becky put her hand to her mouth to stifle a scream. "Oh, my God! Nate, it's John Phelps and he's covered with blood! Is he dead?"

Chapter 16

John Phelps knows too much and wants too much to keep his mouth shut. It's time to eliminate him, thought the silent onlooker. Following John required little effort as he lumbered along in an intoxicated stagger, getting behind the tree and swaying as he waited for Nate Parker. When Nate disabled him without hardly breaking his stride, it had provided a golden opportunity. While the moon played peek-a-boo with the clouds, it had been a piece of cake to retrieve the knife from the bushes where Nate had so carelessly tossed it. Under the guise of helping Phelps stand up, it had been so easy to put the knife in position to plunge into his heart. But Phelps had seen the knife and tried to deflect it, causing it to miss his vital organ. There'd been no time to check and see if the wound was fatal; someone was coming up the path. The only option was to toss the knife back into the bushes and move quickly away into the shadows and out of sight.

Attempting to kill Phelps had been so much easier than the first killing. The old expression, 'practice makes perfect,' was so true. Sheila Rhodes was another fool, turning her back after all the questions she'd asked about that first killing, revealing that she knew too much. The paperweight was lying right there as if asking to be picked up and smashed into the side of her head. Too bad about her computer, though—Sheila had been clever enough to hide it, and there wasn't enough time to do a thorough search. But, no worry. No one would ever find her phone, and *that* was the device with the really damaging information. Really bad luck that Phelps happened to see the meeting with Sheila outside her apartment, them going inside together, and Sheila never coming out. He'd put two and two together and gone to the cottage to check. He'd seen the blood and scuff marks.

Too bad my watch fell off when I hit that nosy bitch with the paper weight, and even worse luck that Phelps found it. He thought he had the magic key to easy money and power over me. Well, he should know, blackmailers seldom get what they want; they get what they deserve. If Phelps doesn't die from this wound, I'll just have to see that something else happens to him. I'll take my chances on the watch. If it's found, no one will associate it with me without Phelps to blab about whom it belongs to and whose blood is on it. If only I knew for sure if Linda Baker saw anything when she was with Phelps and what else she may know. These thoughts ran through the killer's mind while silently retreating and disappearing into the shadows.

****

Becky had turned pale at the sight of John Phelps lying on the path, covered with blood. Nate put a steadying hand on her arm and then squatted beside him and placed a finger on his carotid artery. "Call 911," he told Becky, "he's still alive."

Sheriff Jack McMullen and his deputy Earl Watson arrived within fifteen minutes, and the ambulance was right behind them, sirens blaring and lights flashing.

"What happened here this time?" Sheriff McMullen asked while hitching up his pants.

"This man is injured. He's lost a lot of blood and needs medical attention," Nate said.

Two medics unloaded a stretcher and headed in Phelps's direction. One was a tall, slim man who appeared to be about thirty. He was wearing a badge that identified him as Daniel Greer. The other medic was a petite woman of Asian descent who could have been anywhere from 20 to 40. Her name badge said she was Lynn Biggs. They moved as a fast, efficient team and soon had Phelps loaded into the ambulance. Lynn climbed into the back with him, and Daniel got in front behind the wheel.

"I.V. is started. B.P. is very low and dropping," Lynn informed the driver.

"I've notified the E.R. They know what we have and are ready and waiting," replied Daniel.

"Let's roll," Lynn said.

Daniel Greer backed the ambulance around and headed down the lane. With sirens blaring and lights flashing, they soon disappeared from view.

Sheriff McMullen glared at Nate, "Looks like trouble seems to follow you around. Any ideas about what happened here?" he asked while taking a block of tobacco out of his pocket, cutting off a chunk, and placing it in his mouth.

"Maybe Phelps will come around when they get him to the hospital and get him stabilized. You can take his statement then and find out what happened."

"In the meantime, would you care to speculate as to what kind of injuries could have caused Mr. Phelps to lose so much blood and how he came to have those injures?"

"No, Sheriff, I wouldn't care to speculate, but I will strongly advise you to post a guard with John Phelps, twenty-four hours a day."

"Hey, if you don't care to speculate about this situation, don't be trying to tell me how to run my job," Jack McMullen said, sarcasm dripping from his voice.

"Sheriff McMullen," Nate said, trying to remain patient, "it's obvious the man has a near fatal wound. There's nothing to indicate an accident or that it was self-inflicted. Someone tried to kill him and will very likely try to finish the job. In the meantime, we're going to breakfast. If you have any more questions, you know where to find me."

Everyone was full of questions when Nate and Becky entered the dining room. "What happened? Why was an ambulance here? Why was the sheriff here?" Questions flew at them like arrows, coming from all directions. Nate explained about finding John on the path wounded and bleeding.

"Did he have some kind of accident?" Mattie asked, her keen eyes taking in Becky's shakiness and Nate's self-control. *He's very concerned about something,* she thought.

"I don't think he'd had an accident—there were no rocks or anything sharp he could have fallen on, and he had lost a lot of blood. Hopefully, they'll patch him up at the hospital, and he'll soon be able to tell us what happened," Nate informed the group. He and Becky took a seat at the table with Leah, Sandy, Linda transformed into B.J., and Mattie.

"How are you this morning?" he asked Leah. "Did you sleep okay last night?"

"Yes, I slept well. Once I got in my room and locked my door. How about you? Did you encounter any problems going to your cottage?" Leah asked with a concerned look. Her eyes had a guarded expression that conveyed a certain wariness, as if she feared he was in some way connected with John's injury.

"Nothing serious," Nate answered. "I'll tell you everything later."

"The Portland hospital has a reputation as one of the best in the Northeast. They should be able to stabilize him, and the authorities will get to the bottom of what happened," Mattie said, patting Becky's hand and giving her a reassuring smile.

"Thank you, Mattie. I hope you're right," Becky said, while her thoughts recalled what Nate had said about someone trying to kill Phelps.

Mattie looked around the room at the different expressions on each face. Most were filled with curiosity, while one or two looked at Nate with suspicious, guarded eyes. She noted Leah's demeanor of concern and confusion and wished there was some way she could alleviate the girl's doubts. Mattie would bet the farm that Nate was straight as an arrow and honest as the day is long.

Nate was very much aware of all the ears tuned in their direction. For all he knew, Phelps's attacker was listening to every word they were saying.

When breakfast was over, Leah and Sandy went to their cottage to prepare for the last day of the workshop. Becky said she was going directly to the studio, and Linda/B.J. said she was going back to Jason's when he finished his breakfast duties.

"How about we take a walk and get some exercise before it starts pouring rain?" Ron said, looking at Nate.

"Sure," Nate said. "I could stand to stretch my legs and breathe a little fresh air."

"We need to go by my cottage first. I have something I want to show you," Ron said as they headed outside. They saw Jason on the patio giving Sasha some water. "I heard what you told the group in the dining room about John Phelps. Was he attacked?" Jason asked, looking at Nate.

"It kind of looks that way."

"Any idea what happened?"

"A few," Nate said in a low voice. "I feel like these walls have ears, and I don't trust anyone at this point. Ron and I are going for a walk. Could you join us?"

"I'll be through for the day in about fifteen minutes. I'll run B.J. home and meet you back here in twenty minutes."

"Okay, we'll be at Ron's cottage. Come on up there when you get through," Nate said.

He and Ron went up the lane to Fernwood cottage. Entering the door into the sitting room, Ron turned to Nate, "I hate this damn place. Everything reminds me of Sheila, and it's tearing me apart. They've released her body, and Ron, Jr. is flying up from Texas this afternoon to take her back home. But I can't leave this damnable place to even go home for her funeral."

"I know how you feel, Ron. Hopefully, we're getting close to finding her killer. I think he or she tried to kill John Phelps last night."

"Why would they want to kill him? I thought he was in cahoots with whoever is behind everything."

"That's why I think the killer is getting nervous. I think he or she is cleaning house, getting rid of anyone who knows too much. Whoever it is also thinks Linda knows more than she does. That's why she was kidnapped, and we know Phelps was involved in that."

"I found the flash drive with the info from Sheila's computer. That's why I asked you to take a walk. I wanted to talk to you about it."

"What was on it? Did it have information that gave you any ideas of who the killer may be?" Nate asked.

"There's a lot of stuff on there. Apparently, she'd watched the surveillance tape several times. There were several articles she'd done some follow up research on and a lot of general information she'd checked. I think I'm missing something, I just can't make sense of it."

"How'd you manage to find it?" asked Nate.

"She'd slid it into the opening of the housing at the top of the window blinds. She'd drawn a little heart there also," Ron said with a sad smile.

Jason knocked on the door about that time, and Ron called for him to come in.

"You two sure have serious expressions. Did you discover something new?" Jason said.

"I've found the flash drive with the information Sheila had on her laptop, but I can't make heads or tails of it," Ron said.

"I think we need to get out of here and go for that walk, clear our heads, and do some brainstorming," Nate suggested.

They left Fernwood, went down the lane, around the end of the cove, and up into the woods. Heavy black clouds had gathered over the bay, and sheet lightning flashed across the leaden sky. Low rumbles of thunder echoed across the turbulent water, and boats moored off shore rose and fell like phantom surfers riding each wave. When they passed the spot where Sheila's body had been found, they could hear the moan and sigh of the distant buoys. "It sounds as if they're weeping for Sheila," Ron said, his heart as heavy as the rocks that covered the banks of the bay.

Nate pointed to the sky. "Looks like a gully washer moving in. We better head for high ground. We can sit in the gazebo and pick each other's' brains. Like Hercule Poirot and Sherlock Holmes, we'll use our powers of deduction to solve this crime," he said with a grin, hoping to lighten the mood.

They reached the gazebo just before the bottom fell out. Rain pelted the roof of their sanctuary, but thankfully there was very little wind. The rain seemed to fall straight down from the heavens, rolling off the roof, creating a curtain of water that surrounded them. They sat in silence and waited until the storm subsided. When the rain had finally slowed to a sprinkle, Nate suggested they start at the beginning and think of everything that had transpired in the past four days, regardless of how insignificant it may seem.

"First, and most importantly, Sheila was murdered to prevent her from revealing information she discovered incriminating the killer. She called Susan Porter, probably to confront her with what she had derived from the surveillance videos. The follow up research probably gave her more insight about the Porters, convincing her Susan and her husband were the art thieves."

"Yes, but you don't think she's the killer, do you?" asked Ron.

"No, I think she called someone else and that someone met her at your cottage and killed her," Nate replied. "I'd like to borrow that flash drive and see if I can come up with anything, and also send the data to Harry. He has access to more information than I do," Nate continued. "Sheila found something, and it's got to be in there somewhere—we've just got to figure out what it is and why it was so important that it got her killed."

"Linda was kidnapped because someone thought she knew something that could be incriminating," Jason said. "She told us everything she could remember about the conversation she had at the reception Sunday. She knew the Porters were in the group, but she couldn't remember who else was there. She seemed to think several people came and went during that time."

"She talked about watching the movie about the famous art forger and about reading something about how easy it was for a clever person to make murder look like an accident," Nate said. "I think maybe there's something she's forgetting, but if not, then there's something in what she said that put someone on red alert. We know John Phelps was involved in her kidnapping, but we also know someone else was behind it. Maybe Phelps stumbled on something that incriminated the killer, and that person tried to kill him last night."

"That person also hired two thugs, probably to use any means it took to find out how much Linda knew and if she had told anyone else," Jason added.

"We mustn't forget, those thugs are still out there somewhere and probably looking for Linda." Nate said.

"If we could just find the true motive behind Sheila's death, we'd know who the killer is."

"So, what exactly happened to Phelps?" Ron asked.

"He ambushed me last night on my way back to my cottage and pulled a knife. He was pretty drunk, and I disabled him without hardly any effort. I should have kept the knife, but I tossed it into the nearby bushes. Apparently, someone came along behind me, retrieved the knife, and tried to kill him. They were probably watching Phelps or me from the beginning. I feel sure it's the same person who killed Sheila, and I also feel sure they'll try to finish the job. Hopefully, Phelps will live and tell who his assailant was."

The rain had stopped, and the black clouds had vanished, leaving only remnants of silver-rimmed plumes in a luminous blue sky.

"Look, there's a rainbow," Ron said, pointing to the vaporous pigments, starting directly overhead and disappearing into the bay. "I believe God is sending us a message, a promise that all will be resolved," Ron said in a low voice, almost as if he was whispering a prayer.

"The rainbow was put in the sky as a sign of God's promise, and hopefully it's a reminder that he is with us," Nate said.

When they arrived back at the inn, Ron went to his cottage to call his son and determine what time he would be arriving. Jason went to his house to check on Linda, and Nate went to his cottage, booted up his computer, and inserted the flash drive.

Back at the studio, Andy had just completed his demo painting. This time, he did a self-portrait. He placed a mirror on a pedestal a few feet in front and a little to the left of his easel. He had a light clamped to the left side of the easel with a flexible arm that allowed him to control the direction of the light. He constantly referred back and forth from the mirror to his canvas. Leah watched in amazement as his likeness took shape. He began with a rough sketch, then painted in the dark areas. Already it looked like him, and, as he added mid-tones and lights, he soon had a mirror image of himself. *The eyes…* thought Leah, something about the eyes didn't seem right. She walked up closer and studied the painting, and then looked closely at Andy's eyes. "You've captured your likeness exactly except for the eyes. They're not yours. Why did you change your eyes?" Leah asked as she studied Andy's self-portrait.

"You are a very astute young lady," Andy informed her. "I was wondering if anyone would notice. I painted Rembrandt's eyes staring from my face. He was the world's greatest portrait painter, so I painted my face with his eyes, looking at the world. The eyes are the windows to the soul and my soul is a kindred spirit of Rembrandt's. I, too, shall someday be known as one of the world's greatest painters," Andy said, as if stating a well-known fact. "Now, would anyone like to use my light and mirror and do a self-portrait?" Andy asked the class with a raised voice.

Everyone declined, feeling somewhat intimidated after watching the amazing results of Andy's demonstration. They all chose to paint either a still life arrangement or a landscape from one of the many photos Andy had provided.

Lunch arrived and, after everyone had eaten and set up their gear, the room grew quiet as each one concentrated on their painting.

Leah had chosen an arrangement with a silver teapot, some roses and a lace runner. She did a rough sketch and started laying in the dark patterns. She seemed to be working on autopilot. Her thoughts were on Nate, wondering what happened last night. Was he responsible for John's injuries that had sent him to the hospital and required the sheriff to come? When she came down the path going to the studio, she'd seen Sheriff McMullen and his deputy combing the grounds. Why was she even having these thoughts and concerns? She trusted Nate; if he did anything to John, then it would have been in self-defense. *But, if Nate had not harmed John, then who did?* Leah thought, as the image of Sheila Rhodes' distorted, bloated face filled her mind.

"I've been watching that troubled look in your eyes and the frown on your face. I don't think it's your painting that's causing all that concern. Are you worried about Nate and Phelps?" Sandy asked, walking over to where Leah was standing.

"Yeah, I guess so. I just can't believe Nate would try to kill anyone."

"I think you're right. I don't think he would harm anyone unless it was in self-defense."

"I just hope John recovers and can explain what happened," Leah said.

"Well, we'll keep our fingers crossed and say a prayer," Sandy said, returning to her painting.

Nate had been on the computer since returning from his walk with Ron and Jason. He had gone over and over the information Sheila had discovered. He started again, reading each article, each follow-up research she had done. Apparently, she had seen something that caused her to call someone other than Susan Porter, and that someone had smashed her head in with the paperweight. Nate could see that Sheila had studied the surveillance videos several times, probably leading to her call to Susan. Linda had seen Susan walking up the path with Sheila, but Nate would stake his life that Susan was not the one who struck Sheila down and pushed her into the bay. The person who did it must have had blood on them. Ron had said Susan, dressed as a cleaning lady, had looked no different when she returned to the cottage than when she'd left.

Nate's phone buzzed. He pulled it out of his pocket, and seeing Harry on the caller ID, answered, "What's up partner?"

"I've been reviewing all the data you forwarded to me, and I have a few questions," Harry replied.

"Okay, shoot."

"Did you notice the engagement announcement of Calvin Ross and Judy Mansfield, dated about two years ago?"

"Yeah, I knew they were an item before she married husband number four, but I didn't know it had gone that far. I knew she met Phelps during the time she was involved with Calvin. She ran into him at the resort and brought him to dinner at the inn last night. She left immediately after eating to go check on hubby. I guess Phelps had a little too much to drink and waylaid me on the way to my cottage. He tried to finish me off with a knife."

"I know, and apparently when you disabled him, someone tried to finish him off," Harry said.

"How'd you know about that already?" Nate asked in a surprised voice.

"Why do you call me for info? I see all and hear all. I make it my business to know what's going on," Harry said with a chuckle.

"Well, Mister Fount of Information, what do you make of the obituaries Sheila was researching?"

"And more importantly," added Harry, "what about the research on the murders that were made to look like accidents?"

"You know Harry, it's always a help to toss ideas around with you; get back to me if you think of anything else," Nate said, disconnecting his phone, remembering something he had read.

He went back and reread one of the articles. *I think I have a pretty good idea who killed Sheila and why*, he thought, as he reread a second article. Nate shut down the computer, and, feeling pangs of hunger, headed down the path to the Ledges restaurant. He called Jason on the way and asked him to meet him there.

Nate waited out front of the restaurant until Jason arrived. The hostess seated them in a booth by a window overlooking the lake. After the waitress took their order and left, Nate told Jason about the articles Sheila had been researching but didn't tell him about his suspicions of who the killer was. He wanted to be sure before he started tossing around names, and he also wanted to see if Jason came up with the same idea about who the killer could be.

Jason was siting facing the front of the restaurant, and he could see the main road that ran through the resort. A look of shock and something close to fear filled his eyes. "That black Hummer just went by on the main road going in the direction of my house."

Their food had arrived a few minutes before, and they had only taken a few bites when Jason saw the vehicle with the same two men he and Linda had seen.

Nate took some bills out of his pocket and threw them on the table. "Let's get out of here," he said, rising from his chair and heading for the door. "It's about a ten-minute walk to your house, but I think we'd only lose time if we went up to the inn for my car; let's get there as fast as we can on foot," Nate said, starting out in a swift trot.

By the time they reached Jason's house, the Hummer was nowhere in sight. They hurried up the steps and found the front door standing open. They ran through the house, but Linda was nowhere in sight. Everything was ransacked, drawers pulled open, and closet doors ajar. The clothes Leah had brought to Linda were strewn on the bed along with the toiletries, as if the thugs were saying, "We know Linda is staying here."

"Linda!" Jason called, "Are you here? Are you okay? It's safe! They're gone! There's no one here." He saw blood on the floor and heard a soft moaning sound. Throwing some papers and clothes aside, he found Sasha lying on the floor in a pool of blood. The concealed door to the secret room opened, and Linda stumbled out. She was sobbing as she rushed to Jason, "I saw them coming just in time to go into the hidden room. Sasha was in the house, and she attacked them. I couldn't see what was happening; I just heard Sasha growling and snapping, and one of the men cussed and said he was going to kill that effing beast. Then I heard a gunshot and a thump when Sasha fell to the floor."

Jason grabbed a towel and wrapped it around Sasha. Scooping her up into his arms, he headed for the open door. "We've got to get her to a doctor! Hang in there, girl," he said as they climbed into his SUV. Linda got in the passenger seat as Nate got behind the wheel, turned the Explorer around and squealed off. Driving as fast as possible through the resort, he turned onto the highway. With the hazard lights flashing, he floor-boarded the gas pedal. Jason was in the backseat holding Sasha in his lap with a towel pressed against her head. "Hang in there girl; we're going to get you help," he whispered to her over and over, as Sasha looked up at him with pain-filled, trusting eyes.

Chapter 17

The nearest vet was twenty-two miles away. They screeched to a halt outside the building in less than twenty minutes. Jason was out of the car as soon as the wheels stopped rolling.

Nate was right behind him. He grabbed the door and held it open while Jason rushed in carrying Sasha. "My dog has been shot and needs help now!" he yelled to the girl behind the desk in the reception area.

Everyone seemed to go into motion at once. The door to the treatment area burst open, and an assistant led Jason back to a small room. "The doctor will be right with you," she said as she went out the door. It seemed she had hardly left when she came back with a middle-aged man who introduced himself as Dr. Cox. He was a few inches shorter than Jason, with a slim, wiry build. He had intelligent brown eyes and a shaved head, wearing faded jeans and a sweatshirt that said New England Patriots. He had a compassionate attitude that appealed to Jason.

"What have we got here?" he asked, looking at Sasha.

Jason had laid Sasha on the examining table, still holding the now blood-soaked towel to her head. "My dog Sasha has been shot," he replied in a frantic voice.

Doctor Cox removed the towel and began to examine the wound on Sasha's head. "We've got to get the bleeding stopped first, and then we'll do a complete blood count to determine if she needs a transfusion. In the meantime, if you would go out front and give the girls at the desk your information, we'll take good care of your dog."

"How long will it take? When will I know something?"

"We'll let you know as soon as we get the bleeding stopped, take an x-ray, and get the results of the blood work. Shouldn't take more than fifteen or twenty minutes."

* * * * * * *

Deputy Earl Watson took a pack of gum out of his pocket and put a fresh piece in his mouth. *Boy, what I wouldn't give for a cup of coffee,* he thought, as he paced back and forth outside the cubicle in ICU at the Maine Medical Center in Portland. John Phelps was lying just inside the door. He was hooked up to an IV and a heart monitor that beeped a steady rhythm.

Sheriff McMullen left me here to guard this Phelps guy. He must think whoever knifed him will come back to finish the job. Well, hopefully Phelps would come around and tell them who tried to do him in, Earl was thinking as he chewed the gum with a vengeance. *Damn,* he thought, *Sara Ann's expecting me at four, and it's almost three-twenty. I was just beginning to make some headway with her. Now I'm stuck here at this frigging hospital, and I'll have to stay until sheriff McMullen sends someone to relieve me. Sara Ann just doesn't understand my job isn't nine to five. I have to work when needed.*

Earl Watson was pacing the floor and worrying about how Sara Ann would react to being stood up again, when he saw a familiar face coming down the hall.

"How you doing Earl? How's the patient?" asked the person who had just joined him.

"I think they got him stabilized, but he's not out of the woods yet," he replied.

"Guess you're getting tired and bored. Would you like for me to relieve you for a few minutes, give you a chance to get some coffee?"

"Uh, thanks, but I'm not supposed to leave my post and not supposed to let anyone in here."

"Well, I know rules are rules, but sometimes it doesn't hurt to bend them a little. Do I look like any kind of threat? I was just trying to help you. But that's okay, I understand."

Earl looked at the person standing in front of him, someone he had known for most of his life. *What the hell*, he thought, *it won't hurt for me to take a few minutes to run down the hall for some coffee.*

As soon as Earl disappeared from sight, the intruder stepped over to the bed where John Phelps was lying. Phelps opened his eyes and stared. He tried to raise his arms, but the restraints kept them close to his sides. His heart started racing.

"Don't worry, John. I'm not going to harm you. I just wanted to see how you're doing and let you know I've been thinking about you. I also wanted to tell you I would be very pleased if Nate Parker was put out of commission. You're a smart man; I think you can figure a way to do that."

Again, he tried to raise his arms, and his heart pounded harder, causing the monitor to beep louder and faster. The visitor blew John a kiss and slipped away just as a nurse came rushing to his bedside. She started checking his vitals, but his heartrate was slowing and nothing seemed to be amiss. "What happened? Where's the deputy? Did you realize he's gone and get frightened?"

"I'm right here," Earl said, walking up behind the nurse. He had a cup of coffee in his hand. "I just stepped down the hall for some coffee." He wondered what had happened to the unexpected visitor and why Phelps seemed so upset, but there was no way in hell he would ever tell anyone he had left his post and left someone alone with Phelps. He knew he had screwed up—his instructions were to allow no one to enter the area where John Phelps was isolated.

****

Jason, Nate, and Linda had been in the waiting room about thirty minutes when Dr. Cox came out the door.

"How is Sasha? Is she going to be okay?" Jason asked, jumping to his feet.

"We got the bleeding stopped and did an x-ray. Luckily the bullet didn't penetrate; it just grazed across the top of her skull. There were a few bone fragments in the wound, but we got them cleaned out and stitched her up. She's lost a lot of blood, but her CBC was thirty, so she won't need a transfusion. I've started her on antibiotics and some fluids. She should be fine, but I suggest you leave her here for a few days. We're giving her a strong antibiotic intravenously, along with the fluids and something for pain. She needs rest and quiet to recuperate," Dr. Cox explained.

Jason breathed a sigh of relief. "Thank you, Dr. Cox, whatever you think is best for her. I gave the girls my contact information. I'll be checking on her regularly, but if there is any change, please let me know."

"Don't worry, we'll take good care of her. Was this a hunting accident? It almost looks as if someone tried to shoot her between the eyes and she moved in time for the bullet to just graze the top of her head."

"You might say it happened on a hunting expedition, but it was no accident." Nate pulled out his FBI creds and showed them to Dr. Cox. "You may have heard of the murder over at the Rocky Ledge Inn. We were there investigating an art theft. The victim was one of our agents. Seems we've stepped on some toes and made someone very unhappy."

Dr. Cox looked at the three of them with a concerned expression. "Good luck. I hope you catch them. Anyone who would shoot a dog is a low life scumbag in my opinion."

They returned to the parking lot, and Jason got behind the wheel of his SUV with Nate in the passenger seat and Linda in the back.

"We've got to get Linda to a safe place. The person behind this is not giving up until she's found," Nate said, removing his phone from his pocket. He punched in some numbers, and Harry answered on the second ring.

"What can I do for you, Sherlock?"

"We need to get Linda to a safe place ASAP. What do you suggest?"

"Let me make a few calls and get back to you," Harry answered.

Jason turned the Explorer around and headed out of the parking lot. "Where to now?" he asked.

"We never got to finish our lunch. I think I saw a restaurant on the way here.

Let's go back there, get something to eat, and wait for Harry's call," Nate said

They found the small diner about five miles from the veterinarian clinic. The place was almost deserted. Only one table was occupied with two men wearing work clothes, hard hats, and rugged boots. The trio sat down in a back booth. The waitress came over and handed them menus. She was about thirty, with blond hair that had been dyed so many times it looked like straw. She was wearing a light blue polyester uniform stretched tight across her hips and ending just above her knees. The first three buttons at the top of her uniform were unfastened, showing a lot of cleavage.

"Hi, my name is Lulu. What can I get you to drink?" she asked, looking directly at Nate and winking. Nate ignored the wink and ordered a cup of coffee. Jason ordered coffee also, and Linda ordered tea.

Nate's phone buzzed—he looked at the caller ID and, seeing Harry's name, said, "What you got partner?"

"How far are you from Brunswick?"

"We're on the outskirts at a small diner,"

"I've made arrangements at the Naval Air Station there in Brunswick for Linda to be flown to Pax River, Maryland. An agent will be waiting and will take her to a safe house. Be at the Naval Station within an hour and ask for Commander Nelson."

"Thanks, Harry," Nate said.

The waitress came with their drinks and placed them on the table. "You guys from around here? I don't think I've seen you before."

"We're just passing through," Nate said without looking at her.

"What would you like to eat, honey?" she asked, again looking at Nate with a sultry pout and licking her lips. Nate ignored her innuendoes and ordered a Philly steak sandwich and fries. Jason ordered a burger with fries, and Linda ordered a chef salad. The waitress walked away swinging her hips seductively. The two construction workers were taking everything in, and they called out loudly, "Lulu, get your wiggling ass over here with two more beers."

"Nate, I really appreciate you finding me a safe place, but I've got to get back to my job by next Monday. I can't just take off indefinitely."

"You'll take off permanently if those goons ever find you, and whoever's behind this isn't going to give up. Linda, I wish you could remember exactly who all was within hearing distance of you when you were talking about the murder. I have a pretty good idea who it might be, based on the information Sheila Rhodes was researching the day she was killed, but I need more evidence."

"Well, don't keep us in the dark. Who do you think it is?" asked Linda.

"I don't want to throw out accusations until I'm sure. We'll get you to a safe place, and hopefully you won't have to stay very long."

"If I ever get my hands on that thug who shot Sasha, he'll regret the day he ever set foot in my house," Jason said, as he finished the last of the burger.

"I know how you feel, but try to keep your personal feelings out of this and concentrate on our final goal. I'll call the local police and get them to put out an APB on the black Hummer with a description of the two men."

The two construction workers were still there, drinking beer, probably finished with work for the day and looking for trouble. One of them tipped his bottle in their direction and said, "Hey, where you guys from? Ain't never seen you in here before."

Nate sensed hostility in the man's voice, and he saw Jason's jaw clench. *Damn, we don't have time for this*, he thought. The larger of the two men rose out of his seat and cracked his knuckles. "I don't like the way you looked at Lulu, and I don't like your ugly mug. I think maybe your face needs some rearranging."

Nate looked at the man and smiled, "Seems you have a lot of dislikes. Maybe you should just sit back down and close your mouth."

"You talking mighty big, little man," the worker said, glaring at Nate and flexing his muscles. He was about the same height as Nate but outweighed him by at least fifty pounds. He'd removed his jacket and was wearing a tee shirt with a pack of cigarettes rolled up in the sleeve. There was a tattoo of a mermaid on his forearm that wiggled when he flexed his muscle.

Nate sized him up as a big mouth bully and was irritated at the intrusion. "Look fella, I don't want to hurt you. I'm in a hurry, so why don't you just sit down and cool off."

"Ha, did you hear that, Melvin? He don't wanna hurt me. That's the biggest laugh I've had all day."

"Yeah, Herman, you need to teach that smartass a lesson. Let him know we don't cotton to strangers like them coming in our place and acting all high and mighty. Don't worry about his friend. I got you covered," Melvin said, pushing his chair back and rising to his feet.

Herman lunged at Nate, charging like a bull just released from a pen. Instead of jumping back, Nate made a quick step to the side and stuck his foot out. Herman tripped and went down on one knee. He growled like a mad dog and grabbed Nate around his legs, trying to pull him down. Nate hit him with an uppercut to the chin, knocking him backwards. Herman shook his head, got to his feet, and charged Nate again. Nate grabbed his wrist with both hands and jerked his arm behind his back, dislocating his shoulder. Herman fell to his knees, moaning in pain.

Melvin started over to help his friend, but Jason stepped in front of him, blocking his way.

"Melvin, you want to take your friend to the hospital, or do you want to go as a patient, too?"

Melvin looked at Jason and then Nate and sat back down. "Just don't ever show your ugly faces in this place again," he said, trying to have the last word and save face.

There was a four-wheel drive, three-quarter-ton pickup truck parked in front of the diner.

"Linda, give me your phone," Nate said. Linda reached into her pocket, pulled out her phone, and handed it to Nate. He turned it on and tossed it into the back of the pickup. "Maybe the goons will track our overzealous friends. I'm sure this truck belongs to them. The agency will supply you with a safe phone.

About fifteen minutes later, they stopped at the gatehouse at the entrance to the naval base. The security guard walked up to the window of the SUV and Nate showed his creds. The guard examined Nate's ID and handed it back.

"Okay, Commander Nelson is expecting you. Take this street to the first intersection, turn right, and you'll see a white building with a sign that says "Headquarters." You'll find the Commander there.

They found the building, parked out front, and went inside. A young woman was sitting behind a desk. She had dark auburn-colored hair pulled back into a bun, a pair of dark rimmed glasses perched on the end of her nose, and a name tag that said, "PN2 Sanders." "May I help you?" she asked, removing the glasses.

"We're looking for Commander Nelson," Nate said, flipping open his ID and showing it to the young woman. She put the glasses back on her nose and looked it over. "Oh, yes, he's expecting you. Go down the hall to the right, and it will be the second door on the left. I'll let him know you're here."

By the time they reached his office, the commander was coming out the door. He introduced himself and, looking at Linda, said, "This must be the young lady needing our help."

"Yes," Nate replied. "This is Linda Baker, I'm Nate Parker, and this is Jason Atwell. Linda has some bad people determined to find her, and we need to get her to a safe place. An agent will pick her up when she gets to Pax River."

"We're all set on this end; we can leave anytime," Commander Nelson replied.

****

Leah's hands moved mechanically, putting paint on the canvas, but her mind was not on her work. When everyone starting putting their gear away and cleaning their brushes, she looked at what she'd painted and felt disgusted. "This is pathetic," she told herself, and started painting over what she had done.

"What do you think you're doing?" Sandy asked, walking up behind Leah and looking at the partially completely painting. Leah had slashed gray paint over most of the picture.

"It stinks! I'm covering this sorry excuse of a painting before anyone sees it."

"I heard that," Andy said, joining them. "I've been watching you, and your mind has not been on painting. I've seen you paint this week, and I know you're capable of doing excellent work."

"Well, I guess everyone has an off day now and then," replied Leah. "Maybe I'll come out to the studio later and work on the painting I started the other day."

"If you wish, but don't force yourself if you're not in the mood. I know from experience, if I'm distracted with something and I'm not really motivated, I usually wind up painting over it."

"That surprises me. I would think you could paint in your sleep."

"I probably could, but it wouldn't be up to my standards. So, don't worry about one screw up. You still have two good paintings to put in the critique tomorrow morning," Andy said, patting Leah's shoulder.

Leah finished covering her canvas with gray paint. *Now it'll be primed and ready to paint something different*, Leah told herself. By the time she finished, everyone was gone except Sandy and Becky. They had both cleaned their brushes and put away their materials. "You two go on, you don't need to wait on me. I'm going to get all my materials sorted and put away since we won't be painting tomorrow."

"I can't believe this week is almost over," Sandy said. "Seems it just got started. What with the murder, Linda being kidnapped, and then John Phelps being attacked, it's certainly been an unforgettable week."

Sandy and Becky left the studio telling Leah they would see her at happy hour. Leah went back to the little room where the sink was located and started washing her brushes. She had just finished cleaning them and was about to open the door that led back to the studio when she heard the front door open and two people talking. She recognized Andy's voice but not the other. She had paused at the door when she heard them, and her hand froze on the door knob when Andy shouted, "Damn it Ross! I've told you for the last time, you can count me out of your scheme. Find someone else to do your dirty work."

"You know there's no one else who can do what you do," the unfamiliar voice replied. "Come on, Andy. I came back to Portland so I could come up here and bring you the painting. This is a rare find, and you can turn it into a masterpiece with practically no effort."

"Calvin, you seem to forget one minor point. It is *illegal*," Andy said with a note of sarcasm.

"That may be true, but no one would ever know," Calvin said.

"*I* would know, and I've told you a hundred times, I will not plagiarize another artist's work. Get the guy you used when you found that 'unknown' Boudin."

"He'd be tickled pink to do it. Believe me, he made a chunk on that little scam. But, he's not nearly as good as you; the painting barely slid by the experts."

"Scam—that's the key word, Calvin. It's illegal. When are you going to acquire enough possessions to be happy and satisfied with your life? You've gone from petty stuff as a teenager to major art forgeries. You've got enough legitimate income to live like a king."

"I'll never have enough. Acquiring money and the things it can buy is the ultimate thrill. I've something in the works that would knock your socks off. I'll soon be laying my hands on an authentic masterpiece. You would be green with envy, but I won't be able to let you see it. I've got a buyer wanting it so badly he'll pay a fortune just to have it hanging in his secret gallery."

"Is that the reason you're here Cal? You're going to buy that stolen van Eyck? Who are you buying it from?"

"Oh no, I'm afraid I'd have to kill you if I told you that," Calvin said with a laugh.

"Cal, we were like brothers growing up. We were both poor as dirt and had to struggle for everything we got. But, you got off on the wrong path somewhere along the way. It's like you have to have more and more possessions to prove you're a worthy person."

"What do you know? Everything always came easy for you. Your talent gave you an easy ticket into the good life."

"True, I had some talent, but I worked my ass off to get where I am. Cal, I've always loved you like a brother, and I worry about you."

"Don't worry about me. I'm like a cat. I always land on my feet."

Leah was in a quandary as to what to do. She couldn't open the door and make her presence known, not after what she'd heard. She stood there praying they would leave, when suddenly their footsteps and voices grew louder. They were headed to the back room where she was standing! She looked around for a hiding place. There was a small room in the back corner, just large enough for a toilet. She eased quietly inside it and stood behind the door, hoping and praying it wasn't their destination.

She heard the door to the back room open. "I left my jacket back here. I think I may need it before morning," Andy was saying as they came into the room.

"I might as well use the bathroom while you're looking for your jacket," Calvin Ross said.

Leah's heart stood still. What would she do? There was no place for her to hide in this tiny facility. What would they do if they knew she'd overheard their conversation?

Ross walked into the room and Leah held her breath, expecting him to close the door and expose her hiding place; instead, she heard his zipper as he opened his fly. She stood motionless behind the door, holding her breath. As the sound of urine hitting the water diminished and she heard the toilet flush, she released her breath with a sigh, not realizing she'd been holding it.

About that time, the front door of the studio opened and Sandy entered, calling her name. *Oh no,* thought Leah, *Bad timing, Sandy. Why in heaven's name did you have to show up now?* Andy and Ross walked back into the studio.

"Oh, hi. I didn't realize you were still here," she said, looking at Andy. "Have you seen Leah? I left her here about thirty minutes ago, and she hasn't shown up at the cottage or main house yet."

"Maybe she went for a walk," Andy replied. "She was kind of upset with her painting today. Maybe she's walking off her frustrations. Oh, by the way, Sandy, meet Calvin Ross, an old friend of mine."

"I'm really pleased to meet you," Sandy said, extending her hand. "I've heard of you; don't you have a famous gallery in New York? And, didn't I read about you finding a lost masterpiece? I can't remember who the artist was."

"Well, thank you Sandy. I'm very pleased to meet you, too. Yes, I got lucky and found an unknown Boudin," Calvin said, taking Sandy's hand and holding it a little longer than necessary.

"He was one of the French impressionist painters, wasn't he?" Sandy asked, politely withdrawing her hand from his.

"Actually, he wouldn't be considered a true impressionist, but he *was* one of the first French landscape painters to paint outdoors. He was an important influence to the Impressionist movement."

"Okay, Ross. Quit showing off for the pretty lady; we need to go up to the main house. There's someone there who wants to see you," Andy interrupted.

"Thanks for the art lesson and again, it was nice meeting you," Sandy said as the two men left the studio.

Leah's tensed muscles relaxed, and she took a deep breath but was still reluctant to come out of her hiding place until she was sure the coast was clear. She could hear Sandy moving around in the studio, so she went to the door and peeked out. Sandy was studying the painting she'd done that day. Leah called in a loud whisper, "Sandy, don't scream. It's me. I'll explain later, but check and see if the coast is clear."

"Oh, good Lord!" Sandy said in a shaky voice. "You scared the crap out of me." She went to the front door and looked out. "There's no one in sight," she said, closing the door.

Leah came out of the back room, and she and Sandy eased out the front door and headed up the lane to their cottage. Leah told Sandy about the two men coming in while she was in the back room, overhearing their conversation and then being afraid to make her presence known. "Sandy, you're not going to believe what else I heard."

"What in the world did you hear? They're not gay lovers, are they?"

"Good heavens, no! Andy loves women too much for that." Leah made a face at Sandy. "I never know what direction your mind may take. What I heard could get both of us in a lot of trouble if the wrong person found out what I learned."

"Well, Calvin seems like a real charmer, so what is it? Did he rob a bank?"

"He's here to buy the stolen van Eyck," Leah said.

"Did you find out who he's buying it from?

"No, he wouldn't tell Andy who it is. Apparently, they've been friends since childhood, and he's always operated on the shady side. Andy seemed to be very concerned about him."

About that time, they heard the sound of an approaching vehicle and turned to see Jason's SUV coming up the lane. He stopped beside Leah and Sandy, and Nate got out. "Let me know how Sasha's doing, and watch out for those Hummer guys," Nate said, leaning back into the car.

"I hope they do come poking around my place again. They'll get more than they bargained for this time," Jason replied in an angry huff.

"I just hope the police pick them up before you encounter them. I know you're a big guy and you're strong and filled with anger, but there's two of them and they're big, strong, and mean. They're thugs, Jay. They have no conscience. They probably get their kicks by torturing and killing people."

"I wish I'd gotten their license plate number," Jason said.

"Well, there's not that many black Hummers running around with two muscle-bound thugs. The police will find them if they're on the highways," Nate assured him.

"What's going on? What's happened to Sasha? What about the two guys in the Hummer?" Leah asked as Nate slammed the car door and Jason turned the SUV around and drove away. Nate told the two of them about the men breaking into Jason's house looking for Linda and shooting Sasha.

"Was Linda there? Where is she now? How is Sasha?" Leah asked.

"Linda managed to hide in the secret room before those two goons got into the house. They tore the place apart and shot Sasha, but we got her to a vet in time. She's going to be okay. We also have Linda on the way to a safe place." He turned to Leah and took her hand, "Leah, I've got to talk to you. I want to tell you exactly what happened last night. John Phelps ambushed me on the way back to my cottage. He had a knife and tried to stab me. He'd had too much to drink, so I easily disabled him, but I made the mistake of picking up the knife and tossing it into the bushes. Someone tried to kill him, probably with that same knife, and I'm afraid they'll try again. I'm pretty sure it's the same person who killed Sheila Rhodes. I think they're getting nervous and trying to tie up loose ends. I'm afraid they're going to try and eliminate anyone they feel may be a threat. I want you and Sandy to be very, very careful. Try not to be alone except when behind locked doors."

Leah was about to tell him what she'd heard in the studio when she saw the sheriff's patrol car coming up the lane. It came to a stop beside them. The door on the driver's side opened, and sheriff McMullen climbed out. His deputy Earl Watson climbed out of the passenger side. The sheriff hitched his pants up, and walked over to

Nate. Spitting a stream of tobacco juice on the ground, he asked, "Are you Nate Parker?"

"Well, Sheriff McMullen, something wrong with your memory? You just spoke to me this morning," Nate said with a devilish grin. The sheriff ignored Nate's remark, and the deputy shuffled his feet nervously.

"We're investigating the attempted murder of John Phelps. I'd like for you to come with me and answer a few questions," McMullen said, clearing his throat.

"I'm not going anywhere with you; if you have questions for me, ask away."

"You the one who found him this morning?"

"That's right. My sister and I found him on the way to breakfast and called 911. If you recall, we were the ones who met you there at the scene when you arrived. So what else do you need to know?"

"I need you to go to the station with me for further questioning," the sheriff said in a belligerent voice.

"And, as I said before, I'm not going anywhere unless you're charging me with something."

"Okay, Mister Wise Guy. I didn't want to embarrass you in front of the ladies, but since you refuse to cooperate, I'm charging you with assault with a deadly weapon on the person of John Phelps."

Chapter 18

Leah and Sandy stood in stunned silence as they watched the sheriff's cruiser drive away with Nate handcuffed in the back seat. Sandy broke the silence with a loud expletive, "Damn! I can't believe that idiot sheriff actually arrested Nate."

"I think the sheriff has resented Nate from the beginning. He doesn't like the fact that he's an FBI agent working on a case in his territory. Maybe there's something they consider evidence, or perhaps they think Nate had a strong motive. Maybe they think John ambushed Nate, and Nate got the knife away from him and stabbed him in the heat of anger." Leah paused and took a deep breath, "Sandy, do you think that could have happened? Nate said John ambushed him and pulled a knife. Could he have gotten carried away in the struggle and stabbed John?"

"Leah Dawson, I can't believe my ears! I thought you were a better judge of character than that."

"I thought I was too, until John Phelps fooled me so completely."

"Yeah, but you quickly wised up to him. Did you ever truly trust him? Would you have told him your innermost feelings? He's a smooth operator. He can be so charming and beguiling, but he's also cunning and deceitful. Nate Parker is an open book. He tells you like it is, doesn't pull any punches, and he's a man with principles and integrity. In my humble opinion, he's the best thing that ever happened to you."

"Well, thank you for those words of wisdom. I know that's all true. My heart tells me he's a good man—honest, loyal, and dependable. He's also hot as a sauna and knee-shaking sexy, but my damnable brain keeps worrying me with questions of doubt."

"Leah, follow your heart," Sandy advised.

Some of the people who were in the house having happy hour came out the back door.

"What's all the noise? We heard cars coming and going and people talking. Is anything wrong?" Mary Jane asked. Louise and Joe Williams were right behind her. Liz Walker, Susan and Wayne Porter, Andy and Calvin Ross completed the group inquiring about the disturbance.

"Oh, sheriff McMullen came back; he wanted to ask Nate a few more questions about John Phelps's attack last night." Sandy assured everyone that there was nothing to worry about.

The people drifted back into the house, but Becky had just walked up from her cottage and heard what Sandy said.

"What really happened? If the sheriff had more questions about Phelps's assault, why didn't he question me, since I was with Nate when we found him? And, why did the sheriff take Nate with him?"

"That fool McMullen arrested Nate on suspicion of assault with a deadly weapon," Sandy explained. "I'm sure there's been some mistake and Nate will be cleared."

"Last night when Nate returned from walking you home, he told me about Phelps jumping him and pulling a knife and how he easily disabled him since John had had too much to drink," Becky said, looking at Leah. "If he'd stabbed John, I'm sure he would more than likely have had blood on him. He didn't even look the least bit disheveled. I know my brother, and I know he didn't stab anyone."

"I think I'll go to the jail and see if he needs help. I don't trust that overzealous sheriff. He seems to have a chip on his shoulder as far as Nate is concerned. He probably thinks Nate's invading his territory."

"Would you like for us to come with you?" Sandy asked.

"I'd love to have your company and moral support, but we may not get back before dinner," Becky replied.

"So, we miss a meal or pick up something on the way back."

"You've been awfully quiet," Sandy said, looking at Leah. "I don't understand why, but I know you're feeling uncomfortable about seeing Nate. I'll go with Becky, and you can stay here and think about everything. I'm sure you'll eventually come to the conclusion that your concerns are based more on self-doubt than Nate's innocence," she said, squeezing Leah's hand.

"No, I'm fine. I'd rather go with you and Becky," Leah assured Sandy. But, she had to admit, she *was* nervous about seeing Nate. She knew that he sensed her doubts when he was telling her what happened.

The three women walked around to the parking area in front of Rosewood cottage and climbed into the Jeep Cherokee, Becky in the driver's seat, Sandy in the front passenger seat, and Leah in the back. It took them about thirty minutes to get to the county jail where Nate was incarcerated. Becky pulled into the parking lot beside a one-story brick structure.

"Well, here we are," she said. "It might be a good idea for me to go in alone. I know they won't let us all see Nate and, knowing how Sheriff McMullen feels about him, I may not get to see him either."

Becky got out of the Jeep and went into the building. She entered a large room furnished with a desk and several chairs. There was a deputy seated behind the desk. The name on his uniform identified him as Deputy Charles Bell. He looked up when Becky entered the room and asked if he could help her.

"I would like to see Nate Parker," she said in an authoritative voice. "I'm his sister. He was arrested this afternoon by Sheriff McMullen."

"Oh, I'm sorry, but he's not allowed any visitors."

"Is Sheriff McMullen here?"

"No ma'am, I'm the only one on duty right now."

"I beg your pardon, Deputy Bell, but it's imperative that I see him. He has a medical condition that has to be monitored, and he doesn't have his medication," Becky said in a pleading voice.

"I can take his medicine to him."

"I'm sorry, but it's very complicated. It would take me at least an hour to show you how to monitor his condition to determine the amount of meds he needs," Becky said, hoping she sounded authentic.

"Well, I guess it'll be okay. I'll go back with you. Can you do what you need to do through the bars? I can't allow you to go into the cell with him."

"Yes, I can check him through the bars," Becky replied.

The deputy got her name and relationship and had her sign a ledger. He searched her purse and then led her through a door and down a hall. He unlocked an iron door made of bars, and they went past several cells to the one where Nate was being held.

"Your sister is here to check your condition and give you your meds."

Nate looked at Becky in surprise but caught on quickly.

"Thank goodness! I was really getting concerned that I might have a seizure or pass out if I missed taking my medicine."

Becky had anticipated having problems and had taken a few aspirin tablets out of her purse and put them in a little tin box of throat lozenges, which she had slipped into her pocket.

She took out her cell phone and held it out to Nate. "Okay, put your finger on this spot so I can check your dopamine level." She turned to the deputy and explained that her phone had a program on it that could monitor his dopamine levels by his thumb print. Nate laid his thumb on the edge of Becky's phone.

"They took all my belongings and won't let me make a phone call," he whispered.

Becky placed her fingers on his pulse and raised his eyelid with her other hand to peer into his eye. "What do you want me to do?" she asked in a low whisper.

"Call Harry and tell him to get me out of here."

"Hmmm," Becky said. "Everything seems to be normal right now, but here are your meds. You'll only need one of each to maintain your current level."

"Wait a minute," the deputy interrupted. "Let me look at that before you give it to him."

He walked from his post by the door, and Becky showed him the open tin with a few lozenges and aspirin. "Looks like aspirin to me," he said in a suspicious tone.

"They do look very similar, but they're nothing alike." Turning to Nate she said, "You're almost out of the asperantigaza. Do you happen to remember the pharmacist's telephone number? I'll call them for a refill." Nate understood the message and told her Harry's number and she loaded it into her contact list.

She told Nate good night and to be sure and take his meds, followed the deputy out to the office, and thanked him for being so helpful. When she returned to the car, she told Sandy and Leah what had happened.

"You sure did some fast thinking. Sounds like the deputy was doing some slow thinking," Sandy laughed.

Becky dialed Harry's number, and he answered on the second ring. She told him everything that had happened and gave him Nate's message.

Leah sat in the back seat and thought about Nate being locked behind bars. Regardless of the doubts she'd had, her feelings for him were as strong as ever, and she wished there was something she could do to help. Hopefully Harry would pull some strings, and he would soon be free. Nate was so vibrant and full of life, she couldn't imagine him confined in such a small space.

They got back to the inn a little after six, so they still had almost an hour before dinner. Becky asked Leah and Sandy if they would like to go to her apartment and talk about the situation. They agreed, and Becky drove straight to Rosewood cottage and parked out front. They piled out of the SUV and went into the building. When they entered the front door, Calvin Ross was coming out of the Porters' apartment. He smiled and greeted Sandy. "It's nice to see you again and with two other beautiful ladies."

"This is Leah Dawson and Becky Lawson," Sandy said, introducing them to the man. Turning to Leah and Becky, she explained, "This is Calvin Ross. He owns the famous Ross Art Gallery in New York. He's also been very fortunate in finding some rare paintings."

"Only a couple, but yes, I was very lucky indeed to run across them. I'm always on the lookout for lost treasures. I spend most of my free time browsing estate and garage sales, and I have an assistant who's always on the watch for valuable finds, too. This must be the friend you were looking for," he said, turning to Leah. "Glad you found her; it would be a shame for such a beautiful creature to be lost."

"Thank you. I was walking off my frustrations," Leah said, while mentally comparing him to John Phelps. He had the same smooth and charming demeanor.

"And, you must be Nate Parker's sister," he said, looking at Becky.

"That's right, I've been his sister all my life. I'm surprised you know him," she replied.

"He's a pretty well-known guy, actually. We've never met, but I've heard a lot about him. He has a very impressive reputation. It was a real pleasure meeting you ladies and chatting with you, but I've got to run. I hope to see you at dinner."

"Nice meeting you too," Leah and Becky mumbled as they turned and went into the apartment. Becky uncorked a bottle of wine and grabbed three glasses. "Well, he's a real charmer," Becky asserted, while pouring the wine.

"I don't like that guy. He's too smooth," Sandy observed.

"He reminds me of John Phelps," Leah agreed. She went on to tell Becky what she had overheard between Ross and Andy. "It sounds like he finds old paintings from a particular era and has someone remove the original painting and do a forgery, passing it off as a masterpiece. He was trying to talk Andy into doing one for him."

"Beltracchi!" Sandy gasped.

"What the hell are you talking about?" Becky asked.

"You're right," Leah nodded, "that was the story Linda was telling at the get acquainted reception. She talked about watching the movie about Beltracchi, the most famous art forger of all time."

Becky's head turned from Sandy to Leah in confusion, and then her expression cleared.

"Okay, now I remember Nate talking about someone overhearing what Linda had said and that being the possible motive behind her kidnapping. Do you suppose Andy or Calvin or maybe both could be responsible for her abduction?"

"I think we need to tell Nate about the conversation Leah overheard between Andy and Calvin," Sandy said, while taking a sip of wine.

"And about seeing Calvin leaving the Porters' apartment," Becky added.

****

After Jason dropped Nate off at the inn, he went straight to his house, parked the Explorer, and went inside. When he saw all the chaos and the blood on the floor from Sasha's wound, anger boiled up inside him once more. He could hardly stand knowing those low-life thugs had invaded his home, indiscriminately torn everything apart, and shot his dog. *I hope Sasha bit a plug out of the one who shot her*, he thought, as he started cleaning. He picked up all the paper and debris, as well as the clothes that had been tossed out of drawers and closets. He put all of Linda's things in a box and set it in the hidden room. He thought about Linda and wondered where she was now. He realized he'd liked having her there with him and had grown very fond of her in the short time they'd known each other. The house seemed so empty and quiet now without Linda or Sasha. *Funny, I never noticed it feeling this way before she came. I don't know how two people can be blood and be totally different the way she and John Phelps are*, Jason thought, as he placed a bucket under the hot water faucet, adding some Mr. Clean as it filled. He took the bucket and a mop and went into the living room. Tears filled his eyes as he mopped up the blood and thought of how near he had come to losing Sasha. He knew someone had hired those thugs, and that was the person he really wanted to find. His phone buzzed just as he was putting the mop and bucket away. He reached in his pocket and pulled the phone out to look at the caller ID. He didn't recognize the number. He punched the on button and said hello.

"Jason Atwell, please," said a male voice on the other end. "Speaking; who's calling?" Jason asked.

"This is Sergeant Gerald Hammock with the Maine State Police. I tried to call Nate Parker and got his voicemail. I left a message but figured I should call you since we were given your number also."

"What's up, Sergeant?" Jason asked.

"We picked up two guys in a black Hummer, but we can only hold them a short time on suspicion of a crime. You or Mr. Parker need to come in and ID these fellows and file an official charge."

"I'll be right there, Sergeant. Where are you located?"

"The police department on First Street in Portland."

"It'll take me about an hour to get there." He clicked off and punched in Nate's number. It went directly to voicemail. Jason left a message telling him about the call and that he was on his way to Portland. He then called Becky.

She answered on the first ring. "Hey, Becky. What's going on? Why isn't Nate answering his phone?"

"The county sheriff arrested him for assaulting John Phelps with a deadly weapon. I've called Harry, and he's working on getting him released. Is there anything I can help you with?" Becky asked.

"Damn, that's the last thing we need! That stupid sheriff sure is throwing a kink into everything. I hope Nate gets out real soon. I left him a message, but be sure he knows that I had a call from the police. They picked up two guys in a black Hummer, and I'm on my way to Portland to identify them and press charges."

Jason made it to Portland in fifty minutes. It took another twenty to get to the police station in the afternoon traffic. He went inside and showed his credentials to the officer at the front desk. He was then led back to a small viewing room by another officer. Four men were led out onto a platform, and Jason was asked to pick the two men who had broken into his house. He recognized the two thugs he and Linda had seen the night he rescued her and pointed them out. He was then led back to the front where he filed an official charge. The officer told him the men would probably post bond the next day and be back out on the streets, but a date would be set for a hearing, and they would notify him when it would be.

Jason left the police station and headed back to the inn. He saw a diner up ahead and realized he was hungry. He pulled into the parking lot where several cars and pickup trucks were taking up most of the spaces. He had to pull around to the rear to park. *Must be a popular place*, he thought, as he got out and started inside. He passed a red Mercedes that looked familiar and then realized he'd seen one just like it at the inn. *Looks like the same one. Wonder who it belongs to?* he pondered, as he opened the door and stepped inside. There were booths on each side of the large room with tables in the center. A young woman with long dark hair pulled back in a ponytail and large, very blue eyes approached him. She was wearing tight jeans, boots, and a silky red turtleneck sweater that clung in all the right places.

"Just one?" she asked. He nodded, and she led him to one of the booths on the right side of the room. "Could I get you something to drink?" she asked with a friendly smile that lit up her pretty face.

"I'd like a Bud Light, but you look too young to be serving beer," Jason said with a teasing smile.

"Well, FYI, I'm 23 and in pre-med school," she responded with a pseudo huff, pulling her shoulders back and assuming an important stance.

"What field of medicine are you studying, Candice?" Jason asked, looking at her name tag. "Do people call you Candy?"

"No, they call me C.A. My middle name is Anne, and I'm studying cosmetic surgery. I'm going to be a plastic surgeon."

"Lucky patients, especially if you can make them all look as good as you," Jason said, raising his eyebrows.

C.A. laughed and walked away, returning shortly with a frothy mug of Bud Light. "You ready to order, or do you need a few minutes?" she asked, setting the glass on the table.

"I'll have the Cowboy Burger with everything on it and a side of onion rings," Jason said, handing her the menu.

Jason let his eyes roam around the room and then did a double take, coming back to the woman sitting in a booth across the room. Liz Walker was sitting with her back to him, but he could see enough of her profile to recognize her. He also remembered that she owned a red Mercedes. He debated on whether he should go over and speak to her when she caught sight of him in the mirror at the end of the room and turned to smile and wave. Liz slid out of the booth and started in his direction. She was wearing a black dress made of some kind of soft clinging material. It hit about mid-way of her shapely calves and swayed as she walked. She had on a pair of black, sandal heels and a cream-colored jacket with buttons that glittered and sparkled. Jason had never seen her look quite so glamorous.

"Well, fancy meeting you here, boss; it's a small world. Where you going all dressed up?" Jason asked as Liz walked up to his booth.

"Hi Jason, this is a surprise. I've been to a meeting. What about you? What brings you here?"

"I had some business to take care of in Portland, thought I'd grab a bite to eat before going home."

"Did you hear about Nate Parker being arrested this afternoon?"

"Yeah, too bad. They need to be looking for the one who really attacked John Phelps instead of arresting innocent people."

"I know he's an FBI agent, but that doesn't necessarily mean he didn't attack John Phelps. He'll probably use his connections and get out, though," she said with a disgusted look.

Jason looked at her and wondered why she seemed to dislike Nate so much. Liz's eyes narrowed, and she had a look Jason couldn't define. Anger was there, but something else, too. Maybe frustration? What the hell—who knows what a woman is thinking?

"I don't know. I don't understand what evidence the sheriff could have had to arrest Nate in the first place."

"I think Phelps named him as his attacker, and Nate's fingerprints were on the knife," Liz said.

"How'd you find that out?"

"I've got a friend who works for the sheriff's department."

"Well, that's pretty damning evidence. I don't know if Nate will be able to use his connections to get out," Jason said.

"I hope not. I've got to run. Good seeing you."

Jason watched as Liz left the restaurant and pondered over what she'd told him. *I wonder who her friend is with the sheriff's department. She's lived here most of her life, other than spending winters in New York. Guess it could be most anyone. She sure seems convinced Nate is guilty.* He was just finishing his burger when his phone buzzed. The caller ID showed Nate's phone number. Jason punched the on button, "Hey, Nate. Please tell me you're a free man," he said in a pleading voice.

"Yep, Harry worked his magic and not only got me out, but got all the charges dropped. I'm on my way back to the inn. Where are you? I got your message about having to go to Portland."

"I stopped to get a bite to eat, and I'm about thirty or forty minutes from the inn."

"Good, meet me at my place when you get back. We've got some important things to discuss," Nate said with an emphatic tone of voice.

Chapter 19

Becky had just finished dinner and returned to Rosewood cottage when Nate walked in.

"Thanks for coming to the jail and bringing my meds," he said with a laugh. "I may have never gotten out if you hadn't called Harry. The sheriff refused to let me make my call until he took care of his so-called important business."

"How could he do that? I thought it was the law that everyone has the right to one phone call when they're arrested," Becky said.

"Yeah, McMullen deliberately dragged his feet, said he had something he had to take care of first, and I could make my call when he got back. I don't know what he's up to, but for some reason he sure wanted to keep me locked up."

"At dinner, everyone was talking about you being arrested. They were bombarding me with questions about why, where, and who. They all know you're an agent with the FBI, and they're dumbfounded that a county sheriff could arrest you. Frankly, I'm a little confused myself."

"He must have something that convinced him I attacked John Phelps. I'm sure they found my fingerprints on the knife, and the person who actually tried to kill him probably wore gloves. But my fingerprints can easily be explained. I don't think he would have arrested me on that evidence alone." They heard the front door of the building open, and a few seconds later, Jason was knocking on their door, calling out, "FBI! Open up!"

Becky opened the door and said with a laugh, "Okay, G-man, you've caught us red handed. Whatcha gonna do now?"

"Well, I could use a cup of coffee. I'd gladly give you your freedom for a good cup of java."

"Sounds like a fair exchange—one cup of java coming up," Becky said, heading to the kitchen. She measured coffee into the basket of the coffee maker, filled the carafe with water, and poured it into the back of the machine. It was soon bubbling and spurting, and the aroma of fresh coffee filled the air.

Jason sat down and looked at Nate, "Hey, big fella. Good to see you're no longer behind bars."

"That makes two of us. It's not a good feeling to be confined in a six-by-eight space. What about the two thugs? Are you sure they're the ones who broke into your house?"

"Oh, yeah. It's definitely the two guys Linda and I saw the night I rescued her and the same two I saw go by the Ledges on the way to my house. If we could have gotten there sooner, we probably could have caught them and prevented Sasha getting shot. The sad thing is, they'll probably post bail and be back out on the streets tomorrow."

"Those are two tough guys. Don't ever underestimate them. I'll bet they get off on beating people up. And killing is probably the ultimate thrill for them, especially knowing they'll get paid for doing it. We've got to find the person who hired them. Whoever it is, they're getting desperate."

"I ran into Liz Walker at the diner where I stopped to eat tonight," Jason said, taking the cup of coffee Becky handed him. "She was very informative—she knew all about you being arrested and the reason why."

"Well, now, that is something I truly would like to know. What was the reason she gave and how did she come by that information?" Nate asked with a perplexed look.

"She said she has a friend in the sheriff's department and that John Phelps named you as the one who tried to kill him. She didn't have any nice words to say about you. Sounds like she believes you're guilty and would like to see you stay behind bars."

"Well, that definitely thickens the plot or puts a new light on the situation. However you say it, John Phelps is covering for his attacker. He's even more stupid than I thought. No way will the killer let him live once I'm out of the picture. I sure would like to talk to him, but I wouldn't dare go near the hospital. If anything happened now, I would sure be in deep trouble."

"I could go and talk to him," Becky chimed in. Nate took the cup of coffee she offered him, and looked at her as if she had just arrived from another planet.

"Now, before you say anything, I could take Sandy with me, and we could pretend to be checking on him. If he won't see us or if he's not allowed visitors, then, nothing ventured, nothing gained."

"You know, she's got a point, Nate," Jason said. "Phelps can't do anything to harm them. I mean, what could happen to them in a hospital?"

"I don't know, I just don't like the idea. Let me give it some thought. In the meantime, do you happen to know if the Porters are at home?" he asked Becky.

"They should be away for a while. At dinner tonight, they said something about going to some kind of function with the wedding they're attending Saturday," Becky replied.

"Good, I'd like to search their apartment again, and this sounds like a golden opportunity." Nate drained the last of his coffee and set the cup on the side table. "Jay, would you mind sitting out on the screened porch where you can see the parking lot and warn me if they return?"

"I'd be glad to. It's a nice night, and there's a great view of the bay as well as the parking lot."

"I'll join you as soon as I tidy up the kitchen," Becky said, gathering up the coffee cups. She retrieved two throws from the bedroom. "Just in case we get chilly out there, "she said, handing one to Jason.

Nate opened the door and went down the hall to the Porters'. He knocked on their door and waited a few seconds and knocked again. He eased the door open and called out, "Anyone home?" A lamp on a table by the sofa had been left on, casting a soft glow in the sitting room, but the place had a deserted feeling. Nate went into the bedroom, which was dark except for the ambient light from the sitting room lamp. There was just enough illumination for Nate to see that all the window blinds were closed. He risked turning on his flashlight and went to the closet. Opening the door, he saw the same three wigs sitting on the shelf. It still gave him an eerie feeling—they looked so much like three people standing there in the shadows. He tried to do a more thorough search this time. He pushed clothes aside and checked behind them, as well as in the pockets. He felt on the shelves and looked in shoes. He covered every inch of the closet. There was nothing. He made sure everything was in its proper place and closed the door. The Harlen Coben mystery was still lying on the nightstand. He picked it up and found the phone number he'd seen the first time he searched their apartment. It was now close to the end of the book. Looks like Susan or Wayne had progressed with their reading. He opened the top drawer and saw the gun still in the same place. He shuffled through all the papers and medicine bottles. Nothing. He looked through the chest of drawers and found nothing of interest there.

If I wanted to hide something where I would feel confident no one would find it, where would I put it? Nate thought as he stood in the middle of the room and looked around. He remembered where Ron had found Sheila's computer and flash drive, and started scanning the ceiling, but this ceiling was not made of individual tiles; it was solid drywall. There were no rods on the windows, only plantation shutters. He went in the bathroom and took the toilet paper off its holder and looked inside of it. He started opening drawers and running his fingers over the bottoms. He checked all the drawers in the chest and underneath it. He found nothing, but the nightstand was a different story. *Guess they like to keep everything close,* Nate thought as his fingers encountered what felt like a key taped to the bottom of the nightstand. He pulled it loose and examined the small item. It appeared to be a key to a safe deposit box, but upon closer inspection, he found some letters and numbers on it. He flashed his light directly onto the key. USPS was printed across the top. Under that was *Do Not Duplicate* and then a number: **53967**. *A post office box key*, Nate thought, as he memorized the numbers. He looked at his watch—he had been in the apartment over thirty minutes. Better get out while the coast was clear. About that time, his phone vibrated an incoming text. He read the message Jason had sent. *The Porters just pulled into the parking lot.*

Nate quickly taped the key back in place and scanned the room for any telltale evidence he may have left. They probably wouldn't notice it if he did, there were so many clothes, newspapers, and dishes scattered about. *They were a messy couple, probably used to someone picking up after them*, Nate thought, as he hurried from the apartment.

He hurried down the hall and back into his and Becky's apartment. He was out on the porch with Jason and Becky by the time the Porters entered the building.

"Find anything this time?" Jason asked.

"Maybe. I found a key taped to the bottom of the nightstand. It goes to a post office box somewhere. It would help to know which post office."

"What are you going to do about it?"

"I'm going to find out if they have a post office box in Northpoint first. They probably used a fake name, so I need a good picture of them. If I strike out there, I'll try Portland. There's a number—53967—on the key. I don't know if that's the number of the box or some kind of code number." Nate was interrupted by a knock on the front door. Becky got up and went to the sitting room.

"Who is it?" she asked before opening the door.

"It's Wayne and Susan Porter," a male voice answered

"Oh, hell, what do they want?" muttered Nate as Becky opened the door, and Susan and Wayne Porter walked in.

"We saw your light and figured you were still up," Susan said.

"We were sitting out on the porch enjoying the nice evening," Becky explained. "Is there anything wrong?"

"Oh, no, we just wanted to stop by and invite you to the dance the wedding party is having tomorrow night. The bride and groom wanted to invite all the guests from the inn. It's going to be at the recreational center in Bath and starts at 7 PM. They've got a great band rented. It's going to be a fun evening." Spotting Jason as he and Nate walked into the sitting room, she assured him he was invited also. "I hope you can all come. I know you'll enjoy it."

"Thank you for inviting us," Becky said. "Would you like something to drink?"

"No, it's been a long day. We're going to call it a night," Susan said, turning to go. Wayne opened the door. He had a scowl on his face as if he were not too happy about inviting them to the dance, but he muttered a good night as they left.

Nate called Harry and asked him if he could send another agent to be at the inn sometime the next day. "I need a new face that no one will recognize. I've got a feeling the Porters will make a move tomorrow or Saturday, and I want someone who can take them into custody and hopefully catch the person who's buying the stolen art."

Harry assured Nate he would move mountains to see that his request was granted. Nate laughed, "Love you, Harry. You're the best."

He hung up and thought about the possibility that the key might belong to a box in New York or God only knows where. *Well, so be it. I certainly won't find out if I don't try*, he thought, as he punched in another number. It started ringing and Leah answered on the other end.

"Hello, Leah. This is Nate; did I catch you at a bad time? Are you busy?"

"No, I was getting ready to go to bed and do some reading. Are you back at the inn?"

"Yes, that call to Harry did the trick. He pulled some strings, and I was out within an hour after Becky brought my meds to the jail," he said with a laugh. His voice grew serious as he said, "Leah, I need to see you and talk to you. Will you meet me in front of your cottage?"

"Yes, I'll be sitting in one of the Adirondack chairs when you get here."

Jason left with Nate and walked to where the lane split. He turned left and headed out of the inn property and towards his house. Nate turned right and headed up the lane towards Broadview cottage.

Leah was sitting out front, waiting for him. His heart did a little somersault when he saw her. She had changed into a pair of jogging pants and jacket with a light-colored tee shirt. The pants and jacket appeared black in the moonlight. But, when he drew near, he could see they were a deep blue. He felt a little awkward, but he wanted to touch her and hold her more than anything else in the whole world. She looked up at him, and he took her hand and drew her up from the chair. He wrapped his arms around her, and she laid her head on his shoulder. He put his hand under her chin and lifted her head until her eyes were looking directly into his. "Leah, look at me. Tell me what's in your heart. Do you think I stabbed John Phelps?"

"Nate, you've been on my mind all day. I couldn't even concentrate on painting. I couldn't think of anything but the possibility that you may have stabbed him. My thoughts have been in a whirlwind, but I did come to a conclusion."

"What conclusion did you come to?" he asked in a voice filled with trepidation.

"I decided that if you *did* stab John Phelps, it would have been self-defense. I decided that you are the most honorable man I've ever known and that I would trust you with my life. And, having come to that conclusion, since you said you took the knife away from him and threw it in the bushes, and you and Becky found him almost dead the next morning, then, I believe that is exactly what happened. Now, I want to ask your forgiveness for ever letting shadows of doubt cloud my mind. Will you forgive me?"

Nate's answer was to pull her closer and kiss her forehead, her eyes, her cheeks, and finally her mouth. Leah pulled back and looked at Nate. She touched his face with her hand and let her fingers drift over his cheeks and mouth.

"You have such a rugged, handsome face and expressive eyes. I would love to try and capture your likeness on canvas."

"I'll be glad to sit for you and watch while you attempt to paint this mug. But, I warn you, if you capture the expression in my eyes while I'm looking at you, it may be an X-rated portrait."

Leah laughed, but then her face grew somber. "I still say we live in two different worlds. You have your work, and I have my business. As Kipling said, 'East is east, and west is west and never the twain shall meet.'"

"Yes, but, he also said, 'But there is neither East nor West….when two strong men stand face to face.'"

"You never cease to amaze me. I can't believe you know Kipling."

"I know a lot of things. I know we're two strong people, and we can overcome any obstacles. I'm not letting you out of my life."

They heard footsteps on the path and someone called out, "Nate, I hate to interrupt you, but could you come to my place and meet my son?" It was Ron Rhodes coming up the path from his cottage. "I tried to call you, but your phone went to voicemail. Ronnie and I were sitting on the deck, and I heard voices and thought it was you."

"Sure, Ron. Sorry you couldn't reach me—I left my phone on the charger. I'll be glad to come over. Is there a problem?"

"Ronnie's asking a lot of questions I can't answer, and he's pretty upset. Hello, Leah. I'm sorry to interrupt; would you like to come and meet my son?" Ron asked in an apologetic voice.

"Thanks Ron, but I think I'll call it a night. Maybe I can meet him at breakfast," Leah said, turning to go into the cottage.

"Goodnight, Leah. I'll see you tomorrow; don't forget what I told you," Nate said as he turned to go with Ron.

Nate and Ron walked back down the lane to Fernwood cottage. They entered the front door and went straight through the sitting room to the small deck. A young man who appeared to be around thirty stood up from one of the chairs. He was about six-foot-two with sandy colored hair. He was dressed comfortably in a pair of cargo shorts and a sweat shirt.

"Ronnie, this is Nate Parker, the FBI Agent I was telling you about," Ron said, introducing Nate to his son.

"I'm glad to meet you, but sure wish it was under different circumstances," Ronnie said, extending his hand.

Nate's hand was gripped in a firm handshake, and Ronnie looked at him with eyes so much like Sheila's it caused the hairs on the back of Nate's neck to prickle.

"I'm flying back to Texas with my mother's body day after tomorrow. Can you tell me if there's any chance of getting my father cleared to return for the funeral?"

"I'll do everything in my power to get him released from the restraining order before you leave," Nate assured him.

"Do you have any idea who did this to my mother? I can't believe someone could be so ruthless. She never hurt anyone. She was so kindhearted and loving." His voice broke, and he turned away to hide the tears that were ready to spill from his eyes.

"We're getting very close. There's a lot going on here at this quaint little inn. I know who stole the painting, and that was what brought us here originally. That's what Sheila was working on the day she was killed, but I think she found something else in the course of her investigation that caused someone to silence her."

"Oh, that reminds me," Ron interrupted. "I found something that may be important."

"What did you find?" Nate asked.

"When I was going through Sheila's things and boxing up her clothes, I ran across a sweater that had a slip of paper in the pocket. There were some scribbles on it, kind of like she was jotting down words or phrases she had run across. Maybe something she wanted to pursue more in-depth later."

"Do you still have it?"

"Yeah, I saved it for you. Maybe you can make some sense of it. I believe it's the sweater she was wearing the day she was killed. She was a neat freak, almost paranoid. I think she came back to the cottage when she left the Ledges. Removed her sweater and hung it up before her killer arrived."

Ron went inside the cottage and returned a few minutes later with a slip of paper which he handed to Nate. It looked like a sheet torn from a scratch pad, about five inches long and three inches wide. Nate unfolded it and looked at the words and phrases Sheila had jotted down. There was a phone number at the top of the note followed by what looked like the initials *L*, *W*, and then *C. W.*, followed by some dates from two years ago. There were more words and numbers Nate couldn't make out.

Ronnie had sat back down, and he looked from his father to Nate with a quizzical expression.

"You never mentioned anything to me about finding a note."

"I'm sorry son. We've been so busy since you arrived, I just now thought of it," Ron said in an apologetic voice. Turning to Nate, he asked, "What do you think? Can you make any sense of it? Do you think it's important?"

"This phone number looks very familiar. Did you check to see who it belongs to?"

"Yes, I did and it's the number for Rocky Ledge Inn."

"I guess that explains the *L.W.* Sheila probably called Liz Walker. I'll check with her tomorrow and see if she got a call from Sheila the day she was killed and what it was about," Nate said as he got up to leave.

Chapter 20

Leah left Nate and went straight to her room. She started to knock on Sandy's door, but changed her mind. She could talk to Sandy about most anything and usually felt better after unloading whatever was on her mind. But, she didn't really want to talk to anyone about Nate. She wanted to ponder over everything that was in her heart. She opened her door, switched on the light, and looked around. Since Sheila's murder, she never felt comfortable coming into her unlocked room alone. She pushed the bolt in place to lock the door, went into the bathroom, and checked behind the shower curtain before brushing her teeth. When Nate called, she'd just finished taking a bath and putting on a tee shirt to sleep in. She'd slipped on the jogging pants and jacket before going out to meet him. She now removed them and crawled into the bed wearing just the tee shirt and panties.

She punched the pillow under her head and determined to put negative thoughts out of her mind. She thought of the first time she'd seen Nate. It'd been less than a week since they'd met at the get acquainted reception, but it seemed she'd known him a lifetime. Her lips curved in a smile as she remembered his teasing remark as she was filling her plate and the exciting sensation she'd felt when their eyes met. She thought about how disappointed she'd been when she thought he and Becky were married.

I do trust him, and if he says we have a future together, then I must believe we do. But, he could have good intentions and things still not work out. There are so many differences in our lives, and we live so far apart. Would I be willing to give up everything and move to where he lives? Would he be willing to move to Tennessee? Seems there's so many obstacles to overcome, Leah thought, her mind in turmoil.

Okay, she told herself, *time to turn off the negative thoughts and worries. Just take it a day at a time.* She remembered Sandy's words of advice: *Follow your heart. That's my motto from now on. 'One day at a time' and 'follow your heart,'* she told herself as she snuggled down under the cover and let her body relax. As she drifted off to sleep, she was remembering the way Nate had looked at her and his devilish smile when she mentioned painting his portrait.

****

Friday morning was the last day of the workshop. They were to meet in the studio at the usual time of 9 AM. Andy would be critiquing one or two of each student's work from the past four days. The inn was throwing a farewell celebration lobster bake that afternoon.

Leah awoke early, dressed, and knocked on Sandy's door. They left for breakfast around 7:45, walking down the lane to the main house. Ron Rhodes and his son came out of Fernwood cottage just as they were passing by. Ron introduced his son to Leah and Sandy, and she and Sandy expressed their condolences. "How long will you be here?" Leah asked.

"I'm flying back tomorrow. I'm taking my mother back to be buried in the town where she grew up. I'm just hoping dad will be able to go with me."

Leah looked at his grief-stricken face and wished there was something she could say that would ease his pain. Having his mother murdered and his father accused of the crime had to be a devastating blow. Her heart went out to Ron also. His swollen, puffy eyes were filled with a dull, resigned look of sadness. The sudden and violent death of his wife and then to be accused of killing her had taken its toll on him. It was hard for Leah to imagine the pain he must be going through. *Probably like having someone cut your heart out with a dull knife*, she thought. She felt a rush of anger at the police for arresting him so quickly and not trying to track down the real killer. *God, I hope Nate can find that despicable person in time for Ron to return home to bury his wife.*

"I'm so terribly sorry," Leah said. Feeling the inadequacy of her words, she hugged both of them. "If there is anything I can do, please let me know. I'll be glad to help you pack Sheila's things or anything you think of that you may need."

"Thank you. That's very kind of you, but I think Dad's got everything pretty well packed up." Ron seemed too choked up to reply, so Leah just smiled and patted his arm as she and Sandy went on into the dining room.

Nate and Becky were sitting at a table with Andy and Calvin Ross. When Leah saw the group, she remembered that she had not told Nate about the conversation she'd overheard between Calvin and Andy when she was trapped in the back room of the studio. Becky knew all about it, so perhaps she'd brought him up to date.

Nate looked up and smiled when he saw Leah and Sandy. "Come on, we'll squeeze another chair in and make room for you to sit with us."

"That's okay. I've got to go to the studio and get everything ready for the critique," Andy said, rising from his seat and holding the chair for Leah to sit down.

"I promised I would help you, so the pretty red-haired lady can have my seat," Calvin said, getting up and holding the chair for Sandy.

"Well, thanks for relinquishing your chairs. I don't know when I've ever seen such chivalrous actions," Leah said with an exaggerated southern drawl.

Both men laughed as they left the room. Nate smiled at Leah, "Did you have a good night and pleasant dreams?"

"Yes, thanks. And you?" Leah asked in a formal tone, but with a twinkle in her eyes.

Her expression grew serious, and she glanced around the room. Turning to Nate, she asked in a lowered voice, "Did Becky tell you about the conversation I overheard while in the studio yesterday afternoon?"

"Darn it, I forgot to tell him. There was so much going on last night, and then I went to bed before he came back to the cottage."

"I'll walk up to your cottage with you and Sandy before you go to the studio, and you can tell me then. I feel like these walls have ears."

Becky and Nate were eating what appeared to be omelets with everything in the kitchen thrown in them. "What are you having? It sure looks yummy!" Leah said.

"It's the Farmhouse omelet. It comes with buttermilk biscuits, or you could have one of the other specials: bacon, leek quiche, or gluten-free banana-coconut pancakes with real maple syrup," Becky said. "Guaranteed to clog the old arteries."

"Ah, here comes another two pounds," Sandy moaned. "I've got to try those pancakes."

"I'll have the Farmhouse Omelet," Leah told the girl taking the orders. She helped herself to a cup of coffee and poured Sandy one from the carafe sitting on the table.

Ron and his son had sat down at the table where Louise and Joe Williams and Mattie Wainscot were sitting. *Good*, Leah thought. If anyone can help the Rhodes feel better, it was Mattie. She was one of the wisest and most compassionate people she had ever met. Leah was so amazed at the energy the nonagenarian displayed, not to mention the beautiful paintings she had produced this past week. As Leah was watching the group, Mattie leaned over and said something to Ron and patted his arm. Ron's eyes seemed to brighten for a moment, and a smile spread across his face. Leah's heart swelled at the sight and a sense of appreciation filled her with wonder at the older woman's ability to comfort and console. *She always knows the right thing to say, whatever the circumstances*, Leah thought.

The omelet and pancakes arrived, and she and Sandy dug in. "Yum! This is the best omelet I've ever put in my mouth!" Leah said, almost in a moan of ecstasy.

"Same for the pancakes," Sandy sighed in agreement. "I would marry Jason if I wasn't already married. He is the best chef I've ever known."

"He is an artist in the kitchen," Leah agreed.

"I'm going to see if Liz is in the office and have a word with her while you two finish eating," Nate said, getting up from his chair and heading out of the room.

Liz and Joan Hataway were both in the office. Joan was on the computer, and Liz was looking through some papers. "Good morning, ladies. Sorry for interrupting, but I was wondering if you could clear something up for me," Nate said, looking directly at Liz.

"What do you need?" Liz asked in a not too friendly voice.

"Did Sheila Rhodes call the office the day she was murdered?" he asked bluntly, without preamble, while watching Liz's face closely. A flicker of surprise, maybe even alarm, came and went so quickly that Nate wasn't sure it was even there. *Maybe she was just surprised that he would ask such a question,* Nate thought, *or maybe it was something else.*

"No, not to my knowledge. She didn't call while I was in the office. Do you remember her calling?" she asked, turning to Joan.

"Let me think…that was last Monday. No, I was only here until 9:00 that morning. That was the day I had a doctor's appointment at 10:30 in Portland. The doctor had an emergency, and they kept me waiting for hours. I was so aggravated by the time I got back that afternoon, I was in no condition to work. You remember, Liz, how disgruntled I was?"

"Well, sorry to have bothered you," Nate said, turning to go. "Oh, by the way Liz, will the cottages be available for the people who have to remain in the area until the murder investigation is complete, per police instructions? I know we're supposed to check out tomorrow, but some of us will have to stay longer. We'll need to look for other accommodations if the cottages aren't available."

"This is the last workshop of the season, so the cottages will be available. I normally close everything up and return to New York by the middle of October, but I'll keep the help on as long as they're needed."

"Thanks, that's good to know," Nate said, turning to leave.

"Don't forget, there's a wedding on the grounds here tomorrow afternoon at four," Liz reminded him as he left.

Nate went back into the dining room just as the three women were preparing to leave. The four of them left the house, and Becky went in the direction of Rosewood for a pit stop before going to the studio. Nate, Sandy, and Leah walked up the lane to Broadview cottage. Leah told Nate about the conversation she'd overheard between Andy and Calvin Ross and also about them encountering Calvin leaving the Porters' when they returned from the jail.

"I'm not surprised to hear about Ross's shady dealings, and I already suspected him of being here to buy the stolen Van Eyck. I'm glad to know Andy would not help him with his scam. Unless I've been badly fooled, Andy is a genuinely nice person," Nate said, with a thoughtful expression.

"Well, apparently, Andy and Calvin were both very poor growing up. Seems Calvin started down the wrong path at an early age, and Andy seems to be very worried about him. He said he's always loved Calvin like a brother," Leah said.

They reached Broadview, and Leah and Sandy went inside. Nate told Leah he would see her later that day. She asked if he would make it to the lobster bake, and he told her he had to run over to the fishing village and, depending on what he found there, he may have to go to Portland. "I'll get back, if at all possible. I would love to spend a leisurely afternoon with you. If I don't make it, may I have a raincheck?" Nate asked.

"You've got a raincheck that's good for a leisurely afternoon, and to sweeten the deal, one for a leisurely evening."'

"Ma'am, you sure make it mighty hard for a man to go off to fight the bad guys," Nate said in a bad imitation of John Wayne.

"Go, you're wasting time dillydallying around here. Catch the bad guys and hurry back," Leah said with a laugh, giving Nate a little shove.

****

Harry had emailed Nate earlier, assuring him an agent should be at the inn by noon. He said the agent's name was Harold Ransom and that he had given him Nate's telephone number. Harry had included the new agent's phone number and description. "He's forty-two, five-foot-eleven, medium build, going bald with a fringe of black hair, wears glasses, looks like an accountant. But don't let looks fool you—he's tough as nails," Harry had assured him.

Based on Harry's promise that the new agent would arrive soon, Nate headed for the Northpoint Post Office. As he entered the outskirts of the village, he saw an American flag flying in the breeze atop a tall metal pole. *That has to be the post office*, he thought as he drew near. He pulled into the parking area in front of the one-story brick building, got out of his Cherokee, and went inside. A postal clerk stood behind one of two windows. She was busy serving a customer. The other window was vacant. Nate waited until the customer had finished their business and left before he stepped up to the clerk, who was wearing a name tag identifying her as Sandra Jones. She greeted him with a pleasant good morning. She appeared to be around 50 with short, light-brown hair, streaked with gray and curled in a tight perm. She had on round glasses that echoed the shape of her face and a slightly plump body. "How may I help you, sir?"

"I'd like to speak with the post master," Nate said.

"I'm sorry; he isn't in. Is there anything I could help you with?"

Nate took out his credentials, flipped it open, and showed it to her. "I need to know if Susan and/or Wayne Porter have a post office box here."

The clerk studied Nate's credentials, looked at his picture, then looked at him. Satisfied that he was legitimate, she went to the computer and punched several keys. "No, nothing comes up for either of those names."

"They may have used an alias. Nate reached in his pocket and took out the picture of the Porters. "Do you recognize them?"

Sandra took the picture and studied it, "They look familiar, but I'm not sure," she said with a perplexed frown.

"I have a number—53967. Could be the box number or a code number for the box. Could you check to see if it belongs to anyone?"

Sandra Jones punched some more keys on the computer. "Ah, here it is. The box is registered to William and Sue Ponders. I remember them now. They seemed like a nice couple, didn't talk much, but were very polite."

"Sandra, I don't have a search warrant, but would you mind looking in their P.O. box and tell me if there's anything in there. It's very important. If it's what I think, I may have to get a warrant for search and seizure. But, if the box is empty…."

"I understand. Hold on a second." Sandra disappeared and then came out a door at the end of the counter. She was carrying a key, and she went around the corner to an offset section of the room. Two of the walls were covered with postal boxes. She looked at the numbers, selected one, and inserted the key. Pulling the door open, she reached inside and pulled out what looked like a yellow slip of paper. She put it back into the box after studying it for a few seconds. "It says we're holding a package for them."

"Sandra, you don't know how much I appreciate your help. If you would do one more little thing, I will put you in my will," Nate said with a grin.

"What would that be?"

"Would you just get the package and let me see what size and shape it is?"

"Sure, I don't see what harm that would do," Sandra said, going behind the counter and disappearing in the back again. She reappeared a few minutes later, holding a tube-shaped package about twenty inches long.

"I'd hug you if you weren't behind that counter!" Nate could hardly contain his excitement. At last, he was positive the stolen Van Eyck was in that package. "Will you be open tomorrow?"

"Yes, but only until noon," Sandra answered, with a big grin on her round face.

"I have a feeling the Porters will be coming today or tomorrow to retrieve that package, and I want whoever is working here to be sure they get it."

"I'll be here the rest of today and tomorrow."

"Good, just give them the package. Don't act any differently than you normally would," Nate cautioned her.

"Don't worry, I won't give anything away. Wow, this is the most excitement I've had in the fifteen years I've been working here. Working in a post office in a small village is not the most thrilling line of work."

Nate smiled and gave her a thumbs up as he left the building. He got in his car and punched in Harry's number.

"Well, what's the latest? Have you and Harold connected yet?" Harry asked, by way of answering his phone.

"Not yet, but I hit pay dirt. I'm parked outside the post office in Northpoint. The clerk working here today was very helpful. The Porters do have a box under the name of William and Sue Ponders. The clerk checked the contents of the box for me, and it contained a slip of paper saying the post office is holding a package for them. She showed me the package, and it's a tube about twenty inches long."

"Bingo," Harry said. "What do you plan to do next?"

"I'm going to have Harold keep the post office under surveillance the rest of today. If the Porters don't show up, I'll have him come back tomorrow and Monday if necessary. I'm sure Calvin Ross is here to buy the stolen art. He was overheard telling Barzetti that he's here to buy the Van Eyck and was seen coming out of the Porters' apartment last night."

"Good luck. Let me know if you need anything else. I'm always at your disposal."

"There *is* one other thing you can do."

"And, what might that be?" Harry asked.

"Check the Rocky Ledge Inn's phone records for last Monday."

"Wasn't that the day Sheila Rhodes was murdered?"

"That's right. I'm pretty sure she called the inn before she was murdered, but Joan was out of the office, and Liz says she didn't call."

"I've got Sheila's number, so give me a couple of hours, and I'll let you know what I find."

"Oh, there is one more thing I need you to do. I know it's not going to be easy, but I also know you've got contacts everywhere and can often do the impossible."

"Uh, I don't like the sound of this."

"I need you to check Calvin Ross's bank account. See if he's made any large withdrawals lately."

"You *do* ask for the impossible, but I'll see what I can do."

"Thanks partner," Nate said, disconnecting the call and punching in Harold's number.

"This is Ransom. Where are you? I'm almost to the inn," the agent said, answering his phone.

"I'm in front of the post office at Northpoint. I'll move my car to the parking area next to the little country grocery store. I'm in a Jeep Cherokee."

"Ten-four—I'll see you in about fifteen minutes."

'Ten-four', Nate thought, *is this guy for real?*

Nate moved his SUV to the parking area across from the store. He hoped Harold would be able to keep a low profile. He was afraid he would stick out like a sore thumb in this little fishing village. True to his word, Harold Ransom pulled into the parking lot about fifteen minutes after Nate had spoken to him. He was driving a Chevrolet Silverado pickup that looked to be about ten years old. He opened the driver's door, got out, and headed over to where Nate was parked. Nate couldn't believe his eyes when Harold walked up to his window and asked if he was Nate Parker. Nate was expecting someone in a suit and tie, driving a black sedan. The pickup had mud on it and Harold had on a pair of dirty athletic shoes, faded, ragged looking jeans, a plaid, flannel shirt and a ball cap.

"You look less like an FBI agent than anyone I've ever seen," Nate said, acknowledging his identity.

"Well, that's the idea, isn't it?" Harold said with a wink. "Actually," he continued, "I've got a cabin on a lake a few miles north of Portland, and I was up there fishing. I'm supposed to be on vacation this week. But, when Harry called, I just dropped my fishing pole and came running."

"Harry and I both thank you," Nate said, getting out of his vehicle and shaking Harold's hand. He decided he liked Harold Ransom and would bet money he was an excellent agent. Nate told him about his plan to watch the post office to see if the Porters showed up to collect their package. If they did, he'd follow them to see if they made contact with someone to make an exchange. If so, he'd arrest all of them and take them in for questioning.

"Ten-four," he said again, and Nate tried to keep a straight face as he took out the picture of the Porters and gave it to Harold.

"I may get a little fishing in since the post office is in plain view from that dock. You think I'll be too conspicuous if I do that?"

"I think you'll fit right in," Nate assured him.

Nate climbed into the Cherokee and headed back to the inn. He was about halfway there when he realized there was a car almost on his rear bumper. He hadn't paid much attention to it until he slowed down to let it pass and it continued to tailgate him. He took a good look in his rear-view mirrors and realized it was a black Hummer with two men in the front seat. They sped up about that time and bumped into the rear of the Cherokee. Nate stepped on the accelerator and quickly put some distance between them, but the

Hummer was soon right on his tail again. Nate dialed 911 and told the operator the situation and to notify the police. He gave her his location and, about that time, the Hummer rammed him again. Nate thought about his options. The Hummer was much larger and heavier than his SUV. It was more powerful and faster, and they were on a two-lane country highway. He had no options, other than to try and keep that damn tank of a vehicle off his rear end. He floor-boarded the gas pedal again and shot ahead, but only for a few seconds. The Hummer was coming up on his rear again. But instead of bumping him, it pulled into the other lane and pulled along beside him. He knew they were going to try to run him off the highway. There was a deep ditch on the side of the road, and they were approaching a sharp curve. Nate slammed on his brakes and the Hummer shot ahead just as a massive garbage truck rounded the curve. It smashed into the Hummer head on and tossed it to the opposite side of the road. The front end of the Hummer was crumpled like a tin can. The garbage truck came to a halt about fifteen feet from Nate's Cherokee. The front end was heavily damaged. The grill was crushed, the headlights broken, and the bumper was smashed into the front wheels. Two men climbed out of the cab of the truck and walked over to where Nate was standing, his phone to his ear, talking to someone with 911. "I called a few minutes ago for you to send the police…better send an ambulance too."

Chapter 21

Jason finished his breakfast duties at nine that Friday morning, went to his house, and changed into jeans and a red and white striped, pull-over shirt. He grabbed his windbreaker from the hook by the door as he left his house. The air was so clear and fresh, cleansed by yesterday's rain with a feeling of autumn in the air. Jason took a deep breath and stood for a moment, taking in the beauty of his surroundings. *Such a lovely, serene setting. Hard to believe so much evil has taken place here,* Jason thought, as he hurried to his SUV.

He got into the Explorer, started the engine, and headed through the resort and on to the highway. There was no need to rush this time, so it took him about thirty minutes to arrive at the veterinarian clinic. The girl behind the counter greeted him with a smile, "I bet I know who you would like to see."

"Yeah, how's Sasha doing?" Jason asked.

"She's doing great, other than missing you. Come on, I'll take you back to see her." The girl opened the half door and came around to open the door to the waiting room. Jason followed her to the back of the building where there were several large enclosed spaces. They reminded Jason of small cells, but they were all very clean with a thick, comfortable-looking bed and a container of water. A drain in the center of the floor in each one expedited the cleaning process. A worker was hosing down one of the empty spaces. The subtle scent of a cleaning agent filled the air with a pleasant aroma. It gave Jason a comforting feeling, seeing how well-maintained the area was. Each unit had a hinged door in the back, so the animal could go outside to a fenced run.

Sasha must have heard or sensed Jason's presence. She was standing with her tail wagging. She began whining and barking, her whole body wiggling so hard Jason feared she would reopen her wound. The girl opened the door, and Jason knelt down to hug and pet Sasha, trying to sooth and calm her excitement. "Is Doctor Cox in?" he asked the girl between petting Sasha and telling her what a good dog she was.

"Yes, I'm in. Sometimes I feel like I live here," Doctor Cox said, coming down the hall.

"How's Sasha doing? Do you think it would be safe for her to go home today? "

"Sasha's doing well and healing nicely. But, I think it would be a good idea to leave her one more day, unless you have a way of keeping her confined and quiet."

"No, I don't have anything, and if I tried to keep her in a crate, she would get even more agitated. I know she misses me, but she'll stay quieter here. Would it be okay to pick her up tomorrow morning?"

"Tomorrow's Saturday, so we'll be open until noon. You can get her any time before then."

Jason petted and hugged Sasha once more and told her he would be back tomorrow to take her home. She seemed to understand what he was saying and went and laid down on her bed. She thumped her tail several times, as if to say, "I'll be here waiting for you."

Jason left the clinic, got into his SUV, and started the motor. He shifted into reverse and was about to pull out of the parking lot when his phone rang. He took it out of his pocket and looked at the caller ID. It said unknown caller. Jason pushed the on button and said, "Hello?"

"Hi Jason," Linda said. "How's everything going there?"

"Oh, hi, Linda. Everything's about the same. I'm just leaving the clinic. Sasha's doing great, and I'll take her home tomorrow. Can you tell me where you are? Are you ok?"

"I'm fine physically, but I'm so lonely I could die. I want to come back to the inn and help find out who's behind everything that's happened. This is supposed to be a safe phone, but I was told not to tell anyone where I am, that way no one can be forced to tell. Do you know how John Phelps is doing; any leads on who tried to kill him?"

"That dumb sheriff arrested Nate and charged him with attempted murder. Seems Phelps pointed his finger at Nate and named him as his attacker. Harry pulled some strings and got the charges dropped, and they had to release him."

"Jason, I miss you and Sasha. I hope she'll be ok."

"She'll be fine. You know she really got attached to you. Hopefully we'll get this mess cleared up soon, and you can return to your normal life."

"It's going to take a long time for me to look like my old self again," Linda laughed.

"I kind of like your new look. Everyone tried real hard to turn you into a boy. But, it's hard to hide your femininity."

"I've been thinking a lot about what I might have said that made the killer think I knew more than I did," Linda said on a more serious note.

"Did you come up with anything?"

"Yes, I think someone who heard me talking about murder made to look like an accident has killed before, and they thought I was referring to them. The problem is, I think most everyone at the reception heard at least part of my conversation, so it could be anyone."

"What about the art forgery story you discussed?"

"I just mentioned the documentary I'd seen about the famous art forger and jokingly said Andy could probably out paint him any day. That would make Andy the strongest suspect for kidnapping me, and that just doesn't hold water."

"I agree with that. If only there was a way to get Phelps to tell who tried to kill him. He's a fool to accuse Nate of attacking him. If he thinks the killer will let him off, he's a walking dead man when he gets out of the hospital."

"You be very careful Jason. Whoever is behind this is a desperate person, and desperate people will eliminate anyone who gets in their way," Linda warned.

"I'm always careful. That's how I've survived as long as I have," Jason answered. "By the way, Linda, I miss you too."

****

The two men driving the garbage truck seemed to be unscratched, but when they started walking toward Nate, one of them was limping, and the other had his hand on his chest. "Are you guys okay?" Nate asked, as they approached him.

"What the hell were those crazy fools doing driving on the wrong side of the road? I came around the corner and—WHAM—there they were! I hardly had time to put on my brakes," the big guy who'd gotten out on the driver's side said in a shaky voice. "I was thrown against the steering wheel, hitting my chest, and I may have whiplash—nothing else seems to be wrong. I think Lester's leg got hit by something falling from the dash. Good thing we had our seatbelts fastened."

Lester limped over to Nate and asked, "Did you know those guys? Were you playing chicken or something?"

"Hardly," Nate replied. "They were trying to run me off the road! They bumped my rear end several times, and I called 911 and asked them to send the police. I think I hear them coming now," he said, as the sound of approaching sirens filled the air.

Two patrol cars pulled up behind the garbage truck, and an officer got out of each vehicle.

"What's going on here? Which one of you called 911 and reported someone tailing you and bumping into your rear-end?" the first officer asked.

"I did. My name's Nate Parker, and I'm a special agent with the FBI," Nate said, showing the officer his credentials.

"Yeah, I've heard of you. You're staying over at the inn where the woman was murdered. I'm Lieutenant Daniels, and this is Sergeant Blanco. It's kind of hard to tell the way that Hummer's smashed up, but it looks like there's two guys in there who won't be going anywhere except to the morgue. Did you happen to know them?"

"Not personally, but we've had some encounters. They trashed another agent's house and shot his dog yesterday. We called it in, and they were picked up. Jason Atwell, the other agent, identified them, and they were arrested last night. Guess they got bailed out this morning."

"Oh yeah, we know what you're talking about. Someone did post bond and get them out this morning."

"Do you happen to know who it was?"

"No, an attorney took care of all the legal work, and the bail was paid through a corporation."

"Do you remember the attorney's name and the name of the corporation?"

"The attorney was Michael Fisk. He's defended more crooks than you can shake a stick at."

The ambulance arrived about that time, and two medics got out. They went over to the Hummer and came back in a few minutes. "Those guys don't need our help. It's pretty bad. We'll probably have to cut them out. There's no big rush though—they're both dead as door nails."

Nate's phone beeped an incoming text. He took it out of his pocket and looked at the screen. It was from Harry. He opened the text and read the lengthy message.

"I checked the Rocky Ledge Inn phone records for last Monday. There were quite a few calls. A couple of calls were made from the inn, one at 9:41 to a plumber in Bath, and one at 10:05 to a dentist in Portland. Sheila Rhodes called at 1:19, and the call lasted six minutes. There was a call from the Brunswick Health Clinic at 1:55, lasting thirty seconds, probably went to voicemail. There was a call made from the inn at 2:10 to a number belonging to a burner. It lasted eight minutes. The same number called back at 3:40, and the call lasted ten minutes. I can't determine who the number belongs to, but I called it, and it went directly to voicemail. Calvin Ross transferred $500,000 from his account at the Regional Commerce National Bank in New York to a numbered account in the Cayman Islands day before yesterday."

So, Liz either lied or didn't remember, or someone else answered when Sheila called the inn. Ross was pretty slick; this would definitely make it more difficult to prove he was buying the stolen painting. *We'll just have to catch him with it in his possession*, Nate thought.

"If you guys are through with me, I need to run," Nate said to the officers.

"You can go, but, if you don't mind running by our office in Portland to give your statement and sign the report, we would appreciate it."

"No problem. I'll be glad to help anyway I can. Just give me a call when it's ready." He handed Lieutenant Daniels his card and turned to the two men from the garbage truck. "You guys better get these medics to take you to the hospital and get checked out. You may have injuries you're not aware of yet."

Nate climbed into the Cherokee and eased past the wrecked truck and headed for the inn. His phone buzzed an incoming call. Nate glanced at the caller ID and put it on speaker and answered,

"Hey Jay. What's up?"

"I just left the veterinarian clinic, checking on Sasha."

"How's she doing?"

"Great! I hated to leave her, but Dr. Cox thought it would be best to let her stay there another night. How'd it go at the post office? Did the new agent find you okay?"

"Yeah, he got there, and he's fishing from the dock where he can keep an eye on the post office and blend in with the locals."

"I'm headed to the inn now; can you meet me there in about fifteen minutes?" Nate asked.

"Sure, what's on your mind?"

"Well, to start with, we don't have to worry about the two thugs who trashed your house and shot Sasha." Nate went on to tell Jason about the men tailgating him and trying to run him off the road and the final consequences. "We've got to find out who hired them and, when we do, we'll have our killer. He or she is getting desperate, and I've got a theory that things are going to come together this afternoon. Everyone will be at the lobster bake. I think the Porters will attempt to pick up their package and pass it on to their buyer while everyone is occupied. I've got an idea on how to flush out the killer, too. But, I really need to talk to John Phelps. I need to make a phone call to the sheriff...I'll get back to you."

Nate saw a convenience store at the intersection he was approaching and pulled into the parking lot. He dialed the county sheriff's office and asked to speak to Sheriff McMullen.

"Whom should I say is calling?" came the bored voice of a female deputy.

"This is Nate Parker. I need to talk to the sheriff."

"Sheriff McMullen is busy at the moment; may I ask what this is in regard to?"

"Yes, you may ask, but no, I can't tell you. It's personal. Just tell the sheriff that Nate Parker is calling. I'm sure he'll want to talk to me."

After a moment of waiting, Nate could hear the phone exchanging hands. "Okay, Parker," came the disgruntled voice of sheriff McMullen, "this better be good. What the hell do you want?"

"Sheriff, let's quit playing games. You and I both know I didn't attack John Phelps. He's scared shitless, and he's covering for the person who tried to kill him. The fool doesn't realize he's a dead man if he doesn't speak up and tell the truth."

"And, we both know your fingerprints are on the weapon, and that pretty well corroborates Phelps's accusations."

"Come on, sheriff. You know how my prints got there. Look, I'm not trying to horn in on anything here. I just want to get to the truth, and I want to talk to Phelps."

"Are you crazy? There's no way Phelps will talk to you. Besides you're not allowed to go near him."

"I want a deputy, or you if you prefer, to be there when I talk to him. Then there'll be no question of me doing anything illegal or unethical."

"You're nuts! No way that's gonna happen."

"Okay, Sheriff. I know you want to find out who the killer is as badly as I do, so I'll make a deal with you. I believe if I talk to John Phelps, I can get him to reveal who really attacked him. If we know that, we'll know who the killer is, and you can arrest him or her and take all the credit."

"I don't know what you're up to, Parker. You're blowing smoke up my ass for some reason."

"Look Sheriff, I'm an FBI agent here to do a job. I was sent here to catch an art thief ,and we'll probably arrest them this afternoon. Sheila was an agent assisting with the investigation, and I want to find her killer. It's as simple as that."

"Okay, you have five minutes. Deputy Earl Watson's at the hospital now. I'll call and let him know you're coming and to let you have five minutes with Phelps and to stay with you the whole time you're there."

"Thanks, Sheriff. You're all heart," Nate said, disconnecting the call and punching in Jason's number.

"I'm about three miles from the inn. Meet me there, and we'll go to the hospital in one vehicle," Nate said when Jason answered.

"Did you get it cleared with the sheriff?"

"We've got five minutes to try and pry something out of Phelps, and that's with Deputy Watson hovering over us."

****

Back at the studio, all the students, minus Linda, were gathered for the critique. This was the culmination of their week's work, the time for praise and criticism, a lift up or a letdown. Some of them were thinking, *Why do I waste my time? I can't paint. I need to do something more productive, maybe take up knitting.* Others were eagerly awaiting the time when their paintings would be critiqued, expecting to be praised and thinking, *My work is so much better than what these amateurs have done.*

Andy picked up the first painting leaning against the wall and placed it on an easel. It was the sunset seascape Becky had painted the first day of the workshop.

"Becky's done a great job of capturing the essence of a rocky coast line with the sun either rising or setting on a tranquil bay. The colors are magnificent! Not too bright or garish, but subtle with soft lavenders and grays that really make the splashes of bright color sing. Good job, Becky! The only thing that might improve such an excellent painting would be to add a few highlights on the wet rocks." Andy picked up another painting and put it on the easel, but Leah was thinking about what she had overheard between him and Calvin Ross. She watched him going through the motions of the critique, but her mind kept wandering to the conversation she'd heard. *He's such a wonderful artist and teacher. He's patient and understanding and seems to genuinely care about the people he teaches. It's hard to believe he's a close friend of Calvin Ross. They are complete opposites.* Leah forced her mind back to the present as Andy completed the critique and picked up another painting.

"This was painted by our own Grandma Moses, Mattie Wainscot," Andy said, as he placed the painting on the easel. "I guess you all know, Mattie's 99 years young, and she only started painting when she was 93. She had to give up tennis and decided to start painting and prove her art teacher wrong when he told her she'd never make an artist. Well, Mattie, I think you did a terrific job of proving him wrong. You do have a folk style, but, other than starting to paint late in life, that's where the resemblance to Anna Mary Robertson Moses ends. Your painting is full of energy and life, the colors sparkle, and you have your own individual technique. Your paintings evoke an emotion that people can relate to. Happiness, sadness, nostalgia…they make the viewer want to come back and look again, to try and figure out what's so enticing. The only other comments I have about your work is, keep painting. You should have a one-woman show, and your art should be in a gallery."

Everyone in the room applauded, and Mattie, who was usually so feisty and glib, was speechless as tears filled her eyes. She rallied, swiped the tears away, and stood up. "Thank you, young man. You are an incredible instructor; it's been an honor to be in your workshop class. You're all a great bunch of gals," she said, looking around at the other students. It's been a hoot painting and spending time with you. I hope we all meet again next year, hopefully at another Andrew Barzetti workshop right here at Rocky Ledge Inn.

"Sounds good to me," said one of the students.

"Great idea!" echoed another.

"We'll celebrate your turning 100, and I'll paint your portrait," promised Andy.

"Eat your hearts out, girls. They'll probably put it on the cover of Cosmo," Mattie laughed.

Leah laughed with the others and felt a glow of pride for Mattie as Andy picked up the next painting and continued with the critique.

****

Nate and Jason arrived at the hospital a little before noon. They stopped at the information booth, and Nate asked the person behind the desk what room John Phelps was in.

"I'm sorry, sir, I'm not allowed to give out that information," said a white-haired lady wearing a nametag that said Ida Carver.

Nate took out his FBI credentials, flipped it open, and put it in front of her. "Ms. Carver, please call Deputy Watson and tell him we're here," Nate said in an authoritative tone.

Ida pushed the glasses up from the tip of her nose as she studied Nate's picture on his ID and then looked back at him. "He's been moved to a private room on the 6th floor. He's in number 613. The elevators are around the corner to the right."

"Thank you, ma'am," Nate said, smiling politely.

When Nate and Jason arrived at room 613, they found Deputy Earl Watson sitting outside the door looking through a magazine with a picture of a muscle-bound weight lifter on the cover.

He greeted Nate and Jason, "Sorry, but only one of you is allowed to go into the room."

"That's okay," Nate said, "only one of us needs to go into the room and that would be me. Just don't start timing me until I'm inside talking to Phelps."

Nate opened the door to John's room and walked over to the bed. John was still hooked up to an IV and a heart monitor. The monitor began beeping a little faster when he recognized Nate.

"What the hell! Why are you here, Parker?"

"You know why I'm here. Have you thought about what's going to happen when you get out of the hospital? The person who really attacked you will see to it that you meet with a convenient accident."

"Are you threating me? You gonna try and kill me again?" John sneered at Nate.

"What do you hope to gain by accusing me of something you know I didn't do? I realize you're a low-life scumbag with the morals of an alley cat, but you're signing your death warrant by protecting Sheila's killer."

John's eyes popped open wide with surprise. "What's this got to do with Sheila Rhodes? You stabbed me because you're jealous of my attentions to Leah Dawson."

"And you're full of shit. Leah wouldn't have you if you spit out diamonds every time you opened your mouth. So, let's get to the *real* reason you're protecting the killer. Did you have a visit? Maybe I should ask Earl if he allowed anyone to see you since you've been here? Were you threatened? Did the killer promise you safety if you named me as your attacker?"

Earl was standing at the foot of the bed, listening to everything Nate and Phelps were saying, and he remembered the one time he allowed someone to stay with John while he fetched some coffee. *Could it be possible? Nah, no way,* he thought. But a sliver of doubt remained in his mind. *No way in hell I'll ever admit to letting anyone see Phelps while I went for coffee,* he thought as he watched the two men.

"Do you honestly believe the killer will let you live?" Nate continued. "You know who killed Sheila Rhodes, and I'd bet my last dollar you tried blackmail. Your only hope for safety is to reveal the person who attacked you, because I'm going to find Sheila's killer, and you better hope I do before you're out of this hospital without a guard watching over you 24/7. I'll have you charged with aiding and abetting the murderer of Sheila Rhodes, someone who has killed before and will have no problem killing again."

Nate leaned forward and whispered something. It was too low for the deputy to understand but loud enough for John Phelps to hear. John's eyes widened with surprise. "What do you mean, killed before?"

"Phelps, for someone who is cunning and clever, you can sure be dense. I know you know who killed Sheila, and now you know that I know. So, stop and use your little green cells and ask yourself, why would that person kill Sheila? What would be the motive?"

John opened his mouth to say something and then closed it again. He stared at Nate for a moment with unasked questions in his eyes. before he said in a strained voice, "Get out, and leave me alone."

Nate walked out of the room with Earl Watson behind him. "What'd you say to him when you whispered? It sure got him upset."

"I told him he needed a shave."

He and Jason bid the deputy a good day and walked down the hall. By the time they were on the elevator, John Phelps was calling for Earl. He entered John's room and asked, "What is it Phelps? Something wrong?"

"Yeah, I want you to call my attorney. He's located in Memphis; his name is Michael Bailey. I don't have his number, but you can Google it. Tell him to get someone in this area. I'm sure he has contacts all over the country. I want an attorney here ASAP."

Chapter 22

Harold had been fishing, or at least giving the appearance of fishing, for over two hours. He got up from his place at the edge of the pier and stowed his fishing gear in the tool box in the bed of his truck. He went into the little grocery store and ordered a ham sandwich, keeping his eye on the window where he could see the front of the post office. He got a bottle of tea from the cooler and a package of Sun chips, paid for his food, and walked across the street to the small park. He sat at one of the concrete park tables, unwrapped his sandwich, and took a big bite. *Yum, this ham sandwich is delicious. It's better than what some of those fancy bistros turn out*, he thought, munching on the sandwich and chips.

Harold finished the food, gathered up the paper wrapper and potato chip bag, and threw them in a nearby trash container. He sat back down and continued drinking his Snapple tea. The air was so clean and clear, the sky such a deep blue, it made Harold think of an old song lyric, Bluer than Blue. But, he didn't feel sad. In fact, he'd never felt more relaxed and in tune with nature. The bay was a deeper reflection of the sky, with the sun casting diamond sparkles across each ripple. Colorful buoys were interspersed among the moored boats. He watched two men in a small dinghy coming across the water from an island that appeared to be about a mile out in the bay.

I could get used to this kind of life, Harold was thinking, as he watched the boat bouncing over the swells and heading for the pier.

A white Escalade pulled into a parking space in front of the post office, and a man and woman got out. *Uh oh,* Harold thought, as he pulled the photo of Susan and Wayne Porter from his pocket. "Yep, that's them," Harold mumbled to himself, as he tossed the empty tea bottle in the trash and headed for his truck. Harold sat in his truck and waited. In about ten minutes, Susan and Wayne came out of the post office, and Susan was carrying a tube-shaped package. Harold was expecting the couple to get into their vehicle and drive off. To his surprise, they continued past the Escalade and started to the other side of the street. The two men he'd just seen come across the bay in the dinghy met them about half way. The four of them walked over to the sidewalk and seemed to be having a serious discussion. Harold took out his phone, snapped a picture of the four people, and texted it to Nate, along with the message, *Got complications, need back up. Get here ASAP.*

He headed across the street where Susan and Wayne Porter were talking to the two men. They seemed to be unaware of him as he started walking in their direction. Probably because he looked so much like a local. *That's good,* he thought. It gave him the advantage of surprise.

Susan handed the package to one of the men, and the man handed her an envelope in exchange. The men started walking back towards the pier. Harold was only a few yards from them when he called out, "Wait just a minute, guys. I'd like to ask you something."

The two men stopped, turned, and looked at him. The one who took the package from Susan looked to be about 40. He had a receding hairline, and his remaining hair was threaded with gray.

He was about the same height as Harold but beefier with muscles going to flab. The other man appeared to be a few years younger, maybe 35, tall and slender, with wavy blond hair and a mouth that seemed almost too small for his face. "What can I do for you, fella?" the beefy man asked.

"You can show me what you have in that package," Harold said, pulling out his ID and showing it to the men.

"You're crazy. Why should I show you what's in this package?"

"Because I'm with the FBI, and I believe what you're holding in your hand is stolen property."

"Do you have a warrant? I don't think you have the right to walk up to me out on a public street and demand to see what I have in a package, FBI or not," Beefy said with a belligerent scowl.

"What's your name, and where do you live? I'm taking you in for questioning, and I'll have a warrant by the time we get to headquarters. If you've got nothing to hide, you'll be better off to cooperate now or...."

"Oh, hell, Herb. Show him what you have," Susan interrupted. "He's my brother-in law," she said to Harold, "and he has a summer home over there on Cranberry Island. I bought a painting for him while we were in Paris and had it shipped here so he could meet us and pick it up." She rummaged in her purse and came out with a receipt.

Harold looked at the piece of paper. It was all in French, but he could make out enough to see it was from a gallery in Paris for a painting that cost 2,200 euros. Susan opened the envelope in her hand and pulled out a check and handed it to Harold. It was made out to Susan Porter for $2,500 and signed by Herbert Wolfe. Herb opened the package, reached inside, and pulled out something wrapped in tissue paper. He removed the tissue and unrolled a canvas. It was a still-life oil painting signed by Jean Paul Albinet. "Believe it or not, I'm a collector, and Albinet's work is going to be very valuable one day."

Harold felt like a complete fool. "Sorry folks, my mistake. I apologize for any inconvenience."

Susan snatched the check and receipt out of Harold's hand and turned on her heel, and she and Wayne went across the street in a huff.

"Sorry guys," Harold apologized again and went back to his truck. He climbed into the cab and sat there, pondering what had just happened. He sent a text to Nate and told him not to worry about coming. There was no need for back up; there was no stolen art in the package.

Susan and Wayne backed out of the parking space and drove away. Harold continued to sit and think about what had just happened. He knew Nate was convinced the stolen painting was in the package, and Calvin Ross would be collecting it from the Porters. Based on everything Nate had told him, it seemed like the most likely scenario. Why hide the post office key if it was so innocuous? He Googled Jean Paul Albinet, French artist, and nothing came up under that name. Hmm, if he was such an up and coming artist that people would be collecting his work, then Google should know about him.

Nate drove up about that time and parked beside Harold. "Sorry, I was almost here when I got your last message. So exactly what happened?" Harold explained what had just transpired and added his concerns and suspicions.

"Have the guys left yet?" Nate asked.

"No, they went into the grocery store and haven't come out yet."

"I think we need to talk to them some more. We'll catch them when they leave."

Nate and Harold went across the street and sat on one of the benches in front of the store. Herb and his friend came out about five minutes later. They were carrying what appeared to be lunch. The two men continued across the street to the park table and sat down.

Nate and Harold followed them across the street. "Hey, guys," Nate said "my friend tells me you're an art collector. Do you happen to know Calvin Ross? He owns a gallery in New York."

Nate watched the men's expressions closely, and he detected a flicker of alarm in Herb's eyes, but he recovered quickly, and answered curtly, "I've heard of him but don't care much for his type of art."

"Well, I'm a real enthusiast when it comes to French painters. Could I see your Albinet?"

"We're trying to eat right now," Herb said, opening the sack and removing sandwiches, chips, and drinks.

"I really would like to see what you have in that package," Nate said, indicating the tube-shaped bundle.

"Look, we've already shown the painting to your friend, so why don't you two buzz off and go find some real thieves," Herb said, biting into his sandwich and shoving some chips in his mouth. He turned to his friend, ignoring Nate and said, "What you think, Tony? Is this not the best Ruben sandwich you've ever eaten?"

"I'll have to admit, you didn't exaggerate. It's mouthwatering delicious."

Nate pulled out his phone and punched in some numbers. The men continued to extol the virtues of the food as if he were not standing there. "Hey, Harry, I need you to get me a search and seizure warrant to the Portland field office, ASAP. Harold and I will be bringing in two men for questioning in connection with the stolen Van Eyck." Nate listened for a few minutes to Harry and then replied, "I know you can, that's why I call you. You always come through with the impossible. Thanks, partner."

Nate clicked the phone off and turned to Herb and Tony. "Just because I'm such a nice guy, I'm going to let you finish your lunch, and then we're all going to take a ride down to the Portland office. He pulled out his credentials, flipped them open, and stuck them in Herb's face. He said, "I'm placing you under arrest for questioning regarding possession of what we believe is stolen property."

"Hey, this is an Albinet painting my sister-in-law bought for me in Paris. I have a copy of the receipt right here."

"Well, now, if that's true, you don't have anything to worry about, but we're going to have a real close look at your Albinet when we get to Portland. You have the right to an attorney..." he said, as he began reading them their Miranda rights.

****

Earl Watson found John Phelps's Memphis attorney's phone number. He dialed the number, but he handed the phone to John and let him do the talking. John must have sounded really desperate, because Michael Bailey contacted a friend of his in Portland and arranged to have an attorney there within an hour.

A very attractive young lady arrived around 1:30 that afternoon and announced that she was Carol Ellis with the firm of Jones and Ashcroft. She was tall, slender, and well endowed in all the right places. She had shoulder-length blond hair and brown eyes.

"You don't look old enough to be an attorney," Phelps said.

"I am 25, I'm a paralegal and will be an attorney as soon as I pass the bar exam. I understand you want a document prepared. I am fully qualified to prepare any kind of legal document you wish to make, but if you prefer to get someone else, the decision is yours."

"Okay, okay, I just want to be sure it's legal, and it'll need to be notarized."

"No problem, I'm a notary public—I'll just need some form of ID from you, and the deputy can witness it."

"All right, I'm going to make a statement. I want it notarized and delivered to the police department. And, I want it given to the Captain. Can you handle that?"

"Piece of cake, Mr. Phelps," Carol said, pulling some papers from her brief case.

****

While Herb and Tony finished their lunch, Nate sent a text to Leah explaining a little of what had happened. He apologized for not making it to the lobster bake but said he should be back before dinner. He asked if he could take her to dinner and then to the dance that the wedding was hosting. Leah read his text and felt a stab of disappointment that he wouldn't be able to join them for the lobster bake. But she felt a thrill of excitement at the prospect of having dinner with him and then dancing. The first real date for them. Her heart did little flip flops when she thought about being in his arms again. She'd been feeling a little low, not knowing where he was or how long he would be gone, but now the sun seemed to be shining brighter, and she felt hungry. The food suddenly looked and smelled delicious.

She was sitting at a table with Sandy, Becky, Jason, and Mattie Wainscot. Mattie looked at her and smiled, "You look like a sixteen-year-old who just got her first valentine from the boy of her dreams."

"Guess I kind of feel that way," Leah said.

"I bet we all know who that text was from," Sandy said with a chuckle. "So where is tall, dark, and handsome?"

Jason's phone dinged an incoming text about that time. He pulled it from his pocket and read the message. "Looks like he's on his way to Portland to question a couple of guys and look at the package they got from the Porters. He wants me to find the Porters and take them to Portland for questioning too."

"Maybe we can help you locate them," Becky said, looking around the grounds.

Tables had been set up on the front lawn overlooking the bay. Two men dressed in white aprons and chef's hats were cooking lobsters and grilling marinated chicken. Large bowls of potato salad, slaw, and corn on the cob were arranged on a table. A brisk breeze blowing in from the bay made white caps on the waves splashing against the rocky coast and causing a chill in the air.

A large gust of wind blew the paper tablecloth up at the corner of the table where the group was sitting, knocking over a bottle of ketchup. The lid was open and when it hit the table, it squirted out and covered the front of Leah's white pullover top with red splotches. Leah grabbed some napkins and tried to wipe the ketchup off, but it only smeared and made it worse.

"Oh, for crying out loud! This is one of my favorite tops. I better run up to my room and change into something else and rinse this out before it dries."

Leah went to her room, pulled the top over her head, and took it into the bathroom where she rinsed out the stains and hung it over the shower curtain rod to dry. She opened the drawer in the chest where her tops were neatly folded. She chose a lightweight, red, turtleneck sweater and slipped it over her head. She went back into the bathroom and picked up her hair brush. She stood in front of the mirror, staring at her reflection. Her dark brown shoulder-length hair was mussed a little, but not badly. It was thick, shiny, and healthy—she had a great hair dresser. He'd trim and shape her hair about every six weeks, and all she had to do was shampoo and blow dry. *Wish I could control my emotions as easily as I control my hair*, she thought as she ran the brush over the flyaway strands. Her reflection grinned back at her. "You fool," it seemed to say. "He makes you feel eighteen again. Everyone needs someone, and he's the one you need." *Yes*, she thought, *I need him; I want to wake up every morning and see his face. I want to share my thoughts and feelings with him and hear his thoughts and feelings, share good times and bad times. I was foolish enough to think my career, my home, and my friends were all I needed. I never realized what was missing until I met this man who turned my world upside down. My life would be an empty shell without him.*

But now, her contentious reflection was frowning. "What if you're not the one he genuinely longs for, what if you're just a stand in for his dead wife?"

"No, I don't believe that." Leah slammed the brush down, startled that she had spoken out loud.

She left her room and hurried down the lane. Liz was standing on the back patio when she passed the main house. "Hi, Leah! You sure are in a hurry. Is something wrong?"

"No, some ketchup spilled on my top, and I went to my room to change. I wanted to rinse out the stains before they had a chance to dry."

"Do you have time to come up and look at my apartment? I'm thinking about redoing my bedroom and bath, maybe add a deck off the bedroom. I understand you're an award-winning interior designer, and I'd really appreciate your opinion."

"Well, if it doesn't take long. Sandy and Becky are waiting for me to go for a walk. By the way, I want to thank you for the farewell lobster bake. You really went all out."

"I probably enjoy it as much as the guests. The only sad note, it means the week has come to an end, and everyone will be leaving."

They went inside the house and up the stairs that were in the downstairs sitting room. Leah was pleasantly surprised when they entered Liz's apartment. The door at the top of the stairs opened into a large living area. A fireplace was in the center of the long wall opposite the entrance, with windows on each side. The windows gave a panoramic view of the grounds and the bay. There was an offset at the end of the room containing a compact, efficient kitchen and dining area. The walls were painted a soft beige, and the hardwood floors looked like solid red oak to Leah's trained eye. A sofa was facing the fireplace with chairs on each side, and a glass coffee table was sitting on a Nami Tabriz Persian rug in front of the sofa. There were several antique pieces that Leah felt would be worth several hundred thousand, and the rug probably cost between fifty and sixty thousand.

"You're either an excellent decorator, or you had a professional do this room. It's absolutely stunning," Leah said, "and it's so warm and cozy. I'm sure you love spending time here."

"Yes," Liz answered, "I do love this place. I had it professionally decorated last year, but the decorator worked closely with me and fine-tuned my suggestions."

"I can't imagine any changes you could possibly want if the rest of your apartment is as beautiful as this room."

"Come, I'll show you what I have in mind," Liz said, leading Leah to the bedroom area.

They walked down a short hall where small bedrooms were located on both the right and the left. Farther down, there was a bathroom on the right that opened into the small bedroom and also a large bedroom that extended across the end of the building. "I'd like to convert this small bedroom into a salon bath and walk-in closet. I'd also like to put French doors and a deck off the south wall of the bedroom."

Leah walked through the bathroom, into the bedroom, and back into the bath. There was an old-fashioned claw foot tub, a pedestal sink, and a toilet. "This must be the original bathroom," Leah said.

"Yes, this is where my father slipped and fell. He hit his head on the tub and was killed instantly. It holds very unpleasant memories for me."

They were interrupted by a knock on the door. "Please excuse me, I'll be right back. Go ahead and look around to see what ideas you can come up with," Liz said, as she headed down the hall to answer the door.

Leah heard a murmur of voices and then silence. She expected Liz to reappear any moment. After waiting what seemed like an hour, but was probably no more than five minutes, she started down the hall, calling Liz's name. She was met at the living room door by a man. He was not much taller than Leah but probably weighed close to 300 pounds.

"Excuse me, I'm looking for Liz," Leah said, feeling very confused.

"Liz is not available," the man said in a gruff voice.

"Well, if you'll excuse me, I've got some people waiting for me," Leah said, as she tried to walk around the man. He was standing in the doorway, and he didn't move.

"Sorry, but, you're not going anywhere, little lady," the man said, grabbing Leah's arm.

Leah didn't move; she stood still and weighed her options. She'd had several self-defense classes, and she tried to remember what to do when faced by someone who weighed almost three times as much as you. *Don't show fear,* she thought. *Use your fingers to gouge the eyes, knee them in the groin, and elbow them in the throat.* Leah looked at the mountain of a man with a shaved head and small beady eyes that reminded her of a snake and wondered if he would even feel it if she attempted any of those defense moves. One thing for sure, she wouldn't know if she didn't try. She let her body go limp and looked at him with fear filled eyes. "Please don't hurt me," she pleaded.

His grip relaxed a little and his lips curved more into a sneer than a smile, "Don't worry, little lady, you'll..."

Leah spun around and brought her knee up with every ounce of strength she could summon, smashing it into his groin.

He roared like a lion, but he released her arm and bent double, holding his family jewels. Leah sprinted for the door. She grabbed the door knob and pulled. The door was locked with a dead bolt. Leah looked and saw a key hanging on a hook beside the door. She grabbed it and fumbled until she finally got it into the keyhole. The man was still roaring behind her and the sound was getting closer. Leah turned the key and pulled. A big hand reached in front of her, slammed the door shut, and turned the key. He grabbed her hair and jerked her head back, putting the point of a knife against her throat. "You're going to pay for that little trick, bitch."

****

John Phelps instructed Carol Ellis to close the door to his room. She did as he asked, then pulled a chair up closer to his bed.

"I'm going to tell you in my own words what I want written down, then you can rewrite it in a more professional form. After I sign it and you notarize it, I want you to take it straight to the police."

"Okay, Mister Phelps. I'm ready anytime," Carol said, flipping open a legal pad and reaching for a pen.

"First thing I want to say is that Nate Parker didn't attack me. The person who tried to kill me is the same one who murdered Sheila Rhodes." He went on to explain that he had actually seen the killer going into the cottage with Sheila Rhodes the afternoon she was murdered. He had also seen the killer come out of the cottage, looking disheveled. He'd gone to the cottage to check on Sheila and had found a blood-covered watch lying on the sitting room floor. He'd seen that watch before; it belonged to the person who'd just fled from the cottage. He had put the watch in a safe place and confronted the person. Of course, they'd denied it, scoffing and calling him a fool.

Then, the attempt had been made on his life. The killer came to the hospital and threatened him again but promised if he named Parker as his attacker, everything would be okay. He then revealed the name of the killer.

"Is that all Mister Phelps?" Carol asked.

"Just be sure no one sees this until you get it to the police—my life won't be worth two cents if it falls into the wrong hands."

Chapter 23

The man's face was so close Leah could smell the onions he'd had for lunch. He kept the knife pressed against the side of her neck.

Snake Eyes, as Leah now thought of him, pulled a roll of duct tape from his pocket and gave her a shove. "Get moving," he said while pushing her in the direction of the bedrooms. When they reached the end of the hall, he pushed her into the bathroom. "Okay, get your ass in the bathtub." Leah hesitated, certain the man was going to kill her.

"I said, move it, bitch," he pressed the knife deeper, pricking the skin on her neck. Leah felt a sharp stinging sensation as a trickle of blood ran down her throat and into the red turtleneck she had so recently put on.

"Why are you doing this?" she asked. "Liz will come back and call the police."

"Liz won't be coming back, and no one's calling the police. Shut your damn mouth and get in the tub, now!" he ordered. "Wait," Snake Eyes said, "give me your cell phone first."

Leah reached into her pocket and pulled out her phone. Snake Eyes grabbed it, took the batteries out, and threw it down on the tile floor. He then stomped it until it was smashed flat as a pancake. "Now get," he said.

Leah climbed into the tub, and he handed her the duct tape.

"Put your feet together and wrap the tape around your ankles. Wrap them good, or I may have to do a little carving on your pretty face."

Leah pulled the end of the duct tape roll loose and wrapped it around her ankles several times. "Okay, hold the end out," Snake Eyes said, leaning over and quickly slicing through the tape, leaving about six inches. "Alright, stick the rest of the tape down, then put your hands behind your back." Leah pressed the rest of the tape around her legs but deftly folded one corner under so it wouldn't stick. It was on the back part of her ankles, out of his view. She put her hands behind her back.

"If you think I'm going to put this knife down to tape up your hands," Snake Eyes said, "you've got another thought coming. Take that roll and start it around one of your wrists."

Leah did as instructed, and he took the roll in his free hand to continue wrapping it around her wrist until she was tightly bound. He then cut off a strip about six inches long and placed it across her mouth. "Now, don't worry. I won't leave you long enough for you to start missing me. I'll be back after dark and you and I will go bye-bye."

He locked the bathroom door on the bedroom side and tried to lock the door going into the hall, but it had an old-fashioned bolt lock that only worked on the bathroom side. "Oh well, you're not going anywhere. We'll have some fun when I get back," he said, chuckling to himself as he left the room. He picked up the remnants of her phone and took it with him. Leah heard the front door open and close, and then she heard a key turning in the lock.

****

Herb and Tony took their time eating their sandwiches. As they finally finished and gathered up their clutter to toss into the trashcan, Nate started in Herb's direction with handcuffs, while Harold headed towards Tony with cuffs. Herb was wearing a loose-fitting shirt that hung out over his cargo shorts, and he reached behind his back, his hand coming out with a Glock.

"Don't come any closer," he said, pointing the weapon at Nate's chest. "Okay, Tony, take the package and head for the boat," Herb said, getting to his feet and backing away from Nate. Harold was reaching behind his back for his weapon when Herb quickly turned in his direction, "Keep your hands where I can see them!"

Nate assessed the situation quickly. Tony was running across the street with the painting, and Herb was standing at the edge of the park about thirty feet from him. He and Harold were standing at least twenty feet apart. There was no way Herb could shoot both of them unless he was an expert marksman. Nate's gut told him he wasn't. Harold looked at Nate and a silent signal passed between them. Nate drew his weapon and Harold ducked at the same time. Herb fired the Glock when he saw the look pass between the two men, but the bullet went over Harold's head. Nate fired about the same time, and the bullet hit Herb in his right shoulder. The Glock dropped to the ground and so did Herb. Tony stopped mid-stride and spun around.

"Keep going!" Herb screamed at him. 'They won't shoot an unarmed man!"

"Stop!" Nate commanded, "don't listen to your friend; I will shoot you if you don't halt right now." Tony stopped running and raised his hands. Nate dialed 911 and called for an ambulance.

Harold cuffed Tony and put him in his pickup. People had come out of the nearby houses, and a crowd of about fifteen curious onlookers had gathered outside the store. Harold took out his ID and held it up for everyone to see. "FBI," he said, "please go back to your homes or go inside the store. An ambulance is on the way; everything's under control."

Nate had removed Herb's shirt and was applying pressure to the wound. "Any of you know these two guys?" he asked the crowd in general. Several of the people said they'd seen them around the village but didn't know who they were. They figured they were some of the summer people who stay on the island.

The ambulance arrived, and Nate handcuffed Herb's good arm to the bar on the gurney. "I'll follow this one to the hospital, and you take the other one to the field office along with the painting. We should have a warrant by the time you get there."

"I texted Harry a picture I took of those two when they were talking to the Porters, and he said he'd get back to us as soon as possible."

"Good work, Harold. Glad you thought to take a picture of them. Harry will find out who they are and any other information that's available and probably some more," Nate said.

****

Jason walked up to Rosewood cottage, went inside and knocked on the Porter's door. Their Escalade wasn't in the parking lot, but he was hoping to find at least one of them at home. No one answered his knock. He knocked again and then opened the door. The apartment had a deserted feeling. He went into the bedroom, but it also looked unoccupied. No clothes were scattered about, no personal items in view. He opened the closet door and stared into emptiness. He went back into the bedroom and looked though all the drawers. There was no evidence that anyone had ever occupied the apartment. Jason left and walked up to the main house. He went into the office. Joan Hataway was sitting at the desk working on the computer.

"Is Liz here?" Jason asked.

Joan looked up from the computer, "No, I haven't seen her in the last hour or two. Guess she's busy with the lobster bake."

"Can you tell me if the Porters have checked out?"

Joan got out of the program she was working on and punched several keys. "No, they're registered to stay until Sunday."

"Thanks, Joan," Jason said. He left the main house and went back to the table where Sandy and Becky were sitting. They were talking to Mattie Wainscot, all of them expressing concern about Leah.

"She's been gone over thirty minutes. How long does it take to change a top?" Sandy said. "I'm going to walk up to our cottage and see if she's okay."

"I'll go with you," Becky said

Sandy and Becky walked up the lane to Broadview cottage, went inside and back to Leah's room. Sandy opened the door, and she and Becky went inside, calling Leah's name. They found the wet top hanging over the shower curtain rod that Leah had rinsed earlier. "I don't understand," Sandy said. "Leah said she was going to go change her top and would be right back."

"Do you suppose she went for a walk, hoping to see the Porters?" Becky said.

"No, that's not like Leah. Let's find Jason and see if he has any ideas."

They met Jason on the path as they went around the main house in the direction of the side lawn. He had a distracted, concerned expression on his face. "The Porters have cleared out; all their possessions are gone from their cottage, and no one seems to remember when they were last seen."

"Well, here's something else to add to your worries," Sandy said. "Leah has disappeared too. Do you suppose the Porters took her with them?"

"I think they were already gone when Leah went to her room. They may have loaded everything before they went to the Northpoint post office. If that's the case, they've had almost an hour head start."

"What can we do?" Becky asked

"I've put out an APB with a description of them and their car. The FBI and the police will be on alert. They'll cover all the airports in a hundred-mile radius, plus trains and buses. Unless they've holed up somewhere in this area, I don't think they'll get far."

"What about Nate? Do you know where he is? Do you think you should tell him Leah is missing?" Sandy said.

"Nate should be in Portland by now. He and the other agent, Harold, are taking the two guys who picked up the package in for questioning. I think we should scout around before we tell Nate. He's got enough to worry about right now, and there's nothing he can do until he gets back, which should be within an hour or so."

****

Harold arrived at the Portland headquarters with Tony and the package. Tony was fingerprinted, photographed, and put in a holding cell. The search warrant was delivered via a local judge, and the package was opened and examined. The stolen Van Eyck was found glued to the back of the Albinet.

While in route to the hospital, Nate received a text from Harry. He gave Nate the low down on Herb and Tony. They both had a rap sheet as long as their arms. Drug dealing, racketeering, you name it, and they were lovers, been together five years. "Good grief, to each his own," Nate thought.

He followed the ambulance to the Maine Medical Center in Portland, parked his SUV, and went into the ER. "Seems I can't stay away from this place," Nate thought, remembering his and Jason's visit with John Phelps earlier that morning.

A policeman met Nate in the ER, "I've been sent to relieve you. I or another officer will be here with the prisoner until he is able to be taken into custody and questioned."

"That's good to know," Nate said. "Things go much smoother when the police and the FBI work together."

Nate waited until a doctor had looked at Herb. "He's very lucky," the doctor said. "The bullet went through the meaty area above his armpit, no damage to nerves or bone. He'll probably only need to stay overnight. He's lost some blood, but he'll be okay with antibiotics and rest."

"He's going to have lots of rest where he's going," Nate said.

He left the hospital and went to headquarters. Harold met him when he entered the building.

"Well, what's the latest with our boy Tony?" Nate asked.

"He's singing like a bird," Harold said. "The Porters hired them to pick up the painting and deliver it to Calvin Ross at his studio in New York. He's pretty sure Ross has already paid the Porters, and he was supposed to give him and Herb a big tip when they got the painting safely to him."

"The Porters sure went to some elaborate measures to throw us off track," Nate said.

Nate's phone beeped an incoming text. He looked at the message and frowned. "What now?" Harold said.

"A message from Jason. Seems the Porters have packed up everything and taken to the hills. He's put out an APB, and the police and FBI are searching for them."

****

Leah sat in the tub and listened. She heard no sound other than the ticking of a grandfather clock. She struggled to her feet and sat on the edge of the bathtub, then swung her legs over the side and onto the floor. She tottered to the floor and sat down, then rolled over on her stomach. Bending her knees and bringing her feet up, she was able to reach down and grab the piece of duct tape that didn't stick. Pulling and unwinding it, she soon had the tape unwound from her ankles, making her able to stand up and walk now. She had to find something to get the tape off her wrists. She walked into the kitchen and looked around. She saw a wooden butcher block of knives, but they were sitting on the counter top, too far back for her to reach. Turning around backwards, she started opening drawers. The third one had several sharp paring knives ranging in size from about six inches to ten inches. She felt around until she got the longest one in her hand and held it by the handle with the blade positioned where she could move it up and down in a sawing motion. After what seemed like an eternity, the knife cut through the tape and her hands were free. She jerked the tape from her mouth and debated on screaming but then had second thoughts. The sound might bring the wrong people. She tried the door, but, as she had expected, it was locked and no key in sight. *People usually keep a spare somewhere in a safe place,* she thought. *All I have to do is stay calm and find it.*

She searched the drawers and cupboards in the kitchen with no luck. In the process of searching the living room, she found a rope ladder. She remembered something about some kind of code specifying that all apartments have more than one exit. *This must be the second exit since there's only one door in Liz's apartment. Guess I can climb out one of the windows if I don't find a key.* She headed down the hall to the master bedroom and began searching the bureau drawers.

No luck. There were several purses in the closet, and she searched each one, but none contained a key. She also saw several jackets and sweaters, and she began searching through the pockets. In one of the sweaters, she felt a familiar object. She pulled it out and looked with disbelief at what was in her hand. It was a cell phone. Her heart began to pound—maybe she would be able to call Nate or Jason, if she could remember their numbers. Their numbers had been programmed in her phone, so there was no need to memorize them. She pushed the on button, but nothing happened. *Oh hell, its dead.* She remembered seeing what looked like some charger cables in one of the drawers. *Now which drawer were they in?* She began rummaging through dresser and bureau drawers and found the chargers in the dresser. There were three chargers, and the second one fit the phone perfectly. She went into the bathroom and found an outlet and plugged the charger in. It took about five minutes for the phone to come to life. *Now what? I can't even remember Sandy's number.* The phone was an iPhone. She punched the phone app, and the contact list popped up. There were many names she didn't recognize, but there were also several that she did. She stared, disbelieving at Nate's, Jason's and Ron Rhodes numbers.

What was Liz doing with a cell phone with those numbers programmed in it? She considered the possibilities and could come up with no answer. *Liz should have everyone's number in the files in the office. There should be no reason she'd have them in her personal contact list.* Leah brought up Nate's name and punched the number. It began ringing and Nate answered on the second ring. "Who the hell is this?"

"It's me," Leah stammered.

"Leah, where are you? Whose phone is this?"

Leah's knees went weak, and her heart began to pound. Words spilled from her mouth so fast Nate had to tell her to slow down. When she finally managed to explain everything that had happened, Nate was filled with alarm and frustration.

"Leah, call Jason, and get out of there as fast as you can. Be sure and keep that phone with you. Is there not another door or way to get out?"

Leah told him about the rope ladder.

"Use it. Find a window that's hidden from view if you can. Leah, you've got to get out of there. Call Jason now and call me back as soon as you can."

Leah disconnected, pulled up Jason's name, and punched his number. He answered on the first ring with the same tone of disbelief and alarm. She explained the situation, and he told her to check the windows and find one with the least amount of exposure. "We've been looking for you. Sandy is worried sick!" Jason said. "I'll be watching for you, so hurry. Get out of there!"

Leah ran from window to window, checking the locations. She found one in the offset end of the living room where the dining area was located. It had no screen, and there were hooks on which the ladder could be secured. There was another window in the bedroom with the same set-up, no screen and hooks. The bedroom window looked out on the side where the lane led to Broadview cottage. The one in the dining area was on the bay side, and there was a tree that partially hid the window from casual observation. Leah raised the window and looked down. She felt a wave of dizziness—the ground looked so far away. Suddenly, she was ten years old and her cousin was daring her to climb the black walnut tree in her back yard.

You're a yellow bellied, chicken livered coward, Donna Jean said, as she grabbed the lowest limb of the tree and pulled herself up. She reached for the next branch and went up higher, laughing and chanting, *Leeaah's a fraidy cat, Leeaah's a fraidy cat. Leah can't climb a tree. She's so scared, she'll probably pee.* Leah had gritted her teeth and reached for the lowest limb and pulled herself up. She didn't look down but kept going, determined to show Donna Jean she wasn't afraid. But she was. She went up higher and higher until the limbs grew too small to support her weight. She stopped in a fork of the tree branches and wrapped her arms around the limb. Donna Jean had climbed down and was standing on the ground looking up at her. *I'm sorry, Leah, I didn't mean what I said, you shouldn't have gone up that high… come on back down.* But Leah couldn't move. She could feel gravity pulling at her, and when she tried to look down, the whole world spun like she was on a merry-go-round. But, she wouldn't cry. If she fell to her death, she wouldn't cry. She'd never let Donna Jean see how terrified she was. Leah clung to the limb and tried to ease her foot down to the next branch, but it only encountered air. She heard the sound of pounding feet and thought Donna Jean was probably running away so she wouldn't witness Leah plunge to her death. But the next thing she knew, her father was climbing the tree and telling her everything was okay; all she had to do was back down, and he would see that her foot was planted firmly on each limb, and he would be right below her. Leah didn't know if the tree climbing episode had brought on her acrophobia or if that was the reason she'd been so terrified when she'd climbed the tree. She'd had several sessions of therapy because there were times when working on a project, she'd needed to use a ladder. She'd finally reached the point where she could climb a small step ladder without breaking into a cold sweat, but she still feared high places.

She grabbed the rope ladder and put one end over the hooks, then threw it out the window. It fell within two feet of the ground. *I can do this. I've got to do this. It's my only way out.* Leah kept repeating this like a mantra. She looked down at the ground below. Jason was standing there. He beckoned for her to hurry.

Leah climbed into the window and, once again as when she was ten years old, she gritted her teeth, backed out of the window, and put her foot on the first rung. Slowly, with a pounding heart, she backed down the ladder. Jason was standing there waiting when she reached the last rung. He reached out and lifted her down to the ground. Sandy was right behind him. She grabbed Leah in a bear hug. "I was so worried about you," she said, her eyes brimming with tears that threatened to spill over and run down her cheeks.

Leah hugged Sandy back, "I'm okay now."

"We've got to get you to a safe place, and the closest place I can think of is Nate and Becky's cottage. I think we can get you over there without anyone seeing you," Jason said.

Rosewood cottage was around a bend and a short way down the path from the main house. Jason got on one side of Leah, and with Sandy and Becky on the other, they walked around the path and went into Rosewood cottage.

"I don't know who to trust, so we're not taking any chances. You're staying out of sight until we catch the guy who tied you up. Nate's on his way back from Portland, and he's going to be waiting for him when he comes back for you," Jason said.

"How's he going to get in?" Leah asked.

"By the same way you got out—those ladders are designed to hold a lot of weight, so let's hope no one sees it before he gets back and into Liz's apartment."

"Now," Jason said, "we've got a lot to talk about."

****

Nate switched on his hazard lights, and drove like a mad man. He had to get back to the Inn before the man came back for Leah. He felt so helpless and frustrated. He would like to kill the scum bag who hurt and upset Leah, but he had to keep his head and get some answers to the questions that were filling his mind. He thought about when Leah had called him and he'd seen the name on the caller ID. He couldn't believe his eyes, but it all made sense now. That phone would be the proof he needed to expose the one he'd suspected of the murder of Sheila Rhodes.

Chapter 24

On John Phelps's instructions, Carol Ellis delivered the document she'd prepared to the Portland State Police Headquarters. She'd arrived at an opportune time. The Captain was not busy and was in a good frame of mind. His wife had just called and informed him the dinner party he was dreading had been cancelled. Carol was shown right in to the Captain's private office. She waited while Captain Jenkins opened the envelope and pulled out the papers. He placed a pair of reading glasses on his nose and began scrutinizing the statement.

"This is very interesting, young lady. I'll email it to the state's attorney and we'll go from there."

"Please sir," Carol said, "this is very important. Mr. Phelps hired my firm to see that his confession was duly processed and the alleged killer arrested for questioning. He says the person he named in that document came to the hospital and threatened him if he didn't accuse Nate Parker of attacking and trying to kill him. He fears for his life once he's released from the hospital."

"Okay, Ms. Ellis. I'll see what I can do. But, first, I'm sending an officer to the hospital to question John Phelps about this accusation. The person he's accusing is a highly respected and well thought of individual in this area. Certainly not someone I would think of as any kind of threat to such a man."

****

Susan and Wayne Porter were cruising down Interstate 95, maintaining the speed limit, maybe four or five miles over because that's what most people did. They definitely did not want to do anything that would draw attention. They had just passed a sign saying the Portsmouth exit was five miles ahead when a state trooper cruiser appeared in the rearview mirror. Susan had seen the patrol car parked on the side of the interstate, and she watched as it pulled out and gathered speed. "He's coming after us," she said to Wayne. "Maybe you should speed up and try to outrun him."

"Are you nuts? That's the last thing I should do. He would definitely pursue us then and have every cop in the state looking for us."

"I knew Nate Parker was trouble the first time we met. We should've just forgotten about everything and gone back to New York. We could've picked up the painting another time," Susan said in a whining voice.

"Would you just shut up? It's a moot point now, water under the bridge, nothing we can do to change things. That trooper is getting awfully close. Oh, hell," he said as the flashing lights came on along with a siren.

Wayne pulled onto the shoulder of the interstate. The trooper pulled up behind him and sat in his car a few minutes before getting out. A second patrol car pulled up right behind the first trooper.

"Probably running our license number through the system. Damn, I didn't see that other squad car. Where the hell did it come from? They must be sending out the whole fucking department." Wayne waited for the policeman to get out of his car. He rolled his window down as the trooper walked up to the Escalade. "What's up, officer? I wasn't speeding, was I?" Wayne asked, with a big smile on his face.

The officer ignored his question. "Are you Wayne and Susan Porter?" he asked.

"Why, yes, we're the Porters. Is there a problem?"

"You're under arrest. Both of you get out of the car with your hands in the air."

Wayne started to open his door and get out when Susan pulled a revolver from her purse, pointed it at the trooper and pulled the trigger. The bullet hit him on the right side of his chest. He staggered back and fell to the ground. The second officer drew his weapon and began running toward the Escalade.

"Get out of here!" Susan shouted at Wayne, both their ears still ringing from the loud gunshot. Wayne had not turned off the motor, and he floor-boarded the accelerator. The tires spun, then gained traction. The car shot onto the interstate.

"You idiot! What were you thinking? Every cop in the state will be looking for us!" Wayne yelled.

"I'm not going to jail," Susan said. "Take the Portsmouth exit. We'll get rid of the car and take a taxi to the Portland airport."

The back-up officer, Pete Fletcher, fired at the Escalade as it sped away, but it was already out of range. He was shouting into his Bluetooth as he ran, "Gun shots! Officer down!"

The trooper Susan had shot was not only Pete's partner, he was his friend. His name was Dave Gibson, and he and Pete had worked together five years. Pete was thinking of Dave's wife and two small children and saying a prayer as he examined his partner and looked for blood, trying to determine his injuries. He placed his finger on Dave's neck and felt for his pulse. It was beating strongly but very rapidly. Dave moaned and opened his eyes. He gasped and began taking deep breaths. "She hit my Kevlar vest—it knocked the wind out of me, and I think I have some broken ribs," he said.

"Hang in there, buddy. Help is on the way," Pete said.

Susan and Wayne took the Portsmouth exit and drove into town. They parked their car in a Walmart parking lot, got out, and opened the trunk. Susan rummaged in her luggage, pulled out a gray wig and slipped it on. She then found an oversized dress and slid it over the outfit she was wearing. She wrapped the revolver in a blouse and put it in her luggage. Wayne was going through his bag, and he pulled out a ball cap, put it on his head, and slipped into a pair of coveralls. They got their luggage out of the trunk, locked the car and walked around to the front of the store. Wayne googled taxis and called for one to pick them up. The taxi arrived about ten minutes later. They climbed into the back seat and instructed the driver to take them to the Portland airport.

****

It was almost five by the time Nate turned into the lane that led to Rosewood Cottage. He parked the Cherokee, got out, and hurried inside. Entering the apartment, he found Leah and Sandy sitting on the sofa with Jason and Becky in chairs facing them.

"Thank God you're here! I was afraid you wouldn't get back in time," Leah said.

Nate crossed the room and pulled her into his arms. He held her for a few minutes without saying anything. His thoughts swirled. He was seeing all the possibilities of what could have happened, what could still happen. He knew he cared deeply for Leah, but he didn't realize how important she was to him until this afternoon. When she called him from that phone, it had been such a shock seeing the name Sheila Rhodes on his caller ID. When he answered and heard Leah's voice, he'd thought his heart would stop beating. He knew something was terribly wrong.

"Thank God you got out of that apartment," Nate said, pushing a strand of Leah's hair behind her ear and trailing his hand down her cheek. "You're not only beautiful, you're smart and brave. Just a few of the things I love about you."

Leah leaned her head back and looked into Nate's eyes. Could it be true? Did he really love her?

"Don't look so surprised," Nate said, "I care about you, not Jackie, not Jackie's ghost. You, Leah Dawson, you're a unique individual….."

Jason coughed and cleared his throat. "I hate to interrupt this touching scene, but we've got plans to make."

"I've already made plans. I'm going up that rope ladder and be in the bathroom when that low-life scumbag returns. I'd like to kill him with a slow torturous death, but he's just a hired muscle. I want to get to the true culprit, the one behind all this madness."

"I think all the workshop people left this afternoon after the lobster bake. Well, other than us, and Mattie Wainscot. Her granddaughter's picking her up tomorrow. Andy's staying through tomorrow also. Ron Rhodes would love to leave with his son if he could get the murder charges against him dropped," Leah said.

"We don't know what's going to happen, but hopefully the real murderer will be behind bars by tomorrow morning," Nate said. Nate's phone beeped an incoming text. He pulled it from his pocket and read the message. "It's form Harry. The Porters were stopped on Interstate 95; Susan shot the officer, and they got away. The Bureau has agents watching all the airports, train stations, and bus depots. They have pictures of Susan from the surveillance video showing her in several of her disguises. Hopefully, they'll be apprehended soon."

"Jason, how about walking over to the main house with me and keeping a look-out while I climb up into Liz's apartment and get the rope ladder out of sight," Nate said. He pulled Leah back into his arms and whispered into her ear, "Kiss me for good luck. Not that I need it; I'm already the luckiest man in the world."

Leah put her hands behind his neck and drew his head down until it was level with hers. She kissed his mouth and brushed his hair back from his forehead. He held her for a few moments, then pulled away and grinned, "Good thing there's a room full of people here. Otherwise, I'd never be able to leave and go after the bad guys to fight for truth and justice and the American way."

"Go, Superman," Leah said with a laugh. "Round up the bad guys and hurry back—we're supposed to have a date tonight."

"I'll have to find a white horse, so I can sweep you off your feet and ride off into the sunset with you."

She touched her finger to her mouth, then placed it on Nate's lips. "Be careful, and hurry back to me."

"It'll take more than a short, fat slime-ball to keep me away," he said, then turned and motioned to Jason.

Nate and Jason left Rosewood cottage, and walked down the path to the main house. They rounded the curve and headed to the side of the building where the ladder was still hanging from the window.

"That thing looks sort of flimsy," Nate said, looking at the ladder and up at the window.

"Yeah, but, it's stronger than it looks. It'll support your two hundred plus pounds," Jason said with a grin.

Nate grabbed the bottom rung and placed his foot on it. He reached for a higher rung and started climbing. The ladder swayed and bumped the building a few times, but it held, and Nate was soon in Liz's apartment. He pulled the ladder in and waved at Jason before closing the window. He rolled the ladder up and put it in a nearby chest, then scanned the room to be sure nothing was out of place. He found the tape Leah had removed from her ankles and wrists lying on the floor. There was a paring knife on the counter top in the kitchen. Nate figured Leah had used it to free her hands. He put it back in a drawer and gathered up the duct tape and put it in the trashcan under the kitchen counter. *Quite a layout Liz's got here,* he thought as he continued looking through the apartment. Nate figured he had at least twenty or thirty minutes before dark, when 'Fatso' was supposed to return. Leah had described him as about her height and probably 300 pounds. That meant he may be very strong, depending if he worked out regularly or not. Nate was counting on him being clumsy. He'd seen a few heavy men who were light on their feet, but usually that wasn't the case. But, Nate had the advantage of surprise and a Glock 40 caliber revolver.

****

Jason started back to Rosewood cottage when he noticed Calvin Ross walking toward the studio. He called headquarters and reported his sighting. He was informed that they would be sending a couple of agents to pick up Calvin Ross and bring him in for questioning.

Andy Barzetti was in the studio packing up his painting supplies when Calvin walked in. "Are you leaving tonight? Do you need a ride to the airport?" Calvin asked.

"No, I'm not leaving until tomorrow. I think Leah, Sandy, and I are going to share a taxi to the airport. We're all flying to different destinations, but our flights are within an hour of each other."

"Where are you off to this time? Do you have another workshop scheduled?"

"No, I'm going to Italy. I'm going to spend the winter there, do some painting, and visit my relatives."

"That's good. You need to take some time off, just paint and hang out. I don't guess you'd reconsider my offer, would you? With your expertise and talent, you could do it in a few days."

"Calvin, I've told you before, I'm not going to plagiarize someone else's work. I know we go way back, friends since first grade, but we've taken separate paths. We were both so poor growing up, like hungry kids looking in the candy store window, but it was always out of reach. It bothered you much more than it did me. I just wanted to be able to paint, and you wanted to live in a big house and drive a big car. You always thought if you acquired enough 'things' people would look up to you and respect you. I worked at any legitimate job I could find in order to buy painting supplies and study art. You, on the other hand, started running with some pretty bad characters. I worried about you, but you turned a deaf ear to me and went your own way, always one step ahead of the law."

"Don't give me that holier than thou shit," Ross said. "You were the talented one. Things always came easy for you."

"No, Calvin, I worked my ass off to get where I am. Do you think I just picked up a paint brush and, wham, painted a masterpiece? I worked hard to learn to paint as well as I do. You have a successful, even famous gallery. Revered artists would consider it a privilege to hang their work there. Why can't you be happy and satisfied with that?"

"Because, it's not enough. I want more. I want my own plane, and a yacht. I want an apartment in the Dakota building with a view of Central Park."

Andy just stared at Calvin and shook his head, with a sad expression on his face. "You'll never have enough, Calvin. There's an emptiness inside you that you're trying to fill with material possessions. It's like a sinkhole; you'll never be able to acquire enough to find the peace and satisfaction you seek."

"Hey, don't look at me with that hound dog expression. I've got the world by the tail, and I don't intend to let go," Calvin said, as he opened the door and went outside.

An unmarked car with two FBI agents had just pulled up in front of the studio. The doors opened, and they both got out. The driver looked at Calvin. "You Calvin Ross?" he asked.

"Yeah, that's me. What's the problem?"

"You're under arrest for questioning involving the theft of a stolen museum painting."

"I don't know what you're talking about. I don't have any stolen art."

"You'll have your opportunity to explain, but right now you're going to headquarters," the agent said, grabbing Calvin's arm and placing a cuff on his wrist. The agent quickly cuffed the other hand and pushed Calvin into the back of the car.

Jason sent Nate a text telling him about Ross's arrest and asking him to call if it was safe for him to talk.

"What's on your mind?" Nate asked, when Jason answered his phone.

"I think it would be a good idea for us to stay connected. That way, I can hear everything from your side and come to your rescue if you need help. I'll mute my phone so no one can hear anything from my end."

"Good idea," Nate said. "I'll clip my phone to my belt so it will be out of the way, but you can still hear everything."

Jason went back to the apartment and told Leah, Sandy and Becky about Calvin Ross's arrest.

"Once they catch the Porters, that'll pretty well wrap up the job you and Nate were sent to do," Leah said.

"Yeah, as far as the art heist, but there's still a lot of unanswered questions. I still can't figure out why Linda was kidnapped and where John Phelps fits in. Why was he involved in Linda's abduction?"

"Linda seemed to think someone overheard her talking about art heists and art forgeries at the get-acquainted reception," Leah said. "She believed they thought she knew more than she did. Everyone involved with the robbery has been apprehended. So, none of them seem to have a motive for kidnapping."

"Maybe it was something else she talked about," Sandy said.

"That's right," Leah said, "she also talked about some murder she'd read about that was made to look like an accident. Maybe someone thought she was referring to them."

"Hopefully, we'll have more answers when Nate catches Leah's assailant. I'm going to Ron's cottage where I can keep an eye on the house. I'll also have Ron as back up in case Nate needs help," Jason said, getting to his feet and heading for the door. "You gals stay in here out of sight, and keep the door locked."

"No way," Becky said, jumping to her feet, "we're going with you."

"That's right," Leah said, "we're not about to stay here by ourselves."

"Lead the way, Sherlock, we're right behind you," Sandy said.

****

Nate heard a key turning in the front door and hurried down the hall and into the bathroom. He climbed into the old-fashioned tub and pulled the shower curtain closed. He pulled his Glock out of the shoulder holster, and held it down by his side. Footsteps came down the hall and entered the bathroom. A hand pulled the curtain back. Liz Walker stood there with a .38 revolver pointed at his face.

"You planning on taking a bath?" she asked.

"Hello, Liz. Fancy seeing you here. Where's your big, fat, ugly sidekick?"

"He'll be along shortly, as soon as he takes care of your dear sweet Leah. Unfortunately, he'll have to do away with any witness so, sigh, guess that includes your sister and Sandy."

"My, my, he's going to have his hands full. He'll have to do something about Jason, too."

"You think you're so clever, sneaking up here. I came back to check on Leah and saw the ladder and duct tape your sweetie left behind. It didn't take a rocket scientist to figure you'd be back to try to catch her attacker."

Nate shifted his weight from one foot to the other, and Liz moved closer and pointed the .38 at his face, which was a mistake. It put her within Nate's reach. "Stand still, and put your hands out where I can see them."

Nate raised his hands and pointed the Glock in Liz's face. "Looks like we're at a standoff. You shoot me, I'll shoot you, and bang, bang, we're both dead. But guess what Liz? I'm faster than you," Nate said, raising his left hand and grabbing Liz's wrist, raising it above her head and twisting it until her weapon clattered to the floor. Liz started to bend down to retrieve it, but Nate stepped out of the tub and twisted her arm behind her back. She started kicking her feet backwards trying to hit his shins. She kicked and snarled like a wild cat. "Don't make me have to hurt you," Nate said, while kicking her gun out of reach.

"You wouldn't hit a woman; you're not the type. You're the kind who comes to the rescue of the fair damsel. You'd never hit me," she said, trying to reach behind her head and scratch his face.

"Don't count on it. I will knock you out if I have to. You killed Sheila Rhodes, and you killed your father. I would have no qualms about knocking the hell out of you. You're a sorry excuse for a human being."

Suddenly, all the fight went out of her, and she collapsed on the floor sobbing. "I didn't mean to kill him. He was going to sell Rocky Ledge Inn. He knew I loved this place, but he didn't care. We were arguing. I was trying to convince him the workshops were a good thing, how people learned and grew as artists. How much everyone loved coming here, but he turned and walked away, saying, 'It's not making a profit.' He went into the bathroom and told me there was nothing more to say; he was going to take a bath. I followed him, and he told me to get out, the subject was closed. I lost it. All I could think of was all the times he had rejected everything I ever did. I never met his expectations, and he never bragged on any of my accomplishments. He only criticized my failures, no matter how small or large." Liz laid her head on the side of the tub and ran her hand along the edge. "I ran at him and began pounding his chest with my fists. There was some water on the floor, and he slipped and fell, hitting his head on the side of the tub."

"What happened then?" Nate asked, "Was he killed instantly?"

"No," Liz said, "he was dazed and unable to move. He asked me to help him. I went over and took his head in my hands and looked into his eyes. I told him about all the times he had belittled and hurt me, and then I slammed his head against the tile floor. When I knew he was dead, I called 911. There was never any suspicion of foul play. Everyone felt so sorry for me, sending condolences and expressing concerns. Did you know more accidents happen at home than anywhere else?" Liz asked, as though her father's death had really been an accident.

"Didn't you feel any regrets or remorse at all?"

"No, I felt a wonderful sense of freedom. The ironic thing, even though my father never loved me, he left me everything."

Liz looked up at Nate and laughed. He could see the madness in her eyes now as she continued gloating. "The inn now belonged to me! He left me his apartment in Manhattan and all his paintings. I could legally make and sell as many prints of his works as I wished, and after his death, they more than doubled in value. But here's the real clincher—he had an insurance policy for one million with double indemnity in the case of an accidental death. Of course, his death was ruled an accident. I was suddenly a very wealthy woman."

"But, why did you kill Sheila Rhodes? She was investigating an art crime. She shouldn't have been any threat to you."

"She ran across the accident report about my father's death and began digging around and found out about the insurance. She called me and asked a lot of nosy questions. I went to her cottage to talk to her, and she just seemed to be getting too close to the truth. I didn't plan to kill her. The paperweight was sitting there on the table, and it just seemed like the best thing to do. The bitch should have kept her nose out of my business." She glared at Nate with hate-filled eyes, "Why did you have to come here and ruin everything? Alonzo will be here soon, and you'll wish you'd never seen Liz Walker or Rocky Ledge Inn."

"Alonzo?" Nate said with a laugh, "I didn't know anyone was actually named that."

"Everyone calls him Snake, but that's his real name."

"How do you find all these sleaze balls?" Nate asked.

"You can find people to do anything you want when you have enough money," Liz said.

"One last question, Liz, while you're confessing. Why did you have Linda Baker kidnapped?"

"My father used her law firm for years. When she started spouting off about a murder that was made to look like an accident, I thought she was referring to my father's death."

"Probably your guilty conscience over-reacting. That is, if you even have a conscience," Nate said.

"Maybe so, but I had to know for sure. I knew John Phelps had a connection to her. I paid him to go and talk to her, find out what she knew. He was useless, though. He didn't find out jack shit."

"What were you going to do with her when you found out what you wanted to know?"

"Oh, she'd have to die, of course," Liz said nonchalantly. "But, I had to know if she'd talked to anyone else first. She was standing with John Phelps at the edge of the inn property when he saw me go into Sheila's cottage, and I needed to know if she'd seen me also."

"I sent Jagger and Knox to get the information out of her by whatever means necessary. I thought about having them finish off Phelps too, but he'd found my watch, and he'd told me if anything happened to him, he'd left instructions as to where it was hidden."

"What do you mean, found your watch?" Nate asked

"It fell off my arm when I hit Sheila, and according to Phelps, it had her blood on it. He found it when he saw me coming out of Fernwood and went to check on Sheila. He was trying to blackmail me, but I don't intimidate easily. I was following him the night he confronted you. I was sick and tired of his threats, so I meant to kill him and take my chances and hopefully frame you for his murder. But, you managed to rescue Linda and get Jagger and Knox killed. They were my most dependable helpers, and you, oh, how I wish

John Phelps had killed you that night. I hate you. What did you do with Linda? Where is she now?"

"She's in a safe place. The party's over for you, Liz. You'll probably spend the rest of your life in prison or a mental institution."

Liz looked at him, and her eyes darted around the room like a trapped wild animal. She spotted her revolver lying on the floor a few feet away, and before Nate could stop her, she rolled over, stretched out, and grabbed the gun. She pointed it at Nate and backed herself against the wall with a crab-like crawl. "We're back were we started—you can shoot me, but I can shoot you, too," she said, pointing the gun at Nate's chest.

"Give it up Liz. Jason's heard everything. My phone's an open line straight to his phone."

Liz stared at Nate with unmitigated hate. She seemed to hold that expression for minutes, but it was actually only seconds when it changed to one of introspection. She looked almost the way she had in the portrait Andy painted of her. Tears began to run down her face as she raised the gun slightly, and her finger tightened on the trigger. Nate tensed, ready to reach for her gun, but she turned the weapon, placed it against her chest, and pulled the trigger.

****

Jason and the three women were almost to Ron's cottage when they heard the loud explosion of the gun shot. They didn't know what to expect. Had Liz shot Nate?

"I'm okay. Call 911," Nate said, "Liz shot herself."

Chapter 25

Jason, Leah, Sandy, and Becky arrived at Ron Rhodes's cottage and sat on the screened porch, where they could see the main house and the lane going in both directions. They had all listened to the exchange between Nate and Liz. They'd heard her tell Nate that Snake was going to kill Leah and any witnesses. They weren't sure if it was the truth or if Liz was bluffing. But, they knew Snake had promised Leah he would return for her. They should be able to see him approaching from this vantage point.

When Liz managed to retrieve her weapon, they'd all listened in horror and then heard the gun shot. Nate had immediately reassured them he was okay and to call 911. Jason made the call and told the operator someone had been shot, send the police and an ambulance.

They saw Snake coming around the bend about that time, heading toward the main house. Jason and Ron left the porch, went through the cottage, and headed down the path. They saw Snake enter the building and picked up their pace. As they eased up the stairs, still listening to the sounds coming from Nate's phone, they heard Snake's gruff voice telling Nate to drop his gun.

"I said drop your gun and get your hands in the air!" Snake said for the second time.

"Your boss is dead; she just shot herself. Who's going to pay you for your dirty work now?" Nate said, laying his gun on the floor.

"Killing you will be just for fun. You'd be another notch in my belt. And, I'll really have fun before killing your lady friend. That'll put a bigger notch in my belt and raise the price of my future jobs."

"News flash, Snake. You kill me, there'll be no future jobs."

"That's pretty big talk for an unarmed man."

"Two FBI agents are outside listening to everything that's being said, and the police are on the way. You won't be doing any jobs or going anywhere, except prison. You might get to do some jobs there. Make furniture or license plates or maybe you'll get lucky and get to work in the kitchen. You look like you love to eat, so you'd feel right at home there," Nate said.

The front door burst open about that time and Jason yelled, "FBI! Drop your weapon!"

"I've got this .38 pointed right between your partner's eyes. He's a dead man if you don't drop *your* gun right now."

Jason bent down and carefully laid his pistol on the floor. Snake was watching his movements closely, and while his attention was diverted, Ron stepped from behind the door and fired his 9 mm

Glock three times. The first bullet hit Snake in the right shoulder, the second in his neck, and the third in his chest. Snake clung to his weapon as though it were glued to his hand. He fired it twice before falling to the floor, but the bullets went wild, hitting the ceiling and wall.

Nate walked over and removed the gun from Snake's hand as he checked for a pulse. "He's still alive."

They heard the sound of sirens and saw flashing lights through the window. "That should be the police and ambulance," Jason said.

"Good, I hope this guy pulls through. The police will need to question him," Nate said.

"I'll go and show them the way up," Ron said, heading out the door. Ron met Leah on the path outside the main house, Sandy and Becky right behind her.

"Please tell me everyone's okay," Leah said.

"We heard the gun shots and were scared shitless." Becky said, "We didn't know who was doing the shooting."

"Nate and Jason are fine. You already know about Liz. I shot Snake, but he's still alive. Hopefully he'll pull through to answer some questions," Ron said, heading down the path to where the police cars and ambulance had parked.

Ron told the medics one person needed immediate attention, and one was probably beyond help. They took two stretchers and headed toward the main house. He directed them and the police to Liz's upstairs apartment.

The medics checked Snake's vitals and started an IV. It took four of them to get him loaded on the stretcher. A medic checked Liz and shook his head. The police took pictures of everything and drew a chalk outline around Liz's body. The officer in charge frowned and looked at the policeman who was assisting him. "This sure gives me a creepy feeling. I was here investigating the scene when her father died, in this exact same spot."

Nate and Jason were standing in the living room when the medics came through carrying Snake on the stretcher. "Good luck going down those stairs with him," Nate said.

"Yeah, he's a heavy weight. Like carrying a slab of stone," one of the medics said.

They struggled through the door and could be heard grunting and cursing all the way down the stairs. Two of the officers came out of the bathroom, and Nate recognized Sam Spencer, the detective who had arrested Ron and charged him with the murder of Sheila.

"We've got to quit meeting this way, Detective," Nate said with a sardonic smile.

Spencer ignored Nate's comment, "this is Charlie Shaw, the county medical examiner. Can you tell us what happened here?"

"Well, it's fairly obvious. Liz shot herself. Before doing that, she admitted to killing her father and Sheila Rhodes," Nate said. "She hired that tub of lard the medics just toted out of here to kidnap Leah Dawson. She counted on me coming to the rescue, but she didn't count on Leah escaping. Snake was supposed to find out where Linda Baker is and then kill both of us."

"That sounds like a far-fetched story," Detective Spencer said. "Liz Walker's been a respected member of this community for many years. For all I know, you killed her and made it look like suicide and shot her friend when he tried to help her."

"I think when your forensic team investigates the scene and Mr. Shaw does his thing, you'll find that everything I've told you checks out."

"So, you know where Linda Baker is? Did you kidnap her or maybe kill her too? Funny thing, you came here to our peaceful community to investigate a so-called art theft, and suddenly we have murders and kidnappings. That FBI badge doesn't put you above the law," Detective Spencer said with a belligerent snarl.

"Look, Detective, I don't know what got your shorts in a wad," Nate said, trying real hard to maintain his composure, "but you need to get that chip off your shoulder and look at the evidence with an open mind."

"Nate and I had our phones connected so I could hear everything that was going on while he was up here," Jason said, interrupting Nate and the detective. "I had my phone muted so no one could hear anything from my end, but I could hear everything from Nate's side."

"So, am I supposed to be impressed with your brilliant detective work?" Spencer asked, looking at Jason with a scornful expression.

"No Detective, you're not supposed to be impressed. You're supposed to ask me what was said. There were also three more people who heard the exchange between Liz and Nate prior to her shooting herself and Snake bursting in and almost killing Nate."

"Snake?" Spencer said, "Who is Snake?"

How in the world did this guy ever make detective, Nate wondered, but he kept calm and explained that Snake was the man the medics just hauled away.

"Detective, I'm sure you'll be glad to know I recorded the conversation that took place between Liz and Nate. I'll download it to a flash drive and give it to you."

"You know a recorded phone conversation is not admissible evidence in a court of law," the Detective said.

"Okay," Nate said, "I've had enough. Look, Detective Spencer, I've never tried to horn in and take over this case, but I could very easily have the FBI take charge of it. An agent was murdered, and you arrested her husband and charged him with her murder with no real evidence. You've never put any effort into finding the real killer, and when Linda Baker disappeared, you did nothing to try and locate her."

"We sent out her description and pictures to all the airports and issued an APB," Spencer said, interrupting Nate.

"Fine, I'll tell you what. I won't have this case turned over to the FBI if you'll get that burr out of your butt and quit trying to pin everything on me. You'll only come out looking like a fool. So, open your eyes; look at the evidence with an open mind, and you can take credit for solving the case. But, in exchange, drop all the charges against Ron Rhodes so he can take his wife's body back to Texas tomorrow and bury her with dignity."

"Did you say three other people heard that phone conversation?" Spencer asked.

"That's right," Jason said

"Would they be willing to testify?"

"Of course, they will. Can you round up the district attorney and have a preliminary hearing tonight to get all this mess cleared up?

Snake's a hired killer, and I'm sure he has a record as long as your arm. If he lives, he'll probably spill his guts to save his worthless hide. That'll be another star in your crown. You might even make captain after this is all over," Nate said.

"Okay, as soon as we wrap everything up, all of you come to headquarters. I'll see what I can do about getting the charges against Rhodes dropped."

****

Andy Barzetti saw the unmarked car sitting in front of the studio when Calvin Ross opened the door and went outside. He also heard the agent tell Calvin he was under arrest. "I wonder what he's gotten himself into now." Andy thought as he watched the tail lights of the car disappearing down the lane.

Andy and Calvin had been best friends growing up. Calvin, like Andy had been dirt poor but, unlike Andy who had loving parents, Calvin had an overbearing, abusive father and his mother had run away when he was four years old. His father treated Calvin as though it was his fault she'd left. He beat Calvin every day of his life until Calvin turned fourteen and was bigger and stronger than him. One day when he came home from school, his father started accusing him of anything from being stupid to stealing money from him. He came at Calvin with a walking stick he always carried and had used many times to leave marks on Calvin's back. Calvin had taken the stick away from him and smashed it against the floor until it was a pile of splinters. He'd grabbed his father by the front of his shirt and pulled him up until they were almost nose to nose.

"If you ever touch me again, I'll kill you," Calvin had said, and then he dropped his father to the floor and walked out. He'd never gone back. He stayed with Andy some, but most of the time, he hung out with a gang of boys that were always just one step ahead of the law. Andy didn't know how Calvin had made all his money, and he didn't want to know. He'd restored several old paintings Calvin had managed to find. They'd brought a nice sum when auctioned, and Calvin had paid him well for his work. But, when he asked Andy to forge a masterpiece on an old canvas, Andy had drawn the line. *He never has enough, no matter how much he accumulates*, Andy thought as he walked to his cottage, feeling a deep sadness for his friend.

He heard the gun shot as he entered his cottage. He went inside, put his load of materials on the sofa, and pulled out his phone. He dialed 911 and reported the gunshot. *Should I go over and find out what's going on or should I wait for the police to arrive?* Andy gave this careful thought, making his decision quickly. He decided to wait, and about five minutes later, he heard three more shots. *Oh, my God,* he thought, *what is going on?*

He heard the sirens and saw the flashing lights. He took off running toward the main house, dreading what he might find.

****

Nate and Jason went downstairs to wait for the police to finish with the crime scene. They met the rest of the group standing in a huddle on the back patio. Nate walked over to Leah and put his arms around her.

"Hold me," Leah said. "I was so afraid I'd never see you alive again. I felt so helpless. I wanted to help you. But, I knew there was nothing I could do but wait and pray."

"I'm going to be around for a long, long time. You may start wishing Liz *had* shot me."

"How about we all go to Ron's cottage and wait for the police to finish upstairs?" Jason said.

"That's an excellent idea," Nate said, taking Leah's hand and walking in the direction of Fernwood cottage.

"Hey guys, wait up," Andy called to them as he came around the curve in the path. "What's going on? Is everyone okay?"

"How much time do you have? It's a long story, but we're all fine. Come on and join us at Ron's and we'll fill you in," Nate said.

They all went into the cottage and out to the screened porch. Jason brought some chairs from the kitchen and everyone was seated.

"I don't know about you guys, but I could use a stiff drink right now," Ron said, looking around the group.

"Yeah, so could I," Nate said, 'but I think we better wait. If Spencer comes through with his part of the deal, we'll all have to go to headquarters and testify tonight."

Nate began telling Andy the story of what had happened, beginning with Leah being tricked into going to Liz's apartment and ending with Liz shooting herself and Ron shooting Snake.

Andy was so surprised and shocked; he was speechless for several seconds.

"And I thought this was going to be just another relaxing and educational workshop," he said. He then told them about Calvin being arrested and some of Calvin's background. They heard the back door of the house open and saw Detective Sam Spencer come out followed by the county Medical Examiner. Nate went through the cottage and met them in the lane.

"We've finished with everything upstairs," Spencer said. "I've put yellow tape across the door—no one is to enter the apartment until the investigation is completed. I also made some phone calls, and the District Attorney has agreed to meet with us for a hearing at 9:30 tonight. All of you need to be there."

"We'll be there," Nate said.

The two police cars left, and the medics loaded Liz's body in the back of the forensic van to be transported to the M.E.'s facility in Portland. When all the vehicles had pulled away and their lights disappeared from view, an unearthly stillness seemed to fall over

Rocky Ledge Inn. Then the mournful sighing of the buoys broke the silence.

A collective prickling chill passed over the group of people sitting on Ron Rhodes's screened porch.

Nate was the first to break the silence. "It feels as though the inn and the bay are mourning the loss of their owner. This inn is probably the only thing Liz ever truly loved, and she did manage to make a beautiful place even more beautiful."

"Yes, she loved it enough to kill for it," Jason said. "I think the three main motives for murder are love, money, and pride. All three could easily apply in Liz's case."

"It's been a long day, and it's not over yet," Nate said. "I think we all need some food before heading to Portland and the hearing."

"I agree," Jason said, "why don't we go over to the Ledges and get something to eat. They're open until 9:30 or 10:00."

Ron's son had returned from Portland, where he'd made final arrangements to have Sheila's body shipped to Texas the next day. Ron filled him in on everything that had happened. He said he'd eaten on the way back from Portland and would stay and keep an eye on everything while they went to eat and on to police headquarters. "Good luck, dad. I'll say a prayer for you," he said, as he hugged his father. "Hopefully, we'll be flying back to Houston together with Mom tomorrow."

Everyone seemed to rally somewhat after they'd eaten. They'd seen Mattie Wainscot at the Ledges and filled her in on what had happened. Andy said he would walk back to the inn with her and see her safely to her cottage. Leah, Sandy, and Becky got in the Cherokee with Nate. Ron and Jason followed in his Explorer.

They arrived at police headquarters around 9:15. Benson Cartwright, the District Attorney, and Detective Spencer were waiting in a private hearing room. The group was told to wait in a separate room, and someone would call them one at a time to be questioned. Nate was the first to be called. He was questioned about fifteen minutes then shown to another room where he was instructed to wait. The procedure was repeated with Jason next, then Ron, followed by Leah, Becky, and Sandy.

Sandy was the last to come out and join the others in the private waiting room. "Wow, I feel like I've been put through the wringer," she said, taking a seat next to Leah.

"I think we all feel that way," Leah said.

They'd been waiting for what seemed like hours when an officer came and instructed them to follow him. They were led back into what they had come to think of as the interrogation room. The

District Attorney and Detective Spencer were still in the same seats at the head of a long table, but to their amazement, John Phelps was seated in one of the side chairs.

"Come in. Everyone have a seat," Detective Spencer said.

They all filed in and took seats around the table. Detective Spencer cleared his throat and said, "You've all met District Attorney Cartwright. You'll be happy to know he's reached a decision in the case of State v. Ron Rhodes charging Mr. Rhodes with the murder of Sheila Rhodes. Mr. Rhodes has been cleared of all charges." He looked at Ron. "You are a free man. We apologize for any inconvenience or distress this may have caused. You have our condolences in the death of your wife."

"We've looked at all the evidence and are convinced Liz Walker did willfully and deliberately kill Sheila Rhodes and then take her own life." He removed some papers from a briefcase sitting on the table. "I have in my hand a signed and notarized statement made by John Phelps. He states that he saw Liz Walker and Sheila Rhodes enter Sheila's cottage together the afternoon Sheila was murdered. He goes on to say Liz Walker came out of the cottage alone about fifteen minutes later. She looked disheveled and had what appeared to be blood on her clothing. I am reading this statement at Mr. Phelps's request. He would like to say a few words to some of you before you leave." The detective sat down and nodded in John's direction. "The floor is yours, Mr. Phelps."

John stood up and looked first in Nate's direction. "I want to apologize for naming you as my attacker. I know an apology is inadequate, but I am trying to make amends, and it's the best I can do at this time. I made that statement in order to clear you of all charges and name the one who actually attacked me and also killed Sheila Rhodes. I did a very stupid thing. I attempted to blackmail Liz, and that is why she tried to kill me."

He then turned to Leah. "I know an apology can never atone for the misery and pain I've caused you, but I hope that in time you will forgive me. I did follow you up here, determined to have you as my own. I'm closing my business in Tennessee and moving everything to New York. You will never see or hear from me again. I give you my word."

John paused and let his eyes roam over the group sitting around the table. "I know it's hard for any of you to believe that I've truly changed. I had a lot of time to think while lying in the hospital. I guess when you come close to death, your viewpoint of life changes. I thought of the wealth I've accumulated by whatever means it took and the people I've trampled along the way. I tried to count the number of true friends I have, and I could not think of one single person who would've shed a tear had I died. The hospital chaplain visited me several times. He is a good and wise man. For the first time in my life, I was shown passages from the Bible and told about God. I realize it won't be easy, but with the help of that God the chaplain introduced me to, I shall make amends for the evil things I've done."

Leah was too stunned to reply. She inclined her head slightly, acknowledging his apology.

Nate glared at John trying to decide if he was truly sincere. "I will accept your apology, but if you ever bother Leah or upset her or cause her distress of any kind, I'll make you wish you'd never been born."

"Fair enough," John said.

"You're all free to go, except you, Mr. Phelps," the district attorney said to the group.

"Oh, by the way, Mr. Parker, there's one other thing you'll be interested to know," Detective Spencer said, looking at Nate.

"What is that?" Nate asked, as he rose from his seat.

"The Porters were picked up at the Portland airport about thirty minutes ago. They're being questioned and charged with shooting an officer of the law and fleeing from the scene."

"Well, hang onto them. The Bureau will be charging them with numerous art crimes."

After they had filed out, District Attorney Cartwright turned to John Phelps. "I've read your statement and listened to your apologies. I'm taking into consideration the fact that you came forward with this information and seem to genuinely want to make amends and turn over a new leaf. I'm not going to send this to the grand jury. What I'm going to do is retire it to a file without prejudice. If you commit a crime, these charges will be brought back up."

"Thank you, District Attorney Cartwright. I intend to seek psychological counseling and learn to use the abilities God gave me to help others and make restitution for all the crooked, underhanded things I've done in my lifetime."

****

Saturday morning, Jason prepared breakfast for the last time, and his helpers served the group gathered in the dining room. It had been very late when they got back to the inn the night before, and everyone had slept in. Sandy, Leah, Nate, and Becky were seated at one table, and Ron Rhodes, his son, Andy, and Mattie were seated next to them. Jason came out of the kitchen and sat down next to Nate.

"I wonder what will happen to the inn now that Liz is dead," Sandy said.

"It will probably be sold. I understand she had no children or living relatives," Jason said.

"I hope someone buys it and continues with the wonderful workshops. It's such a perfect place," Mattie said.

"I've always wanted a place like this. I just might buy it myself," Andy said.

"Sounds like a great plan to me. Remember, you owe me a 100th birthday present portrait," Mattie said, looking at Andy.

"Well, we'll just see what happens."

"I don't know if I would want to return here after all the terrible things that have happened," Leah said.

"You'll feel different in time. Just remember all the good things. You've done several beautiful paintings, and you've acquired new friendships that will last a lifetime," Andy said.

"Changing the subject," Jason said, "I didn't have Linda's number, but I called Harry and he contacted her. She called me back, and she'll be here around noon today."

"That's great," Leah said "We'll all be glad to see her."

"Ronnie and I will be leaving for the airport right after breakfast." Ron said. "Give her my regards, and tell her I wish her well."

"Are you returning home today?" Nate asked, looking at Leah.

"Yes, I've got to get back to work. Sandy and I plan to share a taxi with Andy to the airport. My flight leaves at 4:20, Sandy's around 4:30, and Andy's a little before 5."

"Don't bother getting a taxi. I'll take you to the airport. You'll all fit in my SUV."

"That's nice of you, Nate," Leah said.

"I'm not being nice. I want to spend every moment with you until you leave. But rest assured, this is a temporary parting. You'll be seeing a lot of me. I will be camping on your doorstep soon; that is, if you'll let me."

After breakfast, Jason went to his house, changed into jeans and a sweat shirt, grabbed Sasha's leash, got in his SUV, and headed for the veterinarian clinic. When he entered the waiting room, the girl behind the counter smiled, "I know someone who is sure going to be glad to see you."

"She won't be any happier than I will to see her," Jason said. Sasha must have heard Jason's voice. They could hear her barking as they started down the hall to the dog pens in the back of the building.

The attendant opened the door to Sasha's pen, and Jason squatted down. Sasha ran over to him and put her head on his lap and whined. Jason rubbed behind her ears, careful to avoid her wound, and told her they were going home. She seemed to understand what he said. Her eyes seemed to light up as she wagged her tail and started down the hall. She stopped and looked back at Jason. "Okay girl, I'm coming, but let's get your leash on first. I don't want you running and exerting yourself yet."

When Jason got back to his rented house, he removed Sasha's leash and put out fresh water. Sasha ran from room to room, sniffing and smelling everything. "Don't worry, girl, the bad guys are gone, and they won't be back. But, there's someone coming you're going to be very happy to see."

Sasha stopped what she was doing, came over, and sat down in front of Jason. She cocked her head to one side and looked at him with questioning eyes. Jason had boxed up all Linda's things and left the box sitting on the floor in the room where she'd slept. Sasha ran into the room and began rooting around in the box. She pulled out a sweater Linda had last worn and ran back into the living room and laid it down in front of Jason. Jason laughed, "Yep, you're right! Linda will be here soon, and she'll probably be happier to see you than she will to see me."

Sasha thumped her tail on the floor several times and gave a happy bark, then leaned her head against Jason's leg and licked his hand as if to say, *you'll always be number one to me.* Leah and Sandy had gone to their rooms and got everything packed and ready to go. They'd boxed their painting materials and made arrangements for FedEx to pick them up the following Monday. Leah walked through the bedroom and bath that had been her home for the past week. It looked pretty much the way it did when she'd arrived.

Seems it should look different, Leah thought. *I wonder what will happen to the inn. It still looks the same, but so much has changed.* She rolled her bag out the door of the sun porch for the last time and joined Sandy, who was standing just outside the cottage, looking out towards the bay. The sky was a clear azure blue, boats were moored off shore, and colorful buoys bobbed with the ebb and flow of the current. Sea gulls circled and squawked.

"How has it only been a week since we checked into this cottage and admired this same beautiful view?" Sandy asked as Leah joined her.

"So much has happened; it seems a lifetime ago," Leah said. "Do you think any of us will ever be the same?"

"Oh, yes. I'll go home, and Al and the boys will be so glad to have me back they'll be extra attentive. Then we'll settle into our old routine, and life for me will continue as before. Now, with you, it's a different story. Life for you will never be the same. Not because of any of the bad things that happened, but because of the wonderful man you met and fell in love with, and he with you."

"Well, let's go find that wonderful man. He's going to take us to the airport," Leah said with a grin.

Six Weeks Later

Leah hit the remote and watched as her garage door slide open. She pulled her SUV inside, got out and opened the door that led into her kitchen. Once inside she kicked off her shoes, laid her brief case on the countertop, and looked in the refrigerator. Today was the day Mrs. Berryhill came with her crew to clean Leah's house. She usually prepared one of her special dishes and left it in the refrigerator. *Bless her heart,* Leah thought, as she pulled out a covered casserole dish. There were also salad fixings and some homemade dressing with olive oil, balsamic vinegar, garlic, honey, and black pepper. Leah began to salivate thinking of the culinary treat awaiting her. She placed the dish in the oven and set the temperature. Whatever it was, it would be delicious. Mrs. Berryhill had taken Leah under her wing and sometimes acted like the mother Leah never had. She was always fussing at her, telling her she didn't eat enough, she worked too hard, and was getting too skinny. She always ended the argument by telling her she needed to find the right man and get married.

Leah opened a bottle of pinot grigio, poured some in a wine glass, and carried it into the sunroom. *Yeah, she's right… I do need the right man, and the right man is Nate Parker. But, he's in Virginia, and I'm in Tennessee.* She lit a match and placed it under the wood and kindling already laid in the grate. Mrs. Berryhill's husband made sure the fireplace was cleaned and always ready for the next fire.

Ahh, this feels wonderful. Leah put her feet on the foot stool and leaned her head back. The kindling caught, and flames licked around the logs, flickering and growing higher. Leah took a sip of wine and watched as a small log fell apart, sending a shower of sparks shooting up the chimney. It had been unseasonably cool for early November, and the fire and wine filled her with a sense of warmth and contentment.

She'd been busy designing a new kitchen for a historic mansion in mid-town Memphis. The mansion was owned by a very demanding couple who seemed to think Leah should cater to them exclusively, as if they were her only clients. She'd hardly had time to think about the week in Maine that had literally changed her life.

Her snooty clients had finally approved the latest plans she'd presented, and the contractor was ready to start Monday. They would be gutting the old kitchen in preparation to start the new one.

She took another sip of wine and thought of Nate. She didn't realize she could miss someone so much. It became a physical pain in the region of her heart. She'd known him for such a short time, but she couldn't imagine life without him. *But, how can we be together with his work in Virginia and mine in Tennessee?* He'd called every day to tell her how much he missed her. But, she hadn't heard from him in three days, and she was getting concerned.

Her cell phone rang. She pulled it from her pocket and looked at the caller ID. She felt a twinge of disappointment when she saw Sandy's name instead of Nate's. Feeling a little guilty because of her disappointment, she answered warmly, "Hi Sandy, how are you doing?"

"Things are finally getting back to normal. Al and the boys are taking me for granted again," Sandy said with a sigh.

"I'm sure they missed you terribly and are very happy to have you home safe and sound. You know some men aren't very verbal in expressing their feelings, but I'm sure he shows it in many other ways."

"Yeah, when I told Al what had happened at the inn, he thought I was making it up because nothing had been on the news. When he realized it was true, he became so over-protective I thought I would smother to death. He said he didn't want me ever going away without him again."

"Well, I guess he'll just have to come with you when you visit me in January."

"Oh, he'll get over it after a few weeks of being joined at the hip. By the way, what's the latest with Nate? Have you heard from any of the other guys in the workshop?"

"I talked to Mattie the other day, and she's painting up a storm, getting ready for a one-woman show. She told me Andy is buying Rocky Ledge Inn and will continue with the workshops. Nate has been calling everyday telling me how much he misses me, but Sandy, I haven't heard from him in three days. I think he's forgetting me already."

"Have faith, Leah. I've seen the way he looks at you. The man is crazy about you. He'll work something out, and I'm sure you'll be hearing from him soon."

"Well, he's not trying very hard. How can he go three days without talking to me if he *really* cares? Oh, I almost forgot! Nate told me Jason has moved to New York, and he and Linda are 'making plans.' When I asked what kind of plans, were wedding bells involved, he said Jason didn't elaborate, but he wouldn't be surprised."

"Well, I'm not surprised," Sandy said. "You couldn't help but notice how they looked at each other with moon eyes."

Leah's doorbell rang about that time. "Someone's at the door, Sandy. I'll talk to you later."

"Okay, girlfriend. Be careful, and don't open your door until you know who it is."

Leah disconnected the call and slipped her phone back into her pocket. She walked to the front door and looked through the peephole. Nate was standing there, grinning from ear to ear and holding the biggest bouquet of daises she'd ever seen.

She opened the door, and Nate stepped inside. He swept her into his arms, daises falling on the floor and crushing between them as he pulled her close and kissed her.

Leah pulled her head back long enough to stammer, "What are you doing here? Why didn't you let me know?" Nate was kissing her again, stopping her questions. She simply gave up, wrapped her arms around him, and returned his kisses. It was heaven, like a banquet for a starving person. She couldn't believe he was actually here, and she was in his arms. She must be dreaming.

"If I'm dreaming, please don't wake me," she murmured between kisses.

"You're not dreaming. If you are, I've been having the same dream for the last month," Nate said, stepping back and gathering up the daisies from the floor. "Let's do something with these. Put them in some water before they start wilting."

Leah led him to the kitchen, retrieved a vase, and filled it with water. Nate put the flowers in the vase and took her in his arms again.

"Oh, no," Leah said, pulling back. "You've got some explaining to do. She got a wine glass and filled it from the bottle she'd left on the countertop. She handed it to Nate and led him to the sunroom.

Nate sat his wine on the coffee table and put his hands on Leah's shoulders. "I've got a surprise for you," he said, brushing a strand of hair behind her ear and trailing his hand across her cheek. He outlined her lips with his fingertip, and Leah took his hand and kissed it.

"What kind of surprise?" she asked in a dreamy voice.

Nate sat down in the chair Leah had been occupying. He pulled her onto his lap and kissed her neck. "You smell like fresh air and summer rain."

"The surprise?" Leah asked again.

"You may not like it."

"Try me."

"I'm moving to Tennessee and practicing law here. I've got a friend who's been trying to get me to join his law firm for years."

"But what about your work with the Bureau?"

"I'm still with them. I can work on their projects from Tennessee as well as I did from Virginia. You know there's not an art crime every day. So, maybe when I do have a case, you could go with me. Maybe I could get you cleared to be my assistant. The Rhodes weren't official FBI agents. They worked art theft crimes for the Bureau in a special capacity."

"Yes, and look what happened to them…"

"Hush," Nate said, taking Leah's hand, turning it over and tracing the lines in her palm. "This is your lifeline," he said, running his finger down the long line that bisected her palm. "See this other line running alongside it? That's me, and that's where I always want to be. By your side. I love you Leah; I no longer feel like a complete person without you."

Leah put her hands on each side of his face and looked into his amber-green eyes. She saw her reflection and she saw love and safety and desire. She knew he was seeing the same reflected in her eyes. " I love you with all my heart, Nate Parker! I want to spend the rest of my life with you. Hold me and never let me go."

Made in United States
North Haven, CT
25 May 2023

36956971R00267